ISBN 978-1-5276-4458-8
PIBN 10877734

1 MONTH OF
FREE
READING

at

www.ForgottenBooks.com

By purchasing this book you are eligible for one month membership to ForgottenBooks.com, giving you unlimited access to our entire collection of over 1,000,000 titles via our web site and mobile apps.

To claim your free month visit:

www.forgottenbooks.com/free877734

English
Français
Deutsche
Italiano
Español
Português

www.forgottenbooks.com

Mythology Photography **Fiction**
Fishing Christianity **Art** Cooking
Essays Buddhism Freemasonry
Medicine **Biology** Music **Ancient**
Egypt Evolution Carpentry Physics
Dance Geology **Mathematics** Fitness
Shakespeare **Folklore** Yoga Marketing
Confidence Immortality Biographies
Poetry **Psychology** Witchcraft
Electronics Chemistry History **Law**
Accounting **Philosophy** Anthropology
Alchemy Drama Quantum Mechanics
Atheism Sexual Health **Ancient History**
Entrepreneurship Languages Sport
Paleontology Needlework Islam
Metaphysics Investment Archaeology
Parenting Statistics Criminology
Motivational

THE BOOKCASE.

VII.

THE GLACIER LAND.

THE GLACIER LAND.

FROM THE FRENCH OF

ALEXANDRE DUMAS.

BY MRS. W. R. WILDE,

TRANSLATOR OF "PICTURES OF THE FIRST FRENCH REVOLUTION,"

"THE WANDERER AND HIS HOME," "SIDONIA," ETC.

LONDON:

SIMMS AND M'INTYRE,

PATERNOSTER ROW; AND DONEGALL STREET, BELFAST.

1852.

INTRODUCTION.

EVERY traveller thinks it necessary to inform his readers why he travels; and I have too much respect for my illustrious predecessors—from M. de Bougainville, who made the tour of the world, to M. de Maistre, who made the tour of his chamber—not to follow their example.

Besides, two very important things will be found in this introduction, vainly to be sought elsewhere: a cure for cholera, and a proof of the infallibility of newspapers.

On the 15th of April, 1832, on returning to my room, after taking leave of my two excellent and celebrated friends, Litz and Boulanger, who had been quaffing strong black tea with me as a remedy against the prevailing plague, I suddenly felt a weakness in my limbs; a tremor passed through my frame; my head reeled; and I had to grasp the table to prevent myself from falling. In a word, I had the cholera.

Whether it was Asiatic or European, epidemic or contagious, I am entirely ignorant; but this I know, that, feeling a few moments more would deprive me of the power of utterance, I made one last effort, and called for sugar and ether instantly.

My housekeeper, an intelligent woman enough, having frequently seen me dip sugar in rum, after dinner, and swallow it, concluded I now wished something of the kind; and, filling a liqueur-glass with pure ether, into which she popped the largest lump of sugar she could find, brought in the beverage, just at the moment I had thrown myself on the bed, freezing in every member.

Scarcely conscious, I mechanically extended my hand, felt something placed within it, and heard the words, " Swallow this, monsieur; it will do you good." So I raised this something to my lips and swallowed it—that is to say, half a phial of pure ether.

To describe the convulsions caused by this diabolical liquid, as it traversed my torso, would be impossible, for I lost all consciousness almost immediately. An hour after, I came to myself, and found that I was rolled up in blankets and furs, with a jar of boiling water to my feet, while two persons, each holding a brazier of live coal, stood by, rubbing my members with all their might.

For a moment I believed myself dead or in hell. The ether burned me within, the friction scarified me without. At last, after about a quarter of an hour, the cold acknowledged itself vanquished. I broke out into a perspiration, and the physician declared that I was saved. Just in time, truly: two hours more, and I would have been roasted alive.

Four days after, the manager of the Porte Saint Martin Theatre stood beside my bed. His theatre was in a state of health even weaker than my own, and the dying called the recovering to his aid.

"In a fortnight at latest," exclaimed M. Harel, "I must have a piece that will produce fifty thousand crowns at least;" adding, to ensure my assent, that the feverish state in which he found me was admirably adapted for the production of an imaginative work, in consequence of the cerebral excitement which accompanied it.

This reason appeared so conclusive that I began the work instantly; gave it to him in a week, in place of a fortnight; and brought a hundred thousand crowns to his exchequer, in place of fifty thousand. True, the effort nearly drove me mad.

Scarcely had I recovered in some degree when I learned the death of General Lamarque, and next day was named one of the chief directors of the funeral by his family. All Paris beheld this procession, made sublime by order, respect, and patriotism. What changed this order into disorder, this respect into violence, this patriotism into rebellion? I know not, and will never know, until the day when the royalty of July, like that of Charles IX., renders up its account to God, and that of Louis XVI. its account to man.

On the 9th of June I read in one of the Legitimist papers, that I had been taken with arms in my hands at the affair of St. Méry, tried by court-martial during the night, and shot next morning at three o'clock.

The paragraph had such an official look about it, and the recital of my execution (which, indeed, I had borne with exemplary courage) was given with such detailed minuteness, all the particulars being fully authenticated, that for a moment I almost doubted my own existence. Besides, the editor appeared quite in earnest, and spoke kindly of me, for the first time in his life. It was evident, therefore, he sincerely believed that I was dead.

I threw off the quilt, leaped from the bed, and ran to the glass to ascertain the fact. At the same instant my door opened, and a letter from Charles Nodier was handed me, which ran as follows:—

" DEAR ALEXANDRE,

" I have just read in one of the papers that you were shot this morning at three o'clock. Pray send me word if that will hinder you from coming to dine with me to-morrow."

I answered, that as to my being dead or alive I had not quite made up my mind; but that in any case I would dine next day with him, as punctually as the statue of the commandant with Don Juan.

Next day it was unanimously agreed that I was not dead. Still, I had gained but little, for health had not returned: seeing which, my physician ordered me—what physicians always order when they have nothing more to say—a tour in Switzerland.

Consequently, on the 21st of July, 1832, I quitted Paris.

THE GLACIER LAND.

MONTEREAU.

NEXT day, while the coach stopped at Montereau for the passengers to breakfast, I proceeded to visit the bridge, twice celebrated in history, as having, within an interval of four centuries, witnessed the agony of two dynasties; one of which was saved by a crime, and the other could not be saved even by a victory.

These two pages of history are important enough to deserve a record. Let us cast a glance, therefore, at the topography of Montereau, the better to comprehend the events in which John the Bold and Napoleon played the principal parts.

The town of Montereau is situated about twenty leagues from Paris, at the confluence of the Yonne and Seine, where the former loses its distinctive name and becomes absorbed in the latter. To the left rises the mountain of Surville, crowned by the ruins of an old château, while at the base lies a kind of suburb, separated from the town by a river. In front, a wedge-shaped tongue of land extends between the two streams, and to the right lies the graceful city, amid its houses and vineyards, whose green and yellow trellises extend, like a rich Scotch mantle, far away out of sight over the verdant plains of Gâtinais. The bridge which has attained such historical importance joins the suburb to the town, spanning the two streams, and resting one of its massive feet upon the point of land above mentioned.

CHAPTER I.

JOHN THE BOLD.

On the 9th of September, 1419, two men might have been observed on that portion of the bridge that spans the Yonne, engaged attentively in watching the proceedings of some workmen, who, guarded by military, to prevent the approach of the populace, were rapidly erecting a kind of wooden pavilion, that extended across the entire breadth of the bridge, and for twenty feet or so over its length.

The elder of these two personages, whose office evidently was to superintend the mode of construction, seemed about forty-eight. His bronzed face, shadowed by long black hair, was surmounted by a cap of some dark stuff, from which one long end floated scarf-like. His furred mantle was of the same hue, having large falling sleeves that showed two stout mail-clad arms beneath. Long leathern boots covered his limbs, attesting by the mud on them the rapidity with which he had hastened to preside at the elevation of the wooden building. From his belt hung an embroidered purse, and beside it, in place of sword or dagger, a small axe inlaid with gold, and crested by a curiously-wrought head of an unhooded · falcon.

His companion, who seemed scarcely five-and-twenty, was dressed with an attention to effect not quite compatible with the sombre expression of his drooping, melancholy head. He wore a rich mantle of red velvet, furred with ermine, a doublet of gold brocade, and a cap of azure velvet, bordered with ermine likewise; from which floated a peacock's plume, fastened by an agraffe of rubies, that glittered in the sun like an aigrette of emeralds, sapphires, and gold. The costume was completed by tight blue hose, embroidered on the left thigh with a " P." and " G." surmounted by a knight's crest; and long Spanish leather boots turned over at the knee with red plush, from whence they were connected by gold chains with the long pointed toe, after the fashion of the day.

Meanwhile the people watched with no small anxiety the preparations making for the interview between the Dauphin Charles and Duke John; for though peace was desired by all, yet, to judge from the mingled murmurs that arose among the crowd, doubt and fear as to the result seemed the prevailing feelings. The last conference which had been held between the rival parties, was followed by such disastrous consequences, that nothing short of a miracle, it was thought, could effect a reconciliation now between the two princes. Still some few hopeful spirits amongst the spectators believed, or feigned to believe, that the pending negociations would be successful.

"*Pardieu!*" said a broad-faced, rubicund man, with his hands stuck in the belt that encircled, not his waist, but the vast rotundity of his paunch; "*Pardieu!* but I'm glad monsieur the prince, whom God preserve, and my Lord of Burgundy, whom the saints protect, have chosen our town of Montereau for their treaty of peace."

"Ay, mine host," replied a less enthusiastic neighbour, clapping him on the back; "ay, 'tis well, no doubt; for thereby crown pieces will fall into your till, but hailstones upon our town."

"How so, Pierre?" exclaimed the bystanders.

"Why, don't you know what happened at Ponceau? How, when the meeting was over, such a terrible storm burst from the sky, where not a cloud was seen before; and how the very tree was lightning-struck beneath which the duke and dauphin had embraced, while the one beside it remained unscathed, though they sprang from the same root? And see," added Pierre, extending his hand, "why does the snow fall now, and we only at the 9th of September?"

Every head was raised instantly, and there truly were the first white flakes descending of that early snow which next night covered the entire of Burgundy like a winding-sheet.

"You are right, Pierre," said a voice. "It is a bad omen, and foretels terrible things."

"Know you what it foretels?" replied Pierre: "that
God is tired at last of the false oaths of men."

"Ay, ay; true enough," answered the voice. " But
why not let His thunder fall upon the perjurers in place
of on,the poor tree that only sheltered them?"

This exclamation made the younger of the two super-
intendents look up; and at the same moment his eyes
rested upon the workmen, who were busily employed
placing a barrier in the centre of the wooden pavilion as
a mutual safeguard to the rival parties. The precaution, however, did not seem to meet the approbation of
the young knight; for his pale face flushed crimson, and
starting from his habitual apathy, he sprang towards the
men with such a volley of sacrilegious oaths, that the
one who held the plank meant for the barrier let it drop
from his hands in his haste to bless himself.

"Who ordered this barrier here, caitiff?" exclaimed
the knight.

"No one, my lord," replied the trembling workman,
cowering with fright: "no one; but 'tis the custom."

"Custom is a fool, then. Dost hear, fellow? fling me
that plank into the river." Then turning to his companion, he added, "What were you thinking of, Messire
Tanneguy, that you permitted this to be done?"

"Like yourself, apparently, Messire de Gyac," replied
Duchâtel, "I was so pre-occupied with the event that I
forgot the preparations."

Meanwhile, one of the men had dragged the plank to
the parapet of the bridge, and was preparing to throw it
over, in obedience to the Sire de Gyac, when a voice
was heard from the crowd which had gathered round.
It was Pierre who spoke.

"Hold!" said he, addressing the carpenter; "you
were right, André, and this young seigneur wrong."

"Ha!" exclaimed Gyac, turning sharply round.

"Ay, my lord," continued Pierre, tranquilly crossing
his arms; "a barrier is a safeguard for all, and needful
is it, especially when an interview takes place between
two enemies. 'Twas ever the custom."

"Ay, ay; always!" shouted the crowd.

"And pray, sirrah, who are you," exclaimed De Gyac,
" that dares to give an opinion against mine?"

"A citizen of the commune of Montereau," answered

Pierre boldly; "free in person and goods; who has had the habit from his youth up of saying the truth plainly, without fear or care of any greater than himself."

De Gyac's hand was instantly upon his sword, but Tanneguy seized his arm. "Hold! you are mad!" he murmured. Then turning round, "Archers!" he cried, "clear the bridge of these people; and if any attempt resistance, remember you carry a bow in your hand and arrows in your quiver."

"Ay! good my lords; drive us off," responded Pierre, who, last to move, seemed to take upon himself the guard of the retreat: "ay, drive us off; but not till you've heard another truth. There is treason brewing—treachery: God receive the victim and show mercy to the murderers!"

While Tanneguy's orders were being executed, the workmen quitted the pavilion, having completed its erection along with that of the barriers, and two strong gates at each extremity of the bridge, through which admittance was reserved exclusively for the personal attendants of the duke and dauphin, the number of whom was limited to ten; while, for the better security of each rival chief, the duke's people were to occupy the left bank of the Seine and the château of Surville, and the partizans of the dauphin the town of Montereau and the right bank of the Yonne. As to the tongue of land between the two rivers, it was neutral ground, not belonging to either party; but as it was almost uninhabited, with the exception of an isolated mill, no danger or surprise could be apprehended from that quarter.

As the workmen quitted the bridge, a troop of armed men advanced simultaneously from either side, as if they had been waiting for that moment, and proceeded to their respective positions.

One, consisting of archers, commanded by the Grand Master Jacques de la Lime, and bearing the red cross of Burgundy, took possession of the suburb of Montereau and the extremity of the bridge by which Duke John was to arrive; the other, bearing the dauphin's banner, took up their position at the barrier reserved for the entrance of the prince.

Meanwhile, Tanneguy and De Gyac continued to converse; but as soon as all arrangements were completed

they took leave—De Gyac to meet the Duke of Burgundy at Bray-sur-Seine, and Duchâtel to present him-
sent himself to the Dauphin of France.

The night was horrible.   Although the season was so
little advanced, six inches of snow covered the ground,
and all the ripe crops were blasted.

Next day, the 10th of September, one hour after noon,
the duke mounted his horse in the court-yard of the
house where he lodged, having at his right the Sire de
Gyac, and on his left the Seigneur de Noailles.

His favourite dog had howled lamentably all through
the night; and now, seeing his master ready to set forward, he writhed and struggled on his chain, with
flaming eyes and hair standing on end, till at length,
as the duke began to move, with one violent effort
he burst the strong double iron chain that held him,
and, springing to the throat of the duke's horse, bit him
so fiercely, that the terrified animal threw his rider to
the ground.

In vain the impatient De Gyac struck him with his
whip.   The dog took no heed of the blows, but sprang
again and again at the throat of the horse, till the duke
at last, believing him mad, seized a small battle-axe that
hung at his saddle-bow, and cleft his skull in two. With
a last effort to prevent the duke's egress, the faithful
animal dragged himself to the gate and died upon the
threshold; but the duke, with one sigh of regret, leaped
over the obstacle, and passed forth with his retinue.

Twenty paces farther, an old Jew, who dealt in
magic, it was said, and was a retainer of the house,
leaped suddenly from behind a wall, and seized the
duke's horse by the bridle, exclaiming—

"Turn back, my lord duke!   In the name of God,
turn back!"

"What aileth thee, Jew?" asked the duke, stopping.

"My lord," he answered, "I have passed the night
consulting the stars; and by my science I know that, if
you go to Montereau, you will never return;" and he
seized the horse by the bit to prevent him advancing.

"What sayest thou, De Gyac?" said the duke, turning
to his young favourite.

"I say," replied the knight, with a flush of anger
mounting to his brow—"I say that this Jew is a fool,

whom we must treat as your dog, unless you do penance for eight days to absolve yourself from his filthy touch."

"Leave me, Jew," said the duke thoughtfully, while he made a gentle sign for him to clear the way.

"Back, Jew!" shouted De Gyac, forcing his horse against the old man with a violence that threw him to the ground. "Back! Do you not hear my lord duke?"

The duke passed his hand over his eyes, as if to dissipate some gloomy thought; and, casting a look upon the Jew, who lay senseless upon the road, proceeded on his way.

Three-quarters of an hour after, he arrived at the castle of Montereau; but, before alighting, gave orders for a hundred men-at-arms and a hundred archers to proceed to the suburbs and relieve the guard of the night before, at the bridge.

At this moment Tanneguy advanced with the intelligence that the dauphin was already in the pavilion, awaiting the interview; but, as the duke set forward, a page rushed to him and murmured something in his ear.

The duke turned to Duchâtel. "By the holy saints!" he exclaimed, "the word to-day from every one is treason. Are you sure, Duchâtel, that our person runs no risk? It would be ill to countenance treachery."

"Most powerful seigneur," replied Tanneguy, "I would sooner be dead than plot treason against you, or aught else. Fear nothing; the dauphin means no ill."

"Well, then, let us proceed," exclaimed the duke. "We trust in God," and he raised his eyes to heaven; "and in *you*," he continued, fixing them on Tanneguy with one of those piercing glances peculiar to him.

Tanneguy sustained it boldly, and then presented a roll to the duke on which the names of the ten men-at-arms selected to accompany the dauphin were inscribed in the following order:—The Vicomte de Narbonne, Pierre de Beauveau, Robert le Loire, Tanneguy Duchâtel, Barbazan, Guillaume le Bouteillier, Guy d'Avaugour, Olivier Layet, Varennes et Frottier.

Tanneguy received in exchange the list of the duke's suite, as follows:—

Charles de Bourbon, the Seigneur de Noailles, Jean de Fribourg, Saint Georges, the Seigneur de Montagu, Du Vergy, the Seigneur d'Ancre, Guy de Pontarlier, Charles de Lens, and Pierre de Gyac; each of whom, in addition, brought his secretary.

As Tanneguy departed with the list, the duke dismounted in order to proceed on foot from the castle to the bridge. He wore a black velvet cap on his head; a light coat of mail was his only defence; and for an offensive weapon he merely carried a small, elegantly-wrought sword with a gold and jewelled hilt.

On reaching the barrier, Jacques de la Lime told him that he had seen a number of armed men enter a house close to the other extremity of the bridge, but on finding themselves observed, they had hastily closed up all the windows.

" Go, De Gyac, and see if it be true," said the duke; "I shall await you here."

De Gyac immediately set forward to the bridge, traversed the barriers, passed through the pavilion, reached the house indicated, and opened the door. Tanneguy was inside, giving instructions to about twenty soldiers armed to the teeth.

"Well?" said Tanneguy, perceiving him.

"Are you prepared?" responded Gyac.

"Quite. He may proceed now.

De Gyac returned to the duke. " The Grand Master has mistaken, monseigneur," he said. "Not a soul is in the house."

The duke immediately set forward with his suite, and passed the first barrier, which instantly was closed behind him.

Some suspicions arose in his mind at this; but, seeing Tanneguy and the Sire de Beauveau advancing to wards him, he disdained to retreat.

" See, gentlemen," he said, showing his light coat of mail and fragile sword; " see how I come to you, trusting"—and here he laid his hand on Tanneguy's shoulder—" *in your honour*."

Then, in a firm voice, he repeated the words of the oath required.

The young dauphin was already in the pavilion. He wore a mantle of light blue velvet furred with sable, and a cap of the same, decorated with a wreath of golden fleurs-de-lis.

On perceiving the prince all doubts vanished from the Duke of Burgundy's mind. He advanced boldly; and though, on entering the tent, he observed that, contrary to all established usage, no barrier separated the rival parties, yet, conjecturing it was but an oversight, he took no public notice of the omission. When the ten lords that accompanied him had entered likewise, the two barriers were closed.

Twenty-four persons now found themselves shut up, with scarcely room to move in the narrow limits of the pavilion.

The duke removed his cap, and bending his left knee to the ground, before the dauphin, said—

"I have come in good faith, my lord, at your command, though some have assured me you only demanded the interview to load me with reproaches; but, in truth, that cannot be, since I have not merited them."

The dauphin folded his arms, without attempting either to embrace or raise the duke, as he had done at their first interview.

"You deceive yourself, my lord duke," he replied severely. "We have grave reproaches to make against you for not holding by your promises. Did you not suffer my good town of Pontoise, the very key of Paris, to be taken? and instead of flinging yourself into my capital to defend it, or die there, as became a loyal subject, you fled to Troyes."

"Fled, monseigneur!" exclaimed the duke, starting at the insulting expression.

"Ay, fled," repeated the dauphin, dwelling on the word. "You have ——"

But the duke sprang to his feet, determined to hear no more; and as the sword he wore had become entangled in his dress while kneeling, he laid his hand on the hilt to replace it properly.

The prince, not knowing what he meant by the action, recoiled a step, while Robert de Loire flung himself between them, exclaiming, "Ah! you touch your sword in presence of your lord!"

The duke tried to speak, but at the instant Tanneguy stooped down, and taking the axe he had worn the night before from beneath the tapestry, raised himself to his full height, and lifting the weapon high over the head of the duke, uttered the words, "It is time!"

The duke saw the blow descending, and tried to parry it with his left hand, while he endeavoured to draw his sword with the right; but there was no time. The axe of Tanneguy fell, striking down the duke's hand, and cleaving his skull in two to the very chin.

For an instant the form of the duke remained standing, like a strong oak swaying before it falls; then, as Robert de Loire plunged a poniard into his breast, he fell heavily to the ground, at the very feet of De Gyac.

Great was the clamour that arose in the tent. "Treason! treason!" shouted the Burgundians. "Kill! kill!" cried the French. Swords clashed and axes gleamed, and in an instant twenty men were engaged in a fierce death-struggle, within a space where two would have hardly found room to fight. Sparks flashed from their arms and blood spouted from their wounds, till the alarmed dauphin was fain to throw himself head foremost over the barrier. The President Louvet rushed forward to aid him, hearing his cries, drew him out by the shoulder, and succeeded in carrying him to the town, though almost insensible, and with his blue velvet robes all stained and splashed with the blood of the Duke of Burgundy.

Meanwhile, De Montagu, of the duke's party, had scaled the barrier and given the alarm. De Noailles would have followed him; but a blow on the back of the head from Narbonne sent him reeling out of the tent, and he expired on the threshold. Saint Georges received a severe wound from an axe, and D'Ancre had his hand cut off.

Still the cries and combat continued in the tent without intermission. They fought foot to foot over the dying duke's body, but none thought of succouring him. At one time the Dauphinois had the advantage; but just then four Burgundians, who had been alarmed by De Montagu's cries for help, arrived to aid their friends within the tent. Three of them flung their swords at the foe inside, while the fourth broke the barrier. The Dauphinois, however, were speedily reinforced by the soldiers who had lain concealed in the house; and the

Burgundians, at last seeing resistance useless, took flight by the broken barrier. The Dauphinois pursued them, and finally but three persons were left within the silent and blood-stained tent: the Duke of Burgundy, who lay extended dying on the ground; Pierre de Gyac, erect and with folded arms, calmly watching his death-struggles; and, lastly, Olivier Layet, who, pitying the sufferings of his unfortunate master, would have ended them by a sword-thrust, if De Gyac, who saw his intention and apparently did not wish to lose one single groan, or a single convulsion of the dying man, had not dashed the sword violently from his hand, exclaiming, with a bitter laugh, "Can you not let the poor prince die tranquilly?" Then, when the duke expired, he laid his hand upon the breast, as if to assure himself of the fact, and disappeared from the tent, unnoticed, and seemingly unconscious of all else passing around him.

Meanwhile the Dauphinois were returning to the tent after having pursued the Burgundians to the castle walls. Inside they found only the body of the duke, extended on the ground, in the place they had left it; and beside it, with his knees in blood, the curé of Montereau, reciting the prayers for the dead.

Their first impulse was to seize the corpse and fling it into the river; but the priest, lifting his crucifix, menaced with the vengeance of heaven whoever dared to lay hands upon the poor form whose soul had been dislodged so violently. Then Cœsmerel, the bastard of Tanneguy, detaching one of the duke's golden spurs, vowed to carry it thenceforth as an order of knighthood: and the Dauphinois, following his example, took off all the rings with which his hands were covered, and the magnificent chain of gold that hung round his neck, to bear away with them as trophies.

The priest remained there till midnight. Then, with the aid of two men, he had the body carried to a mill near the bridge, where it was laid upon a table, while prayers were recited over it during all that night. Next morning, at eight o'clock, the duke was buried in the Church of Nôtre Dame, before the altar of St. Louis. He wore the doublet and hose in which he had been murdered, and his velvet cap was drawn over the face.

No religious ceremony accompanied the inhumatior,

but masses were chanted for the repose of his soul
during the three following days.

The day after the assassination of the Duke of Burgundy, the corpse of Madame de Gyac was found by
some fishermen of the Seine floating down the river.

CHAPTER II.

NAPOLEON.

On the evening of the 17th of February, 1814, the inhabitants of Montereau beheld in position upon every
height, extending over the surrounding plains, and
thronging every portion of their town in numbers that
seemed incalculable, a dense mass of Wurtemberg
troops—the rearguard of the triple army then pursuing the conquered Napoleon, with the fifteen thousand men who still clung to him, though rather as an
escort than a defence. Bitterly these Wurtembergers
seemed to regret the fate that destined them to remain
behind, as they fixed their eager eyes upon the Seine
flowing on to the capital, and shouted "*Paris! Paris!*"
—that fatal cry, whose echo still haunts us all from our
childhood; so strange and terrible was its sound from
the lips of strangers.

Still, during all that day, the roar of the cannon was
heard from Mormant to Provins, though the foreign
troops, in their careless security, seemed to take little
heed of it: one of the defeated generals perhaps still
holding out, like a wild boar at bay, against the Russians.
But what had they to fear? Was not Napoleon the conqueror flying before them? Was he not eighteen leagues
from Montereau, with his harassed corps of fifteen thousand men, and scarcely strength enough left in them
to reach the capital? Night came. Next day the cannon was heard louder and nearer. Each time this great
war-note of battle was struck, it resounded closer to
the town. The Wurtembergers were startled at last.
They listened. The cannon could be only two leagues
from Montereau; and the cry, "To arms!" ran like an

electric shock through their ranks; the drums beat; the trumpets sounded; and the horses of the aides-de-camp pawed the ground with their iron hoofs. The enemy was ready for the combat.

Suddenly a disordered mass is seen flying along by the Nogent road, pursued so closely by the French cavalry that the breath of our horses may be felt upon their shoulders. These are the Russians, who but the day before had formed the vanguard of the army of invasion, and penetrated even to Fontainebleau.

Upon the night of the 16th, Napoleon had wheeled round, got post-carriages to convey his soldiers, and post-horses to drag his cannon. Fresh cavalry from the Spanish army came up and followed him at a gallop. On the morning of the 17th, he and his army had drawn up in battle array before Guignes. There they fell in with the advanced guard of the allied army, defeated them, reached the Russian columns, and routed them completely. The enemy fell back. From Guignes to Nangis it was a retreat, but from Nangis to Nogent a flight. Napoleon, as he galloped past the Duke de Bellune, flung him an order to detach three thousand men from the main body, and await him at Montereau. What need had he of fifteen thousand soldiers to pursue twenty-five thousand Russians? By proceeding in a straight line, the duke had only six leagues' march to Montereau. Napoleon would join him there on the morrow by a circuitous road of seventeen leagues; but Bellune and his three thousand men lost their way, occupied ten hours in accomplishing a march of six leagues, and on reaching Montereau found that, two hours before, the town had been occupied by the Wurtemburg troops.

Meanwhile, Napoleon swept the enemy before him as the tempest sweeps the desert sands, passed them, and, wheeling round again, drove them back upon Montereau, where Bellune and his three thousand men, he thought, were awaiting him. This cannon, then, that startled the Wurtembergers, was his; this cavalry that shook the earth was his; this man, seen everywhere amid fire and smoke, in the van of the pursuers, chasing twenty-five thousand Russians before him with his horsewhip; this man is Napoleon!

But the flying Russians found themselves unexpect-
edly in the arms of their friends, the fresh Wurtemberg
troops; while Napoleon, who calculated on the aid of
Bellune and his three thousand men, to imprison the
Russians between two fires, found instead a body of
ten thousand enemies, a wall of bayonets, and on the
heights of Surville, where the tri-colour should have
floated, eighteen pieces of cannon pointed for his destruction.   In an instant he comprehended his position,
and issued the order to take the guns.   The guard
dashed forward, sustained three discharges from the
battery, but eventually killed the gunners at their posts,
and the position was ours.

The cannon, however, was no longer serviceable, for
the enemy had time to spike their guns; fresh artillery,
therefore, had to be dragged up by main force.   Napoleon directs, places, points it.   The whole mountain
flames up like a volcano; entire ranks of Russians and
Wurtembergers are swept down by the balls.   The
enemy returns the fire; his shot whistles and rebounds
over the lofty platform.   Napoleon is in the very centre
of the iron hail-storm.   His staff try to force him to
retire.   "Leave me! leave me, friends!" he exclaimed,
clinging firmly by one of the gun carriages; "the ball
to kill me has not yet been cast!"   At the smell of
powder the emperor seemed to have given place to the
lieutenant of artillery.   Courage, Bonaparte! Save
Napoleon!

The Breton national guards take the faubourg of
Melun at a bayonet charge, while General Pajol pene-
trates with his cavalry by the Fossard side up to the entrance of the bridge; there, Russians and Wurtembergers are so wedged together that not only the enemies'
bayonet, but the mere pressure of their bodies, obstructs
his advance.   It becomes necessary to clear a way with
the sabre, as you clear a forest with the axe.   Then
came down the full strength of Napoleon's artillery on
this single point, sweeping the bridge from end to end;
clearing a furrow through the dense mass of human
life, like the track of a ploughshare through the field.
Still the crowd seemed unthinned; they stifled between
the parapets.   At last the bridge breaks, and in an instant the Seine and Yonne are covered with dying men

and crimsoned with blood. The butchery lasted four hours.

"And now," said Napoleon, as he leant exhausted against a gun carriage, "now I am nearer to Vienna than they are to Paris." Then he dropped his head upon his hands, and remained ten minutes absorbed in thoughts of ancient victories and hopes of coming triumphs. When he raised his head again, an aide-de-camp was before him with intelligence that Soissons, the very gate of Paris, was open to the enemy, who were now but ten leagues from his capital.

Napoleon listened, as to a thing which had become familiar to him for the last two years, either from the inefficiency or treachery of his generals. Not a muscle of his face moved; not a single evidence of emotion could be detected, by those around him, on the calm brow of the sublime gambler who had staked and lost a world. He made signs for his horse to be brought him; then indicating with his finger the road to Fontaine-bleau, merely said, " Let us proceed, gentlemen." And thus impassibly this man of iron set forward, as if no fatigue could weaken his frame, and no reverses subdue his soul.

Suspended from the arched roof of the church of Montereau may still be seen the sword of John of Burgundy; and, on all the houses facing the heights of Surville, the traces left by the bullets of Napoleon.

CHAPTER III.

LYONS.

NEXT evening we stopped at Châlons, and reckoned on reaching Lyons easily by water from thence. But our hopes were vain. The river was so low that even during the day the boats had to be dragged up by horses, their keels labouring miserably through the mud and sand of the bed of the stream; so we gave up all thoughts of proceeding after that manner. As the coach, however, did not leave till next day, I bethought me of the ruins of a certain château visible from the road, about four or five leagues from Châlons; and, having nothing better to do, we resolved to make an excursion there the following morning, and carry our breakfast along with us.

We found nothing remaining of the ancient castle of Roche-Pot except a circular enclosure, within which were the buildings destined for the vassals and retainers and the service of the château. The date of its erection was evidently after the close of the Crusades; two towers only seemed to me anterior to that period. A perpendicular rock forms the base of the edifice, and the foundations are laid with so much artistic skill, that, notwithstanding the eight centuries which have passed by, it is still difficult to distinguish the precise point at which the work of man is superposed upon that of God.

Groups of cabins are clustered round the base like swallows' nests in the rock, secure under the shadow and protection of the feudal house; but now the castle is silent, deserted, and in ruins, while the huts of the peasants stand erect, still filled with active, joyful life. And yet the lords of the castle were men of note, who have left their traces in history. In 1434, Jacques Pot, Lord of La Roche, assisted with honour at the tournament held by the Duchess of Burgundy.

In 1451, Philip Pot is named chief of the embassy sent to Charles VII. by the Duke of Burgundy. In 1477, Philip Pot, and Guy Pot his son, sign as plenipotenitaries the treaty of Sens between the King Louis XI. and Maximilian, husband of Mary Duchess of Burgundy.

In 1480, Duke Maximilian of Burgundy erased from the list of knights of the Golden Fleece the name of Philip Pot, Lord of La Roche, suspected of being in the interests of Louis XI.

Here I lose the traces of this noble family, and return to the ruins, which now belong to a citizen of Lyons; though it was from having been the victim of a very curious sharper's trick that he became the possessor of them.

Towards the close of 1828, an individual presented himself at the house of the peasant who then owned the ruins of La Roche, with the two or three acres of stony soil in which they stand, and demanded at what price he would consent to sell his title.

The peasant, who scarcely found nettles enough amid

the old bricks and stones to feed his cow, was ready enough to enter into terms, and the price was fixed, after a short discussion, at a thousand francs. Immediately they proceeded to a notary, who drew up the necessary deed, and the money was paid down; the buyer merely requesting that, for some private reason, the purchase-money named in the deed should be stated at fifty thousand francs.

As the seller was not required to defray the expense of the deed, he readily consented, highly delighted on any terms to obtain a thousand francs for an old ruin which only brought him yearly two or three dozen of crows' eggs; and the notary on his side was perfectly content to carry out any fantasy of his employer, however original, as soon as he was told the cost of the deed might be regulated by the simulated, not the real sum.

When the title was made over to him, the new proprietor got a copy of the deed, and proceeded to Lyons, showed it to a notary there, and demanded a loan of twenty-five thousand francs upon this property of La Roche, guaranteed by a first mortgage. The notary having made inquiry at the proper office as to whether the estate were encumbered with any other charges, and receiving for answer, that not a stone of the château owed a sous to mortal, instantly paid down the loan, and ten minutes after the deed was signed, the borrower departed with his money.

The day for repayment arrived, but neither the borrower, the money, nor the least thing resembling them, appeared.

Accordingly, the notary demanded to be put in possession, and obtained it after paying legal costs of a thousand crowns. Still, by the deed of sale, he had got the estate at half-price; and without delay he set off to visit his newly-acquired property.

He found only an old ruin, worth about fifty crowns to an amateur.

On descending to the village, they asked if we had seen the *Vaux Chignon;* we replied, that even the name of this curiosity was unknown to us. So, as noon had scarcely passed, we ordered the postilions to drive there. And truly it was a strange sight. In the very centre of one of those great plains of Burgundy, where the eye ranges on every side over a perfect level to the horizon, the ground is suddenly cleft in twain to the extent of about a league and a-half in length, and five hundred feet in breadth, leaving a chasm, down which, at the depth of two hundred feet or more, you behold a delicious valley, green as emerald, and furrowed by a little, silvery murmuring river, that mingles music with the grandeur and the beauty. After a ten minutes' descent down a gentle declivity, we found ourselves in the middle of this little Burgundian El Dorado, surrounded on all sides by perpendicular rocks that guard and isolate it from the rest of the world.

From thence we ascended the course of the stream, whose name we knew not—perhaps it has none—without meeting a human being or seeing a human habitation. There were harvests growing, apparently for the birds of heaven; grapes in no way defended from the thirsty lips of the wanderer; fruit-trees bending with the weight of their rich ripe burdens; till in the midst of all this silence, solitude, and luxuriant life, one was tempted to believe he had lighted upon some hitherto undiscovered corner of the earth. We continued the ascent of the river till we reached its two sources at the extremity of the valley; one springs from an opening in the rock large enough to admit of its course being traced to some distance through the sombre corridor before it sparkles into light; the other is fed from a higher spring, and falls from a height of about a hundred feet like a transparent scarf of gauze, then gently gliding down the rock leaves a verdant tapestry of moss to mark its passage.

Since then, I have seen the fair valleys of Switzerland, the sumptuous plains of Italy; have descended the course of the Rhine, and ascended that of the Rhone; have seen the Po between Turin and Superga, with the Alps before me and the Apennines behind: and yet, no scene, no sight, however grand, varied, and picturesque, could make me forget my little valley of Burgundy in its tranquil, lonely loveliness, with the silver stream which no one has yet named, and its light cascade showering a dewy rain upon the turf when the breeze sighs over the valley.

Next day we reached Mâeon, and from thence proceeded to Lyons by water. It was about eleven o'clock the following morning, that, on turning a bend of the river, we came in sight of this rival of Paris, throned upon her hill, with her double crown and regal robes of velvet and silk; Lyons, the vice-queen of France, who bends a river round her for a girdle, leaving one end of the cincture to float through Dauphiny and Provence down to the sea.

The approach to the river is grand and picturesque; Barbe Island, which serves for a Sunday promenade to the fashionables of the suburbs, meeting you like a maid of honour that announces the vicinity of a queen. Behind, as if for a protecting rampart to the city, rises the rock called Pierre-Scise, formerly surmounted by a castle that served as a state prison. During the wars of the League, the Duke de Nemours, having failed in his attempt to take the town, was imprisoned there. Ludovico Sforza, surnamed *Il Moro*, succeeded him; then De Thou and Cinq-Mars, both victims devoted to death, one from the hatred, the other from the policy of Richelieu, and who only left the prison to bend their heads to the executioner, who struck five times before they fell.

A young sculptor of Lyons had an idea of chiselling this immense rock into a colossal lion, the city arms, and would willingly have devoted five or six years of his life to accomplish it; but the authorities gave him no encouragement, and now the work has become impossible; for the inhabitants have so excavated the quarries to find materials for their bridges, theatres, and palaces, that in place of a lion, an artist could represent nothing admirably now except his den.

On passing Pierre-Scise, one meets a second rock that awakens softer memories; for in place of a prison, it is surmounted by the statue of a man holding a purse in his hand: a monument of Lyonnese gratitude, erected in 1716 to the memory of Jean Cléberg, surnamed " the good German," who every year devoted a part of his income to marriage portions for the poor girls of his neighbourhood. An accident, however, deprived the statue of its head; and when I was at Lyons the young girls mourned much over the mutilation, which seemed to them a fatal omen.

Three hundred steps farther, you find yourself at the

foot of the hill that formed the nucleus of the infant city. Cæsar halted here with his legions during the period of the Gallic conquest, and dug the trenches of his camp so deep, that nineteen centuries have not been able to efface the traces.

After the death of the conqueror who subjugated three hundred nations, and waged war against three millions of men, a few of his adherents, still faithful to the memory of their general, sought a place wherein to fix themselves and found a colony.

At the confluence of the Rhone and Saone they met with a band of Germans from the Danube, who had retreated before the wild mountain tribe of the Allobroges, and erected their tents upon this spot, so favoured by Providence with every natural advantage. A treaty of alliance was soon formed between them and the proscribed Romans; and in a short time, under the name of Lucii Dunum,* arose the foundations of a city which soon became the capital of Gaul and the centre of communication, by means of those four grand roads traced by Agrippa, which still traverse modern France from the Alps to the Rhine, and from the Mediterranean to the ocean.

Sixty cities of Gaul then recognised Lucii Dunum for their queen, and erected a temple at the common expense to Augustus, whom they reverenced as a god. Under Caligula this temple changed the object of its worship, and became the place where an academy held its sittings, one of whose regulations reveals the character of the imperial fool that founded it. The rule runs, that whatever acamedician be convicted of having written a bad work shall efface the same entirely with his tongue, or, if he prefer it, be plunged into the Rhone.

Lucii Dunum was but a century old, and already rivalled the Greek Massilia and the Roman Narbo in magnificence, when it was reduced to ashes, struck by lightning, some say; but so rapid was the conflagration, that Seneca, the historian of the disaster, says, "Between an immense city and an annihilated city there intervened but a night."

* By abbreviation Luc Dunum, by corruption Lucdunum, from whence Lyons.

Trajan took pity on the fallen queen. Under his powerful protection Lucii Dunum arose from its ashes, and a magnificent building, destined for merchandise, was erected upon the hill. No sooner was it opened than the Bretons hastened there with their painted bucklers, the Iberians with those fine steel weapons they alone knew how to temper. From Corinth and Athens came, by way of Marseilles, pictures painted upon wood, bronze statues, and graven stone. Africa sent her lions, panthers, and tigers, drunk with the blood of the amphitheatres; and Persia her fleet horses, rivalling in reputation those coursers of Numidia which Herodotus tells us were engendered by the wind.

Here we leave the separate history of Lyons, which, after the year 532, became united to that of the Frank kingdom. Three monuments still exist to attest her progress, and likewise her decadence in art after that period: the Church of Ainai, the Cathedral of St. John, and the Hôtel de Ville; the first contemporary with Charlemagne, the second with St. Louis, the last with Louis XV.

The Church of Ainai stands upon the site of the temple built by the sixty nations of Gaul, in honour of Augustus. The four granite pillars supporting the dome were even borrowed by the Christian sister from her pagan predecessor. Originally they formed but two columns rising to double the height of the modern, and must at least have had an elevation of twenty-six feet. The architect of Ainai, however, preferred the reduced proportions of twelve feet ten inches, and so had them sawed in twain.

The Cathedral of St. John does not appear at first glance of the age we have named. The portico and façade belong evidently to the fifteenth century; perhaps they were rebuilt at that period, but the architecture of the grand nave gives undeniable proofs to the antiquary of the era of the Crusaders, when their memories of the East were first immortalized in stone by the western nations. One chapel within it is called, after the cardinal, "The Bourbon Chapel," and his motto, "Neither fear nor hope," is reproduced in all possible ways.

The Hôtel de Ville, however, is the edifice on which

Lyons most prides herself. The architecture is in the massive, frigid, decorated style of Louis XIV.; which is better, however, than that of Louis XV. as that excels the Republic, and the Republic the Empire, and the Empire that of Louis Philippe. Architectural art began to die in the age of the Grand Monarque, and gave up its last sigh in the arms of Perrault and Lepautre, between a group of Cupids, sustaining a vase of flowers and a river-god crowned with weeds.

· On descending the steps of the Hôtel de Ville, the scene of one of the darkest tragedies in the historical archives of Lyons lies before you. There, beneath your feet, fell the heads of Cinq-Mars and De Thou.

But recent memories still more sanguinary are recalled at the Promenade des Brotteaux: two hundred and ten Lyonnais were shot there after the siege of Lyons, and the pyramidal monument, surrounded by a railing, indicates the place where they lie buried.

During the last five or six years Lyons has struggled hard to obtain a literary, as well as a commercial celebrity; and truly admirable are the efforts of the young artists who have devoted their lives to this overwhelming task. They are like miners exploring a vein of gold in a granite mountain: each blow may clear away a mass of rock, but how little of the ore rewards their labours! And yet, thanks to their untiring perseverance, the new literature has already acquired a considerable influence even in that commercial city.

The work of political regeneration has been less slow in its operation: the seed fell upon the popular mind, always so ready to bring forth good fruit, and the results of the republican education were seen in the admirable device inscribed by the workmen of 1832 upon their banner: " Live working, or die fighting," which, in its advance from the wild cry of '93—" Bread or death!"—may in itself be taken as the exponent of the social progress of thirty-nine years. A still more remarkable sign of progress, however, is the establishment of a journal edited and conducted by the workmen themselves, in which all the vital questions concerning the highest interests of commerce are discussed and pronounced on with admirable ability.

The traveller finds three or four days quite sufficient

for the sights of Lyons. I do not speak of the manufactures and trades, but of the monuments and historical *souvenirs*. So, when you have visited the museum; seen the "Ascension" of Perugino, a Saint Francis d'Assise, by Espagnolet, an "Adoration of the Magi," by Rubens, "Moses saved from the Nile," by Veronese, "Saint Luke painting the Virgin," by Giordano; the famous bronze table found in 1529, upon which is graven the speech made by the Emperor Claudius, in favour of Lyons being admitted to the privileges of a Roman colony; when you have thrown a glance at the monastery of St. Clair, where in 1530 the dauphin, son of Francis the First was poisoned by the Count de Montecuculli; explored the ruins of the ancient theatre, where nineteen thousand Christians were massacred in the second century, whose only epitaph consists of eight lines graven on the pavement of a church; then, if you have nothing better to do, take the coach, as I did, for Geneva, at eight o'clock in the evening, and next morning at six you will be awakened by the driver, who has acquired the habit of asking his travellers to walk a bit for the sake of the poor horses. Fear not, however, to accept the invitation, for the scenery is so grand and marked, one could almost imagine himself already in a valley of the Alps. About ten you reach Nantua, situated at the extremity of a lovely little sapphire lake, set in mountains, like a precious jewel Nature was afraid to lose. Some leagues farther, we stopped at Bellegarde for dinner, and afterwards proposed a visit to the spot of the Rhone's disappearance, about ten minutes' walk from the inn. The driver opposed our project, but we all entered into open rebellion against him, including his postilion, whom we bribed with a bottle of wine, and he was constrained at last to succumb to the majority.

By a rapid declivity we reached the river, and stood upon the bridge that spans its banks, one side of which belongs to Savoy, the other to France. Each nation is represented by a custom-house officer, stationed there to see that no article passes without paying the requisite duty; and we found these two good excisemen were smoking away together after the most amicable fashion: a touching sign of the cordiality existing between the two kingdoms.

The phenomenon we came to see is best observed from the centre of this bridge. The Rhone comes onward, deep and foaming, when suddenly it disappears altogether within the transverse cleft of a rock, to re-appear again fifty paces farther, the intervening space remaining quite dry; so that the bridge upon which we stood overlooks, not the river, but the dry rock that covers it. What passes within this abyss where the Rhone precipitates itself has never been ascertained. Wood and cork, dogs and cats, have been thrown into the river at the point where it enters the rock, but they have never re-appeared. The gulf restores nothing it has once swallowed.

On returning to the inn, our driver was furious.

"Gentlemen," he exclaimed, showing us into the coach, "you have made me lose half-an-hour!"

"Bah!" returned our postilion, wiping the wine from his lip with the sleeve of his coat, "what a fuss about your half-hour! We'll soon catch it again."

And truly he lashed the horses with such effect, that in three hours, as we passed through Saint Genis, he turned and said to us, "Gentlemen, you are no longer in France." Twenty minutes after, we reached Geneva.

CHAPTER IV.

THE TOWER OF THE LAKE.

NEXT to Naples, Geneva is one of the loveliest situated cities in the world, as she lies there negligently resting her head upon the base of Mont Salève, while the waves of the lake press forward to kiss her feet, and with nothing else to do, apparently, than fling her sunny glances upon the thousand valleys stretching up towards the snowy peaks on her right, or crowning the summits of the green hills on her left. At a sign from her hand the lake is covered with light barks that glide on the surface of the water, white and rapid as sea-gulls, or with dark steamers tossing the light spray before them in clouds. With the beautiful sky above, and the scene around, it seems as if this fair city had only to breathe and be glad. And yet this lovely odalisque, this languid sultana, in appearance, is the Queen of Industry, the mercantile Geneva, that reckons ninety-five millionaires amidst her twenty thousand children. Geneva, as its Celtic etymology indicates,* was founded nearly two thousand five hundred years ago. Cæsar in his Commentaries Latinised the barbaric appellation into Geneva; Antoninus, in his turn, changed the name in his itinerary to Genabum; Gregory of Tours in his Chronicles calls it Janoba; from the eighth to the fifteenth century it is designated by authors as Gebenna; finally in 1536 the name settled down into Geneva, and has remained so ever since.

Cæsar is the first who gives us any information respecting this town. He established military posts there to repel the invasion of the Helvetic tribes, and built a tower on the island of the Rhone that still bears his name. When it passed under Roman sway, Geneva adopted the gods of the Capitol. A temple of Apollo rose upon the site now occupied by St. Peter's Church, and a rock in the centre of the lake was consecrated by the fishermen to the god of the sea. Towards the close of the seventeenth century, while making some excavations at its base, two small hatchets and a sacrificial knife were found; but in our days this altar to Neptune has degenerated into the plain appellation of Niton's Stone.

Geneva remained under Roman rule for five centuries, then fell into the hands of the Burg-Hunds, or Burgundians, at the time the barbaric hordes inundated Europe, and was made by them the most important city of their kingdom. The domination of the Ost-Goths succeeded that of the Burgundians, but they only held Geneva fifteen years. The king of the Franks retook, and once more allied it to its Burgundian kingdom, of which it remained the capital till 858; when, after many vicissitudes, it was united to the Germanic empire by Conrad le Salique, who had himself crowned there the same year by Herbert, Archbishop of Milan.

It would be tedious to follow its history during the

* *Gen*, passage; *ev*, river.

long struggles between the Counts of Geneva and the Counts of Savoy; but they ended by the city passing definitively, in 1401, under the power of the latter.

It was the epoch when a great social transformation was taking place in Europe. The communes of France had received their freedom in the eleventh century; the towns of Lombardy organised themselves into a republic in the twelfth; and, at the beginning of the fourteenth century, the cantons of Schwitz, Uri, and Unterwalden separated from the empire, and formed the basis of that confederation destined to include all Helvetia.

Placed in the centre of this popular movement, Geneva felt the glow of liberty upon her cheek, and, in 1519, contracted an alliance with Fribourg, followed soon by bonds of citizenship with Berne.

Children were born to her who became great men; apostles appeared who preached liberty at the foot of the scaffold; martyrs, such as Bonnivard, who, flung into the dungeon of Chillon, remained for six years there chained to a pillar; or Pecolat, who cut his own tongue through with his teeth, and spat it out in the face of the executioner who bade him denounce his comrades; or Berthelier, who, when led to the scaffold, and pressed to solicit the duke's pardon, replied, "It is only for criminals to ask pardon: let the duke demand it of God, for he is my murderer!" And he laid his head upon the block.

The reformed religion, which impelled all nations at first to take such mighty strides forward, that, tired with the effort, they have remained stationary ever since, entered Geneva, after having overrun Germany and Switzerland. It was a powerful auxiliary to liberty, for it added religious hatreds to political differences.

In 1535, the Bishop Pierre de la Beaume was expelled from Geneva, and the republic was proclaimed.

In 1536, we find Calvin in high repute there. The council offered him the chair of theology. His austere manners, bold, unscrupulous eloquence, along with the severity of his principles, gave him unbounded influence; and when he died, in 1554, he left the little town of Geneva the capital of a new religious world: it was a Protestant Rome.

The seventeenth and eighteenth centuries were periods

of rest for Geneva. Then rose her commercial power, which increased so rapidly that industry became everything, territorial property nothing; for, if every citizen had claimed a portion of the soil, ten feet square would scarcely have been allotted to each one of them.

Napoleon found Geneva reunited to France, and for twelve years it hung like a golden ornament on his imperial mantle. But when the kings of Europe, in 1814, divided this mantle amongst themselves, the stitched-on pieces likewise fell into their hands. The King of Holland got Belgium; Savoy and Piedmont fell to Sardinia; Italy to Austria; Geneva remained—no one would have her. Still, they did not choose her to remain with France; so a congress made her a present to the Helvetic Confederation, to which, accordingly, she was annexed, by the title of Twenty-second Canton.

Above all the Swiss capitals, Geneva represents the aristocracy of money: it is the city of wealth, watches, gold chains, and fine equipages. Its three thousand artizans furnish the whole of Europe with jewellery. Seventy-five thousand ounces of gold, and fifty thousand silver marks, pass every year, in different forms, through their hands; and their salaries alone amount to two millions five hundred thousand francs.

The most fashionable jeweller is decidedly Bautte: no dreams of imagination could surpass the marvellous beauty of his collection. There are things there to peril souls feminine, to turn the brain of a Parisian, and make Cleopatra tremble with envy in her tomb.

They are subject to heavy duties entering France, but for a brokerage of five per cent. Bautte undertakes their free transmission. This treaty between buyer and seller is even made openly, as if there were no custom-house in the world; and in truth Bautte has a wonderful aptitude for defrauding the revenue, as one anecdote amongst a thousand will testify.

When the Count de Saint Cricq was Director-General of the Customs, he heard so many stories of Bautte's cleverness in this way, that he resolved to test it himself, and went to Geneva on purpose. There he visited the shop of Bautte, and purchased jewels to the amount of thirty thousand francs, on condition they should be delivered, duty free, at his hotel in Paris.

Bautte agreed, merely requiring him to sign a private document, consenting to an additional payment of five per cent. on receipt of the goods. The count smiled, took the pen, signed *Saint Cricq, Director-General of the Customs*, and handed back the paper to Bautte, who read it, bowed, and replied, "Monsieur Director of the Customs, the articles you have done me the honour to purchase shall be delivered on your arrival in Paris." The count, who had now thrown down the gauntlet, scarcely gave himself time to dine; immediately after he ordered post-horses, and departed within one hour of the conclusion of the bargain.

On reaching the frontier, Saint Cricq related the whole affair to the chief-superintendent, and gave strict orders for a watch to be kept along the whole line, promising a reward of fifty louis to whichever officer seized the contraband jewels. Not one of them in consequence closed an eye for three days.

Meanwhile, the count reached Paris, alighted, embraced his wife and children, and then proceeded to his room to change his travelling-dress. The first thing he perceived was an elegant box upon the mantel-piece, the form of which was quite new to him. He advanced, and read upon a silver shield at the top, "M. le Comte de Saint Cricq, Director-General of the Customs." He opened it, and beheld the jewels he had purchased at Geneva.

Beautte had in fact bribed one of the waiters at the hotel where the count stopped to slip the contraband box into the carriage amongst the other packages of the director. On reaching Paris, his valet, seeing so beautiful and ornamental an article amongst the luggage, hastened to deposit it safely in his master's own room, and so the Director-General of the Customs became the first contrabandist in the kingdom.

Although Geneva has given birth to many men eminent in art and science, yet commerce is the only occupation of the inhabitants. Few know or care anything about modern literature; and a partner in a good bank would think himself insulted, probably, by a comparison with Lamartine or Victor Hugo. Society has something vulgar and mediocre in its arrangements, occasional display, and habitual thrift; so that even in the midst of luxury one is perpetually knocking his elbows against some petty piece of straitened economy. In Paris, our ladies possess albums of great beauty and considerable value; in Geneva, a lady hires one for her *soirée*, and that costs ten francs.

There is nothing to see here, except at the library a manuscript of St. Augustine upon papyrus; a history of Alexander by Quintus Curtius; and the household accounts of Philip the Fair, written upon waxen tablets; in the Church of St. Pierre, the tomb of Maréchal de Rohan and his wife, a daughter of Sully; and, lastly, there is the house of Rousseau, in the street that bears his name. You cannot miss it; for on a large black marble slab is engraven, in French, "Here J. J. Rousseau was born, the 28th June, 1712."

The drives about the environs of Geneva are perfectly delicious; and at every moment of the day elegant carriages can be had for hire, to convey the traveller wherever curiosity or caprice may lead him. We entered one, and set off for Ferney, which we reached in two hours.

The first thing you perceive before entering the château is a little chapel, with an inscription that startles one, though it consists of only three Latin words:

"DEO EREXIT VOLTAIRE."

The object of it evidently was to give notice to the world, that Voltaire at length had condescended to acknowledge the existence of a Supreme Being, and the world no doubt felt much gratified at the intelligence.

We crossed a garden, mounted the steps of the house, and found ourselves in the ante-chamber, where the pilgrims who come to adore the god of irreligion pause to collect themselves before entering the sanctuary. Here, too, the attendant goes over his solemn assurances that nothing has been changed in the apartment, not even the arrangement of the furniture, since M. de Voltaire lived there; and his oratory seldom fails to produce an effect. Nothing, in fact, can be more wonderful than the self-possession and prodigious self-importance of the man. It seems that, when a child, he was attached to the service of the great man, and, consequently, has his memory stored with anecdotes concerning him sufficient to throw the excellent citizens who are his auditors into a state of beatitude.

When we entered the sleeping-room, we found an entire family ranged in a circle around him, swallowing eagerly every word that fell from his mouth, as if their admiration of the philosopher extended even to the man who cleaned his shoes and powdered his *perruque*. It would be impossible to describe the scene fully; but, each time the porter uttered in his own peculiar accent the sacramental words "*M. Arouet de Voltaire*," he bowed and touched his cap, upon which the small circle, who perhaps would scarcely have uncovered before the Christ of Calvary, religiously imitated the movement.

Ten minutes after, our turn came for instruction. The circle paid and departed, and the porter became our sole property.

First, he walked us through the garden, from which the philosopher had truly a splendid view; showed us the covered alley in which "the fine tragedy of Irene" was composed; then, leaving us, suddenly cut off a strip of bark from a tree and handed it to me.

Fancying there was some peculiar look, or smell, or taste about it, I applied the fragment successively to my eyes, mouth, and nose. But no; it was nothing more than part of a tree planted by Voltaire, of which every visitor is expected to carry away a memorial. The poor tree, indeed, was near meeting an untimely fate lately, and still looks rather weakly. Some sacrilegious monster entered the park by night, and carried off, not a strip, but three or four square feet of the holy bark. "It was some fanatical worshipper of the 'Henriade,' no doubt, perpetrated the infamous deed," I said to the porter. "No, monsiéur," he replied; "I rather think it was some speculator who had received his orders from abroad."

Prodigious!

On leaving the garden the porter brought us to his own abode, and exhibited the stick of Voltaire, which he had religiously preserved, he said, since the death of the great man; but now, owing to the necessities of the times, he feared he must part from the precious relic, and finally ended by offering it to us for a louis.

I replied it was too dear; for, eight years before, he

had sold the ditto of it to a friend of mine for twenty francs.

So, taking our leave, we re-entered the carriage, and set off for Madame de Staël's residence at Coppet.

No chattering porter there, no chapel dedicated to God, no tree-worship, but simply a beautiful park where every one may roam at liberty, and a poor woman who wept tears of real sorrow when speaking of her mistress, and showing the rooms she had inhabited, where no trace of her now remains.

We asked in vain to see the desk stained with the ink of her eloquent pen—the bed on which she breathed her last sigh: nothing of all that has been held sacred by the family!

The bed-room has been converted into some saloon or other, the furniture removed no one knows where. Perhaps in the whole château there could not be found a single copy of "Delphine."

From this room we passed into that of her son M. de Staël. Death had struck there twice; two beds were empty, a man's and a child's. M. de Staël and his son had died there within three weeks of each other.

We asked to see the family vault, but found that by M. Necker's bill no strangers were permitted entrance.

We had left Ferney with a stock of gaiety sufficient to carry us through a week; we quitted Coppet with tears in our eyes and sadness in our hearts.

The steamboat was just starting for Lausanne, so we lost no time, sprang on board, and were instantly on our way.

Lake Léman is a Bay of Naples: the same azure sky, azure water, and, yet more, the same dark mountains rising one above another like steps of stairs, only each step here is three thousand feet high; while above all towers the snowy forehead of Mont Blanc, like a great curious giant gazing down upon the other mountains, that seem only like little hills beside his colossal proportions.

One can scarcely turn away his glance from all this to examine the northern portion of the lake, which is, nevertheless, rich in soft, luxuriant beauty. Here Nature has flung down all the fruits and flowers she could gather in a corner of her robe, scattering them over parks, and vineyards, and fields. Here, too, we see a village extending eighteen leagues; castles built on every site, and according to every architectural caprice, bearing the dates of their birth sculptured on their brows. At Nyon we find Roman erections built by Cæsar; at Vuflans a gothic manor raised by Queen Bertha; at Morges rows of villas, that seem transported ready-made from Sorrento and Baïa; and, lastly, Lausanne herself with her slender spires—Lausanne with all her white houses, that, seen from a distance, seem like a group of swans drying their wings in the sun; and her little suburb of Ouchy, placed close by the lake, like a sentinel charged not to permit travellers to pass without rendering homage to the Vaudoise Queen.

Scarcely had I touched shore when I perceived a young republican named Allier, who, after the revolution of July, had been condemned to five years' imprisonment for some *brochure,* and took refuge at Lausanne. He had resided in the town for a month, which was a piece of great good fortune for me. My guide was found.

The moment we recognised each other, he threw himself into my arms, not that we had been particular friends, but from an excitement of emotion that betrayed the grief preying upon this poor wandering soul. In short, he was suffering from home-sickness.

The lovely lake, the unrivalled shores, the sublime mountains, the picturesque aspect of the most beautifully-situated town in the world, all were lost on him: he heeded them not. The foreign air was stifling him. I soon found, therefore, the poor youth could give me no information. When I asked of Switzerland he answered France; but he offered to present me to an excellent patriot, a deputy of Lausanne, who had received him like a brother in religion, and made no effort to console him, for the simple reason that the exile cannot be consoled.

M. Pellis was one of the most distinguished men I met in my travels. Learned, patriotic, and courteous, from the moment we touched hands we were brothers; and, during the two days passed at Lausanne, I received the most valuable information from him upon the history, legislation, and archæology of the canton.

The Canton de Vaud, which adjoins that of Geneva, owes its prosperity to quite different causes. Its wealth is not industrial, but territorial. The soil is divided into small portions, so that almost every one possesses a right to some fragment of the land; and out of a population of a hundred and ninety thousand, thirty-four thousand are proprietors—that is, according to calculalation, four thousand more than in all Great Britain.

For military purposes the canton is the best organised of the Confederation, having always thirty thousand men ready for action, or a fifth portion of the population. Did the French army follow the same ratio, its numbers would amount to six millions of soldiers.

Swiss troops receive no pay. It is considered part of a citizen's duty to serve in the army, and by no means an onerous one. For three months in each year they live in barrack, practising military tactics and inuring themselves to hardship, by which means, at the first summons to war, Switzerland can turn out an army of a hundred and eighty thousand men that do not cost the government a fraction, while the budget for our effectual force of four hundred thousand men amounts, I believe, to three hundred and six millions.

No one is made an officer till he has served two years, and no citizen can marry till he possesses arms, a uniform, and a Bible.

The legislative organisation is established upon an equally just and solid basis. Every five years the Chamber of Deputies is subject to an entire, and the Executive Council to a partial change. Every citizen is an elector. The elections take place in the church, and the deputies take the oath before the federal escutcheon, on which are inscribed the two words, "*Liberty, country.*"

The cathedral of Lausanne seems to have been commenced about the close of the fifteenth century; but the Reformation came to interrupt its progress, and the interior has now the usual desolate, unadorned aspect of Protestant churches. A large praying chair rises in the middle of the chancel; and during the time Calvinism made such rapid progress, it was here the Catholics used to come in such crowds to pray for their erring brethren, that the marble pavement still bears the impress of their knees.

The chancel is surrounded by monuments remarkable either for artistic excellence or for the illustrious remains they cover. Those of Pope Felix the Fifth and of Otho of Granson are well worth attention. The statue of the latter wants the hands, and the story of the mutilation runs thus:—

In 1393, Gerard d'Estavayer, becoming jealous of his wife, the beautiful Catherine de Belp, and the Sire Otho de Granson, resolved to revenge himself, and yet dissimulate the true cause of his vengeance, by accusing him of being the author of an attempt to poison the Count Amédée of Savoy, which had nearly proved fatal.

Accordingly, he laid his accusation solemnly before Louis de Joinville, Bailli of Vaud, renewing it with still greater formalities before the Count Amédée of Savoy, and offering the *combat à outrance* to his enemy in proof of the verity of his accusation.

Although Otho was still weak from a recent wound, he accepted the defiance, feeling that his honour brooked no delay.

It was arranged, therefore, that the combat should take place on the 9th of August, 1393, at Bourg in Brescia; that each champion should be armed with a lance, two swords, and a poniard; and further, that the vanquished should lose both hands unless he avowed, if it were Otho, the crime of which he was accused, or if Gerard d'Estavayer, the falsehood of his accusation.

Otho was vanquished, and Gerard d'Estavayer called on him to avow that he was guilty. Otho replied by extending his two hands, which Gerard severed from his arms by a single blow.

This is why the statue has no hands, any more than the corpse of Otho; for they were burned by the hangman as the hands of a traitor.

When the tomb of Otho was opened, in order to transport his remains to the cathedral of Lausanne, they found a skeleton dressed in armour, casque on head and spurs on heel, with the cuirass pierced at the breast, showing the place where the lance of Gerard had entered.

The modern monuments are those of the Princess Catherine Orloff and of Lady Strafford Canning. In commiseration of his profound grief, Lord Strafford obtained permission to have his wife interred within the cathedral, and Canova received orders from his lordship to execute a monument with the least delay possible. In five months the sculptor forwarded the monument completed, which arrived just the day after Lord Strafford had celebrated his nuptials with a second bride.

Our learned and amiable cicerone, M. Pellis, next conducted us to the penitentiary for criminals. We expected to see something like a French prison, but could imagine ourselves only in an hospital. The prisoners were taking their recreation when we arrived: that is, an hour's walk in a fine court set apart for the purpose. We saw them from a window conversing together in groups.

Afterwards we visited the cells; but nothing except the grating reminded one of a prison. Each was furnished suitably, and some even were adorned with a little library; for the prisoners are allowed to employ their leisure hours in reading.

The object of these penitentiaries is not only to provide a place where the guilty can be isolated from society whose laws have been violated, but where a course of moral training and discipline may fit them for a restoration to the place they forfeited.

In general, our French criminals quit their prisons more corrupted than they entered them: the Swiss, on the contrary, leave theirs disciplined and improved; for the prison regulations have been organised by the Vaudois government upon a sound logical basis.

Almost all crime is caused by poverty: that utter poverty when a man finds himself in the middle of society without power to aid himself or obtain means of existence in any one way. To isolate this man for a certain period from society, and then let him loose again to fall into precisely the same position in which he was tempted to crime, is not to make him better. He has been deprived of his liberty for a certain period, that is all. His liability to fall again into crime is even greater than when he was first imprisoned. The only chance of saving him is by placing him in a position in which he will have an equal chance of earning his livelihood with other men.

The first rule, therefore, in these penitentiaries is,

that every criminal shall be taught a trade, or made to practise his own, being allowed to reserve to himself two-thirds of the profits; and an article has been added lately to this philanthropic code authorising the prisoners to give a third of their savings to their parents, or their wives and families.

Thus the chain of natural ties, violently broken by justice, is renewed by these new relations. The money sent home by the prisoner ensures a joyful welcome for him when he returns to his family. Occupation has been taught him; and in place of coming back amongst them disgraced, poor, and naked, he re-enters his home purified from crime by punishment and moral training, and enabled to earn a livelihood for the future by means of the trade he has learned. Numerous instances could be cited from the registry of the house, proving the efficacy of this noble institution in rescuing the criminal from crime and ignorance, and enabling him to achieve an honourable position in society. Could the whole annals of our galleys and prisons shew even one?

When you have visited the promenade, the cathedral, eaten at the "Lion d'Or" of the unsurpassable fish called the *ferra* of Lake Léman, drunk of the white wine of Vevey, and taken some glasses of the best ice in the world at the *café* in the same street, then hire a carriage, for you have nothing more to do, and depart for Villeneuve. On the way look out for Vevey, where dwelt Clara; for the château of Blonay, where Julia lived; and Clarens, where they still show the house of Rousseau; and finally, on arriving at Chillon, look on the opposite shore for the steep rocks of La Meillerie, from the summit of which St. Preux gazed on the deep clear lake beneath, whose waters were death and repose.

Chillon, the ancient state prison of the Dukes of Savoy, and now the arsenal of the canton, was built in 1250. The captivity of Bonnivard has so filled it with his memory, that even the name of the prisoner has been forgotten who escaped from it in so miraculous a manner about 1798. The poor fellow contrived to make an opening in the wall by means of a nail that he had torn from the sole of his shoe; but he quitted his cell only to find himself in one still larger—that was all: a loop-hole, about three or four inches broad, barred with iron, was the only aperture. He tore these away with a force that seems almost superhuman; for his feet, which were the resisting power, have left their mark sunk a full inch into the stone floor at the point of the struggle.

Bonnivard and Berthelier are the heroes of Geneva. The first vowed one day that for the liberation of his country he would give his liberty; the other offered his life. Both were called on afterwards to redeem their pledges, and were found ready. Berthelier ascended the scaffold; Bonnivard was carried to Chillon to suffer the most horrible captivity. A pillar, to which an iron ring is attached, rises in the centre of the dungeon. To this he was fastened by an iron chain passed round his body, and thus remained for six years without power to walk or lie down, except within the limits of the chain, turning round and round his pillar like a wild beast, hollowing out his own footsteps in the stone by the forced monotony of his track, agonised by the thought that even all this suffering was of no avail to his country, and that Geneva and he were alike devoted to eternal chains. How was it that in the long night, never broken by a sunbeam—in the silence only troubled by the waters of the lake dashing against the walls of the dungeon—how was it that thought did not kill matter, or matter thought? How was it that some morning the jailer did not find his prisoner dead or mad? that one idea, one eternal idea, did not break his heart or dry up his brain? And yet during these six years—this eternity—not a groan, not a complaint escaped from his lips, say his jailers; except, perhaps, when heaven unchained the storm, when the tempest roused the waves, and the rain and wind lashed the dungeon walls; then his voice may have mingled with the great voice of Nature; for God alone could hear his cries and groans, but the jailers never fed their eyes with his despair. Each morning he was calm and still as the landscape over which the tempest had passed. Oh! without that transient relief, would he not have dashed his head against the pillar, or strangled himself with his own chain? would he have been living at that hour when his dungeon was flung open and a hundred voices exclaimed, "Bonnivard, thou art free!" And Geneva? "Free likewise!"

Since then the martyr's dungeon has become a temple, and his pillar an altar. Every noble heart to whom liberty is dear turns aside from his path and bends to pray where he had suffered. They visit the pillar where he was chained; they seek upon its granite face, where every one leaves his name, for some word left by the martyr's hand; they stoop to the worn pavement to trace the impress of his footsteps; they pull at the iron ring to test its strength after eight centuries; all other ideas are absorbed in one: here, to this ring, a man was chained for six years: six years! that is to say, for the ninth portion of a human life.

One evening—it was in 1816, during one of those beautiful nights that God seems to have created alone for Switzerland—a boat glided silently over the lake, leaving a silver trail behind her, glittering in the moonlight, up to the white walls of Chillon. Gently, like a swan, it paused; a man stepped on shore, wrapped in a large dark mantle; still one could perceive his bright, piercing eyes; his pale, haughty brow; and, though the mantle touched the ground, that he limped slightly.

He demanded to be shown the dungeon of Bonnivard, and remained a long while there alone. When he departed, a new name was found inscribed on the pillar. It was that of BYRON.

CHAPTER V.

NIGHT FISHING.

AT noon we reached Villeneuve, situated at the eastern extremity of Lake Léman, from whence I proceeded to examine the spot where the Rhone falls, grey and muddy, into the lake, and, after traversing its whole extent, rises up again, clear and azure, at Geneva.

On returning to Villeneuve the coach was ready to start; so I took my place beside the driver, with the cold evening breeze in my teeth, but for compensation the whole splendid panoramic view of the scenery lay before me.

And in truth it was a grand prospect across the blue

horizon of the Alps; this valley opening on the lake to a breadth of about two leagues, then narrowing gradually till at Saint Maurice it is closed by a gate, so straitly is it bound in between the Rhone and the mountain; and the beautiful villages rising on every side, amid vineyards and pine-trees, some cresting a mountain, others lying along the declivity or bordering a precipice, with no mode of approach to them visible; while above all towers, to the left, 7,590 feet above our heads, the Dent de Morcles, glowing as a brick taken from the furnace; and to the right his sister, the Dent du Midi, lifting her snowy brow 8,500 feet into the clouds; both thrown upon the azure background of the sky, and painted by the sun's last rays, one a pale rose, the other tinted deep and fiery as a ruby. This was the glorious vision I enjoyed, and which even made me heedless of the chilling atmosphere while I traversed the enchanted region.

At nightfall we reached Bex, and alighted at one of those pretty inns found only in Switzerland. Dinner awaited us, and the fish was so excellent that I ordered some for breakfast next morning, which led to my witnessing a mode of fishing peculiar to the Valais.

No sooner had we expressed this gastronomical desire than the landlady summoned a great lad of eighteen or twenty, who seemed to hold the various offices of errand-boy, kitchen-boy, and "boots." He arrived half asleep, and took the order in spite of some very expressive yawns—the only protest against active service the poor devil dared offer to his mistress, when she commanded him to go instantly and fish for trout for monsieur's breakfast, indicating me with her finger.

Maurice, such was the name of the victim, threw a sleepy glance at me, so full of undefined reproach, that I became quite melted at witnessing the struggle between his obedience and despair, and began—

"But really, if this fishing would be inconvenient"—here the face of Maurice brightened up—"if this fishing——"

"Bah!" said the mistress, interrupting me; "it can be all done in an hour; the river is not two steps from here. Go, you idle fellow! take your lantern and knife, and make haste."

So poor Maurice resigned himself to fate with the
apathy habitual to those born to serve.

A lantern and knife to fish!   Ah! poor Maurice had
no chance of escape from that moment, for I was filled
with an irresistible desire to see fish gathered like so
many sticks.

Maurice uttered a deep sigh; for truly he had no hope
but in God, and God had seen him so often in a similar
situation without ever helping him, that there was little
chance of a miracle being worked in his favour.   Accordingly, with an energy like despair, he took a garden
knife, hung up amidst some culinary instruments, along
with a lantern of such curious form that I must describe it.

It was a globe of horn, as round as the lamps we sus-
pend in our rooms, but having an iron pipe attached to
it three feet long, of the form and thickness of the
handle of a broom.   As the globe was hermetically
sealed, the lighted lamp within received the air necessary for combustion through this tube, and was kept safe
from all chances of extinction by wind or rain.

"Are you coming, too?" said Maurice, seeing my
preparations for accompanying him.

" Certainly," replied I: " this sort of fishing seems
very original."

" Ay, ay," he muttered; " very original, to see a poor
devil up to his waist in water at the time he ought to be
sound asleep in his bed.   Will you have a lantern and
knife, too?—that would make it more original."

" *What! not gone yet?*" resounded from the inner room
at that moment, interrupting my response to the rather
ironical proposition of Maurice, while the landlady herself was heard approaching, muttering her disapproba-
tion in a manner that boded no good to one of us at
least.   Maurice felt all this, and, opening the door,
bolted out, without ever heeding me, so anxious was he
to escape the wrath of his mistress.   I darted after him,
fixing my eyes upon the lantern he held, which, however, was already at a distance.   Still I kept straight on
in the dark, never losing sight of my beacon, till my foot
tripped over something, and I was flung forward with a
horrible shock into the middle of the road, at the end of
which glittered my polar star.

The noise must have reached Maurice; but, far from arresting his progress, it seemed only to give renewed impulse to his velocity. On went the accursed lantern, dancing up and down, and then threatening to disappear altogether. My chance of overtaking it now seemed quite hopeless. Furious with pain, I rose up aching in every limb from my crash upon the pavement: rage gave me energy; and, in a voice of thunder, I rolled forth a malediction upon Maurice as a last resource.

The result was all I could have desired. The lantern passed suddenly from a state of agitatiou to a state of immobility, that gave it the aspect of a fixed star.

"*Pardieu!*" I said, advancing with my hand stretched out before me as a precaution against further dangers, "you are a strange guide! You hear me tumble with a crash sufficient to break the very stones of your road, and yet you go on and on with your lantern, never minding, never caring. Look at my clothes, all torn; my cheek bruised;" and I exhibited my wounds in succession to Maurice, who, truth to say, sustained the exhibition with wonderfully little emotion; merely saying, as he extirpated a mosaic of gravel from my hands and face, "Well, this is what you get by going to fish at near ten o'clock at night," and he phlegmatically pursued his way.

There was so much deep truth in the *egoism* of this answer, that I would not take up the argument, though it was attackable at three sides, but walked on in silence within the little circle of light radiated by the ill-omened lantern. At length Maurice stopped. "Here is the place," said he;" and I could distinguish the murmur of a little river through a kind of ravine about two hundred paces from us.

While I made my remarks, Maurice made his preparations. He took off his shoes, and rolled up all his habiliments in a tight band round his waist, giving himself thereby much the appearance of a portrait by Holbein or Albert Durer.

"Won't you do the same?" said he.

"Why, are you going into the water?"

"How else could I fish?" he replied; "and if you want to see me, take off your shoes and trousers, unless you prefer walking into the water with them on. There is no accounting for taste." And he commenced his descent of the steep and rocky ravine, at the bottom of which rolled the river where the miraculous draught of fishes was to take place.

I followed, tottering over the stones, and holding on by him as if he were a stout, straight iron pole. About thirty paces we proceeded in this way, when Maurice took pity on my weakness. "Here," said he, "take the lantern." I took it; upon which he seized hold of my arm under the shoulder, and, with that prodigious strength I have never met but in mountaineers, almost lifted me down the perilous descent; and, in spite of all his rancour against me, placed me safely at the bottom by the edge of the river.

I put my hand in the water. It was icy cold. "You are not going into that," I said, "surely?"

"Of course I am," he replied, taking the lantern from my hand, and slipping into the river.

"But the water is like ice," I said, drawing him back.

"Ay, it comes down from the snow up there," he answered, not understanding what I meant.

"Then, Maurice, you shall not go into this water."

"I thought you wanted trout for your breakfast?"

"Yes; but for a caprice of mine I will not suffer that a man—that you, Maurice—stand in this frozen water at the risk of dying in eight days of an inflammation of the chest. Come along, Maurice! come away!"

"And the mistress—what will she say?"

"Never mind; I'll make your peace."

"But it must be done." And Maurice put his second leg into the water.

"What do you mean?"

"Why, if you don't want the trout, another will. They all like it—the foreigners; a horrid fish like that; nothing but bones. What taste you all have!"

"Well! what of that?"

"Why, if I don't catch it for you, I must catch it for others: that is all; and so I had better begin at once. To-morrow night maybe some of you will say at the inn, 'I'd like to taste a chamois.' A chamois! The vile, black flesh! I'd as soon eat a ram; but no matter. When that's said, the mistress calls Pierre; for Pierre is the hunter, as poor Maurice is the fisher; and she says, 'Pierre, I must have a chamois.' He takes his gun and goes off at two o'clock in the morning; crosses the glaciers, the clefts of which might hold the whole village; climbs rocks where you might break your neck twenty times; and about four o'clock in the morning returns with his beast, until the day comes when he never returns at all."

"How so?"

"Why, you see, Jean that was before Pierre was killed; and Joseph, that served before me, died of a cold caught fishing for trout. Still we must go on—Pierre and I."

"But I have heard that all you mountaineers took the greatest pleasure in these exercises, and many of you passed the night on the mountain, watching to catch the chamois at the first dawn, or to fling your nets into the river."

"Ay, true enough," said Maurice; "but then they hunted and fished for themselves."

I was silent. What a bitter argument had this poor toiler unthinkingly flung into the unequal scale of human justice! Here in these mountains, these Alps, this lofty region of eternal snow, of eagles and of liberty, was still heard, without a hope of success, the ever-ceaseless pleading of those who *want* against those who *have*. Here, too, are men trained to do the work of hounds and cormorants, and catch game and fish for their masters, in return for which they are flung a morsel of bread. "Strange!" I thought. "Why cannot men fish and hunt for themselves? Whence springs this universal custom of slavery? If men willed to be free, could they not become free?"

Meanwhile, Maurice, who little thought how his words had set me dreaming, was up to his waist in water, and beginning his operations after a fashion perfectly new to me. First he plunged his lantern down to the very bottom of the stream, holding on by the long tube which kept the lamp supplied with air. In this way a large illuminated circle was formed at the bottom of the river, into which thronged the fish, attracted like moths to the light, knocking themselves against the shining globe, and swimming round and round it. Then Maurice gently raised the lamp higher and higher, the fish following the ascension, till all reached the surface of the water, when he adroitly struck the trout on the head with the knife held in his right hand, and down they fell again, headless and bleeding, to the bottom of the stream, to the surface of which they rose once more, only to be passed incontinently into the bag Maurice had suspended from his neck.

I was amazed.   My superior intellect, of which I had felt so proud five minutes before, was outdone; for it is evident, if I had been cast the night before upon a desert island, with only trouts in a stream for food, and no instruments with me but a lantern and knife, I must inevitably have died of hunger, notwithstanding all my superior intelligence.

Maurice suspected nothing of the admiration with which he was inspiring me, but silently continued to augment my enthusiasm by renewed proofs of his dexterity, choosing the finest and fattest trout as they sailed round the lantern, and leaving the small fry unhurt, as not worthy of his notice.   I could resist no longer; off went boots and pantaloons, and in a second I was beside Maurice in the water, never heeding the temperature, hardly two degrees above zero, nor the stones that cut my feet, but seizing the lamp and knife from my acolyte, fixed my eager eyes on a superb trout.   With all the tact of my predecessor, I lured him to the surface, and then applied the knife with a force sufficient to kill an ox, cutting the poor creature right in two.

Maurice took up the parts, examined them, then flinging them contemptuously into the water, exclaimed—

" That trout is spoiled."

" Spoiled or not," said I, " I'll get that trout and no other;" and so, picking up my fragments, I returned to shore just in time. for I was nearly frozen.

Maurice followed; he had caught eight trouts.   It was enough. |So we dressed and walked rapidly back to the inn.

" Well," thought I, returning, " if any of my thirty

thousand Paris friends could have seen me this night, standing in such a very remarkable costume in the middle of an ice torrent, would not all the journals have announced the next day that the author of 'Antony' had unhappily become quite insane, which (of course they would have added) was an irreparable loss to dramatic art?"

And while making these reflections, and congealing rapidly into ice, I began to think likewise of a certain wooden stool close by the kitchen chimney at the inn, on which I had left an enormous cat, that seemed perfectly incombustible. "Now," said I, "when I arrive, I shall go straight to that chimney, chase away the cat, and take possession of that stool."

The very idea gave me courage to proceed, by giving me hope. So I hastened my steps, keeping up a provisional heat in my fingers by means of the lantern I had taken possession of, and so happily arrived at the door of the inn within which was the blessed stool, the object of all my hopes. I rung vehemently; the landlady herself responded. Without a word, I rushed past her, crossed the parlour, and precipitated myself into the kitchen. The fire was out! At the same moment I heard the landlady following, and asking Maurice, "What ails the gentleman?"

" I believe he is cold," replied he.

Ten minutes after I was in a warmed bed, with a fine potation of hot wine beside me, by which means I escaped with nothing more than an abominable cold; in compensation for which, however, I had the honour of making an important discovery in science, for which I hope the Institute will thank me.

It is, that in the Valais they catch trout with a lantern and knife.

CHAPTER VI.

THE SALT MINES OF BEX.

NEXT day, having eaten the half of my trout, I set forth to visit the salt mines. Maurice and I had made it up, and he directed me towards a pleasant picturesque by-road, which soon brought me to the salt works.

The first part of the way certainly was a little fatiguing, but a delicious chesnut wood, totally unprotected from the appetite of wayfarers, enlivened me not a little. At sight of it, all my old marauding instincts returned, and by the aid of a great stone which I hurled against a tree near me, a shower of the nuts soon fell at my feet. To break them was my next object, and here my school-boy memories served me; for, after the fashion of those days, I began to roll them directly between the turf and the sole of my boot till the pressure combined with the rotation produced a satisfactory result. At the end of ten minutes I had my pockets full, and proceeded on my way, munching the *castaneæ molles* like any squirrel, or one of Virgil's shepherds.

This is an excellent receipt against *ennui*, and I re-commend it to every traveller who finds himself, like me, unsurrounded by any more mental or spiritual dis-tractions. For my soul's nourishment, indeed, I had come provided with three or four odes from Victor Hugo and Lamartine, which I recited aloud, and then began again, until I lost all perception of the sense of the words, but lulled my brain into a delicious intoxication with the mere harmony and rhythm.

a sculptor carving the head of Voltaire upon an oak stick.

Thanks to all these resources, time and distance vanished, and even when the chesnuts vanished too, and the odes became tiresome, I refreshed myself by impelling a stone forward on the road, and that never failed to restore my spirits.

At length I reached the mines, where I found some of the miners themselves ready to conduct travellers over the works. One of them took me in charge, and we made our preparations for the journey. They consisted in each taking a lighted lamp in his hand, and matches, flint, and steel, in his pockets. Thus provided, we proceeded to an entrance cut in the mountain, surmounted by an inscription, stating the day when the first pickaxe was struck into the rock.

My guide entered this subterranean passage, and I followed. I found it was a gallery cut straight through the mountain, everywhere about the same proportion, five feet broad and eight high; all along the sides were inscriptions indicating the annual progress of the miners, who sometimes had to work through a rock so hard that it broke their tools; at others, through a loose friable clay, which had to be supported by scaffolding, or at any moment it might have overwhelmed them.

Two streams ran along in trenches by the sides of the gallery. One was saline, the other sulphureous. The mountain produces both, and great care is taken to separate them. As to the path on which we walked, it was formed of wooden planks laid end to end, and about eighteen feet wide.

After we had progressed about a hundred paces, we came to a little staircase in the rock, which led to the first reservoir. This place was about ninety feet in circumference to nine in height, and the liquid bore the proportion of eight particles of salt to one hundred of water.

A little farther, still along the same gallery, was the second reservoir, to which we ascended by some slippery steps. It had double the circumference of the other, and the proportions were twenty-six in place of five to one hundred.

One of the most remarkable echoes I ever heard in my life is here, except that of Simonetta, near Milan, which gave fifty-three repetitions of a word. Just as I re-descended to the gallery, my guide took hold of my arm, and without warning me, gave a shout. I thought the rocks were falling on our heads, so completely was the entire cavern filled with the noise, and it was long before the last echo died away; still we heard it murmuring hoarsely in the mountain cavities, or dashing violently against the rock, like a bear surprised in the recesses of his den. There was something terrible in this thundering repercussion of the human voice in a place where echoes seem only fit for the trumpet of the last judgment. We proceeded in the same line till we reached a ladder leading perpendicularly down into a gulf.

The guide asked me to descend, but I felt little inclination, I confess, for the hazardous enterprise. However, as he began the descent, I followed, he with the carelessness of a man well used to the road, I nervously counting each step as I descended.

After about five minutes of this agreeable exercise, and when I had counted my hundred and sixty-fifth step, I paused, and looked down at my guide. The lamp he carried threw a humid halo round his head, but beneath and beyond all was darkness. Finding I had stopped, the man looked up. "Well?" said he.

"Well," said I, "when is this pleasantry to stop?"

"We have only gone a third of the way."

"Ah! then we have four hundred and fifty more steps to descend."

"Ay," said the guide, "there are fifty-two ladders altogether, making four hundred and fifty-seven steps yet to go."

"What! fifty-two ladders still beneath me?"

"Ay, sir, in a direct line."

"So that if my ladder broke ——"

"You would fall a hundred feet deeper than if you fell from Strasburg steeple."

A trembling seized me at these words, and I put out my hands to grasp the ladder firmly at each side, forgetting my lamp, which, dropping from my grasp, fell

·down and down, knocking against every step that came
in its way, till the echo of a dull splash showed me that
it had reached the water at the very bottom.

" What is the matter?" said my guide.

" Only a giddiness," replied I.

"Ah, the devil! get rid of it. It does not suit for
these parts."

I felt quite of his opinion, and shaking off the stupor,
began vigorously my descent, with more precaution,
however, than before, if it were possible. As I had no
lamp, I got nearer to my guide, whose light shone like
a glowworm on each step. At the end of ten minutes
we reached the platform at the termination of the ladders, put a foot above the water, then I looked about
for my unfortunate lamp, but in vain. No doubt it had
sunk to the bottom.

Having reached our destination, I became aware of
one thing which fright had hitherto prevented me from
remarking: I could scarcely breathe; the narrow walls
of the gallery seemed stifling me as if in a dream; and
in truth, considering that the exterior air only reached
us from the aperture at the commencement of the gallery, and that at that moment we were 1,600 feet below
the surface of the earth, it is no wonder that I felt suffo-
cating.

This horrible sensation prevented my giving full attention to the guide, who related that a still more abun-
dant source existed farther down, and that the miners
had sunk shafts to 150 feet, when they were stopped by
some obstacle which all their tools could not overcome ;
and the workmen were of opinion that, while they were
resting or at dinner, some enemy to the employers had
thrown a cannon ball down into the tunnel, and so prevented all progress. Still, the source at which we stood
was of excellent quality, containing twenty-eight saline
particles to one hundred of water. Having given all the
explanations in his power, my guide proposed our ascent.
Joyfully I agreed, and we accomplished it successfully.
Having reached the top, we proceeded to explore the
gallery farther, which still penetrated in a right line
through the heart of the mountain, and each time that
I looked back, the sun's rays seemed diminishing to a

point at the entrance. At the distance of about four thousand feet the gallery takes a turn. I looked back a last time—the distant light now only glimmered like a star. I made one step more and it disappeared.

Four thousand feet beyond this we reached a vein of fossil salt. Here the subterranean passage enlarged, and we stood within an immense circular cavity, where all that man could do to drag the saline treasures from the earth had been done. The large flanks of the mountain were excavated on every side; shafts sunk, then abandoned, seeming like the cells of saints or hermits. There was something profoundly sad in the aspect of this ancient deserted quarry. It seemed like a pillaged mansion, with all the doors left open. Some steps onward, a ray of exterior light falls upon a large vertical wheel, thirty-six feet in diameter, which is put in motion by a mountain stream. This wheel works the pumps destined to draw up the saline and sulphureous waters from the wells, and bring them to the height of the trenches through which they flow out of the mine. This ray of light reached us through an enormous ventilator which descends vertically from the summit of the mountain to renew the air within the mine. My guide assured me that one could see the stars at noon-day by means of this gigantic telescope; consequently, I looked through it for the space of ten minutes, with the most scrupulous attention, but must confess that there was more of boasting than veracity in the assertion of my Valaisan guide.

My position, however, under the ventilator, produced one result: it filled my lungs with fresh air, and, thus fortified, I was enabled to continue my progress with renewed courage.

Soon after my guide paused, and asked whether I wished to return by descent or ascent. I asked him to explain what difference lay between them. He said, by the first I had seven hundred steps to descend, by the latter four hundred steps to ascend. I thought of the fifty-two ladders of the well, and decided for advance by elevation.

On reaching the top of the steps, the light of day once more shone down the gallery, and I confess the light gave me no little pleasure; for, though the excursion was curious, it was rather unpleasant.

As we advanced to the upper regions we traversed a wild narrow valley, and half-an-hour after emerged into the full daylight, through the opening by which we had entered. Compensation was now my thought. I had a long journey and a lamp to pay for. I valued both at six francs, and by his thanks I may conclude that my guide was well pleased. Next day, by eleven o'clock, I was again at Bex; and finding that I could reach Martigny before evening, lost no time, merely changed my dress, and was once on the road.

CHAPTER VII.

A BEAR-STEAK.

ABOUT four o'clock in the afternoon I alighted at the inn of Martigny.

"*Pardieu!*" said I to the landlord, placing my iron-shod stick in the chimney-corner, and my straw hat on the stick; "it is a rough trot from Bex to this."

" Only six little leagues, monsieur."

"Ay, as good as twelve French ones; and from here to Chamouny?"

" Nine leagues."

" Thanks.   A guide, then, at six in the morning."

" Will monsieur go a-foot?"

" Of course."   And I saw instantly how my legs rose in the landlord's estimation, though certainly at the expense of my position.

" Probably monsieur is an artist?" continued mine host.

"Why, somewhat," I answered.

"And will monsieur dine?"

"I most religiously observe that ordinance daily."

In fact, the *tables-d'hôte* are dear enough in Switzerland, every dinner costing four francs, from which it is impossible to abate a single item; so, in my projects of economy, I had long wished to retrieve somewhat of the expense of this article, and finally, after long meditation, had found a mean between the exaction of the host and the voice of my conscience. It was, always to eat to the value of *six* francs, by which means my dinner merely cost forty sous. The only unpleasantness was listening to mine host's mutterings as I called for dish after dish—"Ay, truly, he must be an Englishman, though he speaks French so well."

You see, therefore, our landlord of Martigny was not gifted with the physiognomical science of his compatriot Lavater, or he would not have dared to put the rather impertinent question, "Will monsieur dine?"

"Well, then," he said, after hearing my affirmative, "you are in good luck to-day, for we have some bear still left in the house."

"Ah!" said I, not much pleased inwardly at the prospect. "Is it good, your bear?"

Mine host smiled with a knowing look, as much as to say, "Only taste it, and see if you will ever be able to eat anything else."

"Very well," I said; "have dinner at five o'clock, and I shall go off now and visit the old château."

"Would monsieur like a guide to tell him all about it, and who built it?"

"Thanks, friend, but I shall find my way; and as to its origin, why, it was Peter the Great of Savoy who built it towards the end of the twelfth century."

"Monsieur knows our history as well as ourselves."

I accepted the dubious compliment, and he continued : "In truth, our country has been famous. A Roman emperor lived here once, and it had a fine Roman name."

"Ay," I replied, allowing profound wisdom to drop negligently from my lips like the *Bourgeois Gentil-homme;* "ay, Martigny was the Octodurum of the Celts, and its actual descendants are the Veragrians of whom Cæsar speaks. Fifty years before Christ, Sergius Galba, Cæsar's lieutenant, was besieged here. Here, also, the Emperor Maximilian tried to force his army to sacrifice to false gods, which led to the martyrdom of St. Maurice; and, finally, when Petronius was prefect, and divided Gaul into seventeen provinces, he separated the Valais from Italy, and made your town the capital of the Pennine Alps. Is it not so, mine host?"

The excellent man was stupified with admiration. I saw that I had produced an effect, and as I proceeded to the door, he drew himself up beside the wall to let

me pass, hat in hand. I strode proudly out, whistling
carelessly, and as much out of tune as possible—

Come, fair lady;
Come, I wait thee!

but had scarcely descended ten steps when I heard
mine host calling to the waiter, in a most excited manner, "Prepare No. 3 for his lordship; the same room
Marie Louise slept in when she passed through Martigny, in 1829."

Thus my pedantry had borne good fruit; got me the
best bed at the inn—a great consolation, for hitherto
the Swiss beds had been the torment of my journey.
You must know Swiss beds consist simply of a paillasse
and bolster, over which is spread a piece of linen dignified with the name of a sheet, but so short that it
neither covers the bolster at one end nor your feet at
the other. True, you may drag it up or drag it down, so
that head and feet may enjoy its advantages alternately,
but never can they rejoice in its possession simultaneously. Besides, even this delusive sheet is so coarse,
that the horse-hair sticks out in every direction through
it, which gives you the sensation all night of sleeping
on a monster hair-brush.

Filled, then, with a soothing hope of a good night's
rest, I wandered pleasantly about the town and its environs till dinner-hour arrived.

When I entered every one was at table. I took a
rapid glance of the company. Every one was seated
and packed as closely as possible. There was no room
for me.

A cold shudder passed through my veins. I looked
for mine host; he was behind me. I thought a Me-
phistopheles grin was upon his face.

"And I—where am I to go?" I exclaimed mournfully.

"Here," said he, showing me a little table served
apart—"here. A man like you ought not to eat with
common folk."

Oh! the worthy Octodurian! It was as I suspected.
And how it was laid out, my little table!—four dishes
for first course, and in the centre a noble beefsteak, that

would have made an English one ashamed of itself. My host saw it absorbed my attention, and, bending mysteriously to my ear, whispered—

"There is nothing like it in all the world."

"What! this beefsteak?"

"It is a cut of bear. Think of that!"

I had rather it had been a cut of anything else; and, as I stared at it, my thoughts wandered back to the poor, ungainly brutes I had stopped to look at when a boy, dancing heavily round and round, grunting and dirty, while a man held their chain and struck a cracked tambourine for the special delight of a circle of beggar children; and now, to think of eating one! But, courage! I planted my fork in it heroically, and found that it at least possessed one of the gentlest qualities in nature— tenderness. Still I hesitated, turning and turning it from side to side, till my host decided by a persuasive "Taste it; it will astonish you."

So I cut off a bit about the size of a nut, and, smothering it in butter, opened my lips very wide to let it enter with the least contact possible.

Mine host stood watching the effect with all the benevolent impatience of one who has prepared a joyful surprise for his friend. Mine was great, I confess. Still I hesitated to pronounce, but silently cut another morsel double the volume of the first, and sent it the same road with the same precautions.

"Well," said I at last, "is that bear?"

"Ay, truly is it bear."

"Well, then, it is delicious."

At this moment my worthy host was summoned to the large table, and I was left to an interesting tête-à-tête with my bear-steak, by which I profited so much that three-fourths of it had disappeared by the time he returned and renewed our conversation.

"That was a famous animal," said he.

I nodded to the dish as an approving affirmative.

"Weighed three hundred and twenty pounds!"

"A fine weight;" but I would not have a mouthful lost of it, and I continued eating.

"It was hard work to get hold of him, I can tell you."

" No doubt;" and I raised another morsel to my lips.

" Think of him! He ate the half of the man that killed him."

The fork fell from my hand as if I were paralysed. " What do you mean," I said, " by uttering such horrid jests to a man at his dinner?"

" No jest, monsieur; true as you are there."

I felt a deadly sickness coming on me, but my host continued :—

" He was a poor peasant of our village, named William Mona. Well, this bear (though that's the last bit of him now on your worship's fork) used to come every night and steal his fruit, for these beasts eat anything; but, above all, he favoured a great large pear-tree. Now, it so happened the man liked these pears, too, better than anything else in the orchard, and at first thought the children stole them; so he took his gun without loading, just to frighten them, and set himself to watch. Well, at eleven o'clock or so, a great roar was heard in the mountains. 'Why, there is a bear coming,' he said to himself; and, ten minutes after, another roar resounded so close to his ears, that poor William, thinking he would never have time to reach home, just threw himself down flat on his face, with but one hope—that the bear was coming for the pears and not for him.

" And, in truth, the animal was soon in the orchard, advancing in a right line up to the very tree. He passed within ten steps of William, but never heeded him; climbed the tree, and regaled himself there for a full hour, so well that it was evident another visit would finish his work. Then he got down slowly, as if sorry at leaving it, passed close to the man a second time, who with his empty gun didn't much care for a fight, and made off back again to the mountain.

" However, William was a brave fellow, and he said to himself as the bear was passing, 'Go along now, my friend, but you won't get back another time so easily.'

" So, next morning when one of the neighbours called in, he found him busy settling up and charging his gun. 'How now, William?' he said. 'Tell me truly—are you not after some higher game than a chamois?'

" 'Perhaps so,' replied William.

" 'Well, now,' rejoined his comrade, 'take me with you. I know it is after a bear you are going. Two are better than one at that work.'

" 'Maybe so,' said William, as he went on loading the gun.

" 'But listen now,' continued Francis. 'You shall have the skin all to yourself, and we'll only divide the reward between us;' for the government give eighty francs for every bear killed.

" 'I'd rather have it all,' said William.

" ' But you cannot hinder me from watching its track on the mountain; and, if I find it first and waylay it ——'

" 'Well, try,' says William, whistling as he finished the charge, which was double the ordinary quantity.

" ' Then I am not to go with you, William?'

" 'No. Every one for himself.'

" 'Then, good-bye, William. I'll go and seek its track.'

" ' Good-bye, neighbour, and success to you !'

" So they parted ; but, in the evening, again Francis came to him as he was smoking his pipe before the door.

" ' Neighbour,' said he, 'I bear no ill-will to you. I have found the beast's track, so I have as good a chance as you. Let us go together.'

" ' Every one for himself,' said William again.

" The neighbour told me all this himself the day before yesterday. 'And, just imagine,' says he; 'there was our poor William seated so snugly before his door, smoking his pipe; and then to think, after ——' "

" Well, after?" said I, strongly interested in the recital.

"After that, Francis saw no more of him till he was dead. But here was the way of it:—About half-past ten at night William's wife saw him take his gun and a large grey sack in his hand, and leave the house with them. Francis, on his side, having really discovered the track of the bear, had followed it up to the entrance of the orchard; but, as he had no right to enter there, he contented himself by remaining outside, hid in a clump of pine-trees, to watch for the bear's approach. As the

E

night, however, was very clear, he could see everything perfectly within the garden; and, first, William came out of his house, and made over to a large grey rock about twenty paces from the pear-tree. There he stopped, looked round to see that no one was watching him, and then, unrolling his sack, got into it—all except his head and arms—and stuck himself so close against the rock that no one could tell which was which. Presently the roar of the bear was heard; it approached nearer, and five minutes after, Francis beheld it.

"But, probably from some instinct of danger, the animal did not take its usual course, but described a circle, which brought it quite out of his reach, though within ten paces of William's gun.

"William never stirred: one might think he did not mind the savage beast at all, for he let it pass quite close to him; and the bear, on his part, made straight on for the pear-tree. Just, however, as he had placed his two fore-feet on the trunk to ascend the tree, thus leaving all his breast exposed, a tremendous report was heard, and the animal, with a roar, fell mortally wounded to the ground. Not one in the valley that night but heard the report of the double-loaded gun and the roar of the bear.

"William's head and arms were instantly in the sack again, and he drew up close against the rock, while the furious animal passed again within ten feet of him. Francis, meanwhile, was on the watch, and seeing the bear coming his way, kept his carbine steady; though, truth to say, he could hardly breathe, and yet he is a brave hunter; but he confessed to me that just then he would rather have been in his bed than under the pine-trees. As the wounded bear came on, he made the sign of the cross and steadied his piece; it was now but fifty paces from him, roaring with pain and stopping sometimes to roll itself on the ground and lick the wound. The distance between them was rapidly diminishing; two seconds more and the beast must have struck the muzzle of his carbine, when all at once it paused, snuffed the air, and, uttering a terrific roar, dashed back to the orchard.

"'Have a care, William! have a care!' shouted Francis, starting in pursuit of the animal, and forgetting everything but his friend; for he knew that if there had been no time to reload his gun, William was lost: the bear had smelt him. But scarcely had he made ten steps when a shriek was heard—a human cry of terror and agony united—a cry that seemed to exhaust all human force, all prayers to God, all appeals to man, in the terrible utterance of one word, 'Help!' Then nothing more; not even a groan followed the cry.

"Francis did not run, he flew to the rescue; the natural declivity of the ground aided his advance, and soon he could distinguish the monstrous beast moving about in the shade and trampling on the body of William, while he tore it piecemeal with his teeth.

"He was now about four paces from them, but the bear was too eager over his prey to mind him. He feared to fire lest the shot might hit William, supposing he were not dead yet; so he took a stone and flung it at the bear.

"The animal turned furiously round upon his new assailant. They were so near one another that he even raised himself on his hind paws to strangle him, and Francis felt him press on the muzzle of his carbine: mechanically he touched the trigger and the piece went off; down fell the bear on his back; the shot had pierced his breast and broken the vertebral column. Francis left him writhing on the ground and sprang to William; but there was no longer a man to be seen—scarcely a corpse: he found only a mass of bones and torn flesh. The head had been completely devoured.

"Lights now gleamed in all the huts of the valley, and the whole village was aroused. Francis shouted to point out where he was, and all the peasants came thronging to him; the whole population was soon in the orchard. Among others came William's wife. It was a horrible scene. All of them cried like children. But they did what they could for her: a subscription was got up throughout all the valley of the Rhone, which brought her seven hundred francs. Francis gave her the reward and the profits of the bear's skin and flesh. All tried to help her; amongst others, we innkeepers of the country promised to open subscription lists for her at our respective inns; and if monsieur would be kind enough to put down his name ——"

"Of course; quick! bring it to me."

I wrote my name, and was adding my offering, when a strong, fair lad of middle height entered. He was the guide for Chamouny, and came to inquire when and how I would go.   My answer was brief and decisive: " Five o'clock to-morrow morning, and on foot."

CHAPTER VIII.

THE COL DE BALME.

My guide was punctual as an alarum-clock, and by half-past five we were traversing the town of Martigny, where I saw nothing remarkable except a few *cretins* vegetating stupidly in the rising sun before the paternal door. On leaving the village we crossed the Drance, a stream that descends from St. Bernard by the vale of Entremont, and falls into the Rhone between Martigny and Batia. Then, having made half-a-league or so, my guide invited me to turn round and contemplate the view on all sides.

At the first glance I comprehended why Cæsar attached such importance to Martigny, or Octodurum, as it was then called. From its position it became the centre of his operations upon Helvetia by the valley of Tarnade; upon Gaul by the very road we travelled; and upon Italy by the Ostiolum Montis Jovis, now the Great St. Bernard, where he had traced out a Roman way leading from Milan to Mayence.

We stood at the meeting of these four roads, and could clearly follow them as far as the eye reached, except where the fantastic forms of some of the great Alps through which we travelled broke the view.

The first object that attracted as a central point in this grand tableau was the ancient town of Martigny, with a history even since the time of Hannibal, which Cæsar, Strabo, Titus Livius, and Pliny have contributed, and which owes to its topographical position the terrible honour of having received within its walls the armies of the three greatest leaders of the world, Cæsar, Charlemagne, and Napoleon.

From Martigny the eye follows the Simplon, as it plunges down boldly into the valley of the Rhone, and proceeds in so direct a line that it seems like a cord extended between the two towns of Martigny and Biddes. To its left the Rhone, yet but an infant stream, meanders at the bottom of the valley, brilliant and undulating as a silver ribbon floating from some fair girl's *ceinture;* while above rises on both sides the grand double chain of the Alps, which open to enclose the Valais in its whole length, and then meet again at the place called La Furca, where the gigantic bases of Gallenstock and Mutthorn are united.

On turning to the left we could see the road leading to Geneva by the valley of St. Maurice; the Grand St. Bernard, with the path up to the convent; and then, proceeding once more on our way, there was the steep, apparently unbroken ascent to the gloomy summit of the Tête Noir, until arrived at the Forclas. Convinced that nothing intervenes to prevent your scaling immediately this Pelion upon Ossa, you are suddenly stopped by an immense valley two leagues broad, cleaving the mountain in two, whose existence you never could have suspected until the moment of reaching it.

Although accustomed to distrust the testimony of my eyes in these colossal masses, where one loses all idea of distance, I was not the less astonished at beholding this immense cleft, as if the earth had opened suddenly to the depth of two thousand feet beneath me; and there, at the very bottom, twisting and turning, and glittering like a silver thread, ran the torrent that leaps into life from the glacier of Trient, and must needs cleave a mountain from the summit to the base to follow its capricious fancies winding to the Rhone.

The cottages scattered through the valley, with their grey roofs, looked like large beetles lying motionless on the plain; while two lines at each extremity of the village, scarcely visible to the naked eye, were, my guide told me, the two roads that led to Chamouny, one by the Tête Noir, the other, which we meant to take, by the Col de Balme.

On descending to the valley, my guide counselled me to rest a while at a miserable-looking shed, dignified with the name of inn. It was the only place of the kind, however, within three leagues, he said, and rest would be necessary, as two-thirds of the way had still to be traversed. In short, I perceived he wanted some thing to drink; so we entered.

They gave us a bottle of sour vinegar, only fit for seasoning salad, which they habitually passed off for Bordeaux. My guide, however, swallowed it voluptuously to the last drop. Happily, I found for myself, what is everywhere to be had in Switzerland, a bowl of delicious milk, into which I poured some drops of cherry brandy. It was rather a poor breakfast for a man who had still six leagues to go; but my guide, who perceived my melancholy visage, as I dipped a piece of bread, hard and grey as granite, into the acidulated mix ture, comforted me somewhat by assuring me that at the inn of the Col de Balme we should find something more substantial to eat. I prayed God to hear him, and we set forth once more on our journey.

After half-an-hour's walking we reached the entrance of a fine wood, where the beaten track was lost completely. My guide had not deceived me; the true difficulty was only commencing now. Still, so many more difficult obstacles impeded our way, that I scarcely give this a place in my memory. We had already begun the ascent of the steep side of the mountain, and had at one side a precipice five or six hundred feet deep, with beyond a sharp mountain, called by the inhabitants the Needle of Illiers, which had acquired a recent celebrity by the melancholy death of an Englishman killed there while attempting the ascent in 1831. The guide pointed out to me, at about two-thirds of the entire height of the mountain, the place where the unfortunate young man lost his footing; and the terrible height from which he fell, bounding from rock to rock like a living avalanche, till finally he reached the bottom of the precipice, a mass of mangled flesh, no longer retaining the slightest vestige of humanity.

These horrible histories are never agreeable at any time, still less when related upon the very ground where they happened, and over which you have to pass yourself, liable to the same casualties. No matter how phleg-

matic a traveller may be, it is scarcely pleasant to learn
that, on the very spot where you are standing, one man
lost his footing, or another his life; but the guides are
not at all chary of such tales, for it is an implied advice
to the traveller not to move a step without them.   Nevertheless, on this very path where the Englishman was
killed, I saw a shepherd, followed by his whole flock of
goats, dashing down as fast as his legs would carry him,
bounding from rock to rock, and at every bound loosen-
ing some fragment of stone that in its turn sent others
tumbling down the steep, until a whole avalanche of
mingled rocks and stones clattered down the mountain
like hail upon a roof, with an ever-increasing velocity.
Then came an interval of silence, after which we heard
the whole mass precipitated with a dull plash into the
stream that ran at the bottom of the ravine which separates the two mountains.   He continued this work
during half-a-league, increasing the force and velocity
of his movements, without any other motive apparently
than that of displaying before us his mountain daring
and prowess.   According as we ascended, the air grew
colder and fresher, and yet we had scarcely reached an
elevation of seven thousand feet above the level of the
sea.   Here and there we met with large fields of snow,
which showed that we were approaching the glacial
region where it never melts.   We had long left far
below us the mountain woods of beech and pine, and
some scanty pasturage was all that appeared in the direction we were traversing.   From time to time a cold
wind passed chillingly over our frames, and literally
froze the perspiration on my brow.   It was with real
pleasure, therefore, I learned from my guide that we
would soon reach the inn of the Col de Balme; and in
fact, a few minutes after, the veritable red roof and white
walls of this much-desired house stood out clearly from
the blue sky, in a cleft of the mountain which separates
the valley of Chamouny from that of Trient.   A shaggy
dog was seated on the steps of the door, who, with brilliant eyes and tail erect, advanced graciously to meet us,
as if inviting the wayfarers to enter and rest with his
master.   "Thanks, excellent dog! thanks! we shall accept your kindness."

I was so impatient to reach the comforts of a chair and fire, that I rushed into the inn without even waiting to look round upon the glorious beauty of Chamouny, that unrolled before our eyes in all its splendour and extent. However, when the two great enemies of the traveller, cold and hunger, were a little calmed, curiosity re-awoke to life, and I suffered my guide to lead me with bandaged eyes up to the point which commands the best view of the double chain of Alps, in order that the whole scene might startle me at once with its full magnificence. When I opened them it seemed to me as if a curtain had been suddenly rolled up from the universe; and I felt a pleasure, mingled with awe, as I stood, a mere insignificant atom, in the midst of the immense glory of the mighty panorama, while beneath lay the fair, fertile valley, dominated by its lofty domes of snow, like the summer palace of the frost-god.

All around, far as the eye could reach, peak rose on peak, and from each hung pendent, like a flowing silver robe, the glittering undulations of an icy sea. There seemed a strife amongst these frost-giants which would lift its head highest to heaven, or fling down its glaciers most menacingly to earth. There was the Aiguille of Tour, the Aiguille Verte, and the Pic de Géant, and the glaciers of Argentières, Bossons, and Taconnay; while, above all, as if its mass closed the horizon and ended the mighty chain which is prolonged to the Pyrenees, though hidden from our view, obscured by this giant portal, rose the monarch of European mountains, the brother of Chimborazo and the Immaus, the mighty Mont Blanc, overtopping peak and glacier, and lying like a white bear couched upon the icy summit of a polar sea, the last step of this vast staircase by which man can scale heaven. I remained an hour, annihilated in the contemplation of this superb tableau, unconscious even that the air I breathed was four degrees below zero. My guide, meanwhile, who had gazed upon the spectacle a hundred times before, amused and warmed himself at once by running up and down on all-fours with the dog, and making the animal cry by catching hold of his tail. At last he came to me to communicate an idea which had just struck him.

"Had not monsieur better stop here to-night?" he
said, with the tone of a man who would not be sorry to
double his hire by splitting his day.   "Monsieur will
get an excellent supper and bed here."

Ah! the inexpert knave! if he had only left me quiet,
I would have remained sunk in my reverie until too late
to proceed, and then been forced to wait for bed and
supper, though God knows what sort of either I would
have had.   But now I started up in terror at the danger
I ran, exclaiming, "No, no; let us be off instantly."

"But we are still only half-way to Chamouny."

"Well, I am not tired."

"And it is four o'clock."

"Only half-past three."

"And you think we can still go five leagues by daylight?"

"We may travel two of them by night."

"Ay, and lose the scenery."

"But then we'll have a really good bed and supper.
Come!"

My guide had exhausted all his eloquence. He sighed
and was silent, and we continued our journey.

All that I further beheld, as long as day lasted, consisted merely of detail, struck from the grand picture
which I had contemplated in its unity on the Col de
Balme; detail marvellous to contemplate, but difficult
to describe.

Besides, my object in these sketches—if they have any
object—is to speak of persons rather than localities.

It was dark night when we reached Chamouny. We
had travelled nine leagues—a good journey for one day.
So, on arriving, I occupied myself only about three
things, which I recommend to every traveller who goes
the same route in the same time:—The first, to take a
bath; the second, to sup; the third, to write an invitation for dinner next day, with this address—"To Monsieur Jacques Balmat, surnamed 'of Mont Blanc.'" Then
I went to bed; from which resting-place I must tell you
in two words who is this Monsieur Jacques Balmat,
surnamed "of Mont Blanc," if perchance his fame has
not reached you yet: he is the Christopher Columbus
of Chamouny.

CHAPTER IX.

JACQUES BALMAT, SURNAMED "OF MONT BLANC."

THERE are two consecrated objects at Chamouny, which the traveller should on no account omit to see: the Cross of Flegère is one, and the Mer de Glace the other. These two marvels stand facing each other to the right and left of Chamouny, on the summits of the mountains between which lies the village, and from which you can look down on it at a height of four thousand five hundred feet.

The Mer de Glace, which is fed from the snowy heights of Mont Blanc, descends right between the two mountains called L'Aiguille de Charmoz and the Pic du Géant, to the middle of the valley; and having filled the entire space between the two mountains, like an enormous serpent it opens its verdant throat, from which leaps forth the icy torrent of Aveyron. But as you stand on Mont Blanc itself while contemplating this object, its magnitude is lost, as you are unable to comprehend the extent of its colossal mass.

The Cross of Flegère, on the contrary, surmounts a chain of mountains lying opposite to Mont Blanc; so that, as you descend, were it not for the fatigue, you might imagine, in place of your rising, it was the opposite colossus that was gradually sinking down, like a docile elephant at the command of its rider. But when the platform is reached on which stands the Cross, then the grand commingling beneath of mountain and glacier, rock and forest, shows the elevation at which you stand.

The Cross of Flegère is generally the first point of

ascension; at least, this is what the guide told me; and as I, at all events, had no desire for a near inspection of the Mer de Glace, we set off at once for the other wonder of the scene. The path to it was sufficiently difficult. Every now and then, some steep precipice or rapid declivity tested our capabilities as mountaineers; but altogether, I am happy to say, I acquitted myself with considerable honour. As to the distance, it was nothing after what I had already accomplished. Three hours were enough to bring us to the summit.

I have already spoken of the difficulty of calculating distances in a mountain region, and the optical delusions that result from the exaggerated proportions of objects which are under one's very eyes. From the Cross of Flegère I could plainly distinguish the small red-roofed inn we had left in a *crevasse* of the Col de Balme, as if it were almost close to us, and yet it was four leagues off: a distance at which it would be impossible to distinguish any object in a level country.

In commencing the inventory of the mountain paths around us, the first on the list is the Aiguille of Tour, with its glacier rising to about eight thousand feet above the level of the sea. Then comes the glacier of Argentières and peak of the same name, springing up, black and sharp, one thousand two hundred and ninety feet into the air; and the Aiguille Verte, six hundred feet higher again, lifting its snowy head into the sky like the giant in the ballad, who stopped the eagles as they soared past and dashed themselves against his brow; while opposite is the red Aiguille of Dru, and the wondrous Mer de Glace, spread like a carpet on the flanks of Montanvert, whose solid waves seem to have scarcely any elevation from our point of view, though each undulation is a little mountain in itself when you stand on it. But above all rises the summit of Mont Blanc, to an elevation of about fourteen thousand eight hundred and ninety feet, with the two glaciers of Bossons and Taconnay, pendent almost to the valley, from its sides.

In face of this snowy-headed family of giants, the question naturally rises to one's mind—" Has the snow been lying on them thus from all eternity?"

Two theories, the Neptunian and the volcanic, strive

to give the answer. Both of these affirm that the earth was once fluid. The presence of crystalline matter everywhere, from the highest to the lowest level, proves this; for there can be no crystallization without previous liquidity. Besides, the impressions left in the different strata of vegetable and animal substances show that, at some time or other, these rocks must have been in a state sufficiently soft to receive them. Finally, the normal condition of all strata, placed regularly, layer on layer, as successive deposits, except where some cataclysm has caused disorganization, leaves no doubt on the subject.

The next question is—"Was this liquidity the result of intense heat? or was this planet, in its primordial state, a fluid mass? Has the earth sprung from a central fire or a universal ocean?" As each of these theories can be defended by a long array of reasoning, modern geologists have contented themselves with simply collecting and collating facts, from which it is incontestably proved that, either primitively or subsequently, the earth was entirely covered with water. From the limestone mountains of Derbyshire to the highest peak of the Pyrenees, vestiges of marine animals are found. Fossil ammonites are traced in the rocks beneath the glaciers, seven thousand feet above sea-level; and Humboldt discovered them in the Andes, at a height of fourteen thousand feet. Scripture, too, confirms the researches of science. Moses speaks of a deluge, and Cuvier confirms it. At an interval of three thousand years, the prophet and the *savant* relate to men the same geological miracle; and the Academy enunciates as a scientific fact that beautiful phrase of Genesis, which Voltaire looked on as only a poetical hyperbole—

Spiritus Dei ferebatur super aquas.

We may, therefore, consider this truth as established. The earth was once covered with water, which supported a pressure of sixteen leagues of atmosphere, as the present earth does now; but, whether from volatilization caused by central heat, or from evaporation beneath the

action of the sun, that eye of divinity, the mass of dilu-
vial water gradually diminished, allowing the most elevated peaks of land, such as Chimborazo, the Immaus,
and Mont Blanc, to appear above the surface, like islets
in a universal ocean. Contact with light, heat, and air
gave them fertility; and plants, animals, and finally
man, appeared. The traditions of all antiquity place
the first earth-born in a mountain region. It was in
Eden Adam and Eve awoke to life. It was in the Cau-
casus Prometheus found the first man.

From some combination of causes, however, the waters
began gradually to subside; so that not only the tops,
but the sides, of the great mountain ranges became exposed. The atmosphere descended, still pressing on
the surface of the waters, and, consequently, becoming
colder and of diminished density on the high mountain
peaks. This forced the human race to seek lower levels
for their dwellings. The primitive earth, which their
forefathers had seen covered with fruits and flowers, now
became cold, hard, and sterile; the descending waters
carried with them the soft, loose soil; and gradually the
bare, bleak rock appeared in all its ungenial desolation.
Finally men perceived, to their surprise, one day, a
white carpet of snow spread over the summits that had
been their cradle; and, as the atmosphere became still
more rarified, the snow hardened and accumulated by
degrees, descending down the mountain as a conqueror,
and turning all it touched to ice, till men found no refuge or shelter but in the valleys, and there built their
habitations.

Even popular tradition confirms these theories of
science. The peasant of the Furca will tell you how
the Wandering Jew regularly crosses these mountains
when passing from Italy to France; but the first time
he passed they were covered with flowers, the second
time with pines, the third with snow.

After satiating my eyes with the grand panorama, we
re-descended towards Chamouny. On the way I missed
my watch, and wanted to go back for it; but the guide
told me that was his affair, for nothing was ever lost at
Chamouny. So I seated myself on a ridge commanding a noble prospect, and waited patiently while he

went on the search. In about half-an-hour I saw him emerge from the pine-wood, joyous and triumphant, holding up my watch by the chain. I offered him a compensation, which he refused. It was near four o'clock when we reached the village, and as I approached the inn, I observed an old man of about seventy seated on the bench before the door. At a sign from the waiter he rose and met me, and I instantly conjectured he was the guest I had asked to dinner; so I shook the old fellow by the hand. He was, indeed, Jacques Balmat, the intrepid peasant who first set foot upon the summit of Mont Blanc, and prepared the way for Saussure. Courage preceded science.

I thanked him for giving me the favour of his company; but the brave fellow could not comprehend that I looked on him as quite as great a hero' in his way as Columbus, who discovered a new world, or Vasco, who refound one that was lost.

I insisted that my guide also should dine with us, and he took his place at table with as much simplicity as he had refused my money. The dinner was excellent, and my guests seemed content. At the dessert I turned the conversation upon the exploits of Balmat; and as the wine of Montmeillan had rendered him gay and chatty, he asked nothing better than liberty to relate them. Besides, his very surname, "of Mont Blanc," showed that he was proud of his adventure. So he required no second invitation to begin, but first rose, extending his glass, and saying, "With your permission, monsieur."

"Of course," said I: "Balmat, we'll all drink to your health."

"*Pardieu!*" he exclaimed, reseating himself, "you are an excellent gentleman;" and he swallowed his glass, and threw himself back in his chair as if collecting his ideas.

My guide made his preparations likewise as a listener. They were simple but comfortable, consisting merely in a pirouette of his chair, which brought his feet to the fire, his elbow on the table, his head on his left hand, and his glass in the other.

For myself, I got my note-book and pencil, and prepared to write.   So here is the recital, just as I had it
from Balmat:—

"Well, it was in 1786; I was just twenty-five then—
for, look you, I am full seventy-two now—ah! with a
foot like an antelope, and a stomach of iron.   I could
have walked three days then without eating, as, indeed, happened once when I lost my way on the mountain.   I swallowed a little snow, that was all; and
many a time I looked up at Mont Blanc and thought—
'Ah! my fine fellow, you think you're mighty safe up
there; but wait—I'll soon put my foot on your head.
Have a care, then.'

"So this thought haunted me day and night, and I
walked round and round by the base, seeking if there
was no way up at all.   No, not one.   'Bah!' said I at
last; 'this will never do: if there is no path, why, I'll
make one.'   But when night came, then it was easy
enough going up in my dreams: all plain and smooth,
till maybe I'd come to some narrow ledge; but still
onward, onward; or I'd sink down knee-deep in the
snow, and then I must creep on all-fours over some
precipice.   You know the way one has in dreams.
Then I held by the rocks, but they shook in my grasp
like a loose tooth, and I tried to catch hold of a branch
above my head, for I was falling down, down—but I
caught the branch at last; oh! how I gripped it!   It
was a horrible moment.   How well I remember that
dream! for my wife awoke me with a great box on the ear.
What do you think?   It was her earring I was holding
on by, and pulling down her ear like a piece of elastic
India rubber.   Well, I jumped up.   Nothing could
stop me now.   'Where are you going?' said my wife.
'To look for crystals,' I answered; 'and never mind if
I am not back to-night; maybe I'll sleep on the mountain.'   So I filled my gourd with brandy, took a lump
of bread and my stout iron-shod stick, and set out.

"I had often tried to ascend by the Mer de Glace,
but failed; likewise by the Aiguille of Goûter, but
there a great precipice eighteen hundred feet rather
deterred me.   So this time I tried another route, and
at the end of three hours found myself at the glacier

of Bossons. I crossed it; that was not difficult, and in four hours more I had reached the Grands-Mulets; that was something. I had earned my breakfast. So I sat down, ate a crust, and drank a cup of the brandy.

"At that time there was no resting-place made at the Grands-Mulets as now, and I looked about, right and left, for some spot where I could pass the night, but in vain. I had to put my trust in God and go on.

"After two hours and a-half more climbing I hit on a tolerably dry, sheltered spot, about six feet square. 'This will do,' thought I, 'not to sleep on, but to wait for sunrise.' So I ate a second crust, drank some more, and settled myself for the night. My bed was not long in making, you may think. It was now seven o'clock. About nine I saw the dark shadows coming up from the valley like a thick smoke, and slowly gaining on me. In another half-hour they wrapped me round like a shroud. I could see nothing but the last rays of the setting sun still lingering on the highest peak of Mont Blanc: finally, they disappeared too, and I was left in darkness.

" I knew that at one side of me was a precipice eight hundred feet deep, so you may be sure I could not sleep for fear of rolling over; but I had to keep myself awake by clapping my hands and feet together during the whole night, and to get some heat in me likewise. About eleven o'clock the moon rose up, pale and dim, though the fog soon obscured her; and at the same time a deuce of a mist, that could not get at me sooner— for I had seen it travelling down from the Aiguille of Goûter—came spitting snow in my face as hard as it could.

" I wrapped my head up in my handkerchief. ' There, do your worst now,' said I. Minute by minute I could hear the fall of the avalanches echoing through the mountain, and the glaciers breaking with a sound that shook the rock under me. I felt neither hunger nor thirst, but a strange pain that seized me at the top of the head and came down to the eyebrows. The mist, meanwhile, was increasing. My breath froze on my handkerchief; my clothes were wet through and through;

F

and I had to begin to sing and clap my hands harder to chase away a crowd of black thoughts that came into my brain. But my voice was stifled in the snow; no echo responded: all seemed like death in the midst of that icy nature; my own voice even seemed strange to me, and I became silent, for I was afraid.

"At two o'clock the sky cleared to the east, and with the first ray of daylight my courage returned. The sun rose up, fighting his way through the clouds that covered Mont Blanc, and I watched, hoping he would conquer. But no; by four o'clock the clouds had thickened and the sun grown fainter, so I saw at once there was no hope of proceeding higher that day.

"However, not to lose everything, I began to explore the region around me, and that day visited all the glaciers and examined the most promising-looking paths. Then, when evening came on, and the fog along with it, I re-descended a good piece, until night overtook me; but as the cold was much less, I got on far better than the night before, and when day broke I went down again to the village.

"The first persons I met were Paccard, Carrier, and Tournier—three of the mountains guides—each with his sack, stick, and travelling costume. I asked where they were going. To look for some goats, they answered, which had been given in charge to some peasant boys. As these animals are only worth forty sous a-piece, I conjectured they were deceiving me, and that they were really about attempting the ascent, in order to obtain the reward promised by M. de Saussure to whoever would first reach the summit. One or two questions they asked me, also, concerning the best sleeping-place half-way up, confirmed me in this opinion. I told them every spot was thick with snow, and that a resting-place of any kind was out of the question. At this they exchanged glances, which I pretended not to observe, and withdrew to talk a little apart, the result being finally an offer on their part that we should all try the ascent together. I agreed, but said I must go home first to speak to my wife. Well, I got home, changed my clothes, put up some provisions, and telling her not to be uneasy, set out again at eleven o'clock at night, intending to join my comrades at a place we had agreed on, some leagues up the mountain.

"They were all sound asleep. I shook them, when they sprang to their feet, and we four set forward.

"This day we crossed the glacier of Taconnay, and reached the Grands-Mulets, where I had passed the famous night. After that, we got as far as the Dome of Goûter, and here Paccard grew weak, and had to lie down on one of his comrades' cloaks.

"Just as we reached the summit of the Dome, something black moving in the distance caught our sight: whether a chamois or a man we could not make out. We called out, however, and after waiting in silence for a second, these words came to us, 'Wait you, wait; we are going up along with you.' So we waited, and meanwhile Paccard had gained strength enough to come on with us. In half-an-hour they arrived, and we found it was Pierre Belmat and Marie Contet, who had made a bet with the others to reach the Dome of Gouter before them, but they lost their bet.

"While waiting, not to lose time, I had been investigating all the places about for the best path to proceed by, and actually went a quarter of a league astride on the fish-bone-shaped ridge that joins the Dome of Goûter to the summit of Mont Blanc. It was a way just fit for a rope-dancer; but no matter: I'd have gone on to the end, if the Pointe Rouge had not stopped me. It was impossible to pass this; so I returned to the spot where I had left my comrades, but they had gone. Nothing but my own sack was there. 'It is useless to attempt the ascent,' they said; 'let us return; Balmat will overtake us.' So here I was, quite alone. For an instant I hesitated between the desire to join them and the wish to ascend. I was piqued at their leaving me, and something told me I should succeed this time, if I went on; so at last I decided to proceed, and slung my sack on my back. It was now four o'clock.

"I crossed the grand plateau, and got as far as the glacier of Brinva, from whence I could see on to the valley of Aosta, in Piedmont. A mist covered the summit of Mont Blanc, so I would not attempt the ascent, less from the fear of being lost than the certainty that, if I did reach it, no one would be able to see me from the village, and, consequently, would never believe I had been there.

"I looked about, therefore, for some place to pass the night, but not a sheltered spot was to be had. I began thinking of my other pleasant night on the open mountain, and not liking a second, thought it better to descend. It was now near night. I got as far as the grand plateau, but just there a giddiness and rush of blood to my eyes came on me. I had forgotten the precaution of a green veil for my eyes, and the white snow had now affected them to that degree, that every spot before me seemed covered with large patches of blood. I sat down, closed my eyes, and held my head in my hands, trying to recover. At the end of half-an-hour my sight came back, but the night had fallen. There was no time to be lost. I arose for another march.

"However, I had only gone a couple of hundred feet, when I felt with my stick that the ice was broken just before me. In short, I was on the edge of the great *crevasse*, where, you may remember, Pierre Payot (this was the name of my guide), the three others were killed, and from which Marie Coutet was dragged out."

"What is that story?" I interrupted.

"Oh! I'll tell you to-morrow," said Payot. "But go on now, my ancient; go on: we are all attention."

Balmat continued:—

"'Ah ha!' said I, 'I know you well;' for we had crossed it in the morning on a bridge of ice, and I tried to find it, but in vain. The night was growing darker and my sight weaker; violent pains seized me in the head and stomach, and I could neither eat nor drink. However, there was nothing for it but to stay there that night; so I laid my sack on the snow, tied a handkerchief over my face, and prepared myself for a night like the other: worse even, for I was two thousand feet higher up; so the cold was much more bitter. A fine, sharp snow rained down on me also, and froze every limb. I felt a heaviness and irresistible desire to sleep, while thoughts sad as death filled my mind. I knew well what these sad thoughts and this desire to sleep portended. If I closed my eyes now, I would never open them again.

"Far below me, ten thousand feet down, I could see the lights of Chamouny, where my comrades were, no doubt, tranquilly enjoying themselves in their warm beds by a comfortable fire; and I said to myself, perhaps no one is thinking of me down there, or, if any one does give a thought to poor Balmat, as he is drawing the quilt up over his ears, or stirring the fire brighter, no doubt he is saying, 'Ah! that poor fool Jacques! He is amusing himself clapping his heels together to keep life in him.' Well, courage, Balmat.

"But it was not courage I wanted—only strength: man is not made of iron, and mine had been pretty well tried.

"In the intervals of silence that followed, minute by minute, the falling of the avalanches or splitting of the glaciers, I could hear a dog bark at Cormayeur, though the village was a league and a-half from the place where I was. Well, that kept me alive. It was the only sound that rose up to me from earth.

"However, towards midnight the dog became silent, too, and the stillness round me seemed like that of a graveyard; for I do not speak of the falling avalanches —they only made the silence more terrible, seeming like the thunder-voice of the mountain itself, threatening the poor human wanderer in the solitude.

"About two o'clock, the first white streak of day appeared above the horizon; the sun soon followed it; but Mont Blanc had got his wig on, and nothing I saw would make him take it off. He was in a bad humour, that was evident; and I could do nothing else but retrace my steps down to the valley, saddened, but not discouraged, by my two unsuccessful attempts, for the third time I guessed I would succeed.

"After five hours' walking I reached the village. It was then eight o'clock. I found all well at home, and my wife gave me breakfast; but I had need of sleep more than food; so I went to the barn, threw myself down upon the hay, and slept four-and-twenty hours without ever awaking.

"Three weeks passed away without bringing any favourable change in the weather; but still I watched and waited for a day to make my third attempt. Doctor Paccard, father to the guide I mentioned, wished to accompany me, and we agreed to set out together the first fine day.

"At last, the 8th of August, 1786, seemed to me just made for the excursion; so I went to Paccard and said to him, 'Come, doctor, are you ready? Do you fear neither cold, nor snow, nor precipices? Speak out like a man.'

"'I fear nothing with you, Balmat,' he replied.

"'Come, then,' said I, ''tis time to mount the mole-hill.'

"The doctor said he was quite ready; but at the moment of locking his door, I believe his courage failed him a little, for the key seemed to stick in the lock, and he turned, and turned it. 'Listen, Balmat,' said he: 'would it not be wise to take a couple of guides with us?'

"'No,' said I; 'I shall go either just with you or quite alone. I want to be first there, not second.'

"So he thought a minute, then drew the key out slowly, put it in his pocket, and followed me mechanically with his head bent down.

"After a minute, however, he looked up, shook his head back, and exclaimed, 'Well, Balmat, let us on; I trust in you and in the mercy of God.'

"Then he began to sing, not very well, to be sure, but it kept up his spirits, the poor doctor; so I took him by the arm.

"'Now,' said I, 'mind, no one is to know of this except our wives;' though afterwards we had to take the woman into our confidence, from whom we bought the syrup to mix with water for drinking, brandy being too strong for such a journey.

"As she suspected our object, we told her all, and bade her look for us next morning near the Dome of Goûter; for, if nothing adverse happened, we should certainly be there.

"All our little arrangements being completed, we bade our wives good-bye, and set off about five o'clock in the evening, taking different routes at first, not to be suspected, and agreeing to meet at the first village. That night we slept near the glacier of Taconnay. I had brought a quilt, and wrapped the poor doctor up in it, like an infant, by which means he got a tolerable night. I scarcely slept at all, and at sunrise I awoke the doctor. The day was glorious—no mist at all—so we proceeded in high spirits.

"After a quarter of an hour we began to traverse the glacier of Taconnay; and, in truth, the doctor's first steps on this great ice sea, with its immense cavities bridged over by a narrow ridge that cracks under your feet, were rather unsteady; but I got him on, and we crossed it safe and sound. Next, we ascended the Grands-Mulets, and soon left it behind us. I showed the doctor where I had passed the first night, which did not seem to comfort him much, for he kept silence for ten minutes; then, stopping suddenly, said—.

"'Balmat, do you think we can reach the summit of Mont Blanc to-night?'

"I saw what he was about, so I laughed and tried to re-assure him, but without promising anything, and we went on for two hours more.

"Since we left the Grands-Mulets the wind had been rising, and just as we turned the rock called the Petit-Mulet a violent gust carried off the doctor's hat.

"At the terrible oath he swore I turned round, and saw his beaver careering across the mountain, while he watched its progress with outstretched arms.

"'Oh! put on mourning for it, doctor,' said I. 'You will never see it again. It is on its way to Piedmont. A pleasant journey to it!'

"Maybe the wind didn't like my jesting, for just then we got a buffet that nearly sent us after the hat, only we threw ourselves flat on our faces on the ground, and remained that way for ten minutes without power to rise. The wind lashed the mountain, carrying whirlwinds of snow as big as a house over our heads. The doctor grew disheartened, but I was thinking how the woman would be watching for us on the top of Goûter. So the first moment possible I got up, determined to proceed, the doctor following on all-fours, as he would venture no other way.

"When we reached the spot agreed on, I took out my glass to examine the village that lay just beneath us, and there in truth was our friend, with about fifty others, all staring up, and dragging the glasses from each other's hands to get a sight of us.

"The doctor's pride helped him just then, and he stood up alongside of me, when immediately we were recognised, and the whole village saluted by waving their hats. I waved mine in return, but the doctor could do nothing, his being absent without leave.

"This last exertion, however, was all he was capable of, and no entreaties, no desire of success, could influence him to continue the ascent. So, after exhausting all my eloquence, and finding I was losing time into the bargain, I told him to wait for me where he was, but to be sure to keep himself warm by some movement or other. He replied mechanically, 'Yes, yes!' though I saw he scarcely knew what I was saying, from the excessive cold he was suffering. So I left him the bottle, though I was quite numb myself, and set off alone, telling him again to keep up some motion, and that I would return for him.

"'Yes, yes!' he answered; but when I had gone a couple of yards or so, I turned round, and there he was, in place of running up and down and clapping his soles, seated quite still with his back to the wind. However, even that was a precaution.

"As I went on from that point the road presented no great difficulty; but, according as I ascended, the air became less and less respirable, so that I was obliged to stop every ten minutes. It seemed to me as if my chest were quite empty, and that I had no lungs at all. To help myself a little, therefore, I folded my handkerchief like a cravat, and tied it over my mouth to breathe through. Still I made but little way, and, after an hour, found I had scarcely gone a quarter of a league; but I went on with my head bent down, till suddenly I found myself standing on a peak that was quite unknown to me. I looked round, and perceived that I was actually upon the summit of Mont Blanc.

"Then I turned my eyes in every direction, fearing that I had mistaken, and that maybe there was some other

point still higher which I would never have strength to
reach; for already my legs felt as if they were only kept
on my body by the pressure of the pantaloons. But no,
no; I was at the end of my journey. I was standing
where no living thing had ever yet come—not even the
eagle or the chamois; and I had reached it alone, without any other help than my own strong will. All around
me seemed to belong to me. I was the monarch of
Mont Blanc; I was the statue of that immense pedestal.

"Then I looked towards Chamouny, and waved my hat
at the end of my stick till I saw that my signs were answered. My subjects in the valley had perceived me.
The whole village was there to do me homage.

"After the first moment of triumph had passed away I
began to think of my poor doctor; so I descended as
rapidly as I could, calling him all the while by name,
and terribly alarmed at receiving no answer. At last I
spied him. There he was, lying as round as a ball, but
making no movement whatever in spite of all my shouts.
I bounded over, and found him rolled up like a cat, with
his head between his knees, whereupon I shook him
lustily, and he looked up.

"'I have been on the top of Mont Blanc,' I said, but
he never minded—only begged me to let him go sleep
again. 'Come,' said I; 'get up. You must go to the
top too; that's what you came for;' and I pulled him up
by the shoulder; but he seemed like one drunk. It
was all one to him whether he went up or down, to one
side or the other. However, the movement was of use
in restoring circulation; and then he asked me had I
by chance a pair of gloves in my pocket similar to those
I had on. They were made of hare-skin, expressly for
this excursion, with no division between the fingers.

"In such a position one might have refused them to
his own brother; however, I gave him one.

"About six o'clock we both stood together·upon the
summit of the mountain; and though the sun was still
bright, yet the sky above us was a dark blue, through
which we could see the stars shining. When we looked
down nothing was visible but a confused mass of glaciers,
rocks, bare mountains, and snow-covered aiguilles.

There was the immense chain of mountain from Dauphiny to the Tyrol, with its four hundred glaciers
sparkling in the light. You would have thought the
whole earth nothing but ice. The lakes of Geneva and
Neufchâtel were but mere blue points; the Swiss plains
seemed a pretty green carpet. All Piedmont and Lombardy, as far as Genoa, lay to our right; all Italy before
us. But Paccard saw nothing of all this. I told him
everything. As for me, I forgot all my sufferings. I
felt neither pain nor fatigue—not even the difficulty of
breathing, which, only an hour before, had almost made
me renounce my enterprise. We remained thus for
thirty-three minutes.

"It was now near seven o'clock, and we had but two
hours and a-half more of daylight. It was necessary to
think of descending; so I took hold of Paccard by the
arm, and, waving my hat as a farewell to the villagers,
began the descent. There was no track to guide us,
for the wind had swept the prints of our footsteps from
the snow; nothing except the holes here and there made
by the points of our iron-spiked sticks; and as to poor
Paccard, he was a mere child, that I had to help over the
good places and carry over the bad ones.

"Night began to fall just as we crossed the great *crevasse*, and overtook us entirely at the base of the grand
plateau; while every instant Paccard would stop, declaring he could not go an inch farther, and every instant I would get him on a little, not by persuasion, but
by force. Finally, about eleven o'clock, we quitted the
ice region and set foot at last upon the bare earth. But
it was now pitch dark; so I permitted Paccard to stop,
and was wrapping him up in the quilt when I perceived
that he never made use of his hands.

"'What is that for?' said I.

"'Why, how can I?' said he; 'for I don't feel them
at all.'

"And in truth when I removed his gloves, there were
his hands quite livid, like those of a corpse. Mine, too,
on which I had placed his little kid glove in place of
my own, was in the same state. So out of our four
hands three were frozen. However, he never seemed to

care, only begged of me to let him sleep, and bade me rub the frozen parts with snow.

" The remedy was not far off: I began with him and ended with myself. The blood came back slowly, and with it the natural heat, but accompanied by the sharpest pains, as if needles were running into every vein. Then I wrapped the poor doctor in the quilt, rolled him under shelter of a rock, ate a little with him, drank a cup, and then lay down close beside him to get heat, and so we slept.

" Next morning at six o'clock Paccard awoke me.

" ' Balmat,' said he, ' it is very odd; I hear the birds singing, and yet I see no daylight. Perhaps I cannot open my eyes.'

" But, mind you, his eyes were wide open, and so I told him. Then he began to rub them with snow mixed with brandy, which pained him greatly: still, he saw no better.

" ' Balmat,' said he at last, ' I must have grown blind.'

" ' Faith, it seems like it,' said I; ' but come along, at all events: take hold of the end of my sash and follow me.'

" So we got down safe and sound to the village, and there I left the doctor to find his way to his own house by groping along the wall, while I hastened to my wife to show her I was safe.

" But when I got home I looked in the glass. Good heavens! what an object I was! My eyes were blood-red, my face was black, and my lips were blue; while every time that I laughed or yawned the blood would spout out from my cheeks and mouth. In short, I was horrible to behold.

" Four days after, I set off for Geneva to acquaint M. de Saussure that I had succeeded in making the ascent; but he had already heard of it from an Englishman. He returned with me to Chamouny, and we tried the ascent together, but could not get farther than the summit of La Côte, and it was not till the year following that he was able to accomplish his grand project."

" And Dr. Paccard," said I, " did he remain blind?"

"Blind, indeed! why, he only died eleven months ago, at seventy years of age, and he could read without spectacles.   To be sure, his eyes looked rather red."

" In consequence of the ascent?"

" Oh, not at all!"

" And from what, then?"

"Ah ! he had a way of lifting his elbow, so —— "

And Balmat at these words finished his third bottle.

CHAPTER X.

THE MER DE GLACE.

NEXT morning, according to promise, my guide Payot was with me by ten o'clock. Time enough, as we had only seven leagues to travel, going and coming. He had gone home with old Balmat the night before, who was enchanted with me, and proposed spending that evening with me.

On leaving the village, Payot stopped to speak to a woman he met for some minutes, and then ran after us, apologising for the delay, but "he had something to say to Marie."

"And who is Marie?"

"Why, the only woman that ever made the ascent of Mont Blanc."

"Indeed!" and I turned back to look at her.

"Ay, there's a woman for you! One fine morning in 1811 the peasants of Chamouny said among themselves, 'Faith, it's a fine thing always bringing strangers up Mont Blanc to pleasure them: suppose we got up some day for our own pleasure.' No sooner said than done. The next Sunday was fixed on; and the day being fine, the whole party assembled together in one place, seven of us in all, with Jacques Balmat for our captain. At the moment of setting out, two women joined us, to our great surprise, both determined to make the ascent. One was Euphrosine Ducrocq, a married woman, with a baby only seven months old; the other named Marie Paradis, unmarried.

"Balmat would not hear of the married one going at
all, but he took Marie by the two hands, and looking
steadily into her eyes said—

"'Have you thought well of this, my child?'

"'I have.'

"'We must have no woman's tears, mind you.'

"'But I shall laugh the whole of the way.'

"'I don't ask that; for I, who am an old wolf of the
mountain, could not do it. I only require you to be a
brave girl and of good heart, and when you get weak
just tell me; and though I had to carry you on my
back, you shall reach the top with the others.'

"'Done!' cried Marie, clapping her hands. So we
all set forward.

"Towards night we stopped to rest at the Grands-
Mulets; and as young girls sleep restlessly often, and
Balmat feared she might fall into the ravine, we placed
her in the centre and threw all our cloaks over her; so
she passed a good night.

"Next morning, by break of day all of us were on our
feet, blowing our fingers and shaking our ears. So we
got forward until we reached a kind of wall of ice, one
thousand two hundred or one thousand four hundred
feet high, and the way we got up it was this:

"Balmat scrambled up first a piece, and planted his
stick in the ice to hold by; then the second seized hold
of his leg, and drew himself up by that till he caught
hold of Balmat's stick; Balmat then took a second stick
from that man's hand, and scrambled on another piece
till he planted it down in the ice like the first; and so
by this manœuvre we all crept up like ants on a garden
wall."

"And Marie," said I; "who caught hold of her
leg?"

"Oh! Marie mounted the last. Besides, we were
minding nothing then but our lives; for if a stick had
broken, the whole string of us would have been sent
clean down into the ravine. However, we all got safe
up, even Marie; but, whether from fright or fatigue,
just then her limbs began to fail, and she whispered,
smiling, to Balmat, 'Good Jacques, go a little slower;
pretend you are fatigued, for I am nearly fainting.'

Balmat accordingly relaxed his march, and Marie profited by the delay to swallow handfulls of snow, though
we told her such fare would do her no good. But we
might as well have been singing: she never heeded; so,
at the end of a few minutes, violent pains seized her.
Balmat now said she must give over her pride and consent to be helped; so he called another man, and they
each took one arm, and so we carried her on.

" Just then, too, Victor Terraz declared he could go
no farther; so Balmat signed to me to take his place
beside Marie, while he went to Victor, who was already
half asleep, and shook him violently.

" 'What do you want with me?' said Victor.

" 'I want you to come on.'

" 'And I choose to remain here.'

" 'But you shan't.'

" 'And why, if you please?'

" 'Because we set out seven in number; and when
we arrive at the grand plateau, if the people of Chamouny only see six, they will conclude an accident has
happened to one of us, and not knowing which, seven
families will be plunged into grief.'

" 'You are right, Father Balmat,' said Victor, and he
stood up.

" We were already on the top of Mont Blanc before
they overtook us. Marie had almost fainted away; still
she recovered herself enough to stand erect, and, with
her hand shading her eyes, to gaze on the immense
horizon.

" We laughingly told her that all the lands she saw we
would give her as a marriage portion. 'Then we must
find her a husband,' said Balmat. 'Gentlemen, which
of you wishes to be married?' Faith; our heads were
too busy with other things just then, so no one answered
except Michel Terraz, and he even asked half-an-hour to
think of it. However, as we had only ten minutes more
to stay, his proposition was not accepted; and after he
had looked well round upon the scene, Balmat said,
'Now, my children, it is all grand and beautiful; still
we must file off. See! the sun is setting: let us do like
him.'

" Next day we got safe down to Chamouny, and there

were all the women of the village assembled to question
Marie about all she had seen.   So she said, 'It would
be a long story to tell all that,' and she was very much
tired; but the best thing for them, if they were curious,
was to go up themselves.

"Since then, Marie has been the heroine of Chamouny, as Balmat is the hero; and, like him, she has
the surname of 'Mont Blanc,' and all strangers like
to visit her.

"When a party ascends, she goes as far as the village
of La Côte, and has a dinner dressed for them when they
return, which they never fail to enjoy, and with glass in
hand drink to the good success of all adventurers."

"And have there been many serious accidents," I
asked.

"No, God be thanked!" said Payot.   "There have
been none killed but guides.   Heaven has preserved all
travellers."

" Ay.   Balmat spoke of the *crevasse* into which Coutet
fell; but was he not saved?"

"Yes, he was saved, and is now alive and well in the
valley; but three others remained buried there, with two
hundred feet of snow over their bodies.   So in fine
nights you will see plainly three flames hovering over
the chasm, and these are their three souls; for you
know a shroud of ice and a coffin of snow are no fit
burial for a Christian."

"Well, tell me all about this terrible event."

But Payot evinced considerable repugnance to do so.
"Wait, monsieur," he said, "till you meet Coutet down
there in Chamouny.   He will tell you the story."

I saw the poor fellow was affected by mention of the
subject, so I would not insist upon his complying.   Besides, he distracted my attention by making me remark
a little fountain at our right.

"That is the Fontaine de Caillet," said he.

I looked at it attentively: there was nothing remarkable in its appearance.   I immersed my hand, thinking
it might be a thermal source; but it was cold as ice.   I
tasted some drops, thinking it might be ferruginous:
however, in all things it was a mere commonplace fountain.

"Well," said I, at last; "what is there wonderful about it?"

"That is the fountain immortalized by M. de Florian in his romance of 'Claudine.'"

"Ah, the deuce!" said I. "Is that what you make travellers stop for?"

"And, monsieur, because that fountain is exactly half way between Chamouny and the Mer de Glace."

"Ah, my dear friend! that same reason is worth all your immortality. Mind you always tack it to M. de Florian."

In truth, the road was the most execrable I ever travelled. One might as well have been walking on the slippery roof of a house during these three hours in which we were climbing and stumbling up to our destination—the inn over the Mer de Glace; though a little bread and milk was all that rewarded us in the way of refreshment.

However, the first sensation is not of physical need, but of awe at sight of the grand colossal nature in whose presence you stand. Around, on every side, the sharp snowy peaks piercing the sky like lightning-conductors. to the mountain. Before you a sea—an ocean—of ice, frozen amidst the tossings of a tempest, with its thousand-formed waves swelling to the height of ninety feet, or sinking into a depth five hundred feet down beneath your glance. You seem no longer in France, or in Europe, but in an arctic ocean beyond Greenland or the southernmost islands—upon some frozen polar sea, beyond Baffin's Bay or the Straits of Behring.

When Payot thought we had gazed long enough, he proposed our descending to the sea itself, which lay sixty feet below us. This we accomplished by a path as dangerous as that I had so lately trembled over; so I had to balance myself from side to side with my iron-shod stick; Payot, meanwhile, marching on as if it were the finest of high-roads, and never deigning a glance behind at my struggle for a footing. "My brave fellow," said I, at last, giving him an epithet I could not well claim for myself, "is there no road but this?"

"Why, what are you doing there?" said he, turning round. "What ails you?"

"What ails me? Why, I've got the vertigo. *Pardieu!* do you think I came into the world on the top of a steeple? It is all very well for you; but I've no wish to show off just now. Here, give me your hand."

Payot immediately extended the end of his stick to me, and by help of this I got down safely till we came to a rock about seven feet above a level bed of sand surrounding the Mer de Glace. Here, I confess, the desire to show off did seize me. The moment had arrived for proving to Payot that I could leap, if I could not climb; so, without saying a word, and assuming the most unconcerned air in the world, I carelessly jumped from the rock down upon the sand. Instantly a simultaneous cry was uttered by both; for I felt myself sinking, and he thought I was lost. By an instinctive movement, however, I placed my stick crosswise over the sand, as I had often done with my gun when shooting on the moors, and by this means sustained myself for a moment, during which Payot had time to reach me his stick, which I grasped with one hand and then with the other, till finally he succeeded in drawing me up out of the sand, like a fish dangling at the end of a line, and reinstating me on the rock.

"What a fool you are," said he, when I had recovered, "to take a jump into a sandpit!"

"And what a cursed country this of yours, where one can't take a step without risk of breaking his neck! What did I know of your sandpits?"

"Well, you'll know them another time," he answered quietly. "Only let me tell you, if you had not put your stick across, you would have gone down under the glacier, and never come out probably till next summer, at the source of the Arveyron. Now, would you like to see the garden?"

"What garden?"

"Oh! a little triangle of cultivated ground to the north of the glacier of Talètre, that every one goes to see, to say he has been there."

"Well, my friend, I have no wish to see it; so I won't go."

"But won't you take a turn on the Mer de Glace?"

"Oh, certainly. Am I to skate?"

"Come, let me hold you by the arm, and don't be trying any more of your nonsense."

"Oh! as to that, friend, don't fear. I shall religiously pick my steps after you; so proceed."

In this way we travelled for about a quarter of a league; he first, I following, over the colossal waves of this frozen sea, while horrible noises resounded all around from the cracking of the ice, like groans proceeding from the central heart of the earth to the surface.

Perhaps I have a more nervous or impressionable organization than other men; but when in the midst of scenes so grand and terrible, a certain sensation of physical fear comes over me, even though no real danger exists, from the contrast of my frail humanity with the mighty nature around me. A cold sweat covers my brow—I turn pale—my voice trembles; and if I did not hasten from the locality which excited the emotion, assuredly I would faint. Thus it was here. There was really no danger; yet I could not bear to look down into the hollows of the frozen sea, and up at the vast frozen waves suspended over my head. I took hold of my guide's arm, and said, "Come away; let us leave this."

Payot looked at me in some surprise. "Why, truly, you are quite pale," he remarked.

"I am not well."

"What ails you?"

"I am sea-sick."

At this Payot laughed outright, and so did I.

"Come, come!" said he; "you are not so bad when you can laugh; drink a cup, and that will set you all to rights."

However, I did not recover until I stood upon the solid earth once more; and Payot then proposed that we should skirt the margin of the Mer de Glace up to the "Englishman's Stone."

"What stone is that?" said I.

"Ah! we call it so after the first travellers who arrived there. They took refuge under it from the rain, and dined there. It seems they were a couple of English who discovered Chamouny by chance, for the village had lain there shut up in the mountains, and no one knew anything about it; and they and their attendants entered it armed to the teeth, not knowing but they were going to meet a set of wild mountain savages; in place of which, the brave fellows of the village received them with open hearts, and the travellers in return showed them the wonderful beauties of the country; for the men of the vale had never thought of exploring the Mer de Glace. And so, out of gratitude, the stone under which they sheltered has remained ever since consecrated to the memory of the two Englishmen who, by telling the world what they had seen, made the fortune of our land."

By this time we reached the arch in the rock, made memorable by the inscription over it, bearing the name of the travellers, and date of their journey—"Pocox and Windham, 1741."

Having made the circuit of the stone, we returned to the inn; on entering which, I observed a man on his knees blowing the fire with his mouth.

"Hold!" said Payot; "you wanted to see Marie Coutet, the guide that was swept away by an avalanche. Well, there he is, blowing the fire. Ever since the freezing he got up in the mountain, the poor fellow shivers like a marmot."

"What! is that the man who fell into the chasm where the others were killed? Do you think he would tell me all about it?"

"Try him. It is not a very gay subject, but then it is curious, and we are here to satisfy the curiosity of travellers."

There was something bitter in the tone of his last words; but no matter. I called the landlord, ordered a bottle of his best wine, filled three glasses, and approached Coutet with one,

"To your health, my master!" said I; "and may you never fall into such dangers as you escaped from."

He rose up, with a smile as bright as a Savoyard, and took the glass.

"Ah! monsieur means my tumble into the *crevasse?*"

"Exactly."

"Then, in truth"—and here Coutet swallowed the

wine in a parenthesis—"it was the worst quarter of an hour I ever passed."

"Would you tell me a little about it, as a great favour?"

"Everything, monsieur, if you like;" and he put the glass down, and wiped his mouth with the back of his hand.

"Then let us sit down." And I set the example, filled the glasses of my two guides, and Coutet began.

CHAPTER XI.

MARIE COUTET.

"In 1820, Colonel Anderson and Doctor Hamel arrived at Chamouny; the latter being commissioned by the Emperor of Russia to make meteorological experiments upon all the high mountains of the globe. An expedition for the ascent of Mont Blanc was accordingly arranged, with all the necessary precautions; for nine ascents had now been made without any accident happening. On the appointed day, ten guides were ready, with myself as guide-in-chief; making a party altogether, including the two travellers, of thirteen.

"We set off at eight o'clock in the morning, with every appearance of fine weather, and reached the Grands-Mulets at three in the afternoon, There we halted, knowing we could not gain the summit that day, and that no other good resting-place could be had farther up. So we settled ourselves, tolerably, on a kind of platform, where we found the remains of a shed, built by M. de Saussure for his ascent, and proceeded to dinner, bidding the travellers lay in a stock sufficient for twenty-four hours, as, higher up, in proportion as they ascended, they would not only lose appetite, but even the power of eating. After dinner we talked of the numerous successful attempts, and how all difficulties had been overcome. So this put us in good spirits, and the time passed quickly, listening to the different stories of the guides. Evening came, but still we had no apprehensions. We erected a tent, laid our blankets on straw, and lay down as close to each other as we could be packed. Thus we managed to get through the night without any mischance.

" Next morning I awoke first, and immediately crept out from our shelter to ascertain what weather we had. A single glance sufficed to show me that further progress on that day was impossible. 'What ails you, Coutet?' said Devoissou, one of the guides, as I returned, shaking my head despondingly.

" ' Why,' said I, ' the wind has changed, and comes from the south, and the snow is flying before it like dust.'

" When they all found this was so, we looked at one another, and resolved not to go another step that day: a resolution which was strongly combated by Dr. Hamel, who wanted to insist on our proceeding. However, we were obstinate; and all he could obtain from us was a promise to remain where we were for the night, and not go back to the village.

" The day passed sadly enough; for the snow, which had hitherto fallen only towards the summit of the mountain, now began to descend closer and closer to our little shelter, like a friend warning us by degrees of our danger. Night came. We took the same precautions, and got through it without harm to any of us; but the weather, next morning, was worse than ever. So we held a council, the result of which was, after ten minutes' deliberation, that we should all make our way back to Chamouny; and we accordingly informed the gentlemen that such was our intention. To this Doctor Hamel opposed himself strongly. Well, we were under his orders; our time and lives were his, since he paid us for them; so we yielded—merely drawing lots to see which of us should go back to Chamouny for provisions. Three were chosen, and they left our party instantly. By eight o'clock in the morning, Dr. Hamel had got quite tired of waiting for a favourable change in the weather; and, in place of staying where we were, now demanded that we should proceed in the ascent. Had one of ourselves made such a proposal, we'd have simply pronounced him mad, and tied his legs together; but the doctor was a stranger; he knew nothing of the dangerous caprices of the mountain; and so we just quietly told him that, to proceed even a couple of leagues, after all the warnings we had received, was to defy Providence and tempt God. At this the doctor stamped his foot in a rage, and, turning to Colonel Anderson, muttered the word '*Cowards!*'

"There was no hesitating after that; all made their preparations in silence; and in about five minutes I asked the doctor if he were ready to follow us. He bowed his head in sign of acquiescence, for the anger had not left him yet; and we set forth, without even waiting for our companions from the village.

"Against all probability, the beginning of our journey was most favourable; and we reached the Dome of Goûter, and re-descended towards the grand plateau, without any accident befalling us. At this point we had the great *crevasse* to our left, sixty feet broad and one hundred and twenty long; and to our right the steep side of Mont Blanc, rising abruptly to the height of a thousand feet above our heads, while beneath was a bed of newly-fallen snow, through which we sank nearly up to our knees. Besides this, we had now got the wind in our faces, and every step we advanced it became more and more violent. However, we followed each other one by one up the mountain, for our line of march was arranged on this wise:—First went Auguste Terre, then Carrier, and Pierre Balmat the third; after them, Matthew Balmat, Devoissou, and myself; and six paces behind us, Coutet and Folliguet. Last of all came the travellers, Dr. Hamel and Colonel Anderson, who could make the ascent easier, we thought, by following in the track of the eleven guides.

"But the very measures we had adopted for safety proved our ruin; for, by marching in single file, we trod down a line in the snow like the track of a plough; and on account of its being soft and fresh, and the side of the mountain being too steep to preserve it in equilibrium, the snow naturally began to slip down in masses. Then, in a little while we heard all at once a sound as of the rushing of a hidden torrent; and at the same moment the snow above us, as far as the eye could reach, down to the spot where we had hollowed a track ten or twelve inches deep, began to move. Another instant passed, and four out of the five men that preceded me were swept away: one alone remained standing. Then I felt my limbs failing me, and I fell to the ground, crying out with all my force, 'The avalanche! the avalanche! We are lost!'

" I felt myself carried away with the rapidity of a rolling ball, so that in a minute's time I must have gone over four hundred feet at least; then the earth failed beneath me, and I knew that I was falling perpendicularly down some chasm, and I remember crying, 'God have mercy on me!' At the same instant I found myself at the bottom of the great *crevasse*, lying on a heap of snow, and in a little while heard the fall of another person close beside me, but without knowing who it was. For a moment I was stunned by the fall, but a voice above, lamenting and crying, roused me. It was David Coutet, my brother.

" ' Oh, my brother! my poor brother is lost!' he cried.

" ' No, David; I am here,' I shouted out, 'and another with me. Is Matthew Balmat killed?'

" ' No, my brave comrade! I am alive and here, ready to aid thee,' answered Balmat. And at the same instant he let himself slide down the side of the chasm, and fell close to me.

" ' How many are killed?' I asked.

" ' Three; if the one with you is living.'

" ' And which are they?'

" ' Carrier, Terre, and Pierre Balmat.'

" ' And the gentlemen?—are they safe?'

" ' Quite, God be thanked!'

" ' Well, let us look for the man who fell here; he cannot be far off.'. And in fact, on turning round, we saw an arm sticking out of the snow—nothing more was visible of our poor comrade. So we dragged him out, and got his head free as soon as possible; but he was quite insensible, and as blue as if he had been strangled: still, in a few minutes, we got him on his legs. My brother threw us a little hatchet, with which we cut steps in the ice. When we were near up, those above helped us with their hands; and so the three of us got safely out at last.

" As soon as we were on the top the two gentlemen

came over, took our hands, and said, 'Courage! here are two saved; we will save the others yet.'

"'The others are lost,' replied Matthew Balmat. 'It was here I saw them;' and he led us to the middle of the *crevasse*, where we saw indeed there was no hope of saving them, for two hundred feet of snow must have been already lying on the heads of our poor friends. Nevertheless, we groped with our sticks all about, but in vain. We discovered no trace of them.

"Matthew Balmat was the only one of the party who kept himself erect while the avalanche passed. He was a young man of prodigious strength; and when he felt the snow moving under his feet, he stuck his stick firmly in the solid ice beyond, and, swinging himself up from the ground, remained suspended by the force of his two wrists alone, while the whole avalanche, to the length of half-a-league, swept beneath him with the noise of thunder, carrying away his brother and all his companions along with it. For an instant he thought all must have perished, for no one remained standing but himself.

"The first that rose to their feet were the two travellers, and Balmat called out to them, 'Where are the others?' At that moment David Coutet appeared.— 'The others,' said he; 'ah! I saw them all swept into the *crevasse*,' and running towards it, he stumbled against David Folliguet, who lay stunned by his fall. 'Here is one,' said he, 'so five only are missing, but amongst them is my brother, my poor brother!' It was at this moment I heard his voice, and answered from the chasm, 'No, brother, here I am!'

"Still he searched for the other three, but all in vain. Two hours had passed thus, and as evening came on the wind became more icy, our sticks were covered with snow, and our shoes frozen as hard as iron. Then Balmat, despairing of any further search, turned to the doctor.

"'Well, monsieur,' he said, 'were we cowards, think you? Do you wish to continue the ascent? We are ready.'

"The doctor replied by giving the order to return to Chamouny. As to Colonel Anderson, he wept like a child. 'I have been in many battles,' said he: 'I fought at Waterloo; I have seen whole ranks of men swept away by cannon, but they were there to die—it was their duty; whilst here,' and tears interrupted him, 'I cannot go without, at least, finding the bodies of those poor men.'

"We had at last to force him away, for night was coming on, and it was time to descend.

"On reaching the Grands-Mulets, we met the other guides, who had been despatched for provisions, and two travellers along with them, who wished to make the ascent with our party. We related our disaster, and then sorrowfully retraced our steps to the village, which we reached about eleven o'clock at night.

"Fortunately, the three men who perished were unmarried. Carrier, however, had supported his family on his earnings. As to Pierre Balmat, he had only a mother; but, poor woman, she was not long parted from her son. Three months after his death, she died also."

CHAPTER XII.

THE RETURN TO MARTIGNY.

WHEN the recital was finished, Payot and I set forth again on our journey, After half-an-hour's walking my guide stopped. "Hold!" said he; "there is a nice short-cut down from Montanvert in two minutes and a-half, while the ordinary road takes three hours."

"And how do you manage it?" said I.

"Oh! the easiest way in the world. Just cut four pine branches, place them cross-wise, seat yourself thereon, and then slide down gently all the way, holding your stick as a sort of rudder to guide your way."

"Ah! that must be admirable for one's pantaloons."

" Why, truth to say, one generally leaves them behind him in fragments on the road. However, there is another short-cut of about an hour and a-half, only the path is narrow as a wheel-rut. Will you try it?"

" Certainly."

- Payot looked at me in astonishment. " Why, the wine of Montanvert has got into your head. You are not serious."

" Perfectly. I am hungry enough to do anything. So proceed—I follow."

On went Payot, amazed at my temerity; but, in truth, it is only a perpendicular precipice that affects my head. When the slope is at all gradual I can walk on a path as narrow as a horse hair, and feel no inconvenience. In this instance I succeeded bravely, and we reached the source of the Arveyron in a quarter of an hour.

The water springs from the glaciers of Bois, and issues out of an aperture eighty or a hundred feet high. This cavern resembles the throat of a fish, with arch within arch, like so many jaw-bones retreating to the orifice of the throat, whence leaps forth the glittering stream, supple and agile as the tongue of a serpent. Some of the vaulted arcades seem very fragile, and as if they would fall and crush the traveller who ventures within the cavern.

An accident of this kind did happen in 1830, at the very place where we stood. One of a party of travellers who had entered, wanting to detach a portion of one of those icy arcades, fired a pistol, when one did fall with a terrible crash, at the same time blocking up the entrance and obstructing the passage of the water. The travellers mounted the block of ice to examine the cavity left by its fall, but in a moment the increased force of the stream carried away the dike, and the travellers along with it. One of them had his thigh broken, and another was swept on by the torrent and drowned, in spite of all the efforts of the guides to save him.

Payot gave me all these details as we walked along to Chamouny, and we had already traversed a quarter of a league from the source, when we found ourselves on a kind of island between the Arve and Arveyron. Here we looked round for a bridge, which it seems ought to have been there. In the Alps, these constructions are generally of the frailest kind; probably only the trunk of a tree flung over, which gives you one chance of safety and two of death. Here, however, we had not even the two latter chances; the bridge had most likely been kicked into the stream by some morose or ungrateful traveller after he had been benefited by its services; but no matter what was the cause, no bridge existed now.

" Here is a pretty business!" cried Payot.

" Well," said I, " what is to be done?"

" Why, we must go back, and there's half-an-hour lost."

" My dear friend," said I, " that is impossible. I am too hungry to go back."

" But what can you do?"

" Why, you know, good Payot, though I can't climb, I can jump."

" What! ten feet?"

" Just tell me, is there a morass beyond?"

" Oh, none in the world."

"Then adieu, Payot!"

And in the same instant I was across, safe and sound at the other side. I turned round and saw my man looking very bewildered, but making no attempt to follow. "Go your own way now, my brave fellow," said I; "I shall have dinner ready for you when you arrive."

Payot accordingly retraced his steps, and I had reached Chamouny by the time, probably, he was only at the cavern of Arveyron. When the poor devil came in all covered with snow, dinner was ready, and we sat down. I could see that my exploit had made a great impression upon my guide, and he treated me with profound reverence. These children of nature value only the physical gifts of nature. Strength, courage, and agility, are the gods they worship, and whoever possesses them is in their eyes a man of genius.

In the evening Balmat arrived with some crystals he had promised me, and we had a pleasant supper, enlivened with his anecdotes of the different celebrities who had made the ascent or visited Chamouny. Amongst them were Saussure, Chateaubriand, Dolomieu, and Charles Nodier.

Next day Payot left me, and gave his son in place of himself for a guide. The child had brought a mule which we were to ride by turns, and we set off, with our long, iron-pointed sticks, like old Roman mountaineers going to look after their flocks.

At the end of an hour or so we entered the Gorge des Montets, and here the character of the country changed completely. It was rude, sterile, and desolate, with here and there a group of wretched cabins visible, like a band of tattered beggars, where the peasants shelter themselves for four months of the year, and then seek an abode amongst the avalanches of the mountain. From time to time we passed a rude cross, marking the spot where some traveller, or perhaps some entire family, had perished; but even these symbols of death are transitory, for the stones rolling down the mountain often hurl them prostrate on the ground.

From this we passed into the Gorge of Valorsine, or Valley of Bears, to distinguish it from Chamouny, or Vale of Chamois; and here, too, we found signs of a still wilder region than that we had quitted. Enormous stones were placed on the roofs of the houses, as we place marble weights on the papers of our writing-desks, to prevent their being carried off by the mountain tempest. The church was defended by strong bulwarks, like a castle of the sixteenth century, to guard it against the assaults of the mighty avalanches; and many buildings were raised on piles, to prevent the torrents sweeping them away, and to give room for the waters to pass beneath the foundations. The Gorge of Valorsine extends for a league or more beyond the village of that name, and the road passes through a forest of pine-trees, shadowing a torrent, called by the natives the Black Water: not that its pure, clear waters are in the least discoloured, but from the vaulted roof of pine branches, which fling a sombre shade over the stream. Three times you cross this capricious river upon different bridges, till finally you pass from one mountain to the other, and find yourself at the base of the Tête Noir.

At every step now the road became more savage; the pines ceased to be crowded into forests, and stood out alone like sentinels, or like a file of giants who had tried to scale the mountain and been suddenly transfixed as they stood. Many have been laid low by blocks of granite hurled down from the summit, and the victim and conqueror lie side by side. In many places progression was even dangerous; sometimes we had to cross an abyss or a path but half-a-foot broad, and the inhabitants themselves name this part of the way Maupas, or the bad road.

Once through this defile the road becomes practicable even for carriages, and we descended quietly and comfortably to the village of Trient, where we had dinner, and by seven in the evening found ourselves once more in Martigny, the capital of the Valais. On arriving they told us of a tremendous storm that had visited the town the night before, and on looking over the travellers' book we found the fact touchingly recorded thus:—

" M. Dumont, merchant, travelling for pleasure—five daughters, and tremendous rain"!

CHAPTER XIII.

SAINT BERNARD.

AFTER I had inscribed my name, profession, &c. in the same book, I observed mine host approaching with an air of embarrassment and sadness united together.   In fact, the good man had nowhere to put me; his rooms were full, every bed engaged; "but if I only tried a little hay on the kitchen floor—it made an excellent bed, and the odour was very wholesome."   This timid recommendation, however, did not suit my fancy, and I ordered my guide to conduct me to the Hôtel de la Tour.

At this my host made a last effort.   "There was a large room which he had given up to a party of five travellers, and they were content with a mattress each; now, perhaps I could get room enough amongst them, if I put up with a mattress likewise."

"Lead the way," I said; and we proceeded to the apartment, from which most riotous sounds were issuing.   The travellers within were all fighting for separate spots on which to lay themselves to sleep; and as the size of the room did not seem to admit of any such geometrical division, I thought it a bad time to press my claims; but gently opening the door, I perceived first, that the battle was conducted in darkness, the missiles flung by the combatants having extinguished the lights.   This inspired me with an idea: I blew out my host's candle that my entry might not be observed, and telling him I would manage the rest, slipped softly in, shut the door, locked it, and put the key in my pocket.   My movements passing unobserved in consequence of the peals of laughter that accompanied the war, no one knew that an enemy had entered the garrison. However, I had hardly made two steps when several missiles alighted on my head; but this did not deter me: I stooped down, seized a weapon (there were plenty flying about), and managed it with such vigour that I soon cleared my way to a corner, where I rested, knowing it to be an advantageous position. Here I was comparatively safe, and I took advantage of my success, by quietly appropriating a mattress and mantle that just then seemed to have no particular owner; and enveloping myself most comfortably in the latter, I lay down with my face to the wall, totally regardless of the storm that would arise when one or other of the combatants found himself minus a mattress.

And, in fact, the crisis soon arrived. Calm was gradually restored; the laughter ceased; each of them began to fix his mattress, and I felt one placed at my right, another at my left; then came the impatient seekings to and fro of the victim who could find none, till at last a luminous idea struck him, and he cried out—" Gentlemen, one of you must have taken two mattresses."

This accusation was repelled by a unanimous shout of indignation, but I took good care to remain quiet. Half laughing, half swearing, the victim continued his search, then finally rung for a light. I saw the candle through the key-hole, brought by the servant of the inn. "Open the door," said our friend. "It is locked inside," answered the maid. "Ah! where the deuce is the key? Gentlemen, which of you locked the door?" All denied the imputation. "Then, go and get the second key," he called out to the girl; "every door in an inn has two keys."

She retreated. Moments of intense anxiety succeeded, till we heard her step again. "It can't be found, sir."

"This is too bad!" exclaimed the victim. "You may laugh, gentlemen, but I'll have my mattress, whether you will or no."

Here a growl proceeded from each proprietor of a mattress, and every one grasped his bed convulsively.

"How many mattresses did you bring?"

"Five."

"You see, gentlemen, one of you *must* have taken two for his share."

An energetic and absolute denial followed.

"Very well. Bring me a box of matches."

Something fearful was evidently going to be enacted that I could not comprehend, and I trembled. The girl returned with the matches.

"Now," he cried, "light one, and pass it to me through the key-hole."

The operation was performed. I saw the transit of the little blue flame through the orifice, and its brilliant light when it emerged at our side. What a stupid invention these matches!

Another instant and the candle was lighted, and the whole room illuminated. Every one started up on his mattress to pass examination, when a cry of surprise escaped from every mouth, and a voice terrible to my ears as the doom of execution pronounced the words—

"There are six of us!"

A second voice responded, "Call out the names."

"Yes, yes! call the roll!" they all exclaimed.

The victim, being the most interested in detection, accordingly began :—

"Jules de Lamark."

"Present."

"M. Caron, physician."

"Ditto."

"M. Soissons."

"Ditto."

"M. Reimonenq."

"Ditto."

"M. Honoré de Sussy——"

I started up. "Ah! my dear De Sussy!" said I, extending my hand—"how are you? I saw your sister, the Duchess d'O——, a week ago, and she was looking beautiful enough to drive one mad."

One may imagine the singular effect produced by my interruption. Every eye was fixed on me.

"What! Dumas?" exclaimed De Sussy.

"The same, my dear friend. Now, pray present me

to these gentlemen. I shall be enchanted to make their acquaintance."

"Certainly;" and M. de Sussy took me by the hand. "Gentlemen! I have the honour——"

Each one rose up on his mattress and saluted.

"Now," said I, addressing the bereaved one, "allow me to restore you your bed, provided you all permit me to have one for myself in your company."

The response was affirmative and unanimous. So, having summoned the landlord, I soon succeeded in having one brought in, of which I was proprietor.

The party, I found, were bound for St. Bernard as well as myself, and had engaged two carriages, in one of which I was offered a seat. I accepted. The journey was long; we were all fatigued; and as we were to be off next morning at seven o'clock, every one felt the necessity of repose: so we slept.

At seven o'clock, as agreed on, we were all crushed into a couple of those abominable vehicles called *chars-à-bancs;* but hardly had we gone ten steps when the erratic movements of the horse induced me to address the coachman briefly thus:—

"My friend, I believe you are drunk."

"Why, a little, master; but don't fear."

Things went on pretty well as long as we were on a level, and the eccentric proceedings of both driver and horse only made us laugh. However, it was different when we began to ascend the steep mountain side, like a wall, with a deep precipice beside us—a true Alpine path. Here the laughter ceased; and, as the danger increased, our remonstrances became more energetic.

"But, *sacre!* coachman, you are going to upset us!"

"Oh! don't fear, my masters," he replied, whipping the poor horse unmercifully. "Besides," he added by way of encouragement, "Napoleon passed here."

"Quite true; but then he was on a mule, and his guide was not drunk."

"A mule! do you know that? Ay, truly, he was on a mule."

And our coachman dashed on, with his head turned to chat to us, never deigning to cast a look upon the road.

"Ay, sure enough, on a mule; for it was Martin of
St. Pierre that conducted him, and had his fortune
made by it."

"Coachman!"

"Don't fear.—And the First Consul gave him a house
afterwards, and four acres of land ——"

"Coachman!"

Here the wheel of our carriage had actually turned
the edge of the precipice; and Lamark and Sussy, who
were at that side, were literally suspended over the
abyss.

In fact, the affair was going beyond a joke. So I
jumped out at the risk of my neck, rushed to the horse's
head, and seized the bridle. My companions followed
my example; and, in spite of the reiterated "Oh, don't
fear; Napoleon passed this way!" of our driver, we
hurled him from his seat, and, leaving him sprawling
on the road with his vehicle beside him, pursued our
way on foot, which at least secured us from all peril of
our lives.

In two hours we reached the inn for dinner; and,
having procured another vehicle, with a demure horse
and pacific coachman, we pursued our way to St. Pierre
in perfect safety.

Here was the last encampment of the French army
before crossing the Great St. Bernard, beyond which
the plains of Marengo awaited them. The peasants
pointed out to us the different positions of the cavalry,
the infantry, and the artillery; and told how the guns
had been taken from the carriages, and carried on trunks
of hollow pine by bodies of men, who were relieved every
hundred steps. Some amongst them had even seen this
giant work performed, and told with pride how they had
lent a hand. They described the appearance of the First
Consul, the colour of his dress, and recollected even
the most insignificant words that fell from his lips. It
was strange to find the memory of this great man still
living in all its vividness amongst these mountaineers,
while to our young generation, who had never beheld
him, he seemed a fabulous hero of some Homeric imagination.

Having satisfied our curiosity, we returned to our inn

for the night, it being too late at that hour to proceed
to the hospital of the monks; but the inn was crowded
with travellers, who had already seized upon everything
eatable and every decent room; so we were forced to
put up with a hole into which none but a Swiss innkeeper would think of stowing Christian gentlemen.
The rain filtered through the roof, the rats walked over
the floor. In short, we could bear it no longer, and
unanimously voted an immediate departure for the
Great St. Bernard.

The idea was received with enthusiasm, and we descended to seek a guide.

After the lapse of ten minutes he arrived, and received
orders to recruit two comrades and six mules without
delay, as we intended proceeding immediately to St.
Bernard.

" The Great St. Bernard! the deuce!" he exclaimed,
and he went to the window, examined the night, and
returned, shaking his head.

" You want three men and six mules, you say, to go
to-night to St. Bernard?"

" Yes."

" Well, you must have them;" and he turned away.
His expression, however, made me uneasy, and we called
him back.

" Is there any danger?" we asked.

" Danger! to be sure there is. But you want to go,
and of course you must go. However, I advise you to
take six guides in place of three."

"Very well; let us have six guides. But what sort of
danger is there? for there are no avalanches, surely, at
this season."

" No, but we may miss the road."

" Oh! that could be only in the midst of snow, and
remember this is August."

" Ay, but you'll have plenty of snow up there, as high
as your knees. The rain is very soft and gentle here,
but a league higher it will turn to snow, mind ye."

" Well, to the vote!" we exclaimed. " Let all those
who are for St. Bernard raise their hands."

Four hands were raised out of six; the departure was
settled.

"I would not mind," continued the guide, "if you be-longed to ourselves; but you Parisians are delicate, and will have your feet frozen in the snow before long."

"But we won't alight from our mules."

"Ah! but you must."

"No matter. We'll go."

He left us at last, and then we prepared ourselves for the journey, with coats, cloaks, muffles, and, above all, cigars and a match-box. Then we stood round the fire to warm ourselves preparatory to the expected cold.

The guide entered. "Good; warm yourselves," he said; "you will need it. Now, my masters, we are ready; mount!"

We descended, and mounted our mules in high spi-rits, each one trying for the first quarter of an hour to make his mule take the lead; but every one knows how difficult it is to force a mule out of its original position in a file, and the failures gave us high amusement. At length, Lamark succeeded in taking the lead, and setting his mule into a trot, exclaimed, "Don't fear; Napoleon passed this way."

When one mule trots, the whole caravan trots, and the guides, consequently, have to keep up a running accompaniment. To this movement they always evince great repugnance, in which the animals sympathise, no doubt; for in a very short time the leader comes to a dead halt, which gives a sudden check to the entire line; then having waited an instant, the whole caravan sets forward again in its grave and monotonous march.

"With your leave, sir," said the guide, who had now come up with Lamark; "Napoleon did not pass here, but on the opposite side of the mountain: a few cannon only came this way."

"Gentlemen, the snow!" Our guide prophesied truly.

Down it came—a rain frozen to ice.

"Pardieu! snow in August! Let us alight and fight with snow-balls, in memory of Napoleon, who passed this way."

Every one laughed at the repetition of this sacramen-tal phrase; but the guide interrupted: "Gentlemen, I have said before, Napoleon did not pass this way; and as to fighting with snow-balls, I advise you not to lose time, for in a quarter of an hour it will be quite dark."

" Well then, friend, our mules will lead us."

"Yes, if you don't contradict them. God has made everything for its place—a Parisian for Paris, and a mule for the mountain. Let the beast go, let it go. Here you are safe enough, but once past the bridge of Hudri, you will find the path only fit for a rope-dance. Leave your mules alone, then, I advise you."

"Bravo, guide! We'll drink your health. You have spoken well. Halt!"

Every one lifted his bottle to his lips, then passed it to the guide. In the mountains, we all drink out of the same vessel. You don't mind these things when at any moment within six inches of losing your life.

The rum cheered us considerably; and though night and snow were around, the caravan laughed and talked and went joyously on.

It was a strange sight, in the midst of the darkness and frozen desolation, this little file of mules, cavaliers, and guides, plunging gaily into the depths of the sombre, silent, terrible mountain, which did not even send back an echo in response to our songs and laughter. But by degrees the deep gloom of the scene fell on our spirits likewise, and the songs became lower and the laughter rarer. At length the stillness was broken by an isolated voice, "Let us light our cigars."

" Bravo! Who spoke?"

" I, Jules de Lamark."

"Then you shall have a vote of thanks when we reach the hospital."

"De Sussy, give us the match-box."

"By my faith! gentlemen, my hands are too comfortable in my pockets to venture them out in the cold. Some one must come and take it."

A guide having performed this operation, a file of red sparks was soon seen in the darkness all along the line. All now was stillness. Nothing broke the silence but an occasional word of encouragement from the guides to their mules. In short, the gaiety was frozen in our hearts. The snow fell heavily, and a sharp, bitter cold penetrated every pore. No light was on our path save a pale, livid reflection from the snow, which enabled us sometimes dimly to perceive that our mules were picking their steps over precipices where there was scarcely room for two feet together. At last, the leader of one column halted.

"*Ma foi!*" he exclaimed, "I am frozen dead. Let us try a walk."

"I told you so," answered the guide.

Upon this idea we all acted, and dismounted instantly, hoping the motion would invigorate us.

"Now, hold on by the tails of your mules," exclaimed the guides, "or you will lose your way."

Accordingly, we executed this manœuvre, and trusted ourselves implicitly to the instinct of our conductors.

Now I felt the truth of Balmat's relation, for the cold attacked my head with that violent vertigo of which he spoke, and an irresistible desire to sleep. Several of the party felt the same, and proposed a halt.

"On, gentlemen! on!" cried out our guide, authoritatively. "I warn you, he who stops now will never stir more!"

There was a solemnity in his tone that instantly roused us to fresh exertion, and we continued our walk without further objection for the space of half-an-hour, dragged along by our mules, and knee-deep in snow, ῑ all at once De Sussy cried out, "A house!" We abandoned the tails of our mules, and rushed forw to see it, wondering why our muleteers had said nothi about it.

"Perhaps you don't know what house that is?" si the guide-in-chief.

"Were it the devil's house, we'll enter, and rest ot selves for a moment."

Entrance was not difficult, for there were nei doors nor windows. We called; no one answered.

"Ay, call," said the guide; "if you awake those w sleep here, it will be strange."

In fact, the cabin seemed quite deserted. Howev it afforded some sort of shelter, and we resolved to r a few moments, and shake the snow from our garme

"If there is a chimney we could make a fire," . one.

"And if we had some wood ———"

"Let us grope for the fireplace;" and De Sussy extended his hands. "Comrades!" he exclaimed; "a table! but those words were followed by a cry, half fear half surprise.

"Well! what is the matter?"

"There is a man lying on the table. I have hold of his leg."

"A man!"

"Well, shake him, and rouse him up."

"Hallo! friend, hallo!"

"Gentlemen," said one of the guides, advancing to the opening of the cabin; "no jokes here, if you please. This is no place for them. It would bring misfortune upon all of us—you as well as us."

"Where are we then?"

"In one of the dead-houses of St. Bernard," and he withdrew his head from the opening, and rejoined his comrades, without uttering another word. But the greatest orator could not have produced a more startling effect on us than those few words. We all stood petrified, as if nailed to the spot.

"Well, friends, let us have a look, at all events," said De Sussy, at last, and he took out the match-box. The match crackled in the darkness, then a feeble light dawned through the gloom, by which we observed three corpses—one laid on the table, the others crouched in opposite corners of the cabin. Then the match went out, and all was obscurity once more.

The operation was renewed; only this time we all made rolls of paper, and lit them at the transient blaze, then commenced an examination of the place, holding in our hands other matches ready to light.

One must have stood in our position, face to face with these ghastly phantoms, to comprehend our sensations at the moment; seen the livid, distorted features, the hideous grimaces of death, by the flickering light of our improvvised torch; have felt as we did that any moment a like terrible fate might be our own; to understand fully why the cold sweat stood on each brow; and we fled from the appalling scene more rapidly even than we would have hastened to repose and shelter.

After quitting this mortuary hostelry, no word was spoken by our party for a full hour: not even by the guides. The cold, the night, the snow, the distance, seemed forgotten; but one idea absorbed our minds— the silence and gloom of that lone dead-house.

At last, our head-guide uttered a cry peculiar to the mountaineers as a sign of danger, or simply its approach, and which can be heard at immense distances. Now, the sharp sound passed on and on over the fields of snow as if it would never cease; then ceased, as there was no echo, and the mountain became silent.

We proceeded thus about two hundred yards more, when the bark of a dog was heard.

"Here, Drapeau! here!" cried our guide. At the same instant an enormous dog of the St. Bernard breed bounded towards us, and recognising our guide, saluted him with the most energetic caresses.

Happily we had not much farther to go. Ten minutes more found us before the hospital, where the gate stands open night and day for whatever wanderer needs hospitality in these desolate regions. One of the monks received us, and led us into a room where an excellent fire was burning; and while we enjoyed its warmth, he prepared our cells and supper. But we had more need of sleep than food, and lay down after merely partaking of a bowl of hot milk. The monk who served mine told me I was in the chamber where Napoleon had dined. As for me, I shall always remember it as the one in which I enjoyed the best sleep.

Next morning by ten o'clock we were all astir, and I made the tour of the consular chamber, which had fallen to my lot. Nothing distinguished it, however, from the other cells, except an inscription commemorating the passage of the modern Charlemagne. We looked from the window; the sky was blue, the sun brilliant, and the ground covered with a foot of snow. No words could paint the bleak sadness of the view around this dwelling, placed seven thousand feet above the level of the sea, and in the centre of the triangle formed by the three mountains, Dronaz, Velan, and St. Bernard.

A lake fed by ice and snow is seen at a little distance

from the convent; but far from enlivening the scene, it rather adds to the gloom, for its waters seem black by contrast with its framework of snow, and are too cold to nourish any species of fish, and too elevated to attract any wandering bird. It is like a Dead Sea beside a petrified Jerusalem. Each stage of ascent is marked by a diminution in animal and vegetable life, till at the summit nothing seems to live but dogs and men. And it is only with the gloomy prospect before one's eyes that the courage and devotion of these men can be properly appreciated, who have left kindred, family, the lovely valleys of Piedmont, or the blue waters of some glittering lake, to place themselves on the frozen path of the wandering traveller, with only a stick for guide and a dog for company, amidst eternal tempests and threatening avalanches.

While engaged in these thoughts we were summoned to the refectory. As we passed the chapel the last tones of the morning service were dying away, and then our ears were saluted by peals of laughter. Laughter in such a place seemed strange. We opened the door at the end of the corridor from whence the merry sounds proceeded, and found ourselves in presence of a party of young and handsome ladies, who chatted about Taglioni with the cavaliers, and sipped coffee.

We looked at each other for some time with a sort of stupified stare; then we, too, joined in the merry laugh. We had known these ladies in the gay Parisian world, and now advanced to offer our greeting, with all the manners of the most fashionable society. Compliments were exchanged; we sat down to table together, and in about ten minutes had plunged into the usual strain of gay conversation and completely forgotten where we were.

Even our dining-room did not remind us of our locality: the decorations were not only suitable, but even elegant; there were a piano, engravings, vases, and many of those pretty little toys of luxury that one only expects to see in a lady's boudoir; but the secular appearance of the apartments was easily accounted for: all these pretty articles of furniture were presents from different parties who had enjoyed the hospitality of the monks, and wished, on their return to Paris, to prove that kindness was not forgotten.

During breakfast a monk gave us much interesting information about the mountain. Its original name was *Mons Jovis*, from a temple of Jupiter that stood there, of which the ruins are still visible. The hospital was founded in the ninth century, when the mountain re-received the Christian name of St. Bernard. Nine centuries have passed over since then, but the rules of the monastery remain unaltered, and the lives of the monks are still passed, as those of the first founders, in serving God and man.

Four heroes have made the mountain memorable: Hannibal, Charlemagne, Francis I., and Napoleon. Charlemagne and Napoleon crossed it to conquer; Hannibal and Francis to be conquered.

Besides our French party, two English ladies were receiving the hospitality of the convent, a mother and her daughter, who had travelled all Italy and the Alps on foot. We searched the visitors' book for the names of these intrepid travellers, but found only the signature of the younger—"Louisa, daughter of the mountains."

This book lay in an apartment adjoining the refectory, and like it was adorned with many presents of grateful guests. While engaged in examining them, the gaiety of the party in the refectory seemed to increase. De Sussy had been voted to the piano, while the ladies, including the "daughter of the mountains," danced a galop round the table. In the very height of their evolutions the door opened, and one of the brethren appeared. "Ladies," said he, "I am come to know if you wish to see the large dead-house belonging to the monastery."

This proposition stopped the galop all of a sudden. The ladies consulted among themselves—repugnance, perhaps, combating curiosity. At length curiosity conquered, and we all set forth; but on arriving at the external gate, it was found that a foot and a-half of snow lay on the ground. The ladies hesitated, but we gallantly offered to carry them on chairs swung on poles; they consented; and in this manner, amidst much laughter and frequent exclamations, from the awkwardness of the chairmen and the unsteady balance of the vehicles, we traversed the forty paces that led to the dead-house of St. Bernard. And what a spectacle presented itself to our eyes, as we looked through the large, open windows of the vast, sombre vault! A sight more singular or more horrible could not be imagined. We beheld a large, low hall, lit by a single window; the ground covered with a bed of dust a foot and a-half deep—human dust! This dust, which seemed like the dense waves of the Dead Sea, that supports the heaviest objects on its surface, was strewed with a multitude of bones—human bones! And upon these bones—some erect, some crouched against the wall, grouped with the strange intelligence of chance, each with the expression, or in the attitude, that death had surprised them; on their knees, or with outstretched arms, or heads lifted to heaven, or the fists clenched and face bent down—were a hundred and fifty corpses with set teeth and wide open eyes, and in the middle of them a woman, a poor woman frozen to death in the act of suckling her child, and looking now, in the ghastly circle that surrounded her, like a statue of maternal love.

The chamber contained all this human dust, bones, corpses; and at the window of this chamber, in the full light of the bright sun, were a group of young, fair, female faces, in which flashed the life of scarcely twenty years, contemplating the livid forms in which life had been extinct for ages.

Strange contrast! one that will ever haunt my brain; ever! that poor dead mother suckling her dead child!

What more can I say of St. Bernard? There are a church and a chapel, and the tomb of Desaix, and a slab of marble, with an inscription in honour of Napoleon, and a thousand other things besides. But, mark me: go and see all these things before you visit the dead-house, and see the poor frozen mother and her child.

THE city of Aosta is a pretty little town, that pretends to belong neither to Savoy nor Piedmont; and, in fact, it pays no taxes whatever, though obeying the laws of the King of Sardinia. With the exception of their abominable idiom, a Savoyard corruption, the character of the city is perfectly Italian. Everywhere fresco paintings adorn the walls in place of room-paper; and the innkeepers never fail to serve you up macaroni and cutlets, *à la Milanaise*, along with the wine of Asti.

The town was formerly called Cordelles, after a chief who established himself there with a colony of Gauls. Afterwards it was taken possession of by the Romans under Augustus, and an ancient triumphal arch still exists to commemorate the event. Three ancient entrances are still existing, also, built of grey marble. The centre one was reserved for the emperor or consul, and bears this inscription: "The Emperor Octavius Augustus founded these walls, built the town in three years, and bestowed his name on it in the year of Rome DCCXXVII." (727). A short distance from this monument we found the remains of an amphitheatre in grey marble; but all the edifices, ancient as well as modern, may be visited in a couple of hours: at least, we consecrated no more to them.

On returning to the hotel, we found our host had engaged a driver in our absence, who offered to pile the six of us in a vehicle which by right scarcely held four, assuring us that we would all be very comfortable when we were *packed,* and that he would never stop till we reached Pré Saint Dizier. He kept his word but too faithfully; not all our cries and entreaties could induce him to give us a moment's respite till we were indebted for it to accident. A block of ice had fallen into a lake, whose name I have written so carefully in my note-book that I cannot make it out, and thereby elevated the water to such a height that it overflowed the banks, carrying away with it a hut, fifty-four cows, eighty goats, and four men, who all perished in the inundation. We saw the dead bodies floating along the new river that covered the high road, and rendered progress impossible, except by a loose bridge of stones and trunks of trees hastily thrown across the stream. Our driver dare not trust himself to this bridge, and so we took advantage of the stoppage to quit our cage.

I know of no monk, Chartreuse, Trappist, dervise, faquir, living phenomenon, or curious animal of any kind, exhibited for one penny, that makes such a complete abnegation of free-will as the unfortunate passenger in a public coach. From the instant he trusts himself therein, all his wants, his wishes, and his desires, are subordinated to the caprices of the driver. He is only allowed enough of air to prevent himself being asphyxiated; only enough of food to prevent a jury's verdict of " death from total destitution." He may pass the most wondrous works of nature and art upon the road, but he dare not pause to have a look. Verily, public conveyances are an admirable invention for—their owners, and for portmanteaus.

When the time came to resume our journey, two of us declared against further imprisonment—I for one; so we set off to walk the eight leagues, and reached Saint Dizier at nightfall, far less tired than our companions, who had continued their journey in the cage.

Next morning we all uttered cries of rapture and astonishment at the magnificence of the scene. Our night arrival, of course, had prevented our having any idea of the surrounding grandeur; and, as to our host, he was too much used to the view from his parlour window to think about talking of it to travellers.

We found ourselves now at the foot of Mont Blanc, but on the side opposite to Chamouny. Five glaciers descended from the crest of our old mountain friend,

enclosing the horizon as with a wall; and perhaps it was
this strange frame-work to the prospect that made us
think it the most beautiful of all we had yet seen, not
even excepting Chamouny.

While asking the names of the mountain peaks, a
hunter passed with his carbine in his hand and a couple
of chamois on his shoulder, a goat and her kid, both
killed with the one ball, he told us.

Seeing that we had inquiring spirits, our host asked
if we would like to see the thermal baths, and we had
the imprudence to consent; so we were first conducted
to a whitewashed barrack, then through several caves,
where every brick in the kitchen, and every sponge in
the baths, was enumerated, till, thinking the inventory
was completed, we made an effort at last to depart; but
he arrested our steps on the threshold to point out a
nail on which his majesty, the King of Sardinia, had
consented to hang his hat. We fled, giving the Kings
of Sardinia, Cyprus, and Jerusalem, to the evil one; this
naturally led us on to the subject of politics, and this be-
guiled the way till we reached the inn, where the one
amongst us who had most lungs left ordered dinner.
This operation ended, we ordered two vehicles, as four
hours of daylight still remained, and proceeded on our
tour. No place of importance attracted our notice from
that till we reached Chambéry next day, having stopped
for the night at the little town of Moustier. But I cannot tell anything about the intèrior of the public monuments at Chambéry, simply because I wore a white
hat. It seems an order had arrived from the Tuileries,
ordering the severest measures to be taken against the
seditious beaver, and the King of Sardinia yielded to
the wishes of his brother of France rather than have a
war. Energetically did I declaim against such monstrous injustice; upon which the royal carbineers, who
were a guard at the palace, responded facetiously, that,
if I made any more noise, I would soon have a right to
enter one of the public edifices, at all events—namely,
the prison. As I suspected the King of France would
not go to war with Sardinia to recover me, though I was
his ex-librarian, I forthwith held my peace, merely re-
plying to the gentlemen of the guard, that they really

were wonderfully polite for Savoyards, and wonderfully witty for carbineers.

We left immediately after dinner, and arrived in an hour at the baths of Aix, where the first word we heard uttered was, "Long live Henry V.!" pronounced with a force of lungs and clearness of organ that left nothing to be desired. I looked forth from the hotel immediately, to see if the daring Legitimist were apprehended who had manifested his political predilection in so public a manner; but, no—not one of the promenading carbineers made the slightest hostile movement. True, the gentleman wore a black hat.

The three inns of Aix were full to overflowing, for the cholera had sent one frightened multitude there, and the political discontents of Paris another. Aix, in fact, was just then the rendezvous of the aristocracy of money and the aristocracy of birth; one represented by the Baroness Rothschild, the other by the Marchioness de Castrais, one of the handsomest and cleverest of Parisian celebrities. However, I made out a pretty little room at a grocer's for thirty sous a day, and I got my dinner at the hotel for three francs. These are trivial details, but I place them here to benefit, perhaps, some poor wanderer like myself.

I longed to sleep, but at Aix this is impossible before twelve o'clock. My window looked upon the square, and the square was crowded with a set of chattering dandies, who seem to estimate their worth by the noise they make; but, with all their chatter, I could distinguish nothing but the name of *Jacotot* repeated at least a hundred times in half-an-hour. "Who can be this eminent personage?" I exclaimed, mentally; and it is no wonder that at last I descended, hoping to make his acquaintance.

There were two *cafés* in the square; one was empty, the other crowded: one evidently going quite down, the other coining gold.

"Whence comes this difference?" said I to my host.

"It is Jacotot attracts them all there," replied he.

I dared not ask who was Jacotot, for fear of appearing too provincial; but I hastened to the crowded *café*. Every table was occupied: one place, however, remained vacant at one of them, and I seized it, and called, "Waiter!"

My appeal remained unanswered. Then I drew a breath from the very depths of my chest, and renewed the interpellation, but still in vain.

"It seems you are a stranger in Aix," said a person beside me, with a strong German accent, as he smoked and swallowed his beer.

"Only arrived this evening, monsieur."

"Ah!" said he, with a nod; "I thought so." Then, turning his head round to the door of the *café*, he uttered in a loud, sonorous voice, the word, "Jacotot!"

"Coming, sir, coming!" responded a voice. In another instant he appeared. The mystery was solved: Jacotot was the waiter.

The brightest of smiles was stereotyped on his broad, honest face; and, while I gave my orders, twenty other assailed him with—

"Jacotot, a cigar!"

"Jacotot, the newspaper!"

"Jacotot, some fire here!"

But, no matter what was wanting, Jacotot produced it from his marvellous pocket. All things seemed contained in it. Finally, a voice demanded, "Jacotot, twenty louis!"

Jacotot looked round for the speaker, inspected him a moment, when, of course, seeing he was solvent, he plunged his hand in the miraculous reservoir, and drew forth a handful of gold for the gentleman; then disappeared for the fruit I had ordered.

"Have you lost, Paul?" said a young man near me to another.

"Yes, three thousand francs."

"Do you play?" asked my German friend.

"No," said I; "I am not rich enough to lose nor poor enough to wish to gain."

He swallowed his beer, puffed his cigar, placed his elbows on the table, stared me full in the face, then oracularly uttered—

"Right, young man! Jacotot, another cigar!"

The fourth bottle and sixth cigar were brought. My German swallowed the one and smoked the other.

Meanwhile, some of my companions had been orga-
nising a party for the morrow to the Lake of Bourget,
and asked my aid and presence.

" Only tell me how we are to go," said I.

" Make yourself easy on that score," they answered.
"We have arranged everything comfortably;" and I went
to sleep upon that happy assurance.

Next morning I was awakened by a tumult beneath my
window, in which my name seemed as frequently invoked
as Jacotot's. I leaped from my bed, thinking the house
was on fire, and ran to the window. Thirty or forty
asses, each surmounted by a cavalier, extended along
two sides of the square. Sancho Panza would have been
ravished at such a sight; and I found that my place in
the ranks was impatiently expected.

"Give me five minutes," I exclaimed. They were
granted, and I descended.

As a delicate compliment to my drama of "Christine,"
an ass had been reserved for me bearing that appellation.

The Marquis de Montagu, mounted on a beautiful
black horse, led the van; and, with the species of eloquence familiar to all colonels of regiments, gave the
word—

" Forward! four and four. Trot when you like, gallop when you can."

In an instant we were off; the speed of our steeds
heightened by a set of boys who followed pricking them
behind with pins. Ten minutes after, we were at the
Lake of Bourget; only, in place of thirty-five, as the
party set out, we arrived but twelve. Fifteen had fallen
by the way, and eight others had never got their animals beyond a walk. As to Christine, she flew like an
Arab steed.

These Swiss lakes, with their azure waters, into which
you can gaze down for a depth of ninety feet, are certainly wonderfully beautiful; but one must first have
bathed in the mud of the Seine, fully to appreciate the
luxury of the waters into which we now flung our
selves.

A large building was visible exactly opposite to us;
and, as one of my friends rose above the water, I asked
him its name and use.

Placing his hands on my head and his feet on my shoulders, he sent me down to the depth of fifteen feet; then, as I rose to the surface, gave me answer—

" It is the hautecomb or sepulchre of the Dukes of Savoy and Kings of Sardinia."

I thanked him, and disappeared again.

A breakfast was now proposed, after which we were to visit the royal tombs and the intermittent fountain. This latter curiosity, however, was not destined to gratify our eyes; for our boatmen informed us the spring had ceased to flow for the last eight days.

Still we resolved on the breakfast, at all events ; and, considering very judiciously that thirty-five hungry adventurers could hardly be fed with the mere eggs and milk of the village. we despatched a boy and a couple of asses back to Jacotot, telling him to load all with whatever could be found best for breakfast, and that the bill should be paid by whichever of the party tumbled from their asses on the return home.

While waiting the viands, we walked to inspect the chapel of the tombs. It is* a charming little Gothic structure, which might be taken for an erection of the fifteenth century if its walls were only darkened with the shadow which passing ages alone can fling.

The first tomb on entering is that of the founder of the chapel, King Charles Felix. It seems as if, having confided to the chapel the seven generations of his ancestors, he himself, like a pious son, took up his position as watcher and guard at the entrance.

On each side, as you advance up to the choir, are ranged superb marble tombs, upon which lie effigies of the Dukes and Duchesses of Savoy: the dukes with a lion couched at their feet, emblem of courage ; the duchesses with a greyhound, symbol of fidelity. Others, who travelled to death by the saintly road, in place of the warlike, are represented with a hair shirt on the body and sandals on the feet, in token of a life of suffering and humility; and all these monuments are executed with power and beauty, many of them with the finest skill. Not so the medallions placed above each tomb, representing some scene in the life of the sleeper beneath.

These are the work of modern artists, who, disdaining the simple truth of their elder predecessors, have replaced the knightly armour of the middle ages by the flowing togas of Greece or Rome, and represented the combatant in the academic hose of a Romulus or Leonidas. If these gentlemen had no imagination, they might at least have copied truly. May heaven forgive them! An abbey is attached to the chapel, and part of the business of the monks is to watch and pray by the tombs. While engaged visiting the monastery, our provisions arrived; and a splendid collation was immediately organised beneath the mulberry-trees a hundred paces from the abbey. As soon as the good news reached us, we abandoned the reverend fathers and hastened to the more attractive scene, taking a glance on our way at the intermittent fountain, which, however, showed no sign of motion.

There I found my German friend of the night before, with pipe in mouth and hands behind his back, patiently waiting for the fountain to flow. He had been there three hours, he said. Poor man! they had forgotten to tell him that for eight days the stream was dried up.

I rejoined my companions, and found them reclining like Romans at a festival.

One glance at the preparations showed me the supreme ability of Jacotot. He was one of those rare men whose merit equals their renown.

Breakfast over, the wine drunk, and the bottles broke, we began to think of returning, renewing the compact that they who fell were to pay the share of those who kept their seats.

On reaching Aix we found the town in revolution—every one rushing hither and thither to procure horses, or carriages, or places in the diligence—anything to enable them to quit the place. Ladies even assailed us with clasped hands, soliciting our asses; and to all questions we only received the answer, " The cholera! the cholera!"

Comprehending nothing, we summoned Jacotot. He came with tears in his eyes. " Here is the truth," he said: " a merchant arrived yesterday, and began boasting at breakfast how he managed to escape quarantine, when instantly he was seized with horrible pains. Every one started up, thinking they were cholera symptoms, and rushed from the inn as if the house were on fire, shouting, ' The cholera! the cholera!'

"But nothing ailed the poor man but indigestion, which he was well accustomed to, and cured easily by drinking hot tea, or some other simple remedy. So he was making his way back quietly to his lodgings, when, just as he reached the door, there stood the five doctors of the place ranged upon the steps. The merchant was about to salute them, when unluckily a pang seized him, and, in place of touching his hat, he had to apply his hand to the region of the pain. The five doctors immediately interchanged glances, then rushed forward, seized the patient, felt his pulse, and pronounced him in the first stage of Asiatic cholera.

"In vain the poor victim assured them they were mistaken; that he knew his case well; it was merely indigestion; and if they would kindly let him pass, he would order a little tea and be well directly.

"'No,' they answered. ' He now belonged to them; they were the five doctors of the board of health, and had orders to take charge of every stranger who fell sick at the waters of Aix.'

"'Well, then,' pleaded the merchant, ' give me just four hours to try my own remedies, and if not better then, do what you like.'

"'No,' replied the inexorable five: 'your case is evidently malignant cholera; in four hours you will die.'

"During this discussion one of the five had slipped away, but soon afterwards returned, accompanied by four carbineers, and a brigadier, who, twisting his moustache, inquired where was the cholera rascal. The merchant was pointed out. Instantly two carbineers seized him by the head, two more by the feet; the brigadier drew his sabre, and brought up the rear. Behind him marched the five doctors; as to the merchant, he foamed with rage, struggled, kicked and bit whatever he could get at.

"'What terrible progress the disease is making!' murmured the five; ' he is now in the second stage of Asiatic cholera.'

"Every passer-by admired the devoted courage of these worthy doctors, ready to brave all peril of contagion in behalf of the sufferer; and then each one fled as far as he could from the ill-omened *cortége*. It was at this moment of panic we entered the town."

"Is it because the intermittent fountain won't flow that the people are so excited?" asked our German of Jacotot.

Jacotot began his recital all over again, and when concluded, the German contented himself with exclaiming, "Ah!" and instantly set forward to the hospital.

"Where are you going? where are you going?" was shouted after him from all sides.

"To see the patient," replied our German, and continued his walk. Ten minutes after, he returned: every one surrounded him, asking questions of the cholera patient.

"They are opening him," he answered.

"How! opening him? Is he dead?"

"Ay," replied the German, "but not of cholera; only of indigestion, poor man! He had eaten too much breakfast: that was all."

This was the truth. Next day the unfortunate merchant was interred; and the day after no one thought about the cholera.

My next investigations at Aix were directed to the Roman baths. These early possessors of Aix were fully cognizant of the medicinal virtues of the thermal springs, and numerous buildings were erected to facilitate their use. After the irruption of the barbarians, however, the Roman works were destroyed or choked up; and the waters of Aix did not recover their celebrity until the seventeenth century, when a French physician brought them into notice; and the many cures effected led to the publication of a tract, entitled "Marvellous Properties of the Waters of Aix." Since then the celebrity of the baths has been yearly on the increase.

The Roman monuments still existing are an arch, or rather arcade, the ruins of a temple of Diana, and some thermal baths. An altar to Minerva was also recently discovered, along with the sacrificial knife, and urn destined to receive the blood of the victim; but these objects were all destroyed by the curé, in a moment of religious zeal.

The temple of Diana is less perfect than the arch; some of its magnificent slabs have been taken to form the staircase of the Cercle, or bathing-hall; and part of the ancient wall has been introduced into the library, and left uncovered by any tapestry whatever; so that one has a perfect view of the colossal stones of which it was composed. Some of them are two feet high, by four or five broad, and are placed one above the other without any cement, maintained together solely by equilibrium.

The thermal remains consist of a marble staircase leading to a reservoir for water, about twenty feet long, round which are ranges of marble benches for the bathers to recline on. Pipes for conducting heat pass along these benches, and above, the highest of all, are the orifices by which hot air was introduced. The immense marble *lavabo*, destined for the cold water, into which the ancients plunged themselves after bathing, was at the bottom of the reservoir. The *lavabo* itself has been broken, but the detritus contained within it has retained the perfect form of the vessel within which it dried and hardened.

The modern edifices are the Cercle and the baths. The Cercle is the building where all the bathers meet and enjoy life. For twenty francs you can have a general admission to the *salons:* there the ladies can have balls and concerts, and the gentlemen billiards and a library. A magnificent garden is also attached to the building, and is used as a promenade; nothing can be lovelier than the view around it. On one side the white peaks of the Dent du Chat, rising up clear and sharp into the azure sky, and on the other a rich, level country, fading away into the dim blue distance.

On entering the first apartment at the baths, a visitor can take his choice of either of the medicinal waters, there being two spouts labelled "Sulphur" and "Alum;" one at thirty-five, the other at thirty-six degrees of heat. The specific gravity of sulphuric water is a fifth less than that of ordinary water; and a piece of silver placed in contact with it becomes oxydised in two seconds. The thermal waters also retain heat longer than ordinary water; the latter, after reaching eighty degrees of heat by ebullition, loses sixty in two hours by contact with the atmosphere, whereas the former lose only fifteen degrees in twelve hours.

At certain epochs, and, above all, when the atmospherical temperature descends ten or twelve degrees below zero, each of the waters, although the source seems the same, presents a particular phenomenon. The sulphureous water solidifies into a viscous mass, offering all the characteristics of a perfect animal jelly, both in taste and nutritive quality, while the alum water congeals into what appears a vegetable jelly. In 1822 an earthquake was felt throughout the whole chain of the Alps; and thirty-seven minutes after the shock, the sulphureous pipes were filled with a quantity of animal gelatine, and the alum with vegetable gelatine.

The baths have all various degrees of heat, from thirty-three degrees up to the highest, which is called "Hell," from its temperature. The atmosphere is indeed truly infernal, and raises the circulation to a hundred and forty-five pulsations a minute; the pulse of an Englishman who died there was even raised so high as two hundred and ten pulsations, or three and a-half per second. It was there the poor merchant had been conducted, and his hat still hung upon a nail.

One can descend to the source of the waters by an entrance in the town itself: a grated aperture about three feet square, called "The Serpent's Hole," from the numerous snakes that come to bask there in the double heat of the hot vapours and the mid-day sun. They are quite harmless, however, and children feed and play with them without any danger.

My next visit was to the cascade of Grésy, situated a league from the town, which has a mournful celebrity in consequence of the young and beautiful Baroness Broc, lady-in-waiting to Queen Hortense, having met her death there in 1813. The waterfall has worn away immense cavities in the rock, from fifteen to eighteen feet deep, which, when filled with water, are like large

cisterns; planks are laid over them for visitors to pass;
and it was while passing along one of them that the
plank turned, and the baroness was precipitated into the
grave beneath.

Towards midnight, fatigued with my day's labours, I
had sunk into a delicious sleep in my chamber, when a
crowd of gay companions invaded my repose, each
bearing a lighted torch, and declaring they must carry
me off with them that instant to ascend the Dent du
Chat. Some pleasantries awaken a responsive gaiety in
you immediately; but then you must just have risen up
from a hot supper, with laughter and wine, and, unwil-
ling to extinguish the excitement of the orgie in sleep,
you propose, as a frolic, to run up a mountain to see
the sun rise. But I, calmly resting in the hope of a
pacific night, to be awakened at midnight by so incon-
gruous an invitation, could not, I confess, receive the
proposition with any very vivid enthusiasm.

Expostulation, however, was vain. I was lifted on to
the floor, and a jug of water flung over my bed to make
a return to it impossible. If the promenade was not
amusing, it had at least become indispensable; so in
five minutes I had joined the twelve, who, with guides,
made up our party. We took a boat across the lake to
reach the base of the mountain. Millions of stars were
glittering in the azure above, and mirrored in the azure
water below. I felt as if I could thus have lain for ever,
floating in a lonely boat on the lonely lake; but, then,
we had set off to be *amused*, and so I resigned myself
to it. How strange our life!—for ever seeking pleasure
and passing happiness!

We commenced the ascent at half-past twelve, by the
light of our flambeaux, and at two had proceeded nearly
three-fourths of the way; then the road became dangerous, and our guides recommended a halt till day-
break.

With the first dawn we proceeded. The road had
become almost perpendicular, so that the heel of one
touched the breast of another as we marched up in file.
Each displayed his dexterity, catching hold of bushes
and branches, or taking advantage of any inequality in
the rock that gave a momentary footing. We could

hear the stones rolling down the mountain beneath our feet, and plunging into the lake below. Our guides even could give no help except by marking the path, and telling us in brief, decided tones not to look behind us for fear of the vertigo.

Suddenly one of our comrades, who walked immediately behind them, missed his footing and rolled down, passing the whole file.

"Stop him! stop him!" exclaimed the guides. But it was easier said than done. We thought him lost, and looked on transfixed with horror, but powerless to save him. The last of our line was Montagu, and, making a tremendous effort, he stretched out his hand and seized our poor comrade by the hair. For a moment it was doubtful if the two would not fall together; and the second in which they both hovered over a precipice two thousand feet deep, in a struggle for life or death, will probably never be forgotten by those two men. Both were saved, however, and we continued our way through a pine forest, where we made use of the branches to facilitate our ascent; another path was by holes in the rock, forming a kind of natural staircase. The difficulties were greater; but, as it promised a better view, an enterprising comrade and I determined to try it. The others, however, reached the summit first, and, to celebrate their arrival, lit a fire and smoked cigars. After a quarter of an hour they descended, leaving the fire burning, in order to enjoy the picturesque effect of it from the base.

It was three o'clock when we found ourselves back again in Aix, and from the market-place our friends had the proud pleasure of seeing the fire they had kindled, blazing brightly on the mountain peak.

"Now, may I go to bed," I inquired, "since I have *amused* myself?"

As each one felt a like desire for repose, they replied that they saw no objection in the world.

I think I would have slept thirty-six consecutive hours, like Balmat, if an uproar in the street had not aroused me. It was still night, but the whole population was in motion. I ran to the window, and saw them snatching eye-glasses from each other's hands, with their heads up in the air and figures thrown back, to the great danger of the vertebral column.

" There must be an eclipse of the moon," thought I, and ran down, the moment I threw on my clothes, armed with my pocket telescope. The whole sky seemed in a flame; the peak of the mountain was on fire. At the same moment I felt my hand seized; two of our party were beside me.

" We are off to Geneva," they whispered. " Good-bye !"

Instantly I comprehended the affair. Our friends had set fire to the forest on the Dent du Chat, and the King of Sardinia might not quite like the jest.

I turned my gaze again upon this younger sister of Vesuvius, and really found it a very pretty volcano of the second order. A midnight fire upon a mountain peak is, perhaps, one of the most magnificent sights in the world. Round and round the forest trees winds the stream of fire like a glittering serpent; sometimes darting its flaming head on a branch, licking up the leaves; then running up the tree and circling the summit with a fiery crown; then flashing down and lighting up the whole forest suddenly, as if for a grand public illumination. This is what kings cannot command for their fêtes; and how beautiful it is! Then, when the burning leaves fall down, and the wind scatters them like a fiery rain, and each spark, as it falls, lights up a fire, and these fires extend till they meet and unite, and the whole scene becomes an immense furnace with a fiery sky above, the form of each burning tree distinctly defined on the glowing background, and emitting a peculiar light according to its essence; when the fire whistles as the wind, and the wind roars like a tempest—oh! it is grand, marvellous, glorious! Nero must have learned a new pleasure when he burned Rome.

I was withdrawn from my ecstasy by the arrival of a coach escorted by royal carbineers, containing two prisoners. They were our incendiary friends, who, betrayed by the guides, and denounced by the landlord, had been pursued and overtaken by the police of Charles Albert ere they could cross the frontiers of Savoy. Poor fellows! they were now hurrying off to prison; but we all interceded, offered security, and finally obtained permission for their release on parole till the matter was investigated. It would have been a pity to deprive them of the magnificent spectacle they had planned.

The fire lasted three whole days. On the fourth they received notice that government had imposed a fine on them of thirty-seven thousand five hundred francs. This charge for a few pine-trees seemed to them rather exorbitant; so our ambassador at Turin was appealed to, and, by his intercession, the sum was reduced to seven hundred and eighty francs, on payment of which they were allowed to quit Aix; and, having received a quittance, they hurried away, lest next day some additional item might be added to the account.

We all remained a week after, within which time two misfortunes befel us. The first was an execrable concert given to us by a so-called "leading bass and leading barytone" of the Opéra Comique; the second, the departure of our German from his own lodgings, having been startled one morning by finding a snake in his boot, and his coming to take up his quarters next room to mine. As asinine riding parties become tiresome even when one tumbles every five minutes, and gambling is stupid to those who neither want to gain nor fear to lose; and as, finally, madame the bass and monsieur the barytone menaced us with a second concert, I resolved to diversify monotony by a visit to the Grande Chartreuse, about ten or twelve leagues from Aix, intending from thence to return to Geneva, and wander through the Alps to Oberland.

The German and I had a tender leave-taking. He offered me beer and a cigar, and, while we smoked and drank, "Where go you?" said he.

" To the famous Chartreuse," I answered.

" Oh!—ah!" he continued; " droll people these monks of Chartreuse. They eat out of inkstands and sleep in presses."

" What do you mean?"

" You will see."

So we parted. I could get no further information from him.

Then I went to find my friend Jacotot, who had paid

me great respect ever since he heard I was an author;
and now he begged earnestly I would write something
upon the waters of Aix, and mention the *café* particularly where he was head-waiter, that would bring them
in such fine custom. I said the thing was not probable:
however, it was possible; and I religiously promised, if
ever·I wrote ode or novel on the subject, not only to
make mention of the *café*, but also to make him, Jacotot,
personally as celebrated as he could be. The poor
fellow absolutely turned pale at hearing he was to be
mentioned in a book.

On reaching St. Laurent, a village four miles from the
monastery, we had to quit the carriage, the rest of the
way being traversed on mules. This was very well for
Lamark and me, but not for a lady who was of our
party, particularly as but one mule could be had: all
the rest had gone to some fair or other. However, she
took her turn, and we engaged a guide, who took charge
of our three travelling-bags. It was now seven o'clock,
and we had a four hours' journey before us.

The vale of Dauphiny, where the Chartreuse lies, may
bear comparison with the grandest gorges of Switzerland. There is the same richness of nature, the same
ardour of vegetation, and the same magnificence of
prospect; only that the roads are much easier for travelling, in consequence of the flanks of the mountains
being less steep. Day-journeys, therefore, are attended
with no danger; but at night the case is different, especially as we found ourselves with a horrible storm
brewing over our heads. Being rather alarmed, we
asked the guide to find some place fit for shelter. He
replied there was none: we must go on to the Chartreuse at once.

Our position rapidly became more horrible. The
rain poured down in torrents, and a thick darkness fell
upon the entire scene. Nothing was visible but the
light dress of the lady, as she preceded us on the mule,
while my friend and I followed, clinging to the arms of
the guide; for the road here had narrowed to a few feet,
and an immense precipice lay to our right, at the bottom of which we could hear the roar of a torrent. Add
to this the peals of thunder echoing through the moun-

tains, till the accumulated sound seemed to us like the trumpet of the last judgment.

At last we heard the abbey bell, and half-an-hour after the gigantic outline of the old Chartreuse arose before us. Not the least sound was audible from the interior, except the tolling of the bell; not a light gleamed from its fifty windows; one might have thought that the old cloister had been abandoned to ghosts from the spirit world.

We rang, and a brother opened the gate, but instantly shut it again, on perceiving the lady, as if Satan had been there in person. No woman is allowed entrance. One did obtain admission in male disguise; but after her departure every cell in the monastery had to be subjected to all the ceremonies of exorcism, when the infringement of their rule was discovered. An order from the Pope can alone open the cloister gate to a woman, and by this means the Duchess de Berri obtained entrance in 1829.

When the door re-opened, a monk appeared with a lantern, who conducted us to a pavilion about fifty paces from the cloister. It is there any traveller of the gentle sex is obliged to sleep who comes knocking at the gate of the Chartreuse, ignorant of the strict rules of Saint Bruno.

The poor monk who accompanied us was the gentlest, civilest creature in the world. He was called Brother Jean Marie, and began his attentions by giving us a few spoonfuls of a liqueur made by the monks for the use of all frozen travellers like ourselves. Never was there a better occasion for the use of the holy elixir. The effect was marvellous. Scarcely had we swallowed a few drops when our throats seemed on fire, and we ran hither and thither round the chamber, like lunatics, demanding " Water! water!" from the poor brother. I verily believe, if he had held a candle near us at the time, we would all have lit up into a general conflagration.

Meanwhile, the fire blazed on the hearth, and the table was spread with bread, butter, milk, and beer. The monks of Chartreuse hold a perpetual fast, and make their visitors do the same. Just as our frugal repast was ended, the bell rung for matins, and I asked the brother if I might attend. He replied that the bread of the Word of God belonged equally to all Christians. I therefore entered the cloister.

I am one of those upon whom external objects make a deep impression; above all, religious objects; and the sombre Chartreuse, for many reasons, affected my imagination in a peculiar degree. It is the only monastic order which the Revolution left existing in France. It is the last fragment of the creed of our fathers; the last fortress held by religion in the land of infidelity. Yet each day indifference is undermining it within, as time without. In the fifteenth century the walls of the Chartreuse enclosed four hundred monks; in the nineteenth it holds but twenty-seven. For the last six years no new brother has been recruited, the only two novices who entered during that period not being able to support the severity of the discipline. It is, therefore, highly probable that the days of the order are numbered. Death will strike at the cells one by one, and as each monk is borne out, no living form will take his place. The youngest of them will perchance survive to the last, and as he feels his end approaching, will dig his own grave and lay himself therein, knowing that no living hand is near to do him the last offices.

I am not given to a fictitious enthusiasm, got up by order of guide-books and guides. People may see that I give my impressions just as they strike myself: feebly, perhaps, still with genuine sincerity. Well, then, I may be believed when I say that so overpowering a sensation never struck my heart as when I entered the immense Gothic corridor, eight hundred feet long, I beheld the door of a cell open at the end, from which issued a monk with a flowing white beard and wearing the robe of St. Bruno, unchanged as if eight centuries had never disturbed a fold.

The old man advanced, grave and silent, through the arches darkened by the smoke of centuries, in the midst of a circle of vacillating light, projected by the lamp he held in his hand, while before and behind him all was sombre gloom. As he approached I felt my limbs tremble, and at last I fell upon my knees. Perceiving me in this posture, he advanced with a mild, benevolent air, and laying his hand upon my bent head, said clearly, "I bless you, my son, if you believe; and I bless you also even if you believe not." Let those laugh who like, but at that moment I would not have exchanged the benediction for a throne.

When he passed, I arose and followed him to the chapel. There a new spectacle awaited me. The whole community were assembled by the light of a single lamp, shaded by a black gauze. One brother recited the mass, while the others neither sat nor kneeled, but lay prostrate on the marble floor, their hands and foreheads resting on the ground. Each cowl was thrown back, displaying the bare, shaven crown; and one could distinguish old and young men there, some brought by religion, others by misfortune; some by passion, others by crimes. There were temples throbbing as if fire ran in the veins; there were eyes weeping, and lips praying, cold and rigid as if the breath in them was ice. Oh! what a history, the history of those human hearts!

When matters were over, I asked leave to spend the day rambling through the convent, not wishing any external scene to disturb the train of ideas I had fallen into. Brother Jean Marie agreed to be my guide, took a lamp, and we began by a walk through the corridors. I have already said they are immense, extending to a length equal to those of St. Peter's at Rome, and containing four hundred cells, of which three hundred and seventy-three are now uninhabited. Each monk has graven upon the door of his cell his favourite thought, sometimes original, sometimes borrowed from a favourite sacred author. I copy some that interested me the most:—"*Amor, qui semper ardes et nunquam extingueris, accende me totum igne tuo.*" "In solitude God speaks to the heart of man: in silence man speaks to the heart of God." "*Fuge, late, tace.*" "An hour strikes; it has already passed."

"A ta faible raison garde-toi de te rendre:
Dieu t'a fait pour l'aimer et non pour le comprendre." *

* Trust not thyself to weak reason's deceiving:
God has made thee for loving alone, and believing.

We entered one of the empty cells. The monk who owned it had been dead five days. These cells are all formed on the one plan, consisting of a sitting-room and closet, with a little garret above. A book lay open at the place where the dying man had last cast his eyes. It was "The Confessions of St. Augustine." In the sleeping-room there was merely a bed with a paillasse and blankets; the bed had doors which would close in whoever slept within, and I now understood what the German meant by the Chartreuse sleeping in presses. Below was a workshop containing boots and kitchen articles; for every monk is obliged to spend two hours a-day in manual labour, and one in attending to the little garden attached to each cell. It is the only amusement permitted to them.

We next visited the hall of the chapter-general, and saw portraits of all the heads of the order from St. Bruno, who died in 1101, down to Innocent the Mason, who died 1703. From that the succession of portraits is interrupted, and begins again with the present head, Father Jean Baptiste Mortès. In '92, when all the monasteries were devastated in France, the Chartreuse fled, each one carrying away a portrait with him. Some returned, and brought their portraits safely; others died in exile, but still took precautions to have the precious treasure with which they had charged themselves restored safely to the brotherhood; so that now not a single picture is wanting to the collection.

The refectory is divided into two compartments, one for the brothers, the other for the fathers. They drink out of earthen cups, and eat off wooden plates. These plates have somewhat the shape of an inkstand; for in the centre is a hollow that contains their soup, and around lie the vegetables, or fish, which is the only diet allowed the brethren. Again I thought of my German, and why he said they ate out of inkstands.

I had still the cemetery to see, and though it was night, I expressed a wish to be conducted there. Brother Jean Marie agreed, and had just opened the gate when he stopped, and, seizing my arm, shewed me a Chartreux in the act of digging his own grave. For an instant I remained absorbed by the strange spectacle, then asked might I be permitted to speak to the man. My guide made no objection; indeed, seemed rather glad of the opportunity to take a little rest himself. So, sitting down, he left me to advance alone to the unknown monk.

I scarcely knew how to address myself to the mournful digger; for, hearing my step, he had paused, and was now resting on his spade, waiting for my opening words. This increased my embarrassment; but, feeling my silence growing ridiculous, I said at last, "A mournful office, my father. It seems to me that rest at this hour would be more suitable, after all the mortifications of the day, than such a work. Besides, you are still young," I added, smiling: "surely there can be no hurry for a grave."

"My son," he answered, sadly, "it is not the oldest die the soonest here. It is not age goes quickest to the grave; and, besides, when mine is dug, who knows but God will permit me to lie down in it?"

"Pardon, my father," I replied: "I know little of your solemn, holy rules, though I respect all religious observances; but it seems to me that abnegation of the world should not go so far as to make you wish to quit it."

"Man is master of his actions, but not of his desires," answered the Chartreux.

"Yours seem to be gloomy, my father."

"Because so is my heart."

"You have suffered, then?"

"I suffer always."

"Yet, I thought religion and peace dwelt together?"

"Remorse enters everywhere."

I looked at him fixedly, and then remembered he was the same monk whom I had seen prostrated beside me in the chapel, sobbing and weeping. He recognised me.

"You were at matins?" he said.

"Yes, and I heard you groan and saw you weep."

"What did you think of me then?

"That God had taken pity on you, since he granted you tears."

"Yes, yes; his vengeance is relaxing."

"But have you no earthly friend to confide your sorrows to?"

"Each here bears his own. It is enough. Add another's sorrow, and he would sink under the burden. Yet, it would be something to have a heart near to pity, and a hand that would press ours."

I took his hand and pressed it; but he withdrew his, crossed his hands upon his breast, and looked searchingly into my eyes, as if he would read my very soul.

"Is this interest or curiosity?" he said.

I drew back. "Your hand, my father, for the last time; then farewell," and I turned away.

"Wait, and listen," he continued, approaching me. "It shall not be said, that consolation came and I refused it; that God sent you to me and I rejected you. You have done that for a suffering wretch which none have done for six years—pressed my hand. Thanks! You have said that to impart one's sorrow was to lighten it, and that implies that you will give me your sympathy. Listen, therefore, to my history, and do not interrupt me. When the heart's flood once begins to flow, let nothing check it 'Then, when you hear me to the end, depart without seeking to know my name, as I shall not seek to know yours. This is all I demand."

I promised, and we sat down on the broken tomb of one of the generals of the order. For an instant he leaned his head upon his hand, and when he raised it, the movement made his cowl fall back. Then I saw the face was that of a young man, with black eyes and beard. Suffering had made him pale and thin; but what the face lost in beauty it had gained in expression. It was the head of the "Giaour" I saw before me, such as I had dreamed after reading the verses of Lord Byron.

"I need not tell you," he began, "the place where I was born, or where I lived. Enough if I say that seven years have passed since the great, fatal crisis of my life, and that I was then but twenty-four.

"My family were rich and distinguished; consequently, on leaving college I was launched at once into all the brilliant gaieties of society. I entered the world with a resolute character, an ardent imagination, a heart full of passions, and a conviction that nothing could resist a man who had perseverance and gold.

"My first adventures confirmed me in this opinion.

"In the spring of 1825, a country-house beside my mother's was put up for sale, and purchased by General M——: a man I had met in society, and knew to be grave and austere; a regular man of the camp, who looked on men as units and women as nonentities.

"I heard that he had married some marshal's widow. No doubt he might talk to her of Marengo, and of Austerlitz, and I anticipated little pleasure from such neighbours.

"On his arrival, he came to present his wife to my mother. She was one of the divinest creatures heaven ever formed. You know the world, monsieur—its morality, its strange code of honour, that teaches you to respect a man's property, but permits you to rob him of his wife. From the moment I saw Madame M——, I forgot her husband, his fifty years of an unstained life, his twenty wounds received for his country, the despair of his old age, the ridicule flung on the last remnant of an honourable life. I forgot all, and was possessed with but one idea, one hope—to make Caroline my own.

"Our vicinity gave me the favourable opportunity for cultivating the acquaintance, and I eagerly sought the friendship of the old general as a means to rob him of his wife.

"To deceive him was not difficult. He was kind and paternal in his manner to her, but seemed to think more of the future heritor of his name and honour, with which she was about to present him, than of the young wife herself.

"As to Caroline, she was calm and indifferent; evidently resigned to her position; but I could see clearly she did not love her husband.

"This was enough to make me feel secure; but yet all my attentions were received by her with the most frigid indifference. She neither sought nor shunned me—a proof that I inspired neither liking nor fear. I kept my eyes fixed on her continually, but her glance met mine as coldly as if she were unconscious of my presence; all the fascinating powers which other women pronounced irresistible were lost upon Caroline.

"So passed the summer. My love became madness. Caroline's coldness was a challenge which I accepted with all the impetuosity of my nature. I could not speak of love, because she always received my first words with a smile of incredulity. I therefore resolved to write to her; and one evening, before taking leave, laid my letter in her embroidery, knowing that next morning it would be discovered. I was present, apparently in earnest conversation with the general, when she unrolled her work, and my letter fell to the ground. Eagerly I watched her movements. She stooped, took it up, smiled slightly, and put it in her pocket. All day I watched and waited for some acknowledgment, but in vain. In the evening she sat at work with some ladies round a table; the general read the newspapers. I was seated in an obscure corner of the room, from whence I could watch her every movement. I saw her raise her eyes and look round, as if in search of me. 'Ah! come here, monsieur,' she said, on perceiving me; 'I want you to draw two letters for me: C and M in the Gothic character. They are for the corner of my pocket-handkerchief.'

"'Yes, madame, I shall have that pleasure.'

"'But I want them immediately; come here and sketch them beside me. I can make room for you.'

"I rose, took a chair, and placed myself beside her.

"'Here is a pen,' she said.

"'But you must give me paper too, madame.'

"'Ah! true,' she replied: 'this will do;' and she took a letter from her pocket, and handed it to me. At first I thought it was an answer to mine, and opened it with as much calmness as I could affect, but instantly perceived it was my own letter returned. During this time she had risen and moved away.

"'Madame,' said I aloud, holding the letter up to attract the attention of those present, 'you have given me by mistake a letter addressed to yourself; permit me to return it: the envelope is sufficient for my purpose.'

"The general instantly looked up from his paper. I saw she was alarmed; for she advanced hurriedly, took the letter from my hand, looked at the address, and said, 'Oh, yes; a letter from my mother.'

"The general turned his eyes once more upon the

Courrier Français. I began to draw the letters, and Madame M—— left the room.

"All these details tire you, monsieur,' said the Chartreux, interruping himself; "and you are astonished to hear them from one who wears this robe and digs his own grave; but the heart is the last thing to quit the earth, and memory the last thing to quit the heart."

"These details are all natural," I said, "and therefore interesting. Continue."

"Next morning I was awakened at six o'clock by the general. He was in hunting costume, and asked me to join him. At first the sight of him alarmed me; but his frank air and voice soon assured me that he was without all suspicion, and I accepted his invitation.

"As we rode on, he talked of indifferent matters until he reached a spot where it appeared time for us to charge our muskets. During this operation he looked at me steadily.

"'What are you thinking of, general?' I said, feeling a little alarmed at the expression of his countenance.

"'*Pardieu!*' he replied; 'I am thinking what a fool you are to make love to my wife.'

"You can imagine the effect such an apostrophe produced on me.

"'*I*, general?' was all I could answer.

"'Yes, you. Do you mean to deny it?'

"'General, I swear ——'

"'Swear nothing, monsieur; falsehoods are unworthy of a man of honour.'

"'But who told you?'

"'My wife. Here is the letter you wrote her yesterday;' and he held forth a paper which I could scarcely recognise, I was so agitated. When he saw I was unable to take it, he very coolly rolled it up for wadding, and rammed it down his gun.

"'Now tell me?' said he, advancing and laying his hand upon my arm, 'are all the agonies you have described there real? Are your days indeed miserable and your nights sleepless?'

"'Ah! general, that agony is my only excuse.'

"'Then, my young friend,' he continued, in a kind tone, 'you must seek a remedy. You must leave us.

Travel ﹐ go to Italy or Germany, and you will return cured.   Money, or letters of recommendation, are at your service, for I speak as if I were your father.   Well! you cannot decide all at once.   So be it.   We'll try the game, and talk no more.'

"As he spoke he shot a partridge ten paces off, and I saw my letter smoking from the barrel.

"We returned at five, and the general insisted that I should go in and dine.   Caroline was at her embroidery.

"'Here is a young man,' exclaimed the general, 'come to take leave of you before setting out for Italy.'

"She looked up quite coldly, and merely said, 'Ah! indeed?'

"At dinner, every one talked of my sudden journey; and Caroline did the honours of the table with perfect grace.

"At night the general took a kind leave of me, and as I quitted the château I felt almost as much hatred as love for the woman I had left.

"I travelled afar; saw Naples, Rome, and Venice; and each day felt, to my surprise, that a passion I believed eternal was gradually fading from my heart.   At last I thought myself cured, and returned to France.   At Grenoble I agreed with a young man, whose acquaintance I had made at Florence, to visit the Chartreuse, and thus beheld for the first time the destined residence of my life.

"Turning to Emmanuel (so my friend was called), I said, laughing, 'Had I known this cloister when I was in love, methinks I should have turned monk.'

"I returned to Paris, where my mother had purchased a house, and began again my old life of gaiety and pleasure.   The past seemed like a dream.   I met the general, who received me with all kindness, and offered to conduct me to his wife.   Some slight tremor came over me at the idea of meeting her, and it was rather a relief to me to find she was out.

"But some days after I met her and the general face to face: there was no escaping the meeting, and I paid my respects to her.   Caroline looked more beautiful than ever ; her paleness and languor had passed away, and she was now in all the bloom of fresh glowing health.

"Her manner, too, had changed. There was no longer coldness and indifference, but something soft, even to tenderness. I fancied she pressed my hand even when we met. A tremor ran through my frame; I looked at her, and she drooped her eyes. As I walked my horse beside her, the general asked would I not go down to the country and visit them, particularly as our own country-house was sold; but I refused. 'Do come!' said Caroline, turning her eyes on me. Her very voice seemed seductive. I was unable to answer. What change had a year brought about in this woman's heart!

"'Perhaps monsieur fears being dull with us,' she continued, addressing her husband. 'Give him leave to bring a couple of friends, and that will decide our petition.'

"'Willingly,' replied the general. 'Bring any one you like. Do you hear?'

"'Thanks, general,' I answered; 'but really I have particular engagements.'

"'Oh, you prefer other people to us?' said Caroline, with a pretty petulance I would have given my life to have excited a year before. That decided me. I accepted the invitation.'

"Emmanuel had been my constant friend at Paris. I told him, therefore, of my proposed visit. 'Ah!' said he, 'I was very near going there too.'

"'How? Do you know the general?'

"'No; but I was promised an introduction. My friend, however, has been taken up with other matters, and I have lost a very pleasant excursion.'

"'No, no,' I said, remembering the general's permission. 'Come with me. I have leave to bring a friend.'

"He assented willingly, and next morning we set off for the general's château.

"On arriving, we found the ladies and some company in the park. Emmanuel was received with marked coldness by Madame M. though her emotion was visible on meeting us. All this I interpreted in my own favour, particularly as she said to the general in my hearing, 'You see, monsieur did not think our company suffi-

cient; he has brought a companion;' and she turned
away with a slight frown on her brow.

"This little ill-temper enchanted me. I offered my
arm to Caroline, and we walked together. At dinner
she placed me next her. I was half-mad with ecstasy;
and the passion I had thought conquered blazed up
again in my breast fiercer than ever.

"Day after day passed in the same interesting dream
of mutual love; for I was convinced she loved me. The
general then announced that he was summoned to Paris;
and his absence seemed all that was wanting to complete
my happiness. He went, and every minute of that day
I was beside her. A thousand times her hand touched
mine; a thousand times her hair touched my cheek. I
was in a frenzy—a delirium of joy; and when I threw
myself on my couch at night, I could only exclaim, 'She
loves me! she loves me!'

"But rest was impossible. I arose and went to the
window. There lay the park beneath me where we had
wandered through the day. The air was calm, the
night beautiful; I could not resist the desire to visit the
places she had consecrated with her foot, and I descended. Her windows only were illuminated of the
château; they belonged to her room; and I could distinguish her figure as she passed to and fro between me
and the light. 'Caroline! Caroline!' I murmured, as
if she could hear and respond to the burning love of my
heart. Suddenly she paused and seemed to listen, then
sprang to a door close by the window, opened it, and in
another instant a second shadow passed the window and
was clasped in her arms. The light was extinguished.
A cry burst from my lips, and I remained with my eyes
fixed on the now darkened window, as if my glance could
pierce its secrets."

The monk laid his damp hand on mine. "   ieur,
were you ever jealous?"

"You killed them, I suppose?" said I.

He laughed convulsively; then, lifting his hands above
his head, threw himself backward, uttering groa   of
anguish.

I rose and held him up. "Courage!" I said.

"I loved this woman so! I would have give   my

blood, my life, my soul for her, and I have lost this world and the other for her sake; for, monsieur, my thoughts here are not of God, but of *her*."

"Well, my father? you killed them?"

"I did worse. I betrayed them. Next day, she and her lover were found dead together. They killed themselves. The lover was Emmanuel!"

CHAPTER XV.

CHARLES THE BOLD.

HAVING wandered back to Geneva, sailed once more on the blue lake, seen Moudon and Aventicum, we reached Morat, proudly celebrated in the Swiss annals for the defeat of the Duke of Burgundy, Charles the Bold. An ossary, built up of the skulls and bones of the Burgundians, was the trophy erected by the town before one of its gates, in commemoration of the victory. For three centuries the temple of death remained standing; the blanched fragments still showing the marks of the conquerors' swords, and bearing a triumphal inscription in Latin, which may be translated thus:—"To God, the all-powerful and the all-good. The army of the valiant Duke of Burgundy, when besieging Morat, was destroyed by the Swiss, and left here this monument of its defeat. Anno 1476."

In 1798, when France invaded Switzerland, a Burgundian regiment destroyed the trophy; and to efface all memorial of the national shame, flung the bones into the lake, which sometimes casts up a few now and then on the shore, when a tempest stirs its depths. A column was erected in 1822, by the republic of Fribourg, on the site of the ossary, having a new inscription, which runs thus:—

"The republic of Fribourg consecrates this new trophy to the battle won by their ancestors on the 12th of June, 1474."

About a hundred steps from this column is the best place for viewing the field of Morat. There the whole town lies before you, rising as an amphitheatre from the borders of the lake that bathes its feet; to the right are the heights of Gurmels; to the left, Mont Villy, all covered with vines; while all beneath, on the very ground you stand on, is the scene of the last sanguinary act that closed the funereal trilogy of Duke Charles, which commenced at Granson and finished at Nancy.

A first defeat had shown the duke that, if he still preserved the title of the Bold, he had lost all right to that of the Invincible. A stain had been flung on the ducal blazon which nothing but blood would wash out. A desire for vengeance replaced the conviction of his force. Courage remained, but confidence was gone. Pride urged him on to his destruction, and he rushed upon the rocks like a vessel driven by the tempest.

Before three months were over he had assembled a new army, as numerous as that which had been destroyed; but the fresh levies were all drawn from different quarters: Picardy, Burgundy, Artois, and foreigners, and, naturally, divisions and dissensions sprang up between them. In other times the unvarying good fortune of the duke would have united them by a common confidence; but evil days had begun to cast their shadows, and his troops marched to battle murmuring and undisciplined.

Meanwhile the Swiss had dispersed, according to custom, after the victory of Granson, and each followed his banner to their respective cantons, for the season was approaching which summoned the soldier-shepherds with their flocks to the mountains.

When the Duke of Burgundy fixed his camp on the 10th June, 1476, at the little village of Faoug, situated at the western extremity of the lake, the Swiss had nothing wherewith to oppose his entire force, except the insignificant town of Morat for a rampart, with a garrison of twelve hundred men. Instantly messengers were despatched in all directions with tidings of the advance of the hostile force; signal fires blazed on all the mountains, and the summons to arms resounded through all the valleys,

Adrien de Bubemberg, who commanded the garrison of Morat, beheld the progress of this army, thirty times greater than his own, without betraying the least symptom of fear.   He assembled the inhabitants and soldiers together, showed them the necessity that existed for mutual support and assistance, so that all united should act and feel like one armed family, and give each other aid like brothers.   And when these noble emotions were aroused within them, he dictated an oath, by which they solemnly swore to die amidst the ruins of their town if they could not conquer.   Three thousand voices were raised at once to repeat the vow.   Then one voice alone rose amidst the crowd, proposing that death should be the punishment of whoever spoke of surrender.   The voice was that of Adrien de Bubemberg.

Having taken these precautions, he wrote to the Bernois:—

"The Duke of Burgundy is here with all his power; his Italian hirelings and German traitors; but, fear not, citizens and compatriots.   Let the minds of all our Confederates rest in peace.   I will defend Morat."

Meanwhile the duke surrounded the town with the two wings of his army, commanded by the Count de Romont and the Bastard of Burgundy, he himself commanding the centre; and, from a superb lodge which he had caused to be erected on the heights of Courgevaux, he could retract or extend their position as a man folds or extends his arms.   The town, consequently, was accessible but on one side—that of the lake; but, every night, boats glided silently to the shore, charged with men and all the muniments of war for the besieged.

Neither were the Swiss idle on the other side of the Sarine, to the rear of the duke's position; for they organised not only a defence, but even an attack.   The little towns of Laupen and Gumenen were fortified so as to resist a sudden attack; and Berne, protected by them, was made the rallying point of the Confederates.

The duke saw no time was to be lost.   He summoned the town to surrender; and, on the refusal of the commandant, the Count de Romont unmasked seventy large pieces, which in about two hours opened a breach in the wall sufficient for the assault.   The Burgundians, thinking the place was now their own, rushed forward, shouting, "The town is taken!"   But behind the breach they found a second wall, more difficult to overthrow even than the first—a living wall, a wall of iron—against which the Count de Romont's eleven thousand men dashed themselves five times in the space of eight hours without being able to break it. Seven hundred perished in the first attempt, and the commander of the artillery was killed. Then, like a wounded boar, the Duke of Burgundy turned fiercely upon Laupen and Gumenen. The shock was felt even as far as Berne, which for an instant trembled for itself. Instantly six thousand men were enrolled under her banners, and sent to the succour of the two towns. They arrived just in time to behold the flight of Duke Charles.

The Burgundian's anger was now at its height. Besieged himself in some sort between the three towns he was besieging, he seemed like a lion struggling in a triangle of fire. No one dared to offer advice. His generals, when he summoned them, approached him trembling; and at night, those who watched by his tent-door heard him groaning with terror, and breaking his arms to pieces.

During ten days the artillery resounded without any cessation, destroying the ramparts and ruining the town, but without weakening the constancy of the inhabitants. Two assaults, conducted by the duke in person, were repulsed. Twice Charles the Bold reached the summit of the breach, and twice had to descend.

Adrien de Bubemberg was everywhere, and seemed to have diffused a portion of his soul into the breast of every soldier present. Then, when the day was over in which he had repelled victoriously every attack, he wrote to his allies:—

"Be calm, friends; fear not. While a drop of blood remains in my veins, we shall defend Morat."

Nevertheless, the cantons were in motion and uniting their forces. Men from the Oberland, Brienne, Argovie, Uri, and Entlibuch, had already arrived. The Count Oswald de Thierstein joined them, bringing a contingent from the Archduke Sigismund; Count Louis d'Eptingen encamped under the walls of Berne, with the troops furnished by Strasbourg, as an ally; and, lastly, the Duke René de Lorraine had made his entry into the town at the head of three hundred cavalry, having beside his horse a monstrous bear, marvellously trained, to whom he gave his ungloved hand to lick as he would have done to a dog.

The troops from Zurich alone were wanting. They arrived on the 21st of June, at night, accompanied by the men of Turgovie, Baden, and the free bailiwicks.

All this was beyond even the hopes of the Confederates. Berne was illuminated, and tables covered with viands were placed before the door of each house to refresh the new arrivals. Two hours of rest were granted them; then, in the evening, the whole Confederate army, full of hope and courage, began their march, each canton chanting its own war-song.

In the morning they heard mass at Gumenen; then extended their line of battle along the opposite side of the mountain, where the duke had placed his lodge.

Hans de Hallewyl commanded the advanced guard. He was a noble and brave knight of Argovie, whom Berne had enrolled amongst her citizens as a reward for the high feats of arms he had accomplished in the armies of the King of Bohemia, and in the last war of Hungary against the Turks. Under his orders marched the mountaineers of the Oberland, Entlibuch, of the ancient leagues, and eighty volunteers of Fribourg, who, in order to be recognised by each other in the contest, cut branches of the lime-tree, and stuck them in their caps and casques in place of plumes.

After them came the commandant of the centre, Hans Waldman de Zurich, and William Herter, captain of the men of Strasbourg, who had been placed in that position to honour the faithful allies who had brought such timely succour to the Confederation.

Under their orders marched all the cantons, ranged under their separate banners, each one of which was specially defended by eighty men, chosen from among the bravest, and armed with cuirasses, pikes, and battle-axes. Lastly came the rear-guard, commanded by Gaspard Hertestein de Lucerne. A thousand men scattered along the flanks of the army served as guides through the woods that covered the declivity, extending from Gumenen to Laupen. In June, the whole Confederate army amounted to about thirty or thirty-four thousand men. The Duke of Burgundy commanded an almost equal number of troops; but his camp seemed much more considerable, in consequence of the number of women and camp-followers who encumbered its march.

That evening there was a movement amongst this vast multitude; for the news spread that the Swiss had crossed the Sarine. Great was the duke's joy on hearing the tidings. The whole army was put in motion; and he would have marched them instantly to the crest of the mountain to meet the enemy, if the rain had not fallen, and forced every one to return to quarters.

Next day the duke executed this movement, and from the brow of the hill looked down upon his enemies entrenched in the forest. The sky was clouded, and the rain falling heavily: it seemed no time for a battle, and the Swiss never stirred from their quarters. Three hours the duke waited in vain. At last, when the generals complained that the men were worn out with fatigue, the bow-strings of no use from the damp, and the powder spoiled by the wet, he gave the signal for retreat.

This was the moment anxiously awaited by the Confederates. Hardly had they seen the movement effected by the duke's army, when Hans de Hallewyl shouted to the advanced guard, "Down, children! on your knees to prayer!" Every one obeyed; the centre and rear-guard followed the movement; and the voices of thirty-four thousand men, praying for their liberty and their country, were heard at once ascending to God.

At this moment, whether from chance or as a visible sign of protection, the dense veil of clouds was suddenly rent asunder, and the sunlight flashed back glitteringly from the arms of the kneeling multitude. Then Hans de Hallewyl, rising, drew his sword, and pointing to heaven, cried—

" Soldiers, behold the sign from God! Think on your wives and children!"

The whole army sprang to their feet at these words, like one man, shouting, " Granson! Granson!" then marched boldly forward to occupy the crest of the hill abandoned but a few instants previously by the duke's troops. A pack of mountain-dogs accompanied them, which, encountering at top a pack of hounds belonging to the Burgundian knights, fell on them as furiously as if conscious who were their masters; and being accustomed to combat with bears and wolves, soon sent the weaker foe scampering down the mountain to the camp —an omen which was looked on as highly favourable by the Confederates.

The Swiss army was divided into two bodies, in order to conduct two separate attacks. One, consisting of ten or twelve thousand men, crossed the Sarine a little above its junction with the Aar, and held watch over the Count de Romont, to prevent his bringing succour to Duke Charles. Hallewyl, who commanded one of these brigades, and Waldman, the general of the other, combined their movements in such a manner, that, setting out from the same point and extending their lines like a V, they were ready to attack the camp at the same instant, Hallewyl on the right, and Waldman on the left. All round the Burgundian position were deep fosses and trenches, guarded by a threatening line of black-mouthed mortars and culverins.

This line remained mute and gloomy until the Swiss had reached within half cannon-shot, when suddenly a red girdle of fire encircled the camp, and the cries of the Swiss showed how the messengers of death had swept their ranks. Hallewyl's troop, above all, suffered from this first discharge; and René de Lorraine, with three hundred horse, flew to his assistance. At the same instant a troop of Burgundian cavaliers issued from the camp and fell upon them with their lances. At the first shock René de Lorraine's horse was killed, and he himself thrown to the ground. It was thought he was killed likewise, but Hallewyl sprang forward and saved him.

Waldman, on his side, had advanced to the very edge of the fosse, then been forced to retreat by the Burgundian artillery, but had re-formed behind a hill for a second attack.

It was then a messenger was despatched to Duke Charles that the Swiss were attacking. So little did he imagine such audacity possible, that he never even quitted his tent at the sound of the firing, thinking it proceeded from his own troops continuing their assault upon the town.

The messenger found him in his chamber only half armed, his head and hands bare, and no sword at his side. At first he would not believe the tidings, but when the man assured him that he had with his own eyes seen the Swiss attacking the camp, he started up with furious imprecations, and struck him with his fist. At that moment a knight entered, wounded in the brow, and with his armour all stained with blood. This was evidence the duke could not resist. He seized his casque and gauntlets, leaped upon his war-horse, which stood always ready caparisoned at the door; and when some one reminded him that he was without a sword, he shook the heavy mass of iron that hung at his saddle-bow, saying that such was fitter to strike such rabble; then galloping to the highest point of the camp, he rose in his stirrups and surveyed at a glance the whole field of battle. There the ducal banner was planted, and the instant it was recognised, the Duke of Somerset, captain of the English troops, and the Comte de Marle, hastened to him to demand orders. "Do as I do," answered the duke, dashing forward to a part of the camp which had just been forced. It was by Hallewyl and his vanguard: repulsed at one place, they had tried another where the defences seemed weaker; had succeeded in effecting an entrance within the enclosure, and, seizing the enemy's guns, had swept down the Burgundians with their own artillery.

It was to this spot the duke directed his course, and the engagement took place just where the road to Fribourg passes now. Charles fell like a thunderbolt into the midst of the combat. With every sweep of his iron mace he felled a circle of enemies as a butcher fells oxen, and the tide of battle seemed turning in his favour, when shouts and tumults were heard on the right. It was Hertestein with the Swiss vanguard, who, following the circular plan of attack agreed on by the leaders, had succeeded in turning the camp and attacking it at the place where it joined the lake. This point was defended by the Bastard of Burgundy, and his valiant defence would probably have been successful, if Adrien Bubem-berg had not issued from the town, and so placed him between two fires.

Meanwhile Duke Charles had not succeeded in recapturing the artillery from the Swiss, every discharge of which swept away whole ranks of his men; but as the *élite* of his troops were still around him, no one dreamt of retreat. He had his mounted archers, his bodyguard, and the English volunteers. With these he might have held his ground a long time, if Count René, who was remounted, had not thrown himself with his three hundred horse into the middle of the butchery, aided by the Counts Eptingen, Thierstein, and Gruyère. The Duke of Somerset and Count Marle were the first to fall; but it was against the ducal banner, above all, that Count René directed his efforts, as if it were a mortal enemy. Three times he spurred his horse so close that he had but to extend his hand and seize it, and three times a fresh cavalier sprang between him and his prize. One by one he slew them. The last who held it was Jacques de Maes. René killed his horse, and while the knight fell with the dying animal, and in place of defending himself, pressed the banner of his master close to his breast, the count, perceiving an opening in his armour, took the hilt of his sword in both hands, and, driving it through with all his force, pinned his enemy to the ground, while one of his súite, gliding in between the horse's legs, dragged the banner from the hands of the loyal cavalier, whose hold only relaxed in death.

From that moment the day became a second Granson: no longer a retreat, but a total route. Waldman, too, was conqueror on his side, and aided to increase the disorder. Duke Charles and the few soldiers who remained with him were surrounded on all sides; and the Count de Romont, harassed by the enemy himself, and ignorant of what was passing in other quarters, was unable to advance to his assistance. There remained but one hope for the duke, therefore: to pierce a way through the living wall, whose density he could not calculate, and, arrived at the other side, trust to the fleetness of their horses to convey them on to Lausanne.

Sixteen cavaliers surrounded the duke; and, putting their lances in rest, they dashed boldly through the entire depth of the Confederate army. Four fell by the way; the twelve who remained in their saddles succeeded in reaching Morges with their master, having travelled twelve leagues in two hours. This was all that remained to Charles the Bold of his great and powerful army.

From the moment the duke gave up the battle, all contest ceased. The Confederates ranged as conquerors over the field of battle, striking down all who came in their way, and giving the last blow to those already fallen: no quarter was shown except to women. The Burgundians who attempted to escape by the lake were pursued in boats; the water became dense with corpses and red with blood; and long after, fragments of armour and broken swords were drawn up by the fishermen in their nets.

The duke's camp, with all it contained, fell into the hands of the Swiss; and the tent of the great Charles, with all its rich stuffs, furs, and precious arms, was given to Duke René de Lorraine by the victors, as a testimony of their admiration of his courage during the day. The artillery the Confederates divided amongst themselves; each canton which had sent a contingent to the army obtaining some pieces as trophies of the battle. Morat received twelve.

I went to look at these old *souvenirs* of a memorable defeat, in the place where they are at present, and remarked that the guns are not cast in a single piece, but formed of rings, alternately salient and hollow, soldered to each other—a mode of fabrication to which they owed much of their solidity.

In 1828 or '29, Morat demanded the loan of some cannon from Fribourg, in order to celebrate brilliantly the fête of the Confederation. For some reason the request was not acceded to, and the young men then bethought themselves of the cannon of Duke Charles, which were accordingly dragged in triumph from the arsenal, where they had lain during four centuries. No thing seemed worthier to celebrate their new compact with liberty than these trophies of victory, which they owed to the old Federation, and great was the joy and shouting with which they were dragged to the esplanade. At the first discharge, however, a culverin and bombshell burst, killing or wounding five or six of the young men who stood near.

Thus was Duke Charles avenged.

CHAPTER XVI.

FRIBOURG.

WE found two hours quite enough to spend upon the curiosities of Morat; so, about three in the afternoon, remounted our little travelling chaise and proceeded towards Fribourg. After half-an-hour's progress through a flat country, we reached the foot of a hill, which our coachman advised us to ascend on foot, in order to enjoy the view; but the fact was, in truth, that he wanted to save his horse. However, I always give in to these little plots without seeming to fathom them, and willingly alighted, when I found that our guide's invitation had really some plausible motive.

The view, which embraced the whole field of battle, the town, the two lakes of Morat and Neufchâtel, was indeed magnificent. On the very spot where we stood, the Duke of Burgundy had erected his pavilion. Half-an-hour's walking brought us to the crest of the mountain, on rounding which, we beheld beneath us the place where the whole Confederate army had made their morning prayer.

For the rest of the way nothing remarkable attracted us, except the pretty valley of Gotteron, which joins the high-road about a league before Fribourg, and extends up to the gates of the town. On the opposite summit to that we traversed, our guide made us remark the hermitage of St. Madeleine, which he invited us to visit next day, and at the bottom of the valley a Roman aqueduct, which serves, even now, to conduct the water of the Sarine to the forges of Gotteron.

The gate of Fribourg is most daringly imagined,

being suspended over a precipice two hundred feet deep; so that, in case of attack, the inhabitants have only to destroy this gate to render the town impregnable on that side.

Fribourg altogether is built in a most fantastic manner, as if the result of an after-dinner dream of some intoxicated artist. It is the most hump-backed town I ever beheld: the ground has been taken just as God made it, and man has built thereon—that is all. On passing the gate, one descends, not a street, but a staircase of twenty-five or thirty steps, leading to a little valley paved with stones and bordered with houses on both sides. Before ascending to the cathedral, which is right before you, there are two objects to contemplate: at the left, a fountain; at the right, a lime-tree. The fountain is a monument of the fifteenth century, and curious from its simplicity, representing Samson killing the lion, and bearing the jaw-bone of the ass, stuck in his girdle like a sword. The lime-tree is a trophy of the same age. Here is the tradition of its existence:—

We have mentioned how eighty young Confederates were sent from Friburg to the battle of Morat, and that, to distinguish each other in the fight, they had placed branches of the lime-tree in their caps and casques. When the victory had been gained, one of this little band of brothers was despatched to Fribourg with the news. Like the Greek of Marathon, the young Swiss never paused till he reached the town, where, sinking down exhausted in the public square, he waved the branch of lime-tree above his dying head, and shouted "Victory!" From this branch, planted by his compatriots over the spot where the young soldier fell, sprang the colossal tree existing to this day.

The church-steeple of Fribourg is one of the loftiest in Switzerland, being three hundred and ninety feet high. In general, there are few of these erections in the Alps. Since Babel, man has renounced a struggle against God; mountains have crushed temples. What madman would dare to emulate the altitude of Mont Blanc, or of the Jungfrau?

The porch is highly ornamented, bearing a representation of the last judgment in all its details. There is the Almighty rewarding or punishing those awakened by the last trumpet, while angels are employed in separating them into two groups, and placing the elect in a castle to represent paradise; while the condemned, amongst whom figure three Popes, are sent down the throat of a serpent that represents hell. The interior of the church offers nothing worth notice except a Gothic chair beautifully carved: as to the high altar, its execution does not go beyond the ordinary sculpture of the time of Louis XV.

Fribourg is the Catholic city, *par excellence*—credulous and prejudiced as if still but in the sixteenth century. This gives a mediæval colouring to the ideas and manners of the inhabitants, which makes the national character possess a decided individuality. To them the papacy of Gregory VII. and Boniface VIII. is still the same; and were it necessary, they would be found willing at this day to take down the arquebus of Charles IX. or relight the pile for John Huss.

Next morning I sent forward the chaise to await us on the road to Berne, and inquired for a guide to the hermitage of Saint Madeleine, the road being impracticable for carriages. Our guide offered his nephew, a fat youth, who was sacristan by profession, and guide in his leisure moments. Passing by the lime-tree of Morat, he told me its history; then he descended a street of one hundred and twenty steps, which led us to a bridge thrown over the Sarine. From this point we turned to look at Fribourg, rising like an amphitheatre, with all its fantastic outlines; a true Gothic city, built for war, and placed on the summit of a steep mountain, like the eyrie of a bird of prey. One sees what military genius can do for a locality that seems designed by nature as a retreat for the chamois rather than as a dwelling for man, and how a girdle of rocks can be converted into a girdle of ramparts.

To the left of the turn on the mountain crest, like streaming hair flung back from a brow, waves a forest of old pine-trees, while the waters of the Sarine wind between, like a silver ribbon to bind the floating wild tresses.

On the opposite side of the mountain is a Roman

gateway—like all the constructions of that epoch, heavy, square, and massive; but near it is a pretty little chapel with fourteen saintly statues, bearing date 1650. The ground seems especially holy, for the walls of the interior are literally tapestried with votive offerings to the Virgin Mary, and attestations of the miracles performed by her on behalf of the inhabitants. These miracles are represented sometimes by rude drawings. One interested me. It was a sketch of a child falling down a precipice, but preserved from injury by outspread angels' wings beneath. I asked to be shown the spot where this accident took place, and found that the child had really fallen from a height of nearly two hundred feet, without sustaining any hurt.

On returning to the Berne road, our sacristan pointed out the place chosen by the engineers for the suspension bridge which is to connect the town with the opposite mountain. This bridge will be eight hundred and fifty feet long, with an elevation of one hundred and fifty, and rise ninety feet above the roofs of the highest houses in the valley. The idea of embellishing the ancient Fribourg with this modern erection afflicted me as much as it seemed to rejoice the inhabitants. This kind of iron dancing-cord called a suspension-bridge would harmonize badly, it seemed to me, with the severe Gothic city, which leads our thoughts wandering back to the times of faith and feudalism. Such discrepancies pain one as much as a frock-coat at Constantinople, or top-boots with the flowing garments of the Ganges.

At three o'clock we regained our chaise, and packed ourselves into it with the sacristan in front: proceeding thus to the hermitage of St. Madeleine, till, the path becoming too narrow, we alighted and continued our journey on foot.

The weather was magnificent. Nevertheless, the worthy servant of St. Nicholas had not failed to bring with him an enormous umbrella, which seemed, by the predilection he manifested for it, to be the ordinary companion of his travels. It was an ancient affair enough, robed in blue calico, with patches of grey, and when unfolded to its full extent had a circumference of about eight feet—a venerable ancestral umbrella, whose race exists no longer except in the depths of Brittany or Lower Normandy.

We all laughed much over our guide's precaution, while he, good-humoured and stolid as a true German-Swiss, stared, unable to divine the cause of our hilarity. At length, after a quarter of an hour, he said, as if talking to himself, "Ah! I see; it is my umbrella. I understand."

After ten minutes or so of ascent, the heat became excessive; down came the vertical rays on our defenceless heads. It was then we turned to look at our guide, and found that he had unfolded his apparatus like a great war-machine, beneath the shadow of which he was moving tranquilly along a side-path, sheltered as a holy sacrament beneath its daïs. Now we perceived that his affection for his blue cotton friend was not as disinterested as we had at first imagined, and we paused, watching his ascension with an envious eye, as he moved in the centre of the immense shadow, like a planet in its atmosphere.

Having reached the top, he turned to look at us, and stared at seeing our exhausted condition, as we passed a bottle of kirschen-wasser from one to the other, and wiped the perspiration from our foreheads. At length a thought struck him: "Ah!" said he, "I see you are hot; it must be the sun." Then he continued his progress within the shadow, as calm as ever.

On entering the carriage, like a horseman who looks after his horse before thinking of himself, he had carefully selected a place for his valued friend, for which, indeed, I was beginning to entertain a veneration almost as profound as his own. Carefully and symmetrically he arranged its folds, drew down the metal ring to the extremity of its cord, then placing it in an angle, he took his seat on the edge of the cushion, with all due marks of deference to what he felt was owing both to us and it. When we stopped, in order to traverse on foot the three-quarters of a league between us and the hermitage, the umbrella was the first to alight, and no step did its master take until a scrupulous examination had convinced him of its sound condition. The inventory was not without a show of reason, for the sky had become gra-

dually overcast, and the distant rolling thunder seemed
to come nearer at every step.   Soon large drops of rain
fell heavily; but we were already half way, and boldly
plunged into the wood behind which we expected to find
the hermitage.   After proceeding fifty steps or so, the
rain fell in torrents; another five minutes and we were
all drenched to the skin.   Still we never slackened foot-
step till standing beneath the shelter of the hermitage
trees.   Then we raised our eyes to look for our sacristan.
Behold him there advancing calmly under the vast circumference of his tent, picking his steps deliberately
over the stones that formed little island archipelagos
amid the pools of water, so that from head to foot his
person was intact.   No drop of rain damped his hair;
no spot of mud stained his shoes.   What a contrast to
us!   No wonder on reaching us he grasped in wonder
at our dripping forms, apparently as if our condition was
wholly incomprehensible.   Then after a little reflection
the truth dawned on him.   "Ah!" said he, "I see you
are wet; it must be the rain."

The fellow! we could have strangled him.   Indeed,
I believe the propriety of doing so was put to the vote;
but fortunately we were turned from these evil thoughts
by the sound of a bell close to us, that seemed to shake
the earth.   It proceeded from the hermitage, which we
had reached at last.

The storm was a mountain storm, and passed as
rapidly as it came.   The rain was over, the sky serene;
we shook our clothes and issued from shelter, leaving
our sacristan in search of a fitting place wherein to dry
the umbrella.   In a few moments we found ourselves
face to face with the most extraordinary work, perhaps,
executed by the patience of one man.

In the year 1760, a peasant of Gruyère, named Jean
Dupré, took the resolution of becoming a hermit, and
excavating a hermitage for himself such as the fathers
of the desert had never dreamed of.   Having sought a
long while through the adjacent country for a fitting
spot, he at length fixed on the mass of rocks near to
where we stood, finding them at once both solid and
friable enough for the execution of his project.   To the
south they present a perfectly perpendicular face, over-

looking the valley of Gotteron to a height of two hundred feet, while the summit is crowned with magnificent trees.

Dupré decided on attacking this mass, not merely to excavate a single grotto, but a complete habitation with all its dependencies, limiting himself, besides, as a penance, to a diet of bread and water during the whole time the work lasted. For twenty years he proceeded assiduously in the task, but his tragic death interrupted the completion. It was thus it happened:—

The singularity of Dupré's vow, the perseverance with which he fulfilled it, and the boldness of the project of excavating a mountain, attracted numerous visitors to the Madeleine; and of the two modes of approach, that by the valley of Gotteron, being the shortest and most picturesque, was generally preferred by the sight-seers. To reach the hermitage, however, it was necessary to cross the Sarine; but even this difficulty was removed by Dupré, who built a boat, and exchanged the pickaxe for the oar every time a new troop of visitors desired to see the hermitage.

One day a set of young students claimed the services of the pious boatman; and while in the middle of the river, one of them, out of a jest, to alarm his comrades, placed his feet on the two edges of the boat, swinging it from side to side in despite of the remonstrances of the anchorite. His warnings were prophetic; the boat capsized; the students, being young and vigorous, reached the shore safely, notwithstanding the rapid current of the river; but the old man was drowned, and the hermitage remained uncompleted.

Having descended four or five steps, we entered the grotto by a postern cut eight feet deep into the rock; from thence we passed out on a terrace which led to the chapel of the hermitage, an excavation about forty feet long, thirty wide, and twenty high. Mass is celebrated twice a-year here by a priest from Fribourg; and when filled with the neighbouring village population, it must remind one of the catacombs where the early Christians celebrated their mysteries. Some wooden benches and a few holy images form its sole decorations. At each side of the altar are doors—one leading to the sacristy, a little chamber in the rock, about twelve feet square; the other to the belfry, which, unlike its more ambitious brethren, scarcely appears above the level of the ground. Viewed from above, it seems a well; viewed from below, a chimney. The bell itself is hung between the mountain trees, about four or five feet above the surface of the soil, and the rope employed to set it in motion is seventy feet long.

Facing the altar is also another door, leading to a chamber, from which, by a descent of eighteen steps, you reach a garden; the wood-house and kitchen are likewise in this quarter.

However miserable the fare to which the anchorite condemned himself, yet he by no means neglected all the important accessaries necessary for the sustenance of others. Indeed, by a very singular and disinterested predilection, he seems to have bestowed more care upon the culinary department of the hermitage than upon any other.

On entering, we could for a moment fancy ourselves in one of those caves which the genius of Scott has created in the Scottish mountains, inhabited only by a dishevelled sorceress and her idiot son. In fact, the first object we beheld was an old woman seated in the shadow of the vast chimney, from which the smoke escaped by a funnel eighty feet high, excavated perpendicularly in the rock. She was busied scraping vegetables to throw into a pot that was boiling on the fire, while her son, a great, full-grown lad, sat on a stone opposite with his feet extended, never heeding that they rested in a great pool of water which the storm had sent down the chimney, so intent was he in watching with greedy eyes if there were anything eatable in the rinds his mother threw down one after the other.

We stopped an instant at the door to contemplate this strange scene, lit up by the red glare of the fire alone, in which burned and crackled a young pine, torn up green, with all its leaves and branches, and now blazing from the root to the summit.

A Rembrandt only could have thrown on canvass the rich picturesque colouring of the scene. He only could have adequately comprehended its poetry; seized the bright resinous light as it was reflected from the wrinkled face of the old woman, and played with the white locks of her hair. While striking only the profile of the young man, it threw one side into complete shadow, while the other was inundated with light.

We had entered unobserved; but on some movement made amongst our party the old woman looked up, shading her eyes with her hand from the effects of the dazzling glare beside her, and then perceived us all ranged against the door. Concluding, of course, that we had come to see the place, she applied a rather vigorous kick to the young man's foot, pointing at the same time to us; on which he rose, stood for some moments gazing stupidly at us with his idiot eyes, then yawned, stretched himself, and taking a flaming branch of pine from the hearth, motioned us to follow him, uttering, at the same time, some guttural, unintelligible sounds, which certainly did not belong to any human idiom.

He led us first to a corridor eighty feet long and fourteen wide, the object of which we could not comprehend. It was lit by four windows pierced like loopholes in the thickness of the rock. The idiot held up his torch to the door, exclaiming, "Here! here!" his mode of giving us notice when any object required our attention; and there we beheld some indistinct letters, in which, however, after some difficulty, we made out the name of Maria Louisa, the daughter of the German Cæsars, who at this epoch—1813—the wife of an emperor and mother of a king, had inscribed her name there; now almost effaced from history as well as from the door.

At the termination of the corridor is the anchorite's cell, where his wooden couch still remains, occupied now by the old woman; while beside it on the humid floor lies a bundle of straw, scarcely sufficient for a dog in a kennel, but which served as a litter for her idiot son.

The entire length of the excavation made by the anchorite in the rock is three hundred and sixty-five feet. There we stopped, out of compliment to the days of the year. The height of the roof is fourteen feet.

On returning to the chamber contiguous to the chapel, we descended the eighteen steps leading to the garden, where some miserable vegetables are reared by the idiot lad. Hearing him utter his habitual "Here! here!" we turned to a rock towards which he pointed, from which issued a spring of most excellent water. It is called "The Cave of Eternity."

Having seen all the details of this singular construction, and the weather having quite cleared up during our visit, we thought it advisable to pursue our course to Berne without delay; so, issuing from the postern, we set off in search of our guide, hoping he had procured us something to stop the cravings of a devouring hunger.

We found our worthy clerk of Saint Nicholas seated under the shadow of a tree before a large stone, on which lay the remains of what evidently had been an excellent repast. The bones of a demolished fowl were strewed around, and beside him lay an empty flask, the contents of which had just been transferred to a receptacle still more elastic and capacious.

This was a sight to exasperate the meekest spirit. We demanded if no refreshments of a similar kind could be had for us. He made us repeat the phrase several times; then, having reflected some seconds, said, with the tranquil perspicacity which marked his character, "Ah! I see. You are hungry: it must be the exercise." After which he raised his eyes to heaven, and said grace with the unction of a man who felt that he had really enjoyed the goods of the Creator; rose, shut up his knife, grasped the umbrella, and proceeded to lead the way to the chaise, as phlegmatically as if unconscious that two hungry stomachs were following his full one.

On rejoining our driver, we consulted how much should be given to our guide, and a thaler having been agreed on, I took one from my pocket and presented it. Our sacristan examined the piece attentively, weighed it, then, having put it up, extended his hand for more. This time I seized it with the most violent cordiality, and giving him a squeeze sufficient to send the blood from his finger-ends, said, in my best German, "*Gut reis, mein freund.*" The poor devil made a horrible grimace, and, while he rubbed the nearly dislocated member with the other hand, muttered something we did not understand. However, we left him, mounted our chaise, and, after a quarter of a league's driving, bethought ourselves of asking the driver if he knew what our guide had said.

"Yes, gentlemen," he replied. "The man wondered how you could only offer a thaler to him after his suffering heat, and rain, and hunger for you all in one day."

It may be imagined with what total insensibility we heard this complaint—we, who had really been baked, drowned, and starved; however, the answer naturally reminded us to inquire if there were no inn near.

Our driver's reply drove us to despair. Two hours longer we rolled on, and then he stopped and asked would we like to visit the field of the battle of Laupen.

" Is there an inn on the field?" we demanded.

" No, gentlemen. It is simply the great plain where Rodolph d'Erlac, at the head of the people, conquered the noblesse in 1339."

"Ah! that will do. How many hours' drive yet to Berne ?"

" Five."

" Well, a dollar for *trinkgeld* if you bring us there in two."

The driver lashed his horse with a vigour that never relented till, in an hour and a-half, we beheld the lights of the capital of the Bernois canton glittering in the distance like glowworms in a meadow, and ten minutes after, our chaise rolled into the court of the Hôtel du Faucon.

CHAPTER XVII.

THE BEARS OF BERNE.

THE clatter of numerous voices beneath the windows awoke us early next morning, and, applying our noses close to the pane, we perceived, to our great joy, that the market was held just before the hotel, which gave us an excellent opportunity of enjoying the picturesque scene displayed by all the peasants, men and women, in their pretty national costumes.

Nothing had disappointed us more in Switzerland than the invasion of modern fashion upon the ancient modes, not only amongst the higher classes—always the first to desert the manners of their ancestors—but also amongst the lower, generally the religious observers of all paternal traditions.

However, we were now well repaid for our long waiting, by seeing gathered under our windows all the prettiest peasants of Berne and the neighbouring cantons. There was the Vaudoise, with short hair, and large pointed straw hat shading her rosy cheeks; the women of Fribourg, whose only coiffure is their long hair rolled three times round the head; the Valaisane, who comes from Mont Gemmi, with her knotted hair, and little hat bound with black velvet, from which depends down to her shoulder a broad ribbon embossed in gold; and, lastly, the Bernoise herself, the most beautiful of all, with her little straw hat wreathed with flowers placed coquettishly on one side; her long fair hair falling in plaits from beneath; her plaited chemise, and bodice embroidered in silver, with the band of black velvet ribbon round her throat.

Berne itself—the old, grave, sad town of Berne—seemed this day also to have put on its festal robes, and adorned its gloomy streets with groups of bright young girls, as a coquette trims her ball-dress with flowers. The joyous crowd passed to and fro through the sombre arcades, lighting up the old grey stones with their gay, variegated dresses, and flinging chequered shadows across the sunlight; while here and there were groups of young men with caps, meerschaums, long fair hair, large, solid heads, and frock-coats plaited on the hip, proclaiming them true German students, fresh from Jena or Leipsic, smoking and promenading gravely through the streets, with the federal cross ornamenting the tobacco-boxes that hung suspended from their girdles.

We shouted "Bravo!" from the windows, and clapped our hands, as if the curtain of a theatre had just been lifted, and the scene represented for our amusement; then lighting our cigars, in token of fraternity, we went straight up to two of the young men, and asked them to show us to the cathedral.

In place of merely pointing, as a Parisian would have done, one of them offered, in very Tudescan French, to accompany us, and, turning with his companion, led the way.

After proceeding about fifty paces, we stopped to contemplate one of those old, complicated clocks, to the adornment of which an ingenious mechanician of the fifteenth century consecrated his life. "Will you wait to hear it strike?" said our guide, smiling: "eight o'clock will soon sound."

Accordingly, in a few moments the cock which surmounted the instrument clapped its wings, and crowed three times with its automatic voice, at which appeal the four evangelists came out, and each struck a quarter of an hour with the hammer he held in his hand; then, while the last stroke was resounding, a little side-door opened, from which issued a strange procession, that defiled round in a semicircle, and disappeared by another door just as the last stroke ceased to vibrate.

We had already remarked the veneration entertained by the Bernois for bears.

On entering the night before by the Fribourg gate, we observed the colossal statues of these animals, like the horses of the Tuileries, looming out of the darkness; and in our brief morning walk we had passed a bear carrying a banner and clad in knight's armour, while beside him on its hind feet, stood a little bear, dressed as a page, while it ate a bunch of grapes with the help of its fore paws; also a monument on which two bears were sculptured, supporting the arms of the town, like two unicorns—one of them employed in flinging down the riches of commerce to a group of young girls, while the other was graciously extending its paw to a warrior of the time of Louis XV.; and now we beheld a procession of bears issue from the clock, some playing the flute, the clarionet, and the violin, while others marched with swords by their sides, carbine on shoulder, and banners flying. There was something so ridiculous in the whole exhibition that we laughed aloud, and our good-natured Bernois friends seemed enchanted with our hilarity. When the scene closed we demanded the reason for this continual reproduction of animals which, from their nature and form, had never yet elsewhere been adopted as models of grace and refinement, and requested to know for what properties beyond their skin and flesh the town valued them so highly.

" The bear is the patron of our city," they answered.

Then I remembered there really was a Saint Ours in the Swiss calendar; but I always imagined he belonged to the biped race, though his name, unfortunately, linked him with the quadruped species. Besides, he was the patron of Soleure, not of Berne, and I politely suggested this to my guides.

"True," they replied; "we should have said godfather, not patron; for the bear has really given his name to our town—Berne, or *Baer*, in German signifying bear; and then they proceeded to give us, in the best French they could muster, the legend of the christening.

The city of Berne was founded in 1191, by Barthold Duke of Zœringen; and, as soon as it was finished, girdled by walls and defended by gates, he began to consider of a name for his new town, as earnestly as a mother seeks one for her new-born child. But, unluckily, imagination was not the most brilliant faculty in the noble seigneur's mind, and he puzzled his brain long and uselessly about it. At length he summoned all the neighbouring nobility to his aid, and gave them a grand entertainment.

The dinner lasted three days: still, nothing had been decided respecting the baptism of the town. Then one of the guests rose, and proposed, to end the matter, that next day there should be a grand hunt in the adjacent mountains, and the first animal they killed should give its name to the town.

The proposition was carried by acclamation.

Next morning, they were all astir by break of day, and in about an hour a shout of victory was heard. The hunters ran to the spot, and found that one of the duke's archers had first brought down a stag.

Barthold, however, was anything but pleased that fate should have selected this animal, and swore roundly that his fine, strong, warlike town should never bear the name of a creature which was the symbol of timidity. But some ill-mannered jesters whispered that he had another cause of repugnance towards the symbol; for Duke Barthold was old, and his wife young and handsome.

The archer's feat was therefore declared null and void, and the chase began anew.

Towards evening the hunters came across a bear.

By all the saints! here was an animal whose name could neither compromise the honour of a man nor that of a town! So the poor beast was killed without mercy, and the new-born capital baptised with its blood.

The authenticity of this etymology is affirmed by a stone, still existing, about a quarter of a league from Berne, bearing this simple inscription in old German:

ERST **BAER** HIER FAM.*

No one could doubt after the testimony of such authority; and I gave the most entire faith to our young

---

* Here the first bear was taken.

student's history, which prefaced one still more singular, that I shall relate presently.

Meanwhile, we had traversed a large square, and found ourselves opposite the cathedral.

It is a Gothic structure of remarkable design, though opposed to all the architectural laws of the time, having a belfry, but no steeple: at least, the steeple is truncated at the height of about a hundred and ninety feet, which gives it the aspect of an enormous loaf of sugar from which the peak has been removed.

The edifice was begun in 1421, under the superintendence of Matthias Heins, whose plans had obtained the preference over those of a competitor now nameless.

This man dissimulated his resentment at the humiliation he experienced; and when the structure had obtained a certain elevation, demanded leave from Matthias to accompany him to the platform. Having no suspicions, Matthias granted the request, with a readiness that proved he had more vanity than prudence, and led the way up to the loftiest point, still excited onwards by the treacherous encomiums of his rival. At length he ventured out upon a plank sixty feet from the ground, whose extremities lay supported upon two walls, so that it formed the base of an angle. Here a scream was heard, and the unfortunate architect was precipitated to the ground.

No one witnessed the accident but the rival of Matthias, who said, " The plank had turned from not being properly balanced, and thrown his friend to the ground before he was able to offer him any assistance."

Eight days after, he received directions to complete the edifice, whereupon his first work was to erect a magnificent statue to his rival, on the spot where he fell: an act which gained him a great reputation for modesty throughout all the town of Berne.

The interior of the church is as uninteresting as the generality of all Protestant temples. It contains only two monuments, one of which belongs to Duke Barthold, the founder of the town.

Our next visit was to the promenade, or terrace, as it is called: a walk formed within the town, at an elevation of a hundred and eight feet, and presenting one of the finest prospects in the world.

Beneath, like a chequered carpet, lie the houses, between which winds the rapid and capricious Aar, whose blue waters are fed from the ice of Finster-Aarhorn, and surround Berne on all sides—this citadel, of which the surrounding mountains are the advanced posts. Then, higher still, rises the Gürthen, a hill three or four thousand feet high, and which serves to conduct the eye up to the grand chain of glaciers that closes the horizon, like a diamond wall—a glittering girdle, beyond which one might dream of a world bright as those fabled in oriental romance. It is a brilliant vision, flung on the air like a many-coloured scarf, which, in the morning, lit up by the rising sun, takes all the hues of the rainbow, from the deepest purple to the palest rose; and in the evening seems a fantastic palace, glittering with the last light of day, while the town and valley are shrouded in complete darkness. This magnificent platform, with its avenues of trees, is the interior promenade of the town. There is a *café* at each end to supply ice to the pedestrians, and in the centre of the terrace an inscription graven on the stone records an almost miraculous circumstance. A fiery horse once leaped with its rider, a young student, from the platform to the street below; the horse was killed upon the pavement, but the young man escaped with only a few bruises: the perpendicular leap was a hundred and eight feet. The following is a literal translation of the inscription:—

"This stone was erected in honour of Almighty God, and to transmit the memory of his mercy to posterity. From this spot, on the 25th May, 1654, the Sieur Theobald Vëinzœpfli leaped below with his horse. For thirty years afterwards he served the church in the capacity of pastor, and died full of years, and in the odour of sanctity, the 25th November, 1694."

A poor woman, condemned to the galleys, thought to save herself from the soldiers who pursued her, by hazarding the same leap; but, less fortunate than Vëinzœpfli, she was dashed to pieces on the pavement.

Having cast a last glance at the magnificent scene,

we descended by the lower gate to make the tour of
Berne by the Altenberg, a pretty hill, covered with
vines, that rises on the opposite side of the Aar.
While proceeding, we passed a little Gothic inn, bearing a *boot* for its sign, and heard the following story
of its origin:—

In 1602, Henry IV. sent Bassompierre to Berne, in
quality of ambassador to the thirteen cantons, for the
purpose of renewing the alliance formed in 1582 between Henry III. and the Federation.   Bassompierre,
by his frank manners and loyal bearing, so charmed
the Swiss, that he made them not only allies, but warm
friends of France.   Accordingly, as he was departing,
and had mounted his horse to leave the inn, he saw
advancing thirteen deputies from the thirteen cantons,
each holding an enormous *widercome* in his hand, and
prepared to pledge him in the stirrup-cup.   Having
approached and surrounded him, they lifted their thirteen cups together, each containing an entire bottle,
and, pledging France in a unanimous toast, swallowed
the liquor at a single draught.

Bassompierre, astonished at such courtesy, saw but
one way of repaying it.   Calling his domestic, he bade
him draw off his boot; then holding it by the gold spur,
had thirteen bottles of wine poured into this improvvised vase, which he lifted to his head in order to return the pledge, and exclaiming, " To the thirteen
cantons!" swallowed the contents of the thirteen bottles.

Thus Switzerland found that France was worthily
represented.

A hundred paces farther, we crossed the Aar by a
pretty stone bridge, and in half-an-hour reached the
summit of the Altenberg, from which the view equals
that of the terrace, except that the town itself forms the
basis of the tableau.   But, though the prospect was
lovely, we had soon to descend, for the heat was stifling,
and not a single tree offered its sheltering boughs;
while, on the contrary, at the other side of the Aar, we
perceived a magnificent wood crowded with promena-
ders.   Fortunately a ferry was near, and, hailing the
boatman, we were rowed across.

Totally unmindful where we went, so as we saw something new, we followed the crowd who were proceeding to the promenade of Engi, the most frequented in the environs. A great assemblage having gathered before the Aarberg gate, we demanded the cause. " The bears!" was the laconic answer; and in fact we soon perceived a parapet, round which were gathered two or three hundred people, watching the antics of four monstrous bears, who inhabited a grand and magnificent fosse below, flagged like a dining-hall. The amusement of the spectators consisted, as at Paris, in throwing apples, pears, and cakes to the animals, and I followed the national example immediately. The first pear I threw was seized and swallowed by the Bernois bruin, without any opposition; not so the second. An agile competitor, whose form I could scarcely distinguish, leaped from a hole in the wall and snapped up the morsel, under the very nose of the stupified bear; then rushed back to its retreat, amid the loud plaudits of the spectators. Soon, however, the slender head, lively eyes, and black muzzle of a fox appeared at the orifice, watching another opportunity for cheating the master of the domain out of his rights.

This sight made me wish for a second trial, and I bought some cakes, as the dainty most likely to excite the rivalry of the two antagonists. The fox evidently divined my intention, the moment he saw me calling the cake-seller, and never after took his eyes off me. When I had filled my left hand with a good stock, I took one in the right and showed it to the fox, who gave a sort of nod with his head, as much as to say, " Make your mind easy; I have no doubt about getting it;" and then licked his lips with a prophetic relish of the coming feast. However, I determined to give him a little trouble about it.

The bear meanwhile likewise manifested some symptoms of intelligence, and sat down on his hind-legs, rocking himself, in an insinuating manner, from side to side, with his throat open, his eyes fixed on me, and his paws extended. The fox now glided softly, like a cat, out of its hole, watching its opportunity, and I then perceived that an accidental cause, rather than the velocity of his movements, had prevented me at first recognising his species. The poor beast had no tail.

I threw the cake; the bear watched the descent with his eyes, then dropped on his four paws to seize it; but the fox was behind, and bounding over the bear's back with such an exact calculation of the distance that his nose touched the cake, seized the morsel, and, describing a wide semicircle, made for his hole.

The bear, however, knew enough of geometry to avenge himself, and taking the straight line of the segment, met the fox face to face. One rush, and Reynard was secure; in he slipped, victor and possessor, while poor Bruin could only clasp his teeth in rage upon the last seen portion of his rival's retreating figure. And now I knew why the poor devil had no tail. Several times I renewed the experiment, to the great satisfaction of the bystanders and the fox, who carried off two cakes at least out of every four. In another fosse were some younger and smaller bears. I asked the reason, and was told they were the destined heirs and successors to the place and fortune of their elders. This demanded an explanation. Here it is:—

We have told of the foundation of Berne by the Duke Zoeringen, and how the bear stood sponsor at the baptism. From that time bears not only became the arms of the town, and were carved on every edifice, fountain, monument, and clock, but the inhabitants desired their living effigies, likewise, to be supported at the public expense. There was no difficulty in gratifying this desire: one had but to extend his hand to the mountains and catch them. Two young bears were accordingly led captive into Berne, who, by their gentleness and docility, soon became quite objects of idolatry to the citizens of the town.

Amongst the most affectionate of their admirers was a very rich old maid, whose tenderness towards the interesting animals increased with years, till finally she died. All her relations, from far and near, then assembled to hear the will read. It was opened with the usual formalities, when they found she had left sixty thousand livres to her friends the bears, and a thousand crowns to the hospital of Berne, to found a bed there for the members of her family. The next of kin disputed the will on plea of undue influence, and an advocate was named for the defence. He was a man of great talent, and pleaded so effectually that the innocence of the unfortunate quadrupeds, whom it was sought to deprive of their inheritance, was publicly recognised, the testament declared good and valid, and the legatees authorised to enter immediately into possession of their rights.

Nothing was easier. The fortune of the testatrix was in ready money, which was immediately placed in the public funds, and the government declared responsible for the deposit, with the charge of administering the interest to the best possible advantage of the heritors, they being considered as minors. One can imagine that an immediate change took place in the household of the bears. Guardians were appointed for them, who kept a fine house and carriage in their name; gave splendid dinners and balls in the first style; while, as to the heritors themselves, their keepers took the title of valets-de-chambre, and never chastised them but with a gold-headed stick.

Unhappily, nothing is stable here below. Scarcely more than a few generations of bears had enjoyed a luxury unknown to the rest of their species, when the French Revolution broke out; and the history of our heroes immediately became involved with that of this grand catastrophe of nations in a very remarkable and fatal manner.

Switzerland lay too near France not to be somewhat affected by the great revolutionary volcano that shook the world. Still, she endeavoured to resist the stream of military lava that overflowed and furrowed Europe. The Canton de Vaud raised the standard of independence; Berne assembled her troops, victorious at first in the conflict of Neueneck, but conquered afterwards at Straubrunn and Grauholz, where the victorious French, commanded by Generals Brune and Schaunbourg, made their entry into the capital. Three days afterwards the bank was pillaged.

Eleven mules, laden with gold, took the road to Paris, two amongst them carrying away the fortune of the unhappy bears, who, though perfectly moderate in their political opinions, found themselves compromised as aristocrats, and treated as such.

A great example in philosophy was now exhibited to man by these noble animals, who showed themselves as · dignified in misfortune as they had been humble in prosperity; and, respected by all parties, they passed through the five trying years of revolution that agitated Switzerland from 1798 to 1803. When her mountains bowed beneath the hand of Napoleon, as the waves of ocean at the voice of God, in recompense the First Consul proclaimed the act of mediation, and the nineteen cantons breathed freely under the sheltering wing of the eagle of France.

No sooner had Berne recovered tranquillity than she hastened to repair the wrong done to her citizens, and realise her sublime motto—"One for all; all for one." Amongst other acts of reparation, a subscription was opened for the bears, which produced sixty thousand francs.

With this sum, so moderate in comparison to what they once enjoyed, the municipal authorities purchased a lot of ground near the town that brought in 2,000 livres a-year. After being millionaires, the unhappy beasts found themselves now only in the class of eligible voters; yet even this small fortune was reduced one-half by an accidental circumstance, not, however, connected with politics.

The fosse at that time inhabited by the bears was within the town, adjoining the prison. One night a prisoner, under sentence of death, succeeded in making a breach in the wall with an iron nail. After two or three hours' work, he heard some one at the other side of the wall working away likewise. This gave him courage. It must be a fellow-prisoner, he thought, contriving his own flight, and, both together, the labour will become easy. In fact, his unseen assistant worked with the boldest energy, flinging down the stones with apparent contempt of detection, while his strong breathing could already be heard, so close had the workers approached. The prisoner, fearing the imprudence of his companion would betray them, toiled on his side with redoubled assiduity, as every moment might bring discovery; soon nothing remained between the two except one large block of stone, which all the criminal's efforts failed to remove. In five minutes, however, it was thrown down from the opposite side, and the fresh air on his face showed him the passage was free. Instantly he forced himself through the aperture, expecting immediate help; when, to his horror, he found his assistant was a bear, whose instinct of destruction led him to try and force a way into the prison while the man was labouring to get out.

The prisoner found himself now between two chances: either being hung or devoured. The first was certain, the second only probable. He chose the latter, therefore, and escaped. Intimidated by the power which man exercises even upon the most ferocious animal, the beast cowered before him, and let him depart in safety. Next morning, the jailer, on entering the prison, found a strange substitution of persons: the bear was couched on the condemned man's bed.

Without taking time to close the door, he fled alarmed. The bear followed gravely; and, finding no opposition to his exit, walked into the street, and proceeded tranquilly to the adjacent herb and fruit market. One can imagine the effect produced upon the buying and selling crowd by the appearance of this new amateur amongst them. They fled in every direction, leaving the new-comer in a little time perfectly alone, and quite at liberty to select what pleased his palate best. His choice fell on the pears and apples, fruits for which, as every one knows, these animals have an excessive predilection. So, in place of making good use of his time, and escaping to the mountain, which he could easily have accomplished, he lost his opportunity and himself by his fatal gluttony—squatting down to gormandise at his leisure. This was his ruin.

Two neighbours were watching him from a window; and, having consulted together as to the best means of recapturing the fugitive, they heated a couple of pair of tongs red-hot, then issuing forth, stole cautiously behind the marauder, as he sat completely absorbed in the delights of his repast, and succeeded in grabbing him by the ears firmly on each side. The bear instantly perceived he was lost, and accompanied his conductors, without offering the slightest resistance, or protesting against the illegality of this mode of arrest, otherwise than by a succession of plaintive cries.

After this, for fear of new accidents, it was decreed by the town council, that the residence of the bears should be outside the town. Accordingly, the two fosses in which they are now located were built for them outside the ramparts; but the cost of the erection reduced their capital one-half, as it amounted to thirty thousand francs.

Having heard all these particulars, we continued our walk round Berne, and a magnificent alley of trees presenting itself, we plunged into its depths, along with all the promenading world. This led us to the water, which we crossed in a boat, and reached Reichenbach, between a noisy country inn and the old sombre château of Rodolph D'Erlac. The one offered us a good breakfast, the other glorious memories; but hunger conquered poetry, and we entered the town.

It is an admirable invention, a German inn, for those who love waltzing and sauer-kraut. Unfortunately, I only loved the former. However, determined to enjoy my own pleasure, as soon as breakfast was over I plunged into the dance, and offered my hand to the first peasant I encountered, which she accepted without the slightest reserve, though I wore gloves, a luxury known only to myself, amidst that simple and joyous assemblage. Seizing directly the measure of the tripping and rapid valse, I glided into the circle of dancers as easily as if the study of my whole life had been devoted to this one art. In truth, the orchestra assisted us wonderfully; for, though merely composed of village musicians, yet I have never heard, in any Parisian saloon, music more admirably suited for dancing.

The valse over, I asked my partner for a kiss, in very intelligible German, which she granted with excellent good grace. Indeed, the phrase was one of the very few in that difficult language which I could ever imprint on my memory.

The castle of Reichenbach had our next visit. A tradition, half history, half poetry, like all Swiss traditions, is attached to it. It was there old Rodolph D'Erlac reposed after all his warrior toils, spending the last days of a life which had been so useful to his country and honoured by his fellow-citizens.

One day, Rudenz, his son-in-law, came to visit him, as he was wont, when a discussion arose as to the fortune Rodolph had promised to pay him. Words ran high, and finally, Rudenz, quite transported with anger, seized the sword of the victor of Laupen, that lay on the mantel-piece, and laid the old man dead at his feet with one blow. Then he fled; but Rodolph's two hounds, which were fastened to the gate, broke their chains and pursued him to the mountains. After two hours they returned covered with blood, and Rudenz was seen no more.

The young man who related this story accompanied us back to Berne; and having told him all we had seen of picturesque and beautiful about Berne, we inquired if there were anything remaining worth our inspection. He answered, "The Tower of Goliath." The Tower of Goliath is so named because it contains a colossal statue of St. Christopher.

As my readers may not be struck with the justness of the denomination, any more than myself, I shall explain how the names of the warlike Philistine and the peaceful Israelite became united.

Towards the end of the fifteenth century, a rich and powerful noble bestowed a considerable sum on the cathedral of Berne, for the purchase of sacred vessels for the altar. This testamentary disposition was executed religiously, and a magnificent holy sacrament purchased with the money, and enclosed in the tabernacle.

Being possessed of such a valuable treasure, the next thought of those connected with the church was how best to guard it from all danger. A human guard could not be placed in the sanctuary; so they searched amongst the celestial hierarchy for the saint best fitted by strength, vigilance, and devotion, to undertake the charge.

After some discussion, St. Christopher, who had borne the Saviour on his shoulders, and whose gigantic height gave promise of all the necessary strength, obtained the preference over Michael, who was considered too young to have the prudence requisite for such a charge.

So the ablest sculptor in Berne received orders to model a statue, and set it up beside the altar to frighten robbers, as a dressed-up mannikin is stuck in a field of wheat to keep away birds. Impressed with this notion of all that was required from the saint, the sculptor produced as terrible looking a statue as he could imagine. Even St. Christopher himself, if he looked from heaven, must have been astonished at the warrior aspect he had been made to assume. Every one was enchanted. In fact, the statue was twenty-two feet high, with a halbert in the hand, a sword by the side, and was painted red and blue from top to toe: really a most formidable saint.

It was, therefore, with every chance of faithfully fulfilling his mission, and after listening to a long discourse, in which he was exhorted to his duty, that the guardian saint was duly installed behind the great altar, which he overtopped by half his figure. Two months after, the holy sacrament was stolen. What a commotion was now in the town! and how all the blame naturally fell upon poor St. Christopher! The most exasperated said he had been bribed; the more moderate, that he had been intimidated; but a third party, more violent than either of the other two, abused him in the most unscrupulous manner. This was the party of the Michaelites, who, having been in a minority at the discussion, had preserved their rancour, ready to burst forth at the first opportunity.

In short, scarcely one voice dared to undertake the defence of the faithless saint, and he was ignominiously expelled from the sanctuary which he had so badly defended. But, as Berne at that time was at war with Fribourg, they placed him in a niche of the tower of Fernbach, fronting the Fribourg gate, where he now remains, and telling him his duty, charged him on his peril, like a soldier on guard, to be more vigilant this time than he had been the last.

Eight days after, the tower of Lombach was taken.

This unheard-of conduct changed anger into contempt. The unhappy saint was henceforth looked upon, even by the most reasonable men, as a coward, and, worse still, a traitor. Accordingly, he was debaptised by common consent, deprived of the respected name he had compromised; and, to outrage him in all possible ways, he received the abominable appellation of Goliath.

Just before him is now placed a very pretty little statue of David, holding a pebble and sling in his hand, in a menacing attitude.

CHAPTER XVIII.

THE LAKE DE THUN.

OUR second day at Berne was devoted to an examination of the practical and material in the town, the previous day having exhausted the picturesque and poetical.

After the cathedral, we had to visit the Church du Saint Esprit, the exchange, the arsenal, the hospital, &c. which buildings date from 1718 up to 1740. All guide-books proclaim them as magnificent constructions, but all artists as very commonplace barracks. We left Berne at half-past seven in the evening, and proceeded to Thun by the best and least mountainous road in all Switzerland; though everywhere the highways are admirably kept, particularly by the governments of Vaud, Fribourg, and Berne, who evidently consider that roads should be made for the comfort of pedestrians, as well as of those who go in carriages. Accordingly, seats are placed at equal distances, and near them blocks on which porters may rest their bundles.

Two hours after our departure night fell on our path, but with that silver lustre prophetic of a rising moon, as yet invisible to our eyes. The great family of glaciers, motionless and melancholy spectres, that closed the horizon and looked down upon the sleeping plain, rose up between her and us. Soon, however, their summits appeared circled with a light silvery halo, which increased in brightness, till, from behind the snowy head of Eïger, rose up a globe of fire like one of those barrier signals that called old Switzerland to arms. Gradually it assumed the spherical form, and, balancing itself lightly on the sharp, high mountain peak, for a moment, like an aërostat before he springs, took its flight slowly and silently towards the deep blue heavens.

Thus we continued our journey, amid the fantastic enchantments of night, towards the wall of snow. That was our destined point, and from which plaintive and unknown sounds reached us from time to time, caused by the fall of avalanches and the cracking of the glaciers. Sometimes a rushing sound at right hand or left would make us turn our heads. It was some cascade flinging its scarf of silver to the mountain, or some pine wood murmuring to the breeze in a language they who dwell amongst them can understand. All things in the creation have received a voice from God for tears or joy, for praise or malediction: listen to the accents of the ocean during a tempest, or the hymn of the forest trees in a calm night of summer.

At half-past ten we reached Thun, rather grieved at quitting the beauty and scenery of such a night. Fine roads were now replacing paths by mountain and lake, so our payment was proportionably diminished to our driver. He seemed, however, to find considerable difficulty in tearing himself away from us. Was it affection, or a desire for *trinkgeld?* Perhaps the latter; so, being a brave youth, we indulged him, and he departed in high spirits, having found a lady and gentleman to bring back to Lausanne.

Thun contains nothing remarkable but its artillery school; and as we had not come to Switzerland to hear guns fired, we took places in the mail-boat for Interlaken, not as being the pleasantest mode of conveyance, but because I hoped to glean some traditions from the passengers.

We embarked at half-past nine, almost at the inn door, and ascended the Aar for a little. This stream descends from the glaciers of Finster-Aarhorn, and flings itself on the rocks of Handek from a height of three hundred feet; then traverses through their entire breadth the two lakes of Brientz and Thun, between which stands the charming village of Interlaken, as its name imports.

After entering the lake the horizon extended on all sides, contracting a little, however, towards the left, where a beautiful hill,* covered with trees, ran along the whole length of the lake, seeming, from a distance, like a wall mantled with ivy; while to the right soared two distinct tiers of mountains, the lower of which seemed looking upward to the higher; occasionally they parted in twain, disclosing a valley, which from the lake seems like the fosse of a citadel, but when you are near presents an opening of at least a league.

The first striking ruin on the shore is the manor of Schadeau, built by one of the family of D'Erlac. It has no tradition connected with it, unlike the next ruin, that of Strätlingen, about half-a-league distant, which is rich in memories.

The chief of this house, if one credits the chronicle of Einigen, was descended from a Ptolemy of the blood-royal of Alexandria by his mother's side, and on his father's from a Roman patrician family. Having been converted to Christianity by a miracle (for, one day, while hunting, a cross appeared to him between the deer's horns), he took the baptismal name of Theoderic, and flying from the persecution of the Emperor Adrian, presented himself at the court of the Duke of Burgundy, then at war with the King of France.

When the two armies met, it was proposed by the leaders to decide the quarrel by single combat; on which the duke named Theoderic his champion, and the day was fixed. The night before, however, the French champion saw in a vision the angel Michael combating for his adversary, and he was struck with such terror that, on awaking, he declared himself vanquished.

In recompense to Theoderic, who had procured the divine intervention in so remarkable a manner, the duke gave him his daughter Demut to wife, with a dowry of Hübsland, which consisted of part of Burgundy, and the Vandalic Lake, or Lake de Thun. Accordingly, the new lord of this lovely country erected the castle of Strätlingen on the most picturesque spot on the borders of the lake.

---

* By a hill is meant an elevation from three thousand to four thousand feet in height; by a mountain, a mass from six thousand to twelve thousand feet high.

Two hundred years after, Sir Arnold de Strätlingen, a descendant of Theoderic, in honour of the miraculous assistance afforded by St. Michael to his ancestor, dedicated the Church de Paradis to this saint; and while the workmen were placing the last stone, a voice was heard: " Here lies a treasure so vast that none can calculate its value." Immediately a search was made for the treasure, and behind the high altar were discovered a wheel of Elijah's car and sixty-seven hairs of the Virgin, which afterwards worked numerous miracles.

After many revolutions, Little Burgundy was erected into a kingdom, but still remained subject to the same race. King Rodolph and Queen Bertha reigned there about the tenth century in glory and honour, though after their decease luxury and impiety took possession of all hearts. Their successors called the country *Zur Goldenen Lust*, the Golden Pleasure; and their castle on the lake, *Goldener Hof*, the Gilded Court. In short, license and blasphemy increased to such a height that heaven could endure it no longer; so, on the marriage-day of Ulric, the last of this race, when all the court were boating on the lake, God raised up such a violent tempest that the whole flotilla was destroyed. Jewels and flowers for an instant strewed the surface of the water, then were lost for ever in its depths, and not one of all who were present at this mortuary festival obtained grace before the Great Judge.

The same day the wheel of Elijah's car and the sixty-seven hairs of the Virgin disappeared, and were never heard of since. An inscription cut in the rock denotes the place where this event happened.

While a passenger was telling us this tragic tale, heaven seemed preparing for us a catastrophe like to that which had extinguished the whole royal house of Strätlingen. The sky darkened, and heavy clouds fell lower and lower on the mountains, changing their forms so as to make them scarcely recognisable.

Niesen, above all, whose magnificent proportions rose like a pyramid five thousand feet into the air, suffered the most fantastic changes from these capricious children of the air. Sometimes a cloud resting on the summit extended on all sides like a flowing perruque *à la Louis Quatorze;* then, descending, formed a cravat under the chin; finally, the transparent mass, descending and thickening, spread over the massive base, completely veiling the head of the giant, till it seemed an enormous table-cloth laid out for a dinner to which Micromegas might have invited Gargantua.

I was absorbed in the contemplation of this strange scene, when a strong wind, a sort of visible *bise*, that seemed to sweep the ground, came rushing down the valley towards us, more rapidly a thousand times than a race-horse. What rendered it so visible was the cloud of snow-dust which it carried along with it from the summits of the mountains whence it descended. I spoke of it to the pilot, who answered briefly, without ever turning his head, so intent was he in guiding the boat,. " Yes, yes; I see it well. And mind you, it will give us a smart chase, unless we make haste and get under shelter of those rocks.

" On, my children!" cried he to the boatmen; " four arms to every oar, and row for your lives!"

The boatmen obeyed, and instantly our boat skimmed the surface of the water like a swallow. At the same moment the first rush of the wind struck us, messenger of the advancing storm, carrying away with it our pilot's hat, which he never turned to look after.

" Ho, master!" I exclaimed, pointing to the hat that floated on the water like a little foundering vessel, " do you not see?"

" Ay, ay," he answered, still without looking.

" But—your hat?"

" Well, government will give me another. It is in our bargain, otherwise my whole salary would go in hats. That is the fifth this year."

" Very well. A pleasant voyage to it." At the same instant the hat filled with water and disappeared.

While I was occupied watching the shipwreck of the poor beaver, the motion of the boat suddenly slackened, and, looking round, I found the rowers busily employed rolling up the awning that had been drawn over us. At this manœuvre a cry arose from the ladies, who saw themselves left defenceless against the coming rain. Remonstrances were uttered. The pilot turned towards them, and grimly inquired, "Do you want to go along with my hat?"

"No."

"Then keep quiet, and don't talk."

In fact, it seemed doubtful if we could reach the rocks in time, though but fifty paces distant; for the wind came rushing on like a destroying spirit, and its sharp breath, laden with snow, already whistled in our faces. Just then, too, our bark bounded on the water as if a giant were playing ball with it: evidently the whirlwind had caught us, and our little ocean was giving itself all the airs of a tempest. Still the affair was serious enough. The year before, a boat, laden with wood, had been swamped under similar circumstances, and the boatmen only saved themselves by means of the cargo, which, drifting together, formed a kind of little pyramid. On this they rested during the whole night, while the water froze around them, so that next morning they found themselves isolated on a polar isle, and twenty-four hours elapsed before any assistance could be obtained for them. As to us, we had not even this chance of safety, which I comprehended perfectly when the pilot turned to me, and asked—

"Can you swim?"

So I took off my blouse under pretence that I did not like it to get wet, and held myself ready for any event. We were saved, however. The wind struck the boat in the centre, and impelled it across the lake, which we traversed in its entire breadth, landing safely just below the grotto of Saint Beat. Now I thanked the tempest, in place of keeping up any bitterness in my mind towards it, for by its means I was enabled to make a pilgrimage to Saint Béaten Hohle. I therefore took leave of our pilot, and proceeded on foot, accompanied by a boy who offered his services as guide.

I learned from him that the grotto we were about to visit had been the dwelling of Saint Beat, in the third century, who had conquered a dragon that lived there, and bade him give up his residence; to which the docile beast consented. The legend runs that Saint Beat was an Englishman of illustrious birth, who, before his baptism at Rome, was called Suetonius.

After his conversion, under the Emperor Claudius, he quitted Rome with a friend, who also changed his name from Achates to Justus, and both together preached the gospel to Helvetia. There Saint Beat made numerous disciples, which were increased by a miracle he worked. One day the boatmen of the lake refused to carry him across to Einigen, where he was expected by a vast concourse of people; so the saint, extending his mantle on the water, took his seat on it, and by this frail conveyance traversed in safety the two leagues that separated him from the village. After such a proof of his celestial mission, the whole country acknowledged his sway and became devout converts.

The path to the grotto is as *strait* as that to heaven—perhaps the saint liked to symbolise it—and is intersected with numerous little ravines. My guide showed me one called Flocksgraben, into which a man tumbled one night with his horse. Being unable to move, and having both his legs broken, he uttered such shrieks for help that they were heard at the village, a league off. Meanwhile, till help came, being exhausted with a burning thirst, he flung his cloak into the stream near, and kept himself alive by sucking the moisture.

No accident, however, impeded us, and we reached the grotto safely, or rather grottoes, for there are two orifices in the cavern. From the lower springs the Béaten stream, which rushes noisily down the rocks: by the banks of it the saint died in his ninety-eighth year.

Up to 1528, his skull was preserved in the adjacent cave, and held in high veneration by the faithful; but, after the Reformation, the relic was removed by order of the Council of Berne, and interred at Interlaken. Still, however, the Catholics continued their pilgrimages to the grotto; so the entrance was walled up in 1566, though afterwards opened. The cave inside is about thirty feet deep and forty wide.

The Cave of the Stream, though less venerated, is more curious. The arcades through which the torrent rushes, though they gradually become lower and lower, yet offer a practicable path for the space of six hundred feet. We had brought nothing with us necessary for an adventure within the gulf, though, even if we had, the thing was now impossible. In fact, scarcely had we entered the orifice of the grotto when it seemed to me as if the noise inside augmented every moment. I made the remark to my little guide, who listened attentively; then, exclaiming, "It is the review of Seefeld; let us run!" took to his heels with the most incomprehensible celerity. Seeing him run, I ran too, without knowing why or wherefore. When he stopped, I stopped; then we looked at each other and laughed.

At first I thought the urchin was making a fool of me, and I was just about to pull his ears when he pointed to the cavern, and said—

"Look!"

Then, indeed, the phenomenon was explained. The water was rushing from the mouth of the cave in a triple volume, and with, of course, triple augmentation of sound.

Had we advanced even a hundred steps within the orifice, we could not have escaped, such was the violence with which the torrent poured forth. When there are violent rains, this result always takes place, as the water filters through the rock and increases the volume within the cavern. As to the name, "The Review of Seefeld," my guide informed me it arose, first, from the mountain peak above being called Seefeld; and, secondly, from the detonations resembling frequent discharges of musketry, accompanied by the booming of cannon at intervals.

Having heard these explanations, we took leave of Béaten Hohle, and proceeded to Neuhaus, from whence a public coach took us all to Interlaken. We found our fellow-passengers by the boat scarcely yet recovered from their fright. One poor devil, indeed, suffered so much, that on landing he was seized with fever, from which he had not recovered when I returned five days after from my excursion in the mountains.

CHAPTER XIX.

THE VALLEY OF LAUTERBRUNNEN.

On reaching Thun, I think I said 'the *Oberland* commenced there. So now for a few words respecting the country designated by that name.

Oberland signifies the Upper Land. It is to Berne what Dieppe is to Paris—the pilgrimage of the citizen class. Parties are arranged to visit the glaciers, as the worthy denizens of Rue St. Martin and Rue St. Denis promise their families some time or other an excursion to the sea. But the Oberland has a still wider celebrity. Englishmen from London and Frenchmen from Paris come on purpose to see this magnificent country, and nothing else; and then return contented, thinking they have seen all of Switzerland worth notice. True, they have traversed its most brilliant features, if not the most singular.

Interlaken, from its position, becomes the usual point of reunion for all travellers after their excursion tour; consequently, it is not unusual to meet the representatives of eight or ten nations at the dinner-table. Conversation there is a Babel which might confuse the most expert philologist; and at the end of a week you have almost unlearned your mother-tongue.

The difficulty of communicating with guides also becomes greater, as few of them speak French except in the most unintelligible manner. During the five days I rambled with mine, I was forced to the most assiduous study of *patois.*

The preparations for departure occupied all the morning, and noon had passed before we set off for Lauter-brunnen.

We received strict charges not to omit visiting the village of Mattin *en route*, where some curious painted glass windows, three centuries old, still exist. One of these paintings struck me as singular. It represents a bear armed with a club, and bearing two turnips in his girdle and one in his paw. The legend is as follows :—

In 1250, the Emperor of Germany, being at war, demanded a contingent of troops from Oberland. At that time three strong and powerful giants dwelt by the Lake of Brienz, who lived by hunting, and clothed themselves with the skins of bears they strangled in their arms. Oberland sent her three giants to the emperor, and thought she had done well.

But, when the emperor saw them, he fell into a rage, having calculated on the arrival of a large troop. However, the giants bade him not be disquieted. True, they had no arms; but only let them visit a forest, and they would soon be armed enough to defeat a whole host.

So it came to pass, that an hour before the battle commenced, they went to a forest near the place of combat, and each, cutting down an immense beech-tree, stripped it of leaves and branches, and transformed it into a club.

Armed with these weapons, they took up their stations in the army, one at the right, the second at the left, and the third in the centre. Down went rank after rank of the enemy at each sweep of these mighty clubs, till at length victory was proclaimed for the side at which they battled. The grateful emperor then addressed them.

"Ask what you will," he said, "and it shall be granted."

The three giants consulted among themselves, after which the eldest answered—

"May it please your gracious majesty to grant us permission, every time we walk by the borders of the lake in your lands of Bonigen, and that we feel thirsty, to pull three turnips each, one to carry in our hands, the two others in our girdles."

So his majesty granted their demand; and the three giants returned home quite enchanted, and enjoyed the privilege of eating imperial turnips all the days of their lives.

A quarter of a league beyond Mattin, we passed the ruined castle of Unspunnen, formerly owned by a lord of that name, held in high consideration by the Council of Berne.

Many times he tried to persuade old Walter de Waldeuschwyl to add the valley of Oberhasli, of which he was lord paramount, to the territory of the city, but all negociations were vain. Then the young Walter fell in love with the daughter of the Lord of Unspunnen, and tried for her sake to persuade his father likewise. Still the old man was inflexible, at which the Lord of Unspunnen being sore enraged, forbade the young people in his wrath ever to behold each other again. They, however, fled away, and left the old men to continue their dispute as best they could.

About a year after this, old Walter died. Then time passed; and one evening, as the châtelain of Unspunnen sat alone in his castle, weeping and mourning for the loss of his only daughter, two pilgrims from Berne demanded hospitality at his gate. He bade them enter, when, kneeling before him and flinging back their hoods, his son and daughter prayed for the paternal benediction on their marriage, at the same time presenting two papers. One was an absolution from the Pope, the other a donation of the valley of Oberhasli to the city of Berne. Entreaties so enforced could not be resisted; besides, the fugitives had already earned their pardon by suffering.

Half-a-league more of travel, and we entered the valley of Lauterbrunnen, the loveliest valley in all Switzerland.

Nowhere is the verdure so rich or the vegetation more rapid. If but a foot of soil deep enough can be found, a tree springs up, proclaiming, "This earth is mine!" and flings its branches over it. If a rock rolls from the arid mountain height, the wind carries to it the dust of the valley, the rain falls and tempers it to clay, the moss gathers and robes it in her mantle. Then a germ is wafted to the soil, and a mass of fibres winds round the rock in all capricious forms, till they strike deep into the bosom of the common mother; and the oak rises proudly to heaven, gaining strength day by day, until at last nothing less than the tempest of God can dethrone the giant.

For half-a-league we travelled through the strangely beautiful country of fantastic outlines and capricious alternations of light and shadow, then reached the Rocher des Frères, once crowned by a castle belonging to two brothers, Ulric and Rodolph. It was their fate to love the one woman. Rodolph was rejected, but hid his grief and hatred in his heart for an hour of vengeance. The day preceding that fixed for the marriage, he asked his brother to hunt with him in the mountains. Suspecting no evil, the affianced bridegroom consented; but on reaching the rock that now bears their name, and seeing no human help or hindrance near, Rodolph drew his poniard and stabbed his brother to the heart. Then, taking a spade which he had hid among the bushes the night before, he dug a grave, laid the murdered Ulric within, and covered him with earth; but he must now hasten to the streamlet near, for his doublet drips with blood. The water has cleansed the stain, and he returns to take a last look at the grave; but lo! the corpse of Ulric is lying unearthed on the spot where he was murdered. Rodolph digs another grave, lays the murdered one within, and stamps down the earth; but the doublet again drips with blood. Again he rushes to the stream, and the stains are cleansed. He turns, and with a shriek of horror beholds the corpse of Ulric again before him. The grave had given up its dead. That evening, the vassals of Ulric found the body of their lord and bore it to the castle. Rodolph fled to the mountains; but, not daring to ask hospitality from any one, perished from hunger.

An inscription cut in the rock verifies these facts, which might else be deemed but a wild, romantic legend. It runs thus:—"Here the Baron of Rothenfluh was murdered by his brother. The murderer fled, and perished in exile and despair, being the last of his once rich and powerful race."

Opposite the ruins of Rothenfluh, like a colossal pendant, rises the Scheinige Platte, a mountain whose red and rounded summit bears evidence of the primitive waters. It was from the crest of this rock a chamois-hunter was flung three thousand feet down into the valley below, by the spirit of the mountain. Here is the legend, as related by my guide:—

"Once on a time there was a hunter, who excelled all others in the mountains for agility and address in his favourite pursuit, so that his skill was renowned, far and near, through the Oberland. One day he pursued a she-goat, a poor expectant mother, over vale and rock, till they came to a precipice she could not traverse, though at another time she would have crossed it with a bound. The harassed, trembling animal, seeing death before and behind her, and no means of escape, lay down by the edge of the abyss and wept like a stag at bay; yet the sight of her agony never stayed the foot or hand of the hunter. He took his bow and fixed an arrow; but, on looking up, beheld an old man before him, seated by the goat and caressing her, while she licked his hands. The old man was the spirit of the mountain. At sight of him the hunter dropped his bow, and the spirit spake.

"'Man of the valley! to whom God has given the riches of the plain, why come you hither to torment the dwellers on the mountain? I never descend to drive away the ox from your stables, nor the hens from your roosts; why then do you ascend to kill the chamois of my rocks, and the eagles of my clouds?'

"'Because God has made me poor,' answered the hunter, 'and has given me nothing of what he gives to other men, except hunger. I have neither hens nor cows, so I must come up here to seek the egg of the wild eagle, and the chamois of the rock. The eagle and the chamois find their food in the mountain, but no food exists for me in the valley.'

"The old man was silent, and reflected; then, beckoning the hunter over, he milked the goat into a wooden cup, and the milk instantly congealed and took the form of a cheese. This he gave to the hunter.

"'Take it,' he said, 'and eat of it when you are hungry,

and when thirsty drink of the sweat that flows from my brow into the valley. This cheese will never fail you, as long as you leave my eagles and my chamois in peace upon their mountains.'

"The hunter promised, descended to the plain, hung up his bow on the wall, and lived for a year on the miraculous cheese, which he always found entire at every fresh meal. Meanwhile the joyous chamois regained their confidence in man, and came bounding and leaping down the valley with their young kids beside them.

"One evening the hunter sat at his window, when a chamois came so near that he could kill it from the spot; the temptation was too strong; he reached down the bow, and, forgetting his promise to the spirit, shot the arrow and killed the animal. Then he went out, took up the poor beast on his shoulders, and dressed it for his supper. When the last bit was eaten he thought of his cheese, by way of dessert, and opened the press where it lay, but out jumped a great black cat, with the eyes and hands of a man, holding the cheese in its mouth, with which it leaped from the window. The hunter cared little, for the chamois had become so plenty that he could shoot them from the valley; and thus he lived a whole year. Then they grew more strange, and kept up in the mountains; so the hunter had to go seek them among the glaciers.

"One day he stood upon the same spot where, three years before, the she-goat had been saved by the mountain spirit. Again a chamois bounded before him; he drew his bow, and it fell close to the edge of the precipice, down which it rolled in its last agonies; the hunter followed and looked over the steep chasm. Beneath, at the bottom of the gulf, stood the old man; their eyes met, and the hunter could not remove his glance. An indescribable giddiness seized him; he tried to fly, but could not. Three times the mountain spirit called him by his name, and at the third time the hunter, uttering a shriek that was heard all over the valley, flung himself into the abyss."

Having reached the inn at Lauterbrunnen and ordered dinner, we hastened off to see the Staubach, one of the most vaunted waterfalls of Switzerland. We had seen,

at a distance, this immense column precipitated nine
hundred feet from the rock in a perpendicular fall,
though slightly arched from the impetus of the higher
particles. We approached as near as we could—just to
the very edge of the basin; it was hollowed out in the
rock, not by its force, but the continuity of its fall; for,
though compact at the first moment of descent, yet it
reaches the ground but in spray. "It is," says Haller,
"a river that has its source in the air, leaps from the
clouds, and is scattered back into the clouds again,
though a rainbow strives to bind it like a variegated
scarf."

Nothing can be more graceful than the movements of
this magnificent cascade. The curves of a young girl's
form, the wavings of a palm, the windings of a serpent,
have not more suppleness than the glittering undulations of this transparent column. Each breath of wind
sets it floating like a banner, so that often, out of the
immense column precipitated from the height, scarcely
more than a few drops reach the basin below. The rest
is carried away by the breeze, for a quarter of a league
or more, and flung upon the trees and flowers of the
valley, like a shower of diamonds.

It is owing to all the strange caprices and beautiful
coquetry of this graceful cascade that no two travellers
ever see it under the same aspect. Every variation of
the air makes it change its form or robe: sometimes
glittering in all the dazzling splendour of the sunlight,
or frozen by the north wind into a grey icy foam; sometimes it is seized by the south wind and hurled back to
its source, where gathering strength, its waters rush
down the valley with redoubled force. Then winter
comes and freezes the sparkling rain as it falls, till, from
the summit, may be seen two enormous pilasters of ice
gradually lengthening and descending, like the work of
some audacious architect who begins to build in the air
ere he rests his foundation on earth.

CHAPTER XX.

PASSAGE OF THE VENGENALP.

NEXT morning a Tyrolienne chanted under our windows by the guide awoke us at break of day. Since we quitted Berne and entered the German territory, popular airs peculiar to each district had accompanied us at every step. One must travel in Germany to comprehend the universality of musical genius amongst its people. Infants are rocked to sleep with songs, and learn music and their mother-tongue together. Men without culture or method take up an instrument and extract sounds from it that would require an educated professor to equal elsewhere. National songs here are not the hoarse utterances of the children of the plains of France: they are the wild cries of the mountaineers of Savoy. They are infinitely varied modulations, produced in some airs by a few notes, in others by daring leaps from one octave ·to another without any intervening gamut. Frequently they are chanted by six persons, each taking the part that best suits his voice, and embellishing as best suits his fancy, with an ease and brilliancy not equalled even in Italy.

I was making these reflections when my guide thought I was asleep, and so commenced another Tyrolienne in a louder voice. I listened to the end, then opened the window.

"Is the weather promising, Willer?" I asked.

"Yes, yes," he replied; "the marmottes are whistling; but if monsieur wishes to see Grinderwald to-day, and the glacier above it, we had better set off now."

"I am ready," I answered, taking my gaiters and

o

blouse, and proceeding to the inn door, where I met
Willer with a bag on his back and my stick in his
hand.   I took it and we set forth.

So here again I had begun my old mountaineer life;
a pilgrimage of hunter, poet, artist, in one; my album
in my pocket, my carbine on my shoulder, my iron-
spiked stick in my hand.   To travel is TO LIVE, in the
full plenitude of the word; 'tis to forget the past and
the future for the present; 'tis to breathe for once free
as the winds of heaven; to enjoy all, appropriate all in
creation as if it were your own; 'tis to light on mines of
gold in the earth that none have touched; in the air on
marvels that none have seen; 'tis to pass after the crowd,
and gather amongst the grass the pearls and diamonds
which they carelessly overlooked as but mere flashes of
snow or drops of dew.

Certes, to each traveller the same scene assumes a dif-
erent aspect.   Others had passed where I had passed,
seen what I had seen, and yet had not returned with the
thousand poetical memories which my foot disturbed in
the dust of centuries.   Perhaps my habits of historic
research aided me in the patient acquisition of such
details.   I searched my guides like manuscripts, too
happy when I found we spoke a common language.
Not a ruin appeared but I must know its history; not a
name was uttered but I must learn its meaning.   And
all these wild tales struck me with an added charm, when
told in the rude poetry of these mountain children, such
as they heard them in their cradles from their fathers·
and fathers' fathers.   Yet the echo of tale and legend,
that flourished like Alpine roses on every peak, in the
gloom of every ravine, at the foot of every glacier, is fast
dying away on the lips of guide and peasant, shamed
into silence by the incredulous smiles of the highly
informed and enlightened travellers of the day.

Unhappily for me, the Vengenalp has no traditions;
but in recompense for the want of historical or poetical
association, I had one of the most glorious prospects
ever beheld, unrolled before the eyes according as I
ascended.   Beneath lay the valley of Lauterbrunnen,
green as emerald, with its red-tiled houses sprinkled over
the turf; before was the magnificent Staubach, flinging

its waters like a glittering silver scarf across the air, then falling in a shower of diamond dust; to the left, a wall of gigantic snow-mountains, as if the world ended there, and amidst them the rushing cataract of the Schmadribach; to the right, the valley we had left, with the Lutchine river, guiding the eye into Interlaken, which, seen through the blue mountain air, seemed like one of those toy cities in boxes, which children build up on the table with their houses and trees.

At the end of an hour, we halted to combine our admiration and our breakfast. Nothing was easier: a rock was our table, a nut-tree gave us shadow, and an iced stream was near. Willer opened his bag, and at the first glance I could see that its contents were admirable enough to entitle him to the post of commissary-general for a whole caravan.

Another hour brought us to the first summit of the Vengenalp by a zigzag path; but once arrived at this spot, the road took a uniform direction for about a league; then you reach a châlet, and make a halt: you are at the foot of the Jungfrau.

I know not if this maidenly appellation gave it a peculiar interest in my eyes, but certainly no name could harmonise more perfectly with its elegant outline and virginal whiteness. Amidst all its colossal sisters and brethren, it stands the proud favourite of travellers and mountaineers.

It is with a smile the guide points out to your notice two other mountains placed on her mighty breast, called by geographers "Silberhorner," but to which the simple guides have given the more natural name of *Mamelles*. They show you to the right the Finster-Aarhorn, higher again than the Jungfrau, rising to above thirteen thousand feet; and the Blumlisalp, more massive in its proportions. Still, beyond all, the Virgin of the Alps is the true mountain-queen.

This name of Virgin was given to the Jungfrau because no being, since the creation of the world, had sullied her mantle of snow; neither the foot of the chamois nor the wing of the eagle had reached the regions that encircled her lofty head. Man, however, determined to deprive her of this proud title. A chamois-

hunter dared for her what Balmat did for Mont Blanc.
After many hazardous attempts, he at last reached the
summit; and, one morning, the astonished mountaineers beheld a red flag floating on the brow of the
desecrated Virgin. Since then, she has been called,
simply, "The Frau;" for, according to them, she has
lost all right to the appellation of "Virgin."

It was to one of the Mamelles that a lammergeyer
(the great vulture of the Alps) carried up a child belonging to Grinderwald and devoured it, without its
parents or any of the village being able to render
assistance, though they heard its cries.

To the right of the Jungfrau rises the Wetterhorn, so
named because, from the presence or absence of clouds
on its summit, the inhabitants can predict the weather.
To the left extends the Blumlisalp (Mountain of Flowers),
upon a base of many leagues; but the name seemed
to me so thoroughly inappropriate—the Mountain of
Flowers being entirely covered with snow—that I had
recourse to Willer for an explanation, who answered
thus:—

"In olden times," he said, "our Alps were not as
bleak as they are now. The sins of men and the vengeance of God brought the snow on our mountains, and
the glacier in our valleys: peaceful flocks once pas-
tured where the eagle and the chamois dare not rest
now. Then the Blumlisalp was loveliest amongst her
sisters, and merited her name of the Mountain of
Flowers. It was the property of a shepherd, who was
rich as a king, and possessed a magnificent herd. In
this herd was one white heifer that he loved above all,
and built it a stable like a palace, which you reached
by a staircase made of cheeses. One winter's day, his
old mother, who was very poor, and lived in the valley,
went to see him, and reproached him for his prodi-
gality. Then he grew angry, and bade her go back to
her village, for he had no place to lodge her in: still,
she begged hard to stay, even in the stable where he
kept his heifer; but he would not, and made his shepherds turn her out at the gate. Now, there was a damp,
icy wind whistling in the air, and the poor woman, as
she descended to the valley, miserably clad as she was,

and shivering with cold, began to implore vengeance on the head of her unnatural son from all the powers above, and stopped and cursed him then and for ever.

" Immediately the rain changed into snow, and every step the mother took downward, the mountain behind her became white as a winding-sheet. On reaching the valley, she fell dead from cold and hunger, and next day the whole Mountain of Flowers was a mountain of snow."

While Willer told me this tale, a sound like a roll of thunder intermingled with a violent breaking of the ice, resounded through the mountain. I thought we were lost, and looked at my guide. "What is it?" I said.

Then he extended his hand towards the Jungfrau, and showed me what seemed a silver ribbon floating from the flank of the mountain. "What!" said I; "a cascade?"

"No—an avalanche," he replied.

"And was it that produced the terrible detonation?"

"The same."

I could not believe it. It seemed impossible that a stream of snow, like a mere scarf of floating gauze, could have filled the air with thunder; and I looked around for some other more probable solution. When I turned my glance again on the Jungfrau it was calm as ever: The cascade had disappeared.

Willer then told me to fire off my carbine. I did so; and the report at first appeared to me less loud than on the plain; but gradually it struck against the mountain side, and was flung back with added intensity from rock to rock, till the multiplied echoes blended into one thunder-peal; and then, as the last vibrations ceased, a hoarse, hollow, rumbling sound pervaded the mountain, such as I had first heard; and my guide, pointing to one of the Mamelles of the Jungfrau, showed me an improvvised avalanche hurled from the summit by the violence of the vibration, and falling in thunder to the valley.

I now saw how slight a cause could produce such an effect.

Just then, one of the mountain idiots, a double *cre-tin*, appeared carrying a little cannon, which he planted at our feet, and pointed with as much care as if he were going to batter down a town; then applied a match, and in an instant the mountain thunder was again awakened, and another avalanche rolled from the summit to the valley.

In fact, the poor devil was by trade a maker of avalanches, and testified much dismay that I should undertake to make them on my own account with my carbine. However, I reassured him by paying for my own avalanche at the usual tariff of his cannon explosions, and explaining that I had no idea of rivalling him with the travellers of the Vengenalp.

Having satiated our eyes with the magnificent spectacle, we continued our ascent till we reached the most elevated point of the mountain crest. The pine forests of the base had long ceased to fling their shadows over us: at first they stood firm and close in rank and file, like a proud army of invaders; then only in scattered groups, like men fighting their way for life through a hostile land, till at the summit we found the last remnant, bleak and blasted; the mountain ice-breath had conquered, and the dead trunks lay like corpses around.

Before descending, a strange circle attracted my attention, about thirty paces in circumference, perfectly bleak and bare, although all around the earth blossomed with the Alpine rose and purple gentianella. On asking the cause, Willer related the following the legend, telling me at the same time very candidly, he did not believe it:—

" Once on a time, a great magician dwelt in the valley of Gadmin, who made the animals serve him like intelligent creatures. Every Saturday night, he gathered them around him on the high mountain peak: eagles from the clouds, bears from the forest, serpents from their holes; and then tracing a circle with his ring, which they could not pass, stood in the centre, and gave them his orders to the four quarters of the Oberland.

" One night, however, his orders were of such a nature, that they refused their accustomed service, at which the magician grew in wrath, and for the first time uttered a terrible spell to force them to obey; a spell so potent, that he himself trembled in the utterance. Scarcely were the words pronounced when he saw two dragons leave the troop of reptiles, and proceed to a neighbouring cavern. He thought they had gone to execute his mission, but they soon re-appeared, bearing on their backs an enormous serpent, with eyes shining like carbuncles, and a crown of diamonds on his head. This was the king of the basilisks. They all approached to the edge of the circle, and then the dragons, lifting their king on their shoulders, flung him over, so that he passed it without touching. The magician had only time to make the sign of the cross, and exclaim—'I am lost!' Next day he was found dead within the magic circle, upon which no grass has since grown."

Having quitted the accursed spot, we proceeded to Grinderwald, reaching it, happily, without meeting either the king or queen of the basilisks. Then, ordering dinner, we set off for the glacier, about a quarter of an hour's walk distant.

I have already said so much of glaciers that I may pass this one of Grinderwald in silence, merely relating an anecdote connected with it, which illustrates remarkably the courage and devotedness found amongst the mountain guides.

One ascends the glacier of Grinderwald by a set of steps rudely cut in the ice. I scarcely cared to go up; but Willer, who knew my weakness for anecdotes, told me something at the top would interest me, so I followed him.

On reaching the surface of the glacier, I found it broken up into deep cavities, the sides of which met together sixty or one hundred paces down.

Willer generaly leaped over these *crevasses*, and I did the same, till, after a quarter of an hour's march, we came upon one as large and round as the opening of a well, and so deep that a stone was many seconds falling to the bottom.

" Here it was," said the guide, "that M. Mouron, pastor of Grinderwald, was killed in 1821."

And thus it happened :—

M. Mouron, who was a man of both active mind and

body, devoted all his leisure hours to excursions on the mountain for the purpose of scientific observation, and, being a distinguished philosopher and botanist, obtained many valuable results from his meteorological and other investigations; besides which, he formed an herbærium, containing all the Alpine plants classed in families.

One day, while herbalising on the glacier, he paused at this *crevasse* where we stood, and threw down stones to judge of its depth by the echo, resting his iron-pointed stick on the opposite side, and bending over to listen. Suddenly the stick slipped down the steep side, and the pastor was precipitated into the chasm.

The guide who accompanied him, unable to render any assistance, rushed back breathless to the village to recount the accident.

Some days passed, and the tragic death of their beloved pastor became the talk of the whole country. Gradually suspicions arose; and, finally, it was alleged that he had been murdered by the guide, for the sake of his watch and purse, and afterwards flung into the *crevasse*.

Immediately the whole body of guides met to consider a case which dishonoured one of their members ; and it was agreed that one should be selected, by lot, to descend the precipice, at the peril of his life, where the unfortunate pastor had fallen; when, if the watch and purse were found upon the corpse, the guide should be declared innocent.

The lot fell upon one of the strongest and most vigorous men in the country, named Burguenen.

On the appointed day, the whole village assembled on the glacier. Burguenen had a cord tied round his waist, and a lantern suspended from his neck ; then, taking a bell in his hand, to ring whenever he wished to be drawn up, and his iron-spiked stick to aid in his descent, he let himself be lowered by a cable held by four men.

Twice, on the point of being suffocated for want of air, he rang, and had to be drawn up to the surface: at last, on his bell being sounded for the third time, a heavy weight was felt at the end of the rope, and finally Burguenen appeared, along with the mutilated corpse of the pastor. Both purse and watch were found upon the body of the dead man!

The stone erected over the pastor's grave records the mode of his death, and the devotion of the guides who recovered the body for Christian sepulture, after it had lain twelve days in the abyss.

Burguenen estimated the depth of the descent at seven hundred and fifty feet.

CHAPTER XXI.

THE FAULHORN.

NEXT day, at eight o'clock, we set off to attempt the most difficult ascent we had yet undertaken; in fact, we were ambitious of sleeping in the highest habitation of Europe—that is to say, at eight thousand one hundred and twenty-one feet above the level of the sea—five hundred and seventy-nine feet higher than the hospital of St. Bernard, at the last limit of the eternal snow.

The Faulhorn, if not the highest, is at least one of the highest mountains in the chain which separates the valleys of Thun, Interlaken, and Brienz, from those of Grinderwald and Rosenlauwi. Lately, an innkeeper established a small hostelry there, which, however, is only habitable in summer. As soon as October arrives he breaks up his establishment, carries off the door and windows, until the next summer, and then abandons the empty shell to the storms of heaven, which rage within and without till scarcely a beam is left in its place.

Our host of the valley took great pains to assure us, that aliment for natural life was scarce and bad in the lofty regions whither we were going; for, that the innkeeper up there could only get up his marketing once a-week, leaving but a bad chance for those who came to visit him at the end of that period. He, therefore, entirely for our own interest, advised us to return and dine with him. We thanked him for his tender solicitude, but declined; after which, I regret to say, he manifested the most complete indifference about our welfare—even refusing to sell me a cold fowl which I desired, in case absolute starvation should await us at the top.

However, I took my gun, and trusted to chance and skill for a dinner, though success in such matters is very precarious on Swiss mountains, the game having gradually deserted all the paths and haunts of travellers. I therefore took bypaths, plunged into thickets, and watched and listened with the utmost assiduity for some time.

" Hush!" said my guide at last; " do you hear?"

" Well!" said I; " what is it? I hear a whistling sound."

" The marmots," he answered. " Look you, the marmot is a precious dish."

" The devil! if I could but catch this one!"

" Oh, that you never will. Such a taste as they have. You skin and roast them like a hare, and pour broth or cream over them, with a few herbs round, and then, when you have eaten the flesh and sucked the bones, faith, you may lick your fingers."

" Ah! my friend, tell me how to kill one," I exclaimed.

" Impossible! They are too 'cute; but when cold, with pepper and vinegar, and a little parsley, and maybe a glass of wine added, look you, there never was anything in the world so delicious."

" Then, can you not aid me? I must have one for supper this evening."

" No, no, master; the beasts take good care to keep out of the way; they know too well how good they are, roast or boiled. Your only chance is in winter, when you may catch them asleep in their holes, rolled up as round as balls."

As I could not wait for winter to taste a marmot, I set forth incontinently in search of the one near us; but as I approached the whistling ceased. The animal had probably re-entered its hole. Another and another served me in the same way, till, after five or six ineffectual attempts, I at last acknowledged that my guide had spoken truth.

Very mournfully, therefore, I was making my way

back to the road, when an unknown bird started up at
my feet. I fired, and my guide cried out that it was
wounded. Still, the bird continued its flight, and I
began to run after the bird.

No one but a sportsman comprehends the strange
paths one can traverse while pursuing game. I am no
intrepid mountaineer; but truly I now bounded like a
chamois from rock to rock, never minding where my
foot rested, so intently were my eyes fixed on the curves
described by the prey I followed; at last, it fell at the
other side of the torrent. I sprang across, never paus-
ing to calculate the breadth, seized my prize—my supper. It was a magnificent white woodcock.

Turning round with a shout of triumph to my guide,
I perceived for the first time the immense distance I
had run. He was at least a quarter of a league behind
me. To regain the road where we had parted company
was then my object; but how? First, there was the
torrent to recross—a good leap of fifteen feet, though I
had never heeded the breadth in the ardour of the chase.
Now, I took a run at it twice, and twice stopped at the
edge. My guide laughed aloud, and feeling myself
thoroughly humbled, I sneaked up the bank, seeking a
narrower point to cross.

In vain; there was none; and I found myself only
going more and more out of my way. Then I turned
back and tried the other direction, when, getting a hill
between me and my guide, I took advantage of the
secresy cast upon my movements, to sound the stream
with a branch of pine. Finding it but two or three feet
deep, I plunged in boldly, and reached the other side,
saturated up to the waist. Next there was a mountain
to ascend; I looked up, and saw Willer at top. "Bring
me my stick," I roared out, "or I shall never get up this
path." I could have said, "Throw it down to me;" but
in truth, I wanted to give him trouble. Rancour was in
my heart in consequence of certain explosions of laughter at sight of my dripping pantaloons, which had reached
my ears. However, down Willer came, with all the
courtesy and respect one never fails to meet amongst
these brave guides, and helped, and pushed, and lifted,
and dragged me up, till at last, after three-quarters of

hour's toil, I regained the distance which, as a sportsman, I had traversed in five minutes.

Still we had to ascend, and under aggravated difficulties, for a cold, sharp wind began to buffet our faces, carrying with it flakes of snow left unmelted by the summer sun. At another time I would not have minded these little difficulties, but after my cold bath nothing could have been more unpleasant. I began to freeze as we passed a little lake situated seven thousand feet above the level of the sea; so it was no wonder if, at the summit of the Faulhorn, eleven hundred and twenty-one feet higher, I froze completely.

The little tavern was at hand. I rushed in, and totally regardless of all I had travelled so far to see, demanded a fire—nothing but a fire—from the host. In truth, it was small compensation to me, thinking I was located in the highest dwelling of Europe, if destined to die there of inflammation.

"How many pounds of wood do you wish?" asked mine host.

"Eh! *pardieu*, my dear friend!" I answered; "give me a fagot, no matter what it weighs. I am too cold to buy heat by the ounce."

He disappeared, and returned with a bundle, which he threw into a scale at hand.

"Thirty francs for this bunch, monsieur," he said.

Having been born and bred in a forest, the price certainly struck me as extravagant.

"*Dame*, monsieur!" exclaimed the host, comprehending my expression; "when men have to go seek it four or five leagues off, and carry it up on their backs, it's not so much. Besides, one must have wood for the kitchen, which, in truth, makes victuals come a little dear here."

The last phrase foreboded no good to my purse. However, my dinner fortunately was secure, though it cost thirty francs for wood to warm me for procuring it.

My next measure was to retreat to my chamber with the new purchase; and, lighting up ten francs' worth, I changed my dress for one more suited to the climate, and thus enjoyed the thawing efficacy of the fire.

When I had finished, Willer entered to inform me

that I must hasten out to view the magnificent scene
around, or it would all be obscured, as a thunder-storm
was gathering.

We accordingly set forth; and a little ascent of about
fifteen feet brought us to the very highest point of the
Faulhorn.

There before us, towards the north, extended the
whole chain of glaciers that we had seen since quitting
Berne: a range of colossal giants—their snowy mantles
and white hair seeming a personification of the past centuries—hand in hand encircling the world.

Some amongst them, such as the Wetterhorn, the
Finsterhorn, the Jungfrau, and the Blumlisalp, sur-
passed the others by a whole head—the patriarchs of
the giant race; while, from time to time, an avalanche
glided from the summit and wound amongst the rocks,
like an immense serpent with its glittering silver scales
shining in the sunlight.

To the south, the scene had a totally different aspect.
Three steps from the place where we stood, the mountain, cleft asunder perpendicularly by some cataclysm,
gave to view, at a depth of six thousand five hundred
feet beneath us, the whole valley of Interlaken, and two
lakes which seemed like immense mirrors framed in
emerald, for God to behold his face in from heaven.

Beyond, in the distance, rose sombre, detached masses
upon a blue horizon. These were Le Pilate and the
Righi flanking Lucerne, like giants placed to guard
some marvellous treasure; while the Lake of the Four
Cantons bathed their feet; and behind them glittered
the blue waters of Zug, mingling with the blue sky,
which it seemed to touch.

While I gazed, clouds that seemed storm-bringers
rose from the high summits of the Wetterhorn and the
Jungfrau, advancing silently, dark, and menacing, like
two opposing armies who wait till they meet face to face
before opening their destructive fire. I saw that one of
nature's grandest scenes was approaching—a tempest in
the mountains. The clouds moved onwards with extreme velocity, yet no breath of air stirred around: they
seemed impelled towards each other by some invincible,
mysterious attraction. A profound silence reigned over

nature, undisturbed by the cry of a single living thing. All creation seemed awaiting, mute and immoveable, the awful crisis that was approaching.

A flash of lightning, followed by a detonation, echoed back from mountain and glacier, proclaimed that the clouds had met and the combat begun. Suddenly animation seemed restored to the world by the electric shock, and creation started to life with every symptom of affright. A hot, heavy wind passed over us, nearly uprooting a large wooden cross planted on the mountain. The dogs howled; and three chamois, springing suddenly to sight, bounded on a cleft of rock close at hand. I fired, but the shot fell harmlessly on the snow, and never seemed even to attract their attention, so entirely were they absorbed in the terrors of the tempest.

Meanwhile the clouds advanced and struck, flashing lightning for lightning; and from all points of the horizon other clouds of various hue and form rushed upwards to the combat, adding their thunders to the elemental war. Then the entire south glowed with a fiery red, the sky around the sun deepening in colour as if the focus of a fire, till the whole scene was lit up by a fantastic illumination. The Lake de Thun rolled its waves of flame; that of Brienz was tinged a pale green, fringed with coloured lamps like a decoration at the opera; and the waters of Zug and the Four Cantons changed their azure hue for a pale dead white.

Soon the wind redoubled in violence, lashing the clouds before it till they scattered into broken masses, then hurling them down towards the earth, where they formed a dark, dense curtain, veiling the whole scene from our view.

Heavy drops of rain fell, a thick mist was around us, and the lightning ran along my carbine, so that I dropped it as if it were red-hot steel. We were in the crisis of the tempest. Then was a rush for shelter, and the inn. We reached it, but the rain beat the windows, the storm shook it like an earthquake, and the thunder seemed literally to strike upon the door.

Ten minutes passed, and all was over. The sun shone through the mist, the sky was serene, and we ventured forth once more. The storm which had raged above was now beneath our feet: a hundred feet down, the thunder was resounding, and the tempest rolling its waves like a vast sea in an abyss lit up by lightning; while, from the middle of this ocean rose up, like great islands, the snowy heads of Eiger, Monck, Blumlisalp, and the Jungfrau.

Suddenly a living creature appeared battling with the tempest surges, then rising above them. It was one of the large eagles of the Alps seeking the sun; and now perceiving the splendour, it soared majestically to meet it, passing within forty paces of me; yet I never thought of firing, so completely was my attention absorbed in the magnificence of the scene.

Fatigued and excited with all I had suffered and seen, I retired to my chamber, but not to rest. A peculiar cry rising up from the valley startled us all. The guides gathered together and listened. It was a cry of distress. "There are travellers lost on the mountain," they exclaimed; "let us light our torches, let slip the dogs, and hasten to the rescue."

Instantly each hastened to prepare for the task—to seek torches, rum, and whatever else was needed—then, all together, uttering a loud peculiar cry, as a notice to the travellers that help was approaching, they set forward to the rescue.

I took my torch along with the others; not that I had the presumption to suppose I could traverse a path by night which by day I had to cross on all-fours, but I wished to witness the details of the scene. Therefore, seating myself on a ledge of rock, I watched the troop of guides as they proceeded down, then broke up in different directions, their torches gleaming like meteors on a marsh amid the snowy waste. During half-an-hour this wildfire dance was kept up—the lights now gleaming from a ravine, now glittering on a peak, while all the evolutions were accompanied with the shouts of men, the bark of dogs, and the discharge of pistols. Finally, all the lights concentrated at one particular spot, where they rested a space; after which, a long advancing line could be distinguished ascending to the inn. As the light of the torches flickered over the procession, I could make out a confused mass of men, women, children;

mules, horses, and dogs—all speaking, neighing, and howling, after their kind : it was Noah's ark launched into the tower of Babel.

On joining the caravan and anaylsing the contents, I found there ten Americans, one German, and one Englishman; all in the most deplorable state possible. The Americans had been found in the lake, the German in the snow, and the Englishman hanging on by the branch of a tree, over a precipice three hundred feet deep.

But none were lost; and the night closed with the most perfect tranquillity.

CHAPTER XXII.

ROSENLAUWI.

NEXT morning, at eight o'clock, every one assembled—
infantry and cavalry—on the plateau of Faulhorn; the
cavalry consisting of a French lady, an American gentleman with his wife and seven children; and the infantry of the eldest son of this voluminous family, myself,
the Englishman, and six guides.

As to the German, he was unable to stir without uttering the most inhuman cries, so we left him behind at
the inn, where probably he still remains, unless Providence worked a special miracle in his favour, and restored his shattered bones.

As soon as the bottles were filled, and the mules har-
nessed, the little army began its march, with all the
gaiety of spirit caused by reaction after the escape of a
great danger.

Our intention was to proceed first to the glacier of
Rosenlauwi, then on to Meyringen for the night. It
was a long journey; but our ladies were well mounted,
and as to myself and comrades, we had limbs to vie with
the stoutest mountaineers of Oberland. I say comrades,
for we were the best friends in the world before a hun
dred steps were traversed. In fact, I had met the
American before in Paris; and as to the Englishman, he
was gay and frank, unlike the generality of his country-
men, though his face retained the most absurd gravity
in the midst of all his gambols; which, truly, could not
be exceeded in daring, dexterity, and imprudence. Our
guides looked on with visible admiration and wonder,
evidently thinking, "Well done! right well done! but

you will break your neck some day;" while he leaped
over precipices, hopped on one leg across trees flung
as bridges over the torrents, plunged down chasms to
gather wild-flowers, which might have remained there
an eternity before I would peril my life to seek them.

This rashness was the more meritorious as the road
we traversed was detestable in the extreme. At every
step men slipped, mules stumbled, and ladies screamed;
part of the way was on the edge of a precipice one thousand five hundred feet deep, and along a path so narrow
that the guides had not room to walk by the mules. At
this untoward spot the mule which carried the American's eldest daughter became restive, and threw the
young lady out of her saddle. For an instant it was
doubtful at which side she would fall, and death and life
were involved in that moment; but fortunately one of
the guides had the presence of mind to give her an impulse with the end of his staff, which sent her to the
ground opposite the fatal precipice, safe from harm, except from the infliction of a few bruises.

This accident threw the whole caravan into disorder :
ladies leaped from their saddles, and in leaping fell ;
cries rent the air ; every one thought they were going
to be killed, and called upon every one else to help
them ; the dogs barked, the guides swore, the mules
took advantage of the confusion to crop the herbage;
and the Englishman, perched on a point twenty-five
feet above our heads, that would give the vertigo to a
chamois, whistled tranquilly "God save the King."

In an instant, however, order was re-established; our
ladies, dragged from under their mules and placed one
by one under the care of guides, traversed the rest of the
road in safety, and in ten minutes we were securely
anchored on a greensward as rich and beautiful as the
garden of Versailles.

Here we encamped for breakfast. The ladies regained
their carriage, the panic was forgotten, and full of new
courage we proceeded strengthened on our journey.

According as we descended the atmosphere became
more temperate, and the pines re-appeared within their
own peculiar region, which, as if by some enchanter's
wand, they are forbidden to pass; and without any fur-

ther accident, the whole caravan defiled safely through the gate of the Rosenlauwi inn.

Merely stopping to take a warm bath—a process which required no delay, as a thermal spring was at hand—we set forward to visit the glacier, one of the most renowned in all Oberland.

The storm, which the evening previous had rolled beneath our feet, now thundered above our heads, in consequence of our change of elevation; yet we had the courage to proceed in spite of elemental warnings.

The glacier of Rosenlauwi merits its reputation; for, if not the largest, it is certainly the most beautiful in all Oberland. The tint is peculiar to itself, being of the loveliest azure throughout, though the shade varies from the palest turquoise to the deepest sapphire.

From an opening near the base, like the portal of a fairy palace, issue forth the sparkling waters of the Reichenbach; while marvellous columns, so light and transparent that they seem the work of genii, sustain the vaulted roof, interwoven with a glittering fretwork of crystals.

On gazing down into the cavern, within which the torrent foams and frets, one is startled at the fantastic beauty of the architecture: it seems the dwelling of some nymph or goddess, some fairy Undine of the legends of romance.

The noise produced by the rush of water, as it dashes and breaks in foam on the rocks, absolutely made the thundering of the storm inaudible; though the tempest had doubled its force, we had forgotten its existence, until reminded by the dull, heavy plashing of the large raindrops. Then, looking up, we saw the dark sky descending gradually upon the mountains as if it would crush them; then lower, lower, as if it would finally crush us. The air was stifling; we breathed with difficulty, as though under a vast pneumatic machine; but a single flash seemed wanting to light up the whole dense volume of atmosphere into flame.

At last came a thunder-peal, rending asunder the black pall of vapour; and the storm, lashing the air, flapped its heavy wings, dripping with rain, down upon our heads.

Having fled to a tree for shelter, we made a tent with our poles and blouses for the ladies, till the rain poured through like a shower-bath, and we judged it best to make a run for the inn, though at each step the water came nearly to our knees.

"Give us fresh clothes!" we exclaimed to Willer, on arriving, like a file of mountain torrents, at our destination.

"Impossible!" he answered. "I have sent all the luggage on to Meyringen."

"What! not even a pocket-handkerchief left?"

"Not one."

"Then we must all to bed, and dine reclining, like Roman emperors."

And thus we did, falling into peaceful slumber afterwards, from which I was startled, I know not at what hour, by the entrance of the maid with a flambeau in her hand.

"How now?" I exclaimed. "What is the matter?"

"Nothing, monsieur, except that you had better get up, for the stream has been swollen by the tempest, and the bridge carried away, and we are afraid the house will be carried away too."

"The house?"

"Oh, yes, monsieur; it happened once before : not to this one, but to another."

"And my clothes?"

"Just slip them on as quick as you can."

Never was a toilet made with such expedition. I passed my arms through the blouse, ran down stairs, and rushed into the kitchen. The water reached above my knees.

"Here, monsieur!" cried the girl. I did not heed her, but perceiving a door, hastened to it.

"Monsieur! monsieur!" she screamed, "you will be drowned."

I jumped on a table to leap out of the window.

"Monsieur, you are going right into the river!"

"Well, then, where *am* I to go? Better have left me in my bed, if you did not mean to provide a boat."

"But, monsieur, you should have leaped from the window on the first floor."

" The deuce!   And why not tell me that before?"

" I have been telling you so all along, but you would not listen, running about like a madman."

" True; I was wrong.   Conduct me now where you will."

Accordingly, we ascended to the first floor, and she pointed out a plank, one end of which rested on the window, the other on the mountain.

" Is that what I am to escape by?" I demanded. " It looks rather too much like Mahomet's bridge for a good Christian to venture his neck on."

" Are you afraid?   Bah!   Your friend the Englishman passed it in a jump."

" Ah!   And the ladies?—did they jump it too?"

" No; the guides carried them."

" Well, could not they carry me?"

" Why, no; for they have all gone to the mountain for wood to dam the stream."

I found no resource left for me except to brave the worst; but, in place of going afoot, I went astride; so that, had any one seen me during the transit, he would certainly have taken me for a sorcerer riding to a sabbath on a broomstick.   On reaching the end of my plank and alighting on *terra firma*, I perceived a spot illuminated by torches, to which I hastened.   The view from thence was strange and magnificent.   The cascade, whose light, aërial grace we had admired in the morning, was now a foaming, fearful torrent, sweeping down stones, and rocks, and pine-trees in its course; while the guides, naked to the waist, cut down enormous branches, with all the energy of mountaineers, and flung them as a dam to stem the waters; others standing round in a circle, with lighted torches in their hands, to guide the efforts of the workers.   At length, every strong arm was needed; and the torch-bearers, seizing axes in their turn, looked round for some place to fix the torches. Perceiving their embarrassment, I took a flambeau from one of them, and running to an isolated pine that commanded the scene, fired its resinous branches; ten minutes after, the whole trunk shot up in flame from the base to the summit, forming a magnificent candelabrum, perfectly in harmony with the scene it illuminated. Strange and grand, like a scene from the primitive earth, was this spectacle of men warring against the elements; flinging down these mighty trees, which in other countries would have been the sole property of a king, beneath their mountain axes, as if the land and all its produce were their own: just as the first warrers against the Deluge may have worked and striven. As for me, I was seized with a kind of intoxication from excitement, and hewed at a monstrous pine till I laid it low, and shouted a cry of victory. It was the only moment of fatuity in my life; but my strength seemed at the instant supernatural, as though I could have hewn down the whole forest without resting.

But now the cry, "Enough!" resounded on all sides. Every axe fell to the ground. The torrent was vanquished at last; and destruction ceased when it became no longer necessary.

Immediately, all of us returned to the inn to finish our slumber, which was accomplished in perfect safety, a guard having been placed to give notice in case of further danger from the irruption of the waters.

Next morning we proceeded to Meyringen, along a road which bore frightful traces of the last night's storm: fierce and foaming torrents, shattered fragments of rock, mighty trees torn up by the roots, and lying prone with all their branches, formed perpetually recurring barricades, which our ladies and their mules often found it difficult to pass.

At length our caravan reached the peak of a little mountain, dividing the valley of Rosenlauwi from that of Meyringen, where we found a delicious verdant plain, inviting us to repose by the aspect of its velvet sward. Nature is a coquette; and amid the rudest rocks and cliffs, made but for the eagle and the chamois, unveils suddenly some secret beauty to tempt the approach of man. Like a true woman, she is not content without universal homage. That of the lower animals does not suffice her: the lord of creation must likewise be brought to her feet; and therefore some gentle, winning grace is mingled even with her wildest and most terrible moods.

It was on the plateau of Meyringen that these fancies wandered through my head; for Nature's loveliness seemed more lovely when she thus suddenly unveiled her beauty after our long, dreary journey, through torrent, and tempest, and barren mountain walls.

For half-an-hour we gave ourselves up to ecstasy, then proceeded to the waterfall of Reichenbach, whose position we could already distinguish by the cloud of watery vapour that rose up like smoke from a volcano. We reached it by a steep ascent, from which elevation the water plunges down into an abyss eighty feet beneath, rising again in a humid dust so dense, that a hut is built near on purpose for spectators to shelter themselves from the rain, which springs from earth and rises to heaven.

A trade is carried on here in pretty, elegant sculptured toys in wood; cups and vases, wreathed with ivy and oak, can be had to equal those for which Virgil's shepherds disputed; but the prices run high. I saw a pair of vases sell for a hundred francs.

There is a second cascade, about a hundred feet lower, which Ovid's lines in the first book of the Metamorphoses describe to a miracle. I beg, therefore, the reader may seek the description for himself, as it will save me all further trouble.

From Meyringen to Brienz is a journey of two hours, and there the celebrated cascade of Geissbach claims especial notice; but one wearies even of waterfalls; and, truth to say, during the last week I had seen so many of them, that an absolute nausea came over me at the sound of all words ending in *bach*. However, it was our duty to see the Geissbach; so we went, saw its eleven falls, and listened to its thunder, which can be heard a league off. Then, taking a boat, we promised double *trinkgeld* to our rowers if they reached Interlaken before five o'clock.

Thus stimulated, we skimmed the waters of the lake like sea-birds, merely observing, as we passed, the Tanzplatz, for the sake of its story. It is a greensward, where the villagers once held their dances. One ay a young pair of lovers, whose union had been forbi den by their parents, met in a waltz. Their arms entw ed, their lips met; but, at each turn, it was observed ney approached nearer to the edge of the precipice;

the excitement of the dance seemed to reach its height; and, pressing each other in a last embrace, they flung themselves from the height into the lake beneath. Next day the bodies were found, still locked in the death-embrace.

After dinner we took a walk in the Hohbuhl, the pretty promenade of Interlaken. It is laid out in the English style, and offers nothing worthy of notice except a seat upon which Henry of France, Caroline de Berry, and François de Châteaubriand, have engraved their names.

On returning, Willer asked me by which road I proposed to leave Interlaken for the small cantons. There were three: the Gemmi, the Grimsel, and the Brunig. I decided for the Gemmi; but, should I again have to make a choice, the Grimsel or Brunig would have the preference.

CHAPTER XXIII.

MONT GEMMI.

WE left Interlaken at five in the morning, in a chaise, which was to carry us as far as Kandersteg, after which the road was impracticable for carriages. However, our limbs were saved for at least half the way—a luxury not to be disdained, considering that afterwards we had to cross one of the roughest of the Alpine mountains.

About six o'clock we found ourselves in the valley of the Kander, and at ten reached Kandersteg, where my faithful Willer rejoined me. For a league or so we coasted along the base of the Blumlisalp, which, however, no longer bears the name of the Mountain of Flowers, but the more appropriate designation of Wild Frau, in consequence of the maternal malediction associated with it. Yet another legend, still more tragical, filled my mind at the moment; the one on which Werner founded his drama of "The Twenty-fourth of February;" and we were actually approaching the inn of Schwarrbach, where he laid the scene.

Every one knows this drama, in which Fate pursues a family of peasants, as in the ancient trilogies it pursued a race of kings; in which, during three generations, these shepherd Atrides are destined to avenge the sins of the past on the present, at the same day and hour in each year. It is a drama to be read at midnight, while the storm rages and the lamp flickers, till the marrow seems to freeze in your bones from terror: a drama which Werner flung to the world, not for glory, not for the applause of a theatre, but to free his soul from the burden of incessant, unconquerable gloom, that gnawed it like the Promethean vulture.

The story of this poem of darkness and horror is as follows:—

An old peasant and his son dwelt once on a rude Alpine peak; the young man felt the necessity of a companion, and, despite of his father, wedded Trude, the daughter of a neighbouring pastor, who, when dying, left nothing behind him except long sermons and old books. The want of a dower made Trude an unwelcome daughter-in-law, and frequent altercations took place between her and the old man, which were resented by the son, whose feelings day by day became embittered against his father in consequence of his treatment of the wife.

One evening—it was the 24th of February—young Kuntz returned home in high spirits from a festival given at Louëche. Singing the chorus of a jovial song, he entered the house and found his father scolding Trude, who wept bitterly. In an instant anger filled his heart; but, out of respect to the old man, he kept silence. The perspiration stood on his brow, he bit his lips and clenched his hands; still no word escaped him.

This seemed to embolden the father, and he became more bitter and insulting; till at last the son looked at him, and with a low, demoniacal laugh, took down a scythe from the wall. " The grass will soon be ripe," he said; " I must sharpen this instrument:" and he began sharpening it with a knife, while he sang one of those pretty Alpine ditties, as fresh and simple as the wild-flowers of the glacier:—

> " Un chapeau sur la tête,
> De petites fleurs dessus;
> Une chémise de berger
> Avec de jolis rubans."

The old man still raged and stormed; the son continued singing. At length old Kuntz, exasperated to the highest pitch, flung one of those epithets to his daughter-in-law that a husband can never pardon. The young man sprang up, pale, trembling, and furious; the knife, the accursed knife, was in his hand; and, no doubt impelled by the demon, he rushed upon his father. The old man fell, cursed the parricide, and expired!

From that moment misfortune took up its abode beneath the roof. Kuntz and Trude continued to love each other, but with that sombre, gloomy love that bore the memory of blood. Six months after, a son was born to them. The last words of the murdered man had been to curse the child in the womb of its mother; and, like Cain, it bore the brand—a bloody scythe upon the left arm.

Some time after, their cottage was burned down; then disease carried off their herds; and, finally, a slide of snow from the summit of the Rinderhorn covered the ground for two leagues, burying the whole farm and fertile pastures of Kuntz beneath it.

Nothing was left for him now but to turn innkeeper. Five years after the birth of their son, a daughter was born, and they fondly hoped that God's vengeance had ceased; for the child was beautiful, and bore no brand of malediction on its frame.

One evening—it was the 24th of February—when the girl was two years old and the boy seven, the two children were playing on the threshold with the knife that had killed their grandfather. The mother came and took it to cut the throat of a fowl for dinner; the boy watched her; then, with that love of blood that seems instinctive to some natures, said to his little sister, "Come, let us play; I shall be cook, and thou the chicken." Upon which, taking the accursed knife, he drew her behind the door: five minutes after the mother heard a scream, the little girl lay steeped in blood, her throat cut across. Then Kuntz cursed his son, as his father had cursed him.

The boy fled, and no one knew whither he went.

From that day everything went wrong. The fish died in the lake, the corn was blighted, the snow covered the valley, and travellers could no longer come to the inn. Kuntz was utterly ruined. One by one he sold off everything he was worth, even to the cottage that sheltered him, but which he was allowed to keep possession of on condition of paying rent. Then a time came that he could no longer pay rent for the few planks that kept the snow and rain from beating on the head of the parricide.

. One evening—it was the 24th of February—Kuntz returned from Louëche, where he had gone to beg a little more time from the landlord; but a delay of twenty-four hours was all he could obtain. Then he had gone about amongst his rich friends; begged, implored, conjured them by all that was most sacred, to save him from despair: not one extended a hand. He met a beggar by the roadside, who shared his loaf with him; Kuntz brought the bread home, threw it on the table, and said to his wife, " Eat, woman'; I have dined."

Meanwhile the storm raged-outside, the wind roared like a hungry lion, and the snow fell dense and heavy. The scared night-birds came flapping their heavy wings against the window, attracted by the light from the cottage, within which sat the husband and wife face to face, yet scarcely daring to look at each other, or, if their eyes met, each started at the wild, ghastly expression upon the face of the other.

At this moment a traveller knocked; the pair within trembled. Another knock, and Trude opened the door.

A fine young man of about four-and-twenty entered, dressed as a hunter, with pistols in his belt along with his purse, a hunting-knife by his side, and a stout mountain staff in his hand.

Kuntz and Trude both looked at the belt, and then exchanged a rapid glance.

" You are welcome," said Kuntz, extending his hand; " but your hand trembles."

" It is from cold," said the young man, regarding him with a strange expression; then opening his sack, he produced a fowl, fried meat, and a flask of brandy. " Will you not sup with me?" he said.

" I never eat fowl," said Kuntz.

" Nor I," said Trude.

" Nor I," said the traveller.

And all three supped on the other things. Kuntz drank lustily.

Then, supper being over, Trude went to the inner room, put a mattress on the floor, and returning, said to the stranger, "Your bed is ready."

" Good night, then," he replied.

" A good night's rest to you," responded Kuntz.

The young man entered the room, shut the door, and knelt down to say his prayers.

Trude threw herself on her bed. Kuntz bent down with his head buried in his hands.

After a few minutes the traveller rose up, placed his belt under his head, and hung up his clothes on a nail in the wall; the nail was old and rusty, it fell, and the clothes along with it. The young man tried to hammer it in again with his fist, and the vibration caused some article to fall which was hung at the other side of the wall.

Kuntz looked up. It was the knife, the accursed knife, stained with the blood of two murders, which had fallen, and now lay close to the door of the stranger's room. He rose to take it up, and while doing so caught a glimpse of the young man as he lay asleep, his head resting upon the belt. Kuntz kept his eye some time at the keyhole, while his hand held the knife. Then the lamp went out in the traveller's chamber, and Kuntz turned to see if Trude slept.

Trude was sitting up, her head on her hand, her eyes fixed on her husband.

" Rise," he said, " and hold the lamp, since thou dost not sleep."

Trude took the lamp, Kuntz opened the door, and both entered the room of the sleeping man. Kuntz grasped the stranger's belt with one hand, and held the knife lifted with the other.

The sleeper stirred, the knife fell, and so sure was the aim that the young man had only time to exclaim, " My father!"

Kuntz had killed his own son!

The young man had been abroad, had made his fortune, and had now returned to share it with his poor parents.

Such is the drama of Werner and the legend of Schwarrbach.

One may imagine how the tragedy haunted me as I ascended the mountain. In fact, the desire to see the inn where all these terrible events had happened was my principal motive for visiting Mont Gemmi. The scene was in grand keeping with the drama. Behind us the delicious valley, the Kanderthal, young, gay, and verdant; before us the bare rocks and the icy snow; while in the centre, like a stain of blood upon a shroud, lay the accursed inn of many murders. Still, I could have wished that bright blue sky away; the tempest should have been roaring around the cabin, and the heavens frowning darkly above it.

Well, at least, I thought, our host will have a gloomy, sinister aspect, suited to his abode; and I advanced in the full hope of all my worst imaginings being realised. But nothing of the kind: two pretty children, like white and red roses, were playing before the door, cutting holes in the snow with a knife. A knife! How could their parents suffer them to touch so fatal an instrument? I tore it from their hands, and the little ones began to cry.

I entered. The landlord came to greet me. He was a large, jolly fellow, of about forty; very fat and very gay.

" Here," said I, " take this knife away. How can you let your children touch it?"

" Thanks, monsieur, but there is no danger."

" No danger, unhappy man! and the 24th of February?"

Mine host curled his lip as if annoyed.

" Ah!" said I, " you understand me?"

At the same time I looked round and recognised the interior perfectly. There was the sitting-room first, Trude's bed in a recess; beyond, the stranger's sleeping-room where he had been murdered. I opened the door and looked down on the boards for the stains of blood. The dinner-table was laid there.

" Heavens! how can you eat in this room?" I exclaimed.

" Why, sir? a bed is useless there, for few travellers stop the night."

" No wonder," I answered: " terrible scenes ———"

" Here's another of them," muttered the landlord, looking very angry.

" But how had you courage to take such a house?" I continued.

" I didn't take it; it was my father's."

" Then you are the son of Kuntz?"

" No, my name is Hantz, not Kuntz."

" Ah! I see; you changed the name?"

" I never changed my name, and, God be praised, never need to change it."

" I understand : it was Werner changed it."

" What do you mean?" said Hantz.

" Why," said I, too happy to begin, " was it not here——"

" Ah, the devil! Must I have more of this?" interrupted Hantz. " This is the way they have all been going on for fifteen years, till my wife and I are well nigh ruined."

" Crime and its punishment!" I murmured.

" Why, Calvin himself couldn't have stood such a persecution," he continued. " There was no 24th of February, nor Kuntz, nor murders. This inn is as safe as a mother's breast for her child, and no one knew that better than the villain who set the story afloat, for he stayed here a fortnight."

" Who? Kuntz?"

" No, *mon Dieu!* no. Don't I tell you there never was a Kuntz at all in the neighbourhood, but a poor wretch they call Werner, who came here."

" How? the poet?"

" Ay, the poet! that's what all the vagabonds call themselves. Well, monsieur, the poet came one day to my father's—better for us he had broken his neck getting up the mountain. It was in 1813; I remember him well—an honest-looking, worthy gentleman; no one could have suspected him. And he asked my father's leave to stay a week or so; and my father said, ' Yes; but we have only this room to give you; will it do?' ' It will do well,' replied the other, and so he installed himself in this very spot. But we might have suspected something from the very first night, for he began to talk aloud as if he were mad; and when I got up to look at him through the keyhole, he was enough to frighten any one; pale, with his hair thrown back, his eyes now fixed, now wandering, sometimes as immoveable as a statue; then, all at once, gesticulating like a madman, and then writing, writing as fast as the pen would go: look you, no worse sign than that. So went on fifteen days, or rather fifteen nights, for in the daytime he kept prowling all about the house. At the end of that time he said, 'I thank you, good people, for your kindness. I have done.' 'We could not do much for you, sir,' replied my father; 'but you were welcome to all.' Then he paid; and, truth to say, paid right well, and so went away.

"A year passed quietly, and we heard no more of him. Then, one day, two travellers came in, and looked about attentively.

" 'Here is the scythe,' said one.

" 'And the very knife,' said the other.

" The scythe was a nice new one which I had just bought at the Kandersteg; and the knife, an old rusty kitchen one, that we kept hung up on a nail near the door. Father and I stared; then, one of the gentlemen approaching, said—

" 'Was it not here, my little friend, that a horrible murder took place on the 24th of February?'

" 'What murder?' said I.

" 'That of young Kuntz by his father.'

" 'I don't know what you're talking of,' said I.

" 'Don't you know M. Werner?' they asked.

" 'Ay do I,' said I; 'he was a nice gentleman that staid here a fortnight, two years back: only a little odd; he never stopped talking and writing the whole night, in place of sleeping like other folk.'

" 'Well, my friend, here is what he was writing about you and your inn,' said they, handing me a little book, called 'The Twenty-fourth of February.'

"No harm as far as that went. The 24th of February is as good a day as any other. But I hadn't read thirty pages when the book dropped from my hand. Oh! such lies, such horrible lies, about our poor inn! and all to ruin us innocent innkeepers! If we had charged him too much, could he not have said so? But no—he said nothing, and paid—even thanked us; and then, the villain! to go and write a book, and describe our house! Ah! such treachery! such baseness! it makes me mad. But if ever I catch another fellow here that writes books, I will make him pay for his comrade."

" Then, there really was no murder here?"

" None at all. Every word that fellow wrote was pure invention! Oh! the way we were tormented!" (And here our poor host tore his hair with both hands.) " Look you, sir: not a living soul would pass the house but he'd say—

" ' Ah! there is the very spot, and the scythe, and the knife!'

" It was the same song with every one. So my father got provoked, and took them down one day; but no good was in that, for then the next set cried out—

" ' Ah, ha! they have hid the scythe and knife; but see, here is the identical room!'

" In faith, sir, it was enough to kill me, and my father's life was shortened ten years by it. To hear such things said of one's own house—and that to go on now for fifteen years! The fiend! I wish some one had the old barracks; I would sell it, walls, and furniture, and all, for a hundred crowns, and go to live some place where I'd hear no more about Werner, or Kuntz, or the scythe, or the knife, or the 24th of February."

" Well, well, mine host; never mind now. Just get dinner for me."

" And what would monsieur like?" he said, adjusting his apron.

" A cold fowl, if you have it, would be excellent."

" A cold fowl! Ah! there's more of it; why, don't you know he put a fowl into the book too. Just think —a fowl! as if they had done any harm, poor things!"

" Well, my friend, anything you like—only make haste, and I'll go and take a walk."

So I went forth, really pitying my unfortunate host; for such magic vitality have a poet's words, that when once sown, nothing can eradicate them. All I could do was to promise my influence in silencing the *calumny*, as Hantz called it. So, if any of my readers visit the inn of Schwarrbach, pray let them make known that I too have written a book, and therein striven to unsay all that Werner said.

After dining, Willer and I visited the Dauben Lake, the highest, perhaps, in the known world, and consequently desolate, no living thing being able to support the temperature of its waters, even in summer.

Having passed the lake, we entered a defile, at the end of which stood a deserted hut. Willer said the descent commenced there; and, curious to see this extraordinary passage, I ran on to the spot; but no sooner had I reached it than, uttering a cry and closing my eyes, I fell backwards on the ground.

Have any of my readers ever felt that sudden sensation of vertigo one experiences at the edge of a precipice, mingled with the irresistible desire to plunge over? Have they felt their hair standing on end, the sweat pouring from their brows, and every muscle convulsed like those of a corpse at the touch of the voltaic pile? If they have, I need not describe my agony at this moment; they will comprehend it when I say that I had run to the very edge of a rock with a perpendicular descent of one thousand six hundred feet: one step farther, and I must have been precipitated.

Willer ran to my assistance, and seeing that I had half fainted, poured some kirschen-wasser down my throat, and then led, or rather carried me, to the threshold of the cabin.

His look of alarm forced me to the effort of exertion, and I tried to laugh, in order to reassure him; but it was a laugh in which my teeth chattered one against another, like those of the damned in the icy pond described by Dante.

However, I soon recovered, conquering physical weakness by moral strength, and advanced with perfect calmness to take another glance at the terrible precipice. I then perceived a little path about two feet wide, which wound down to the base, and, with a step as firm as my guide's, began the descent; only, for fear of my teeth being broken by their striking one against another, I stuffed my handkerchief into my mouth.

For two hours we continued the zigzag descent, a

perpendicular precipice at each side all the way; and at last, without having uttered a word the whole time, reached the village of Louëche.

" Well!" said Willer; " you see it was nothing after all."

I drew my handkerchief from my mouth and showed it to him, cut through and through as if with a razor.

CHAPTER XXIV.

THE BATHS OF LOUËCHE.

I WAS so fatigued on reaching Louëche that I flung myself into bed, without waiting either dinner or a visit to the baths. But next morning Willer was remorseless, and insisted on my being up at nine o'clock—though I had got only fifteen hours' sleep—in order to witness the very curious scenes of ablution and amusement at the baths.

Twenty paces from the inn, we found the large spring of Saint Laurent, which feeds the baths. There are twelve or fifteen other sources of thermal water in the vicinity, but no use is made of them.

The aspect of the baths at Louëche is quite different from that of any other establishment of the kind I have ever inspected. There are no separate baths for men and women: all are mixed together in a manner quite patriarchal.

Imagine the large reservoir at a swimming-school, with a gallery all round, and two bridges running along in the form of a Latin cross, so as to form four compartments, and in each compartment about thirty bathers, making a total for the four of a hundred and twenty persons, all hermetically enclosed in flannel wrappers, and leaving nothing visible above the surface of the water except a set of heads, wigged or capped according to the grotesque fancy of each individual; while before each head is placed a plank of wood, on which a pair of hands belonging to invisible arms is ever active. People eat, drink, knit, play cards, read, &c. in this manner, and pay visits to each other with the most perfect facility, carrying their seats from one corner of the bath to the other, and drawing their little tables along with them by means of cords.

The foregoing, however, of these migrations varies with the character of the bathers. Some morose individual will stop for two hours in the one spot; another will fall asleep over his newspaper, which quietly drops into the water, until the entire sheet is saturated, up to the very title; but a gayer spirit will make a regular promenade of the bath, having always something to say, apparently, to the person farthest off from him, and stumbling over every one else, in order to reach his friend; flinging a few words, at the same time, up to his child in the gallery, or across to his wife, who is in another compartment.

Amidst the whole crowd, I can recollect but one face that interested me. It was that of a pale, melancholy girl, of about eighteen. Unlike the other bathers, her black hair floated on her shoulders, in place of being confined beneath a cap, and her little table was covered, not with cards and glasses, but with fresh flowers, which she was tying into a bouquet. There was a strange contrast between the brilliant blossoms and her fading cheek. I could have dreamed she was a dying Ophelia, with her head and hands just visible above the stream where she drowned herself. As I turned my glance away from this interesting creature, I heard the physician saying, "In a month she will be dead!"

Dead! So young! so beautiful! Dead in a month!

The air seemed stifling. I longed to quit the place. Heaven had lost its azure, earth its festal robe. Dead in a month! I seemed to be walking in a graveyard, and these words came like an echo from the tombs.

For nearly a league I could think of nothing except this horrible prophecy of science, and walked on, totally oblivious of all surrounding objects, until Willer took me by the arm and said, "We have arrived." In fact, we had reached a kind of grotto, having beneath us the summit of a perpendicular rock eight hundred feet high, at the base of which runs the Dala; and to our left, the first of the six ladders which establish a communication between Louëche-le-Bourg and the village of Albinnen;

for without this aërial road the inhabitants would be obliged to make a circuit of three leagues, in order to reach the market.

One must really see this suspended highway in order to form some idea of the marvellous daring which is characteristic of the inhabitants of the Alps.   After throwing yourself flat on the ground, for fear of the vertigo, to look down eight hundred feet beneath at the foaming waters of the Dala, you rise, mount the first ladder, and by the aid of hands and feet reach the jutting point of rock on which the second is placed; arrived at this spot, you are just in the act of assuring your guide that no human creature could possibly venture his life by such a transit, when a Tyrolienne is chanted above.   You look up, and there, a hundred feet over your head, suspended in the air, appears a peasant carrying his fruit to market.   There, also, is a hunter bearing his chamois, and a mother carrying her infant, and you see them come and go with the same reckless security as if they were traversing the glassy slope of one of our own hills.

Willer asked if I wished to continue the ascent.   I thanked him.   He laughed.   "Why, it is nothing," he said.   "Look at that woman, how bravely she climbs!" And in truth there was a young girl lightly tripping up the ladders we had quitted, merely taking the precaution to draw up her skirt, and fasten it to her waist, so as to form pantaloons in place of a petticoat.

We watched her ascending up to the fourth ladder, when a stoppage occurred; a man was descending: what would she do now?   The position was embarrassing.

"Never fear," said Willer: "you'll see the mountain mode."

Accordingly, in a moment, the man, with a ready gallantry that would have done honour to one of our finished dandies, swung himself lightly round to the inside of the ladder, descending on that side, as the young girl ascended by the other, acknowledging his courtesy by the exchange of a few words as they passed.   It was a sight truly marvellous to behold.

The man passed close to us.   "Look at that fine spark!" said Willer.

"Well?"

"By seven o'clock to-night he will be dead drunk, tumbling twenty times on the smooth road from the baths to the first ladder, yet he will mount every one of the six in perfect safety; and so he has done these ten years back."

"But some fine day he will kill himself."

"Oh, not at all. There is a special god for the drunkards, you know."

"Ah, my dear friend! then I am certainly not in special favour with that particular god, for·my head is turning round already. Let us descend."

"As quick as you please; or maybe you'll end like Monsieur B——."

"Who was this Monsieur B——?" said I, as soon as we touched *terra firma* once more.

"Ah! I'll let you know all about him. First, then, he was a broker from Paris, who had ruined himself and his wife and children, they said, by speculating in the funds. But you ought to know that best, since you are from Paris."

"Well, go on."

"However, he insured his life for a large sum—five hundred thousand francs. I don't know what he meant by it all, but you may."

"Perfectly; go on."

"Well, he came here to Switzerland with a party. 'Let us go see the ladders,' said one of them, a lady. 'Ah, yes!' replied Monsieur B——; 'let us go see the ladders.' So, after breakfast, they all mounted and took a guide. Monsieur B—— had his own plan in his head, however, and would go afoot. Well, they came on here to the edge of this slippery declivity, and Monsieur B—— sat down, bidding the others go on. Then he said to the guide, 'Fetch me a large stone—mind, a large one.' The guide went, never suspecting anything, and got a great big block, as much as he could carry. 'Here, this will do you, I think,' he cried out. But, lo! no one was there!—nothing to be seen except a little track on the grass, down to the edge there. (Don't go so near, it is five hundred feet down, and the place is slippery.) Think how the guide shouted! Every one ran to the spot; but no one would look down. 'Here, my fine fellows,' said a gentleman at last, one of the party, to the guide; 'here is a louis if you look over into that abyss.' He had not to say it twice. The guide ran, holding on by the bushes as well as he could, and looked.

"Well?" said the gentleman.

"There he is," said the guide. "I see him right well; down at the very bottom."

"Then they all returned to the baths. Men were sent for with baskets and ropes; and two hours after a mass of human bones was brought up—all that remained of the Paris broker!"

"And did he kill himself intentionally?"

"No one knows. His family and the insurance company went to law, but the family gained, and the five hundred thousand francs were paid down to them."

I had heard something of this story at Paris; but to stand on the spot where it happened, sent such a shock through my veins that I had to sit down when Willer concluded.

Strange organization of our social system, which has brought commercial development to such extreme excess that a man can even make a traffic of his own death!

On returning to the baths, we found a crowd assembled round one of the springs. A set of travellers were boiling a fowl in the thermal water. So, bidding Willer go and pack up my luggage, I staid to witness the curious operation. At the end of twenty minutes he returned, and found me eating a wing of the thermatical bird with great satisfaction; for the proprietor, seeing the interest I took in the experiment, had judged me worthy to appreciate the result. In return, I offered him a glass of brandy, but the poor devil was only a water-drinker— a hot-water-drinker: worst of all!

After this interchange of courtesy, my guide and I departed for Louêche-le-Bourg. Mid-way, Willer stopped to show me the village of Albinnen, to which the road of ladders conducts. The streets here are so steep that they resemble roofs of houses; and the villagers are obliged to tie their fowls to prevent their tumbling down. At three o'clock we reached Louêche-le-Bourg, where we dined. There is nothing to see here, so at four we

crossed the Rhone, and half-an-hour after I took leave
of my brave Willer, and entered the public coach that
was to convey me to Brieg.

The road we followed is that leading to the Simplon,
at the foot of which lies Brieg. From Martigny, as far
as this town, the road was made by the Valaisans; the
remainder only of this marvellous passage was executed
by French engineers.

On commencing our journey, I had observed a mass of
dull, dark clouds gathered in the gorge of the Haut-
Valais, which lay spread out before me in all its depth.
While day lasted, I took it for one of those local storms
so common in the Alps; but as night came on, the clouds
assumed a sombre reddish hue, till at length the glare
of an immense fire lit up the horizon.

The whole northern forest of the Valais was in flames,
making the icy tresses of Finster-Aarhorn and the Jungfrau to glisten and sparkle through the darkness. As
night fell deeper, every object seemed painted black upon
a deep-red background, and we journeyed on thus for
seven leagues, still approaching the focus of the flames.
At length, the black outlines of Brieg appeared before
us, sketched upon a gigantic background of a blood-red
hue. Then as we advanced the light descended, leaving
the tall spires alone glittering in the ruby light: this,
too, faded; darkness fell upon the scene, and we seemed
entering the gloomy precincts of a subterranean vault.
We had arrived; the gates were passed, and we entered
the calm, sleeping town, which lay silent as Pompeii at
the foot of her volcano.

CHAPTER XXV.

OBERGESTELEN.

BRIEG is situated at the western point of the Kunhorn, and forms the point of intersection between the two roads of the Simplon and the valley of the Rhone. The first and principal highway, which is grand and beautiful, leads to Italy by the gorge of La Ganter; the second, which is but a mean, narrow, capricious path, crosses the plain, cuts right down the southern side of the Jungfrau, and plunges into the Valais, just where the union of Mutthorn and the Gallenstock bounds the canton with the summit of La Furca; then, redescending from the summit, it passes on to meet the road of Uri, in which the poor little path is swallowed up like a streamlet in a great river. It was by this last little defile that I quitted Brieg the day after my arrival there, and as I had eighteen French leagues to travel, I bestirred myself early, and was on the road by five in the morning.

The first village we came to derives its name of Naters, or Natria, from a tradition concerning a dragon that once infested those parts. The monster dwelt in a cave on the mountain, from which it sprang forth to devour men, quadrupeds, or whatsoever living thing passed that way, so that it became the terror of that whole neighbourhood, and no communication between the High and Low Valais was possible because of it.

Many mountaineers attempted the destruction of the beast, but, one after another, they all fell victims to their daring. At length the idea of contest was given up; none would hazard their lives, or offer themselves to certain death, and the horrible monster reigned undisputed monarch of the mountain.

It chanced, then, that a certain smith, who had murdered his wife from jealousy, was condemned to death. The sentence having been pronounced, the criminal demanded leave to combat the monster, on condition that pardon should be granted if he were victor.

The request being acceded to, he prayed permission to delay two months in order to prepare himself. During the period he forged a suit of armour, made entirely of the purest steel; then a sword, tempered in the icy waters of the Aar, and in the blood of a freshly-killed bull.

Thus equipped, he proceeded to the church of Brieg, where he passed the day and night preceding the combat, and received the communion as if he were going to the scaffold; then, at the appointed hour, set forth to the dragon's cave.

As soon as the monster perceived him, it issued from the rock, spreading its wings and beating them with such force, that even those at a distance upon the mountain trembled at the noise.

Then the two adversaries advanced to the encounter, like two enemies to the death-combat; one covered with an armour of steel, the other with one of scales.

When the dragon had approached sufficiently near, the smith lowered the hilt of his sword, which was in the form of a cross, and awaited the attack; while his adversary seemed on his side fully to comprehend that he had no mere mountaineer to deal with.

There was a pause of an instant; then the monster, rising on its hind paws, seemed on the point of seizing and crushing the man; but the sword flashed like lightning, and one of the animal's fore-paws was severed from the body. The dragon gave a roar, and, rising on its wings, whirled round its antagonist, sprinkling him with blood; then descended, as if to crush him with its weight: but the terrible sword again flashed, and a severed wing fell to the ground.

The mutilated creature fell likewise, dragging itself upon three paws, bleeding from two wounds, twisting its tail, and roaring like a half-killed bull beneath the butcher's club; while shouts of joy resounded through the mountain in answer to these roars of agony.

The smith now advanced boldly on the dragon, which lay like a serpent with its head upon the ground, watching all his movements; but, according as he approached, the monster drew in its head, till, finally, it was completely hidden under the enormous coiled-up body. Suddenly, however, just as the smith had approached sufficiently near, the terrible head was darted forth with its fire-glancing eyes, and the teeth cracked upon the stout steel armour. The violence of the shock was too much for the man; he fell to the ground, and at the same instant the dragon leaped upon him.

Now nothing more was visible except a confused, horrible struggle, in which human cries and roars were mingled. Sometimes a wing beat, or the sword flashed; sometimes the steel armour of the smith was uppermost, then the glittering scales of the dragon; but, as the man was unable to regain his feet and the monster could not rise into the air, the combatants were never sufficiently separated at any time for the spectators to distinguish which was conqueror or which conquered.

The struggle lasted a quarter of an hour: it seemed an age to the watching crowd. Suddenly a terrible cry arose from the place of combat, so strange and horrible that none could tell whether it proceeded from man or monster. The living mass heaved like a wave of the sea, trembled an instant, then all was still and silent.

Had the man killed the dragon, or the dragon devoured the man?

The spectators approached slowly and cautiously. Nothing moved. The man and the dragon lay extended one upon another, and for twenty paces around them the grass was red with blood, and powdered with scales glittering like gold. The dragon was dead, the man had only fainted; so they took off his armour and sprinkled him with the iced water of the river, then bore him in triumph to the village, which henceforth, in commemoration of the combat, was called *Naters*.

As to the dragon, he was thrown into the Rhone.

On passing Naters, I saw the dragon's cave and the place of the combat. They showed me also the place where the monster habitually slept, and the traces left by his scaly tail upon the rock.

I stopped at Lax for breakfast, and sat side by side in the *café* with a brave student, who spoke French literally, but who knew nothing of our modern literature beyond "Télémaque." This, he told me, he had read six times. I asked him were there any legends or historic legends current in the neighbourhood.

"Oh, no," said he; "but there is a very fine view from the mountain right before you, except on misty days."

I thanked him courteously, and buried my nose in the *Nouvelliste Vaudois.* The unfortunates who have read this journal can alone measure the destitution to which I was reduced. The first thing I lit on was an account of the execution of two republicans, taken with arms in their hands at St. Méry. My head fell upon my hand, and I sighed. I was no longer at Lax in the Valais—I was at Paris. Is this all we have attained by our struggles and revolutions?—heads still rolling on the scaffold, and tracing in the bloody dust the words, " Royalty or the People!" Oh! when will this book of horrors be closed, and, sealed with the word "Liberty," be flung into the grave of the last martyr?

Filled with these thoughts, I traversed the next five or six villages, noticing little around me; walking on like a man in a feverish dream, who has risen in delirium from his bed of agony. I feared to be taken for the Wandering Jew, and probably I was, as I strode along, silent and gloomy, over mountain and plain. However, down came an Alpine shower on my burning head, and I was refreshed. I sought no shelter, but continued my route with Socratic calmness till I reached the village of Munster.

Here a young lad ran after me, and asked in Italian if I wished to see the glacier of the Rhone.

" Yes," I answered, with a thrill of pleasure at hearing his delicious language; " will you be my guide?"

" Willingly, sir; for five francs I shall conduct you."

" Then I'll give you ten. Come!"

" Yes, when I say adieu to my mother, and get my umbrella."

"Make haste, then. I shall wait for you on the road."

Strange human machine this frame of ours! A few drops of rain had taken the fever from my head and restored my equanimity.

Once, when a rising was threatened, Pétion put his hand out of the window, and quietly saying " It rains, there will be no revolution to-night," went to bed in perfect security; and there was none. If it had rained on the 27th of July, what a difference would have been made in French history! In France they fear rain much more than bullets : a man will rush to fight unarmed, but will not venture out without his umbrella.

I had got thus far in reflection, and half-a-league on my road, when my Italian guide overtook me.

" How is it," said I, " you talk Italian in a German village?"

" Because," he answered, " I was apprentice to a shoe-maker at Domo d'Ossola."

" And your name ?"

" Frantz in German, Francesco in Italian."

" Well, then, Francesco, I am going not only to the glacier of the Rhone, but to the petty cantons. I shall traverse the Grisons, a corner of Austria, see Constance, follow the Rhine to Basle, and probably return to Geneva by Soleure and Neufchâtel. Will you come with me ?"

" I should like it much."

" How much shall I give you a-day?"

" What you like. It will be more, at all events, than my earnings."

" Well, forty sous a-day and your food. That will leave you seventy or eighty francs at the end of our journey."

" 'Twill be a fortune !"

" You agree, then ?"

" With all my heart."

" So, then—write to your mother from the next village, and tell her you will be away a month in place of only three days."

" Thanks."

And Francesco placed his umbrella on the ground and

took a whirl; his mode of expressing contentment, as I afterwards found. So I had made one being happy, at least, and at a very small cost.

On reaching Obergestelen, Francesco and I halted for the night. We had only gone two leagues from Munster, so that all at the inn were his acquaintances: a circumstance that procured for me incontinently the best room and a splendid fire.

I was saturated to my very marrow, so my first thought was a complete change of dress, which I accomplished with all that delicious *egoism* of feeling that accompanies the sensation of shelter and security while the rain is pattering on the window from without.

Hearing a great noise at the door, I went to the window, and saw a guide and mule arriving with four travellers, who had been caught in the storm descending La Furca. Two of them were ladies, who seemed to me young and pretty, in spite of their damp hair and clinging garments; so in honour of the fair sex I stirred up my fire, stowed away my habiliments, and sent a message inviting the party to occupy my room while theirs was preparing.

The offer was gratefully accepted on the part of both ladies and gentlemen, as soon as they had changed their clothes. The gentlemen made their appearance first, and found me occupied in preparation for my dinner, to which they requested permission to add theirs, a proposition I accepted. One of them was a Frenchman, gay, lively, and middle-aged, with an open countenance, and wearing his red ribbon—a regular lounger of the Paris saloons, whom I had come across twenty times without knowing his name; the other was a German, pale, reserved, cold, and distant. I had never seen him before, but in five minutes made out the whole story. The Frenchman was M. Brunton, one of our best architects; the other was chamberlain to the King of Denmark, and called Kœfford.

Just as compliments were exchanged the ladies entered, and M. Brunton, by my advice, repaired to the kitchen to investigate our chance of a certain marmot, whose succulent odour had risen gratefully to my nostrils.

The wives of my new friends presented as strong a

contrast as their husbands. My pretty, lively country-woman, Mme. Brunton, had poured forth her thanks twenty times before her solemn German companion had finished the first reverence demanded by etiquette. She was a large, white, pale, cold woman, without a spark on her whole frame except a faint, dying gleam in the eyes.

M. Kœfford was buried in his guide books, so conversation and the ladies were left entirely to me; however, two Parisians are never in want of a subject as long as the opera exists. To understand, criticise, and analyse its merits and demerits, is the exclusive privilege of good society, and therefore I instantly plunged into the subject with all the ardour of genuine fashionables.

Mme. Brunton evidently did not know me, and by her questions showed some curiosity as to the class of society to which I belonged. First she tried literature, and we passed in review all authors from Hugo to Scribe; then painting, from Delacroix to Pujol; architecture, from Percier to Lebas. I talked learnedly upon all, and my fair friend was visibly puzzled.

After a few moments' silence, some remark about her health sent us full sail into the inexhaustible subject of nerves and depression. My spirited antagonist, of course, suffered from both: every well-bred person does. When a woman says, "I am dreadfully nervous," that means, being translated, "I have eighty thousand francs a-year, and a box at the opera; I never walk, nor rise till about noon." As for me, I sustained the conversation like a man wholly without nerves, but who yet recognised their existence; one, in fact, who had not the honour of their acquaintance, though he had heard much about them. Up to this point Mme. Kœfford had been silent; but now, when a subject relating to general humanity was started, she opened her lips and gave us her experiences. She too, poor woman, had nerves; nerves of the cold north. This gave me an opportunity of establishing a very subtle distinction between nerves of latitude, and after some minutes I must have impressed both ladies with the notion that I had devoted a whole life to the study of the philosophy of sensation.

Who then could I be? This question was evidently in their minds. I was too much a man of the world for an artist, too much of an artist to be a mere man of the world. I spoke too low for a notary, too loud for a physician, and I allowed other people to talk, which proved I could be no lawyer. Just then, M. Brunton returned from the kitchen, and advancing gravely to M. Kœfford, who was plunged in his guide-books, exclaimed, with the most serious comicality of expression—

"My poor friend!"

"What is it?" said the chamberlain, turning full round.

"Have you ever read in any of your guide-books that the inhabitants of Obergestelen were anthropophagi?"

"No, never," returned the other, "but I'll just look;" and he ran his finger down the index till he came to the word Obergestelen, then read aloud—

"Obergestelen, a village of the Haut-Valais, situated at the foot of Mont Grimsel, at an elevation of four thousand one hundred feet above the level of the sea. The houses are all black, in consequence of the action of the sun on the resinous matter in the wood of which they are built. The rise of the Rhone causes frequent inundations during summer," &c. &c.

"Well," said M. Kœfford, gravely, lifting up his eyes from the book; "not a word about human flesh in all that, you see."

"But, my friend, you know I always told you these guide-books were a pack of stuff. Go to the kitchen yourself, lift the cover off the pot, in which they say is a marmot, and tell us what you find there."

Quite elated at the prospect of some new fact for his tablet, the chamberlain rose and proceeded to the kitchen, M. Brunton preserving his serious air admirably all the while, though his wife and I could not restrain our laughter. As to Mme. Kœfford, she was sunk upon the sofa with her eyes fixed on the wandering clouds, plunged in some reverie of other times or places, perchance.

In a few moments, Mme. Kœfford returned, pale and trembling.

"Well, what was in the pot?" we asked.

"Oh heavens! a child!" he exclaimed, sinking into a chair.

"A child?"

"Poor little angel!" sighed forth Mme. Kœfford, who had listened without hearing, or heard without comprehending, and had no doubt seen in her dream some white-winged cherub pass before her with its aureole of gold.

When one has reckoned upon a roast shoulder, or a calf's head at least, and has during a whole hour been appeasing the murmurs of the stomach with the savoury fumes of a marmot, it is very terrible to find this marmot a child; and were it even an angel, as Madame Kœfford suggested, the appetite would revolt from such an equivalent in exchange. Accordingly, I was in the act of rushing from the apartment when M. Brunton held me back, saying, "Never mind; let them serve it up." Almost immediately after, the servant-girl entered, bearing a long dish, upon which was laid, extended on a bed of vegetables, an object which had all the appearance of a new-born infant skinned and boiled.

The ladies screamed and averted their eyes. M. Kœfford rose, approached, examined it attentively, and then pronounced, in a sepulchral voice, "It is a girl!"

"Ladies," said M. Brunton, sitting down and sharpening a knife, "I have heard that, at the siege of Genoa, Massena, who, you know, invited his whole staff one day to dine upon a cat and twelve mice, remarked one regiment alone that preserved its original fat, sleek aspect in the midst of the universal falling away caused by the famine. When the town capitulated, he interrogated the colonel concerning this singular exception. 'Why,' replied the other, ingenuously, 'they asked my leave to eat the Austrians, and I could not refuse them so slight a favour, especially as they sent me all the best bits, being colonel; and, truth to say, his imperial majesty's subjects are no such bad eating after all.'"

The cries of horror redoubled; upon which, M. Brunton very delicately raised the creature's shoulder, and devoured it with as much *goût* as Ceres devoured the shoulder of Pelops.

Just then the servant entered, and seeing but one person at table, exclaimed, "What! ladies, will you not taste the marmot?"

The secret was out.   We breathed freely once more;
yet the very resemblance of the quadruped to the biped
was too striking not to destroy all appetite.   The hands
and feet especially were like the human members; so,
notwithstandiug all Willer's vaunts at the Faulhorn, I
could not bring myself to taste a morsel.

" Have you nothing else?" I inquired of our attendant.

" An omelet, if you like."

" An omelet!" exclaimed the ladies.   " Nothing better?"

" But," said I, turning towards them, " do you know
what a real omelet is?   Permit me to say, that an
omelet is to cookery what the sonnet is to poetry."

" Rather the mere alphabet," they retorted.

" Do you hear?" cried M. Kœfford to the girl; " can
you make an omelet?"

" Oh, yes, sir; and no one ever complains of them."

" Then, let us see."

The girl   retired, made   her   omelet, and in ten
minutes brought us a huge cake covering the whole
surface of a large dinner plate.   At the first glance I saw
its nature; nevertheless, I cut up the thing, and served
a morsel to each of the ladies.   It was rejected with
disgust.   My prophetic fears were realized.   One might
as well have eaten the corner of a quilt.

" Well, my child," said I to the girl, " your omelet
is execrable.   What say you, ladies?"

" Horrible!   We shall die of hunger.   It is enough
to make one despair."

" Then," I answered, " moments of despair require
desperate measures.   Shall I try an omelet?

" An omelet!"

" An omelet," I repeated, bowing modestly.

The ladies stared; but M. Kœfford, starting up, and
grasping the only plank of safety held out, exclaimed,
" Since monsieur has the goodness to offer ——"

" Provided you and M. Brunton assist me," I continued.

" Willingly," they answered, with the alacrity of
famine.

" Then bring fresh eggs, fresh butter, and fresh
cream," I said to the girl.

They came. I assigned to each his post. M. Brunton chopped up some delicate herbs; the German beat the eggs; I held the handle of the frying-pan, and performed the necessary rotations with a gravity that enchanted the ladies. Already the omelet began to brown in the butter, and every one to look on with an increasing interest, when the general silence was broken by M. Brunton saying—

"Monsieur, would it be too indiscreet if we ventured to inquire the name of our gifted cook?"

"Not the least so in the world, monsieur."

"Because I feel certain we have met at Paris."

"So do I. Have the goodness to hand the butter. Thanks." And I slipped a slice under the omelet to prevent its sticking to the pan when turned.

"Perhaps, even if you mentioned your name——"

"It is Alexandre Dumas."

"The author of 'Antony?'" cried Madame Brunton.

"The same," said I, turning out the omelet, beautifully done, and laying it on the table.

There was a pause; so, not hearing a single compliment uttered either on my drama or my omelet, I looked up. The company were stupified. Probably I had overthrown some poet ideal, and the present phase did not please them. Unhappily, too, the omelet was excellent, and the ladies ate it to the last morsel.

CHAPTER XXVI.

THE DEVIL'S BRIDGE.

NEXT morning the ladies appeared perfectly restored after their bad journey and bad dinner. In fact, no one seemed to have suffered except poor M. Kœfford, who had passed the night in the midst of his guide-books and maps.

Strange man our chamberlain! Before leaving Copenhagen he had traced out an itinerary throughout Switzerland for himself, from which nothing was to make him depart. Now, in this itinerary, it was set down that, on the 28th of September, he would be in Oberland and cross the Grimsel. Of course, the elemental chances of rain and storm were not thought of in his philosophy; but it so happened they had power even to derange M. Kœfford's plans. And now we were at the 29th of September in place of the 28th; we were in the Valais instead of the Oberland; and our guides declared that, after the late rains, the party must cross by Mount Gemmi, and not attempt the passage of the Grimsel. Monsieur and Madame Brunton were quite content to try either; but the change completely overturned the whole existence of M. Kœfford.

I did all I could to console him; said the Gemmi was far better worth seeing than the Grimsel; and that, after all, it was only the delay of a day.

"Only the delay of a day!" he exclaimed, with the accent of despair; "and do you call that nothing? To mark one hour, and strike another, like a clock out of order—you call that nothing?"

Monsieur and Madame Brunton now lent their aid to console him; but, like Rachel, he would not be comforted. As to his wife, she knew him too well even to attempt condolence.

However, necessity conquered even M. Kœfford, and he consented to a delay of twenty-four hours and the passage of the Gemmi; upon which I left him, calm, if not resigned.

After my return to Paris, I learned that the unhappy chamberlain did not finally reach Copenhagen until the evening of the 1st of January, in place of the 30th of December; consequently, was not present at the King of Denmark's New-year's-Day reception, for which omission he nearly lost his place at court.

As to me, having no court situation to be placed in jeopardy, I kissed the ladies' hands, and set forth with Francesco to follow my own sweet will.

He was a brave lad and a pleasant companion; joyous and light-hearted; strong as a man of twenty bred in the towns, and sprightly and active as a chamois of the mountains.

We walked on for two hours, following the steep banks of the Rhone, which from a river had become a torrent, and from a torrent a rivulet; yet displaying from its very source all those fantastic caprices and eccentricities which mark its entire course, as the whims of a child denote the future passions of the man.

At last, after a sudden detour, we perceived before us, filling up the entire space between the Grimsel and the Furca, the magnificent glacier giant with its head resting on the mountain, and its feet pendent in the valley; while three streams, like sweat from its flanks, poured down to the base. These, uniting after a certain distance, form one large river, which, under the name of the Rhone, pours its waters into the sea by four outlets, the smallest of which is a league in breadth.

I leaped over these three streams, of which the largest is but twelve feet across; and, having performed this exploit, we commenced the ascent of the Furca.

It is one of the bleakest and saddest mountains in all

Switzerland. The inhabitants say that its sterility is owing to the fact of the Wandering Jew having made it his high-road from France to Italy. I have already mentioned the tradition of its being covered with a wheat harvest on his first passage, with pines on the second, and the third time with snow.

It was in this last state we found it; but I remarked that, here and there, the snow was stained with large patches of red. Perceiving, also, that these spots were produced by springs bubbling up from the surface of the earth, it struck me the water must be ferruginous; and, having tested it, I found such to be the case. The snow, in fact, was rusted where it fell.

While examining this phenomenon and weaving theories on its origin, Francesco advanced, and, with rather an embarrassed air, requested my flask, which he had himself filled that morning at Obergestelen; not, indeed, with kirschen-wasser, as I expected, but with wine. However, the substantial liquor being one of the excellent red wines of Italy, I did not quarrel about the exchange, though unable to divine Francesco's motive in making the alteration.

His request now set me thinking again on the subject: perhaps some hygienic reason made him prefer the wine of Italy to the cherry-water of the Alps, and he was no doubt going to give me a convincing proof of this preference. Accordingly, I watched every movement with the corner of my eye, though without seeming to observe.

But all my conjectures were wrong. Francesco placed himself on the most elevated point of the mountain, and when astride as it were upon its back, made the sign of the cross, turning first to the west and then to the east; then, pouring some wine into the hollow of his hand, he threw up the liquid into the air, letting it fall again upon the snow in a rosy rain.

At last, the exercise being finished, he returned with the flask, never having once raised it to his lips.

"What devilish ceremony have you been at?" said I, as he replaced the bottle by my side.

"Ah!" he replied; "it is a precaution against accidents."

"How so?"

"Why, the wines of Italy pass this way going to Switzerland, France, and Germany, slung in barrels on the backs of mules, which are led by Italian muleteers, mostly drunkards, if the truth be said. Now, the Furca is a wearisome mountain to travel over, and, about half-way, the devil generally tempts them to tap the barrels, which, consequently, don't reach their destination quite as they set out. Of course, such robbers couldn't expect to go to the same place as honest men after their death, and their ghosts come by night to wander round the place where temptation overcame them. See these red patches on every side—they are their foot-prints on the snow. It is they who raise up the tempest, and lead the poor traveller to a precipice with their false meteor-lights. Well, there is but one way of propitiating these evil spirits: it is to make the sign of the cross, and fling them some drops of the wine for which they perilled their souls and went to eternal damnation; and this is the reason why I filled your flask with Italian wine in place of kirschen-wasser."

This explanation appeared so perfectly satisfactory, and withal of such importance to ensure our safety, that I instantly hastened to repeat the ceremony on my own account, strictly adhering to all the formularies observed by Francesco; and it was no doubt owing to these anti-diabolic precautions that we arrived without any acci dent at Réalp, a little village situated at the base of the terrible mountain.

At Réalp I hired a chaise to Altorf, reserving to myself the right of walking when and where I wished during the journey; so, about a quarter of a league after passing Andermatt, I availed myself of this privilege of alighting. We had reached the most curious part of the road: it is a defile formed by the Gallenstock and Crispalt, through which rush the waters of the Reuss—a stream whose cradle I had seen on the summit of the Furca, and which goes on increasing in size till, five leagues farther, it merits the name of "The Giant."

At this spot the road coasts along the granitic base of the Crispalt, and passes through an excavation in the rock from one valley to another. This subterranean gallery, which is one hundred and ninety feet long, and lit by openings looking on the Reuss, is vulgarly called "The Hole of Uri."

Having quitted the gallery, I found myself opposite the Devil's Bridge, or rather the Devil's Bridges, for there are two, an old and a new one: the former, however, has been abandoned, except by some occasional pedestrian like myself. So, leaving the chaise to take the new bridge, which has usurped the traffic and even the name of its ancestor, I climbed, with the aid of hands and feet, upon the veritable remains of the old Satanic one. Each is composed of a single arch, flung over the river Reuss; the new one is sixty feet high, the ancient but forty-five; still it is not the less fearful to traverse, on account of the absence of parapets.

The tradition attached to the name is one of the most curious in all Switzerland. Here it is in all its purity:—

The river Reuss, flowing in its rocky bed sixty feet deep, sadly interrupted all communication between the inhabitants of the valley of Cornera and those of the valley of Goschenen; that is to say, between the Grisons and the people of Uri. How to remove this impediment was the grand problem with the two cantons. They assembled all their most able architects and finally it was agreed to build a bridge at the common expense. But bridge after bridge was built, and none was found strong enough to resist the tempests, the avalanches, and the rise of the water, longer than a year. A last attempt was made towards the end of the fourteenth century, and the bridge having bravely resisted all the elemental assaults for nearly a year, hopes were entertained by the inhabitants of its permanence when, one morning, it was announced to the Bailli of Goschenen that the bridge had given way.

"Well, then," cried the bailli, "none but the devil himself can build one strong enough to last."

Scarcely had he said the words when a servant announced "Monsieur Satan."

"Ask him to walk in," said the bailli.

The servant departed, and ushered in a gentleman of about thirty-five, dressed in the German fashion, with pantaloons of bright red, a doublet of black velvet, slashed with red, and wearing on his head a black cap, from which floated a flame-coloured plume, in the most graceful undulations. As to his shoes, they were in the fashion which a hundred years later was adopted under Louis XII. with great round toes; and to one leg was attached a large cock-spur, which probably was very serviceable whenever his highness took the air on horseback.

After the usual compliments, the bailli took an arm-chair, and the devil threw himself into another; the bailli put his feet on the hob, the devil placed his quite unaffectedly on the fire.

"Well, my good friend," said Satan, "I hear you wanted me."

"Indeed, my lord," replied the bailli, "your aid might be useful."

"For your cursed bridge: is it not so?"

"Why, perhaps so."

"Are you in great want of this bridge?"

"In truth, we cannot do without it."

"Ha! ha!" laughed Satan.

"Suppose, my good devil," said the bailli, after a moment's silence, "you would build us one."

"The very thing I came to propose."

"Then, we have only to talk about the—" and the bailli hesitated.

"The price," continued Satan, with a malicious grin at the bailli.

"Why, yes," replied the bailli, feeling that the affair was becoming serious.

"Oh!" said the devil, balancing himself on the hind legs of the chair, and paring his claws with the bailli's penknife, "I shall not be too hard with you, friend."

"That gives me some comfort," said the bailli; "the last cost us sixty gold marks. Let us say double that sum for your new one, if you consent to build it."

"Eh!" cried Satan. "Gold, indeed! What do you think I want with your gold? Look!" And he took a red coal from the middle of the fire. "Hold out your hand, bailli."

The bailli hesitated.

" Never fear," said Satan ; and he dropped it on the bailli's hand, where it fell an ingot of gold, as pure and cold as if just out of the mine.

The bailli turned it, and turned it over and over. Truly it was a pure gold piece: then he wanted to give it back to Satan.

" No, no, my friend," said the devil, flinging one leg carelessly over the other; "keep it: it is a little present I make you."

" I understand," said the bailli, putting the ingot in his pouch; " gold is of no value to you, who can make it so easily. You would rather be paid with some other sort of money; so, pray, as I cannot know what you would like best, name your own conditions."

Satan reflected an instant.

" Give me," he said, " the soul of the first individual who crosses the bridge I shall build."

" Agreed," said the bailli.

" Then draw up the deed," continued Satan.

" Dictate, then," said the bailli, taking paper, pen, and ink.

Five minutes after, a deed, duly signed and sealed by Satan himself, and the bailli on behalf of his townsmen, was executed.

In it the devil engaged himself to build a bridge in one night, solid enough to last five hundred years; and the magistrate, on his side, conceded to Satan the soul of the first individual whom chance or necessity would force to cross the Devil's Bridge.

By next morning, at break of day, the bridge was built.

Soon after, the bailli appeared on the Goschenen side. He had come to ratify his promise to the devil. The bridge was excellent in all things, just such as was required; and there stood Satan at the other end awaiting payment for his nocturnal labour.

" You see I am a man of my word," said Satan.

" And I, too," replied the bailli.

" What! my dear Curtius," exclaimed the astonished devil; do you mean to devote *yourself* to the good of your town?"

" Not exactly," said the bailli, laying down a sack he

had carried on his shoulder at the end of the bridge, and proceeding to untie the string.

" What is that?" said Satan, trying to divine what was going to happen.

" Prrrrrrrooooou!" said the bailli.

And a dog, dragging a frying-pan at its tail, leaped frightened from the sack, and made across the bridge as fast as it could for the place where Satan stood, running up right between his legs.

" There!" said the bailli. " Catch your soul now if you can: run after it; do, my lord!"

Satan was furious. He had reckoned on the soul of a man, and was not fond to content himself with that of a dog. He could have damned himself at the moment, if the thing had been further possible. However, he was a perfect gentleman, and appeared to take the thing as a capital joke, laughing with all his heart as long as the bailli was there. But as soon as that functionary had his back turned, Satan rushed at the bridge, and began trying to tear it to pieces with his hands and feet; indeed, he was so much in earnest that he turned his nails and broke his teeth, still could not move one single stone.

" What I fool I was!" said Satan. And having made this reflection, he put his hands in his pockets, and descended the banks of the river Reuss, looking from one side to the other, as if he were admiring the beauties of Nature, but, in fact, meditating some project of vengeance.

What he sought was a rock of sufficient size and weight to carry up the mountain, in order that he might then let it fall five hundred feet down upon the newly-built bridge of Goschenen.

He had not gone three leagues when he spied just such as would suit him: a fine rock, about the size of one of the towers of Nôtre Dame. Satan picked it up with as much ease as a child would take a turnip, and proceeded up the mountain, putting out his tongue at the bailli, in anticipation of that functionary's dismay when he found his fine bridge next morning all crushed to pieces.

After he had gone a league, Satan thought he per-

ceived a great concourse of people upon the bridge, so
he laid down the rock, ran on, and then clearly distinguished the whole clergy of Goschenen, with cross
uplifted and banner displayed, who had just finished
breaking the Satanic spell, and consecrating to God the
Devil's Bridge.

Satan saw it was all over with his little project of vengeance; so he descended the mountain very sadly, and,
meeting with a cow, he took hold of it by the tail, and
sent the poor thing over the precipice, just to relieve
his feelings.

The Bailli of Goschenen heard no more of the infernal architect: only, the first time he put his hand in
his pouch, it was burned dreadfully: the ingot of gold had
turned back again into a red-hot coal. As to the bridge
it lasted five hundred years, according to the devil's
agreement.

It is easy to find out the truths veiled by these wild
superstitions, especially in cases where some great work
of toil and science has been accomplished. In fact,
throughout Switzerland, all the great works attributed
to the devil—bridges, castles, high-roads, and the like—
are in reality the work of the Romans.

Contrary to the example of the Greeks, who destroyed
wherever they invaded, the Romans improved and built.
Helvetia was scarcely subjugated by Cæsar when a tower
rose at Nyon, a temple at Moudon, and the summit of
St. Bernard was levelled by a military road, which traversed the whole breadth of Helvetia, and only ended at
Mayence, close to the Rhine.

Under Augustus, some of the wealthiest and noblest
amongst the Roman families established themselves, in
the new conquest, at Aventicum, Arbon, and Curia; and
it was then, in order to render communication easier
between the rich foreigners, that Roman architects, the
best and most daring in the world, flung those wonderful bridges from mountain to mountain, and over the
most terrible precipices, which still exist in so many
places, so admirably were they constructed.

Roman domination lasted, as every one knows, for
above four hundred years in Helvetia. Then, one day,
a new race appeared upon the mountains, nomade con-

querors, coming from no one knew where; seeking a new country, settling themselves, according to caprice, with their wives and children, wherever the land or pasture suited; chasing before them the conquerors of the world at the point of the sword, as the shepherd drives the sheep with his staff; and making slaves of the people whom Rome had adopted for her children. Such were the Burgundians and Alemanni, sent by God as a tempest to desolate Helvetia, and who established themselves from Geneva to Constance, and from Basle to St. Gothard. Wild and uncultivated as the forests from which they sprang, the monuments left by Roman civilization struck them with awe as well as wonder; and, feeling themselves quite incapable of producing anything similar, their pride revolted from acknowledging them as the product of human minds at all. "They must be the work of demons," they said; "and the nation that preceded them must have paid the demon price of body and soul in return for their erection." Such was the origin of all the marvellous legends bequeathed by the middle ages to posterity.

About a league after passing the Devil's Bridge, on descending the course of the Reuss, we crossed a second bridge flung across the stream at a place called "The Monk's Leap."

The story goes, that, once on a time, a monk loved a beautiful young girl, and bore her away in his arms from her father's house. Her brothers pursued; and as their fleet horses threatened every instant to gain upon the fugitives, the monk leaped the river, still holding his precious burden in his arms, though at the risk of his own life and hers. The brothers dared not follow him, and the monk remained in the possession of her he loved.

The leap taken by this Claude Frollo of old times was twenty-two feet across, over an abyss one hundred and twenty feet in depth.

A quarter of an hour before reaching Altorf, we perceived the village of Attingausen, on the opposite bank of the river; and, behind the village steeple, the ruins of the house of Walter Furst, one of the three liberators of Switzerland. We were now leaving the region of fable for that of history. Henceforth no more demon legends or monastic traditions, but the Iliad of a great and noble act accomplished by a nation without any aid but that of her own children, the first page of which we were soon to read at Bürglen, upon the altar of the chapel erected on the spot where William Tell was born.

THE END.

THE BOOKCASE.

Eighteenpence per Volume.

NOTICES OF THE PRESS.

VOLUME I.

"One of the most agreeable works which have appeared on the subject."—*Sunday Times.*

"Most agreeably written."—*Liverpool Chronicle.*

"One of the most remarkable and interesting books on California."—*Dublin Evening Post.*

"Very lively and fascinating."—*Glasgow Examiner.*

"One of the best and most exciting books of travel we ever read."—*Glasgow Sentinel.*

"Exceedingly popular and interesting."—*Plymouth Journal.*

"This narrative of a journey unparalleled for the perils it involved, for the novelty, variety, and sublime wildness of the scenery traversed in its course, stands unrivalled among modern books of travel."—*Liverpool Mercury.*

"Full of lively, stirring incident and valuable information."—*Nottingham Journal.*

"We can, with the greatest confidence, recommend the first number of THE BOOKCASE as one of the most charming productions of the day."—*Doncaster Gazette.*

VOLUME II.

"We cannot tell when we were more thoroughly captivated with a volume of this kind."—*Belfast News-Letter.*

"Every matter likely to strike the eye of an acute observer is seized hold of, and given to the world in the happiest style of the author."—*Sunday Times.*

"The people of St. Petersburg, their manners, customs, and institutions, are, as it were, daguerréotyped in these pages, in which we have a succession of pictures faithfully coloured."—*Cork Southern Reporter.*